Fall of the Western Kings

J. Drew Brumbaugh

Fall of the Western Kings is a work of fiction and any resemblance to persons living or dead is purely coincidental.

Cover by Lynn Forbes, TypePhase Graphics - tygrtygr@roadrunner.com

Copyright 2016 J. Drew Brumbaugh

All rights reserved.
This book cannot be reproduced, scanned or distributed in any printed or electronic format without written permission of the author.

ISBN: 1534733779
ISBN 13: 978-1534733770

Also by J. Drew Brumbaugh

Shepherds

War Party

Foxworth Terminus

Ten More

Girls Gone Great
(A children's book co-authored with Carolyn B. Berg)

More information and active links are at:
www.jdrewbrumbaugh.com

Dedication

Thanks to all the people who were instrumental in making this book possible: to Kat Jordan for her insights in the early going, to Casey Sloop for reading an early version and giving me encouragement, to my brother Bill who read the entire manuscript even though he doesn't like fantasy much, and to my role-playing friends who provided inspiration for some of the characters in this story. Special thanks to my wife, Carolyn, who proofread the entire manuscript despite not liking fantasy, and for making suggestions that prevented some serious plot errors. Any errors that remain are entirely my responsibility.

Chapter 1

Gant's long strides carried him swiftly along the animal trail through the old forest. The cool shade under the leafy canopy was a welcome relief after the hot, sunny meadow where he'd secretly trained in swordsmanship with his uncle. The sweat dried slowly on Gant's sinewy body, muscles developed by swinging a forge hammer in his father's smithy. He had grown into a tall, muscular young man. His light brown hair fell loosely around his ears and his hazel eyes sparkled with enthusiasm.

He enjoyed the walk home almost as much as the sword practice. The solitude gave him time to reflect on his uncle's criticism and advice. Certainly he had improved over the years but he still had lots to learn and doing it in secret limited his practice time.

A warm breeze fluttered the leaves, sending flickering shadows dancing among the roots and ruts at his feet. As he walked along, Gant snapped his wooden practice sword in vicious arcs, visualizing specific moves, defending against imaginary attacks. One day, he thought, he would carry the real sword he'd made that lay hidden under his bed. For now he had to be content to train with his wooden sword in secret and pray for the day that would change.

Voices drifted to Gant from over a slight rise in the trail ahead. Who could it be? What if he was seen? As a commoner sword practice was forbidden. Maybe he should hide or throw away his practice sword. The sounds grew louder, yells for help, sounds of a struggle. He recognized Gwen's voice, his neighbor and friend. The other voice was Wendler, a nobleman's son with a nasty reputation for deflowering peasant girls.

Gant sprinted to the top of the hill. Below he saw Wendler wrestling with Gwen, twisting her by the shoulders, trying to force her down. Gwen fought back, managing to stay on her feet.

"What are you doing," demanded Gant, rushing down the slope toward them.

Over his shoulder Wendler snarled, "I'm about to take this wench. Go away."

Wendler slammed her against a tree trunk. Her breath burst from her body in a single gasp. And then he flung her to the ground like a rag doll and leaped on top, his hands clawing furiously at her dress, ripping away bits of the fabric.

Gant ran up behind Wendler and grabbed him by the collar. He yanked the nobleman to his feet, spun him around and shoved him back away from Gwen.

Wendler staggered for a step and then caught his balance. In one smooth motion he had his sword out. The long, shiny blade flashed in the flickering sunlight. Wendler's eyes flared.

"You've struck a nobleman. For that I am going to kill you. Then I shall finish with the wench."

For an instant, Gant panicked. The sight of sharp steel in Wendler's hand sent shivers down his spine. That lasted only a split second as Gant's training took over. He cleared his mind, concentrated on controlling his breathing and shifted into a defensive posture with the wooden practice sword ready.

"Let her go," Gant said.

Wendler's dark eyes filled with contempt, a sly smile curled his lips. "I shall enjoy killing you."

"We'll see about that."

Wendler poked his sword menacingly in Gant's direction. "Attacking a noble is punishable by death so killing you will not even raise an eyebrow."

Gwen jumped to her feet, stumbled slightly, regained her balance, and screamed, "Gant. No. If he doesn't kill you here they'll execute you for fighting him."

Gant ignored her and inched closer, wooden sword ready, intent on drawing Wendler away from Gwen. "Run," Gant shouted, "run home."

"No," she said firmly, "not unless you go with me."

"Too late for both of you," snarled Wendler and advanced past the girl. "This useless son of a blacksmith has drawn a weapon on me and I shall kill him for his insolence."

Gwen grabbed Wendler's arm from behind. "No. There's been no harm. Let us both go home and nobody need mention it again."

With hardly more than a shrug, Wendler cast Gwen off and closed in on Gant. He beamed with sadistic satisfaction. Lowering his sword tip he lunged in, the point aimed straight at Gant's heart.

Gant could hardly believe Wendler's foolishness. He swept Wendler's sword up and out of the way and danced backward.

"Want to reconsider?" asked Gant. "We could go home and forget this ever happened."

Wendler lunged in again. This time Gant swept the attack aside and smashed down on Wendler's forearm. Wendler's smile turned to a grimace. His sword fell uselessly into the dead leaves at his feet.

"You hit me," screeched Wendler. "I'll have you beheaded."

"No doubt," said Gant, surprised at how easily he'd dispatched his first real opponent.

Wendler picked up his sword with his off hand but made no move to attack.

"Never learned to use your other hand," said Gant. "Too bad. Even I've been taught that."

Gant turned to Gwen who stood petrified near the edge of the trail holding her tattered dress together with both hands. He stepped toward her.

"Look out," she shrieked.

Gant whirled as Wendler rushed at him with his sword raised overhead. Gant parried the weak blow, twisting his wooden sword to deflect Wendler's blade and in one continuous arc brought his practice sword down solidly on the side of Wendler's knee. Crack! And Wendler toppled to the ground.

Gant grabbed Gwen by the hand and ran up the trail dragging her along. "You're coming with me," he said. "Mother will make sure you don't get blamed for this."

Gwen twisted free and ran on her own. "What will you do? They'll execute you."

"Only if I'm around to be caught," he said between rasping breaths. "I'll have to leave Netherdorf, but that's better than letting scum like Wendler have his way with you."

"I'll go with you, help you escape," she said with a weak smile.

"No. Just stay with my mother. Stay safe or this has all been for nothing."

As they ran Gwen asked, "How could you best Wendler? He's a trained swordsman."

Gant glanced at her. "I am too."

"You can't be. Commoners aren't even allowed to own swords."

"True," said Gant and slowed to a walk. "It's my Uncle Jarlz. You know my mother is the king's cousin."

"And your father is a commoner which makes you a commoner. He may be the king's sword maker but that doesn't allow you to be a swordsman."

Gant nodded. "Yes but Uncle Jarlz happens to be the best swordsman in the kingdom and he decided that I should be a swordsman, illegal or not. So, he's been teaching me."

"They'll kill you if they find out."

"And now they'll know. Which is why I've got to get out of Netherdorf."

They crested the last rise into the clearing behind Gant's home. Smoke rose from the smithy's forge fires. The clang of the smith's hammer on hot metal rang like harsh music. They passed the shed and the corral where his father kept horses waiting to be shod, rounded the corner of the house and went in through the front door.

Once inside, Gant lurched to a stop. The adrenaline drained away and his hands shook. Seeing his mother busy cooking made the battle in the woods seem unreal.

His mother turned, took in Gant's face, noticed Gwen's torn dress, and a piercing glare crystallized in her eyes. "Gant," she demanded, "what is going on?"

Gwen stepped in front of him. "It's my fault, really," she started.

"He can speak for himself," ordered Gant's mother. "Now what is going on? Have you two been up to something?"

"No," said Gant. "It's Wendler. I caught him with Gwen in the woods. Trying to force himself on her."

"So you brought her here," said his mother, her mood transforming to serious concern. "Good for you."

"Not exactly," replied Gant. "We got in a bit of a fight. I think I broke his arm." After a moment's pause, he added, "Maybe his leg, too."

Gant's mother's face darkened. "That will mean trouble." She stood silently for a moment, unconsciously stirring the stew. Finally she said, "Come along. I'll take you to the king and we'll get this cleared up."

"No, you won't, " said Gant's father who had entered unnoticed through the side door. "The king will have him executed. He can do no less. It's the law."

"But the king is my cousin. He can't execute my only son."

Gant's father shook his head sadly. "Second cousins really and cousin or not, he'll have Gant executed because the rest of the nobles, especially Wendler's father, will give him no choice. We are near enough to a civil war over the way the king has treated commoners. Letting Gant off after attacking Wendler would be all the excuse they need to rally against the king. And with Barlon massing troops in the mountain castle the king cannot allow civil strife. No matter how much he'd rather let Gant off, he won't risk the kingdom over one person."

Even as he spoke, Gant's father gathered up a side of meat, a loaf of bread, a skin filled with well water, and finally, from the crock beside the fire pit, a few silver coins. He slid the coins into a tattered, leather purse and drew the drawstring shut.

"Well get moving," he roared at Gant. "The king's men will be here soon enough and you'd better be far down the road by then. Get a bedroll, clothes, whatever you think you'll need and can carry. You won't be coming back."

Gant studied the room, his parents' faces, memorizing each facet, knowing he'd never see them again. And then Gwen hugged him.

"Thanks," she mumbled into his tunic.

Gant hugged her back, wondering why he'd never hugged her before. "Tell Chamz I said goodbye," he whispered in her ear.

"Come on, son. Get moving," rasped his father, pushing Gant along.

Gant gathered up his hiking pack, extra clothes, boots, a cloak, hat, socks. Finally he pulled out the sword he'd made from under his bed. He withdrew it from the plain leather scabbard and admired the craftsmanship. It was a good sword sharpened under his father's guidance. Would it be good enough? He'd soon find out. Outside of Netherdorf he could legally carry it, a day he'd dreamed of. It never occurred to him that he'd have to leave home to do it.

Within minutes he had all he could carry strapped around his waist, slung over a shoulder or packed into his backpack. His mother hugged him fiercely, kissed him three times and said, "Stay well, my son. Someday you'll be able to return. I'll see to it. I love you."

"I love you too," was all Gant could manage. His world had come apart. He had no plan, no idea where he would go. He only knew that his life depended on escaping right now.

His father wrapped Gant in a mighty bear hug, almost crushing Gant's ribs. "I love you too, son. Take care of yourself. Go to Blasseldune. It isn't the safest town but you'll be safe there from Netherdorf's soldiers. We'll see that Uncle Jarlz meets you there as soon as he can."

Gant wished he wasn't leaving. Strange how in a crisis people did things they wouldn't otherwise. Gant's father hadn't hugged him in a long time. It felt both good and strange. His mother was crying. Gant hated that. Still, what was done was done. He had to go.

"I love you both," he said, whirling around and dashing out the door.

Tears streamed down his cheeks clouding his vision as he jogged back down the forest trail. He hurried, knowing the trail so well he could navigate it safely even when he could barely see. At least Gwen was safe.

A few yards up the trail Gant broke into a dead run. Blindly he dashed through the woods toward the place where the forest trail connected with the road to Blasseldune. He ran, and ran, trying to blot out the heartache.

Chapter 2

Gant ran until he reached the junction with the main east-west road. He checked left and right for the king's soldiers. Nothing. He turned east toward Blasseldune and settled into a pace that avoided bringing attention to him. There were few travelers and he continued steadily down the rutted dirt road. Periodically Gant glanced over his shoulder for pursuing soldiers. None materialized.

The air was hot with summer's breath and sweat ran down Gant's cheeks even as the sun sank behind the towering trees. The road ahead lay shaded, empty and dusty. His sword pressed into his shoulder blades. His pack straps cut into his back. The realization that he'd never see his family and friends again was depressing. His steps dragged.

The forest became wilder, closing in around the road. Thickets of briars and thorns grew under the overhanging canopy of trees at the edge of the road. Occasionally Gant passed an isolated farm carved out of the forest, surrounded by thick stone walls and locked gates. No soldiers would come to their aid if attacked.

Gant turned at the sound of shouts behind him. A lone wiry figure ran over a distant rise, waving frantically. Gant smiled as he recognized the voice and silhouette of his life-long friend, Chamz.

"Gant, Gant," Chamz yelled, "wait for me."

Chamz sprinted down the gentle slope that separated them, still waving his arms. In a moment he caught up with Gant. He was slightly taller than Gant and much thinner. His face was boyish, making him seem younger than Gant. He wore soft deerskin leggings and a thin leather vest. A heavy pack swung from his back and he had a water skin and hunting knife on his belt.

Gant grinned, both happy and surprised. "What are you doing here? And how'd you know where I was going?"

"Gwen told me what happened," said Chamz, clapping Gant on the back. "You didn't think you were going without me, did you?"

"What do you mean?"

"I'm going with you that's what I mean."

"How can you go with me? Your parents need you in Netherdorf."

Chamz started walking again pulling Gant along by the sleeve.

"I told my father I was going with you to Blasseldune. We both know that's where you're going. You've been dreaming of it forever because of your Uncle Jarlz's stories about the place."

"What did your father say?"

"Well, he didn't say anything. I sort of -- I left him a note."

"Left him a note? You can't write."

"Okay, I told Gwen and she's going to tell her father tonight and then he'll tell my father but by then we'll be halfway to Blasseldune and no one will come after us, least of all my father."

Gant shook his head. "You are crazy."

"Yeap," said Chamz with a smile.

As they walked, Gant considered the future. What were they going to do in Blasseldune? Yes, his Uncle Jarlz had filled their young minds with yarns about the world outside Netherdorf. Many of those stories were about Blasseldune, a free city located between the Kingdoms of Netherdorf, Mulldain, and the Eastern Empire. It was ruled by a loose group of merchants called the City Council. For centuries they had successfully played one power against the other and remained neutral and free. It was a city without a conscience where anything could be bought or sold. Including a man's life.

Gant had dreamed of going to Blasseldune as a warrior, a swordsman. Now, he was an outlaw in Netherdorf and going to Blasseldune was a necessity. He had no idea what he would do once he got there.

Gant looked up and realized Chamz was now some distance ahead. Shrugging his shoulders to resettle his pack, Gant grabbed the sheathed end of his sword to keep it from bouncing, and sprinted to catch up.

"Chamz," he said regaining his friend's side and slowing to a walk, "what are we going to do in Blasseldune? I've only got a few coins and they won't last long."

"You get a job as a guard. I'll load wagons, or something."

Chamz made it sound so easy. Gant doubted it would be. He thought of suggesting Chamz go home but the truth was Gant was glad to have him along.

They walked in silence for a while. Gradually their steps grew longer as the daylight dwindled. Signs of civilization disappeared. There were no more fortified farms. A single merchant's wagon surrounded by guards passed them headed toward Netherdorf. The guards eyed Gant and Chamz with suspicion as they passed. The merchant remained hidden inside the covered wagon.

Gant and Chamz continued eastward through the old forest. The sun dropped lower and the day's heat waned. Slanting flickers of sunlight barely penetrated the fluttering leaves.

Chamz finally broke the silence. "I think the king should rethink the law when it comes to you."

"Why is that?"

"Why? Because he'll need every warrior he has including you. With Barlon taking the Mountain Castle, it's only a matter of time before Netherdorf will be at war. He'll attack us next."

"And for that you think King Tirmus should ignore the law that outlaws swords from commoners. A law that's a hundred years old?"

"Yes. A law that never should have applied to you. I mean, your mom's related to the king. How much more noble do you have to be?"

Gant didn't have an answer. What if this went badly for his mother and father? He couldn't change what he'd done. All he could do was hope his parents were all right and make the best of things. Maybe he'd see his parents again someday.

"I'm telling you he'll call you back with a full pardon," said Chamz, carrying on the conversation without Gant. "Your mother's a noble. You're half noble. The king's made a mistake. And he'll see that when he's under attack."

Gant shook his head. "The king will do what he has to do. Stability within the kingdom is more important than I am. I'm sure there are plenty of nobles crying for my head right now."

Chamz laughed. "Mark my words those same nobles will be crying a different tune when Barlon comes down out of the mountains."

"And exactly what makes you think Barlon is going to attack Netherdorf?"

"Don't you ever go to the pub? Almost everyone there says it's just a matter of time. Barlon is power hungry and we're next. That's what they say."

"Pub talk," scoffed Gant and shifted the sword on his back to alleviate the irritation.

They walked on. Gant thought again about his fight with Wendler. He had violated the law. What was he supposed to do? He couldn't let Gwen be raped. Could he have done something different to stop Wendler? Nothing came to mind.

And what about Gwen? She'd been Gant's friend since they were toddlers. They'd played together in the fields, behind the smithy, around the chicken coups at her house. Gant was going to miss her. Maybe one day, they'd see each other again.

Chamz rattled on. "Wendler deserved it," he said with conviction. "He's been trying to pick a fight with you for years and now he got one. I think he hated you because the king allowed you to attend Uric's classes in the castle. And for knowing the answers when he didn't."

Gant stopped, grabbing his friend by the sleeve. "How would you know who knew what in Uric's classes? You weren't there."

"I hear things," said Chamz laughing. "There are plenty of commoners working in the king's castle and we aren't blind or deaf. Come on, hurry up or we'll never get to Blasseldune."

Gant hurried on, thinking about the times Wendler had tried to goad him into a fight. Mostly in the schoolyard. And how Uric, the schoolmaster, had always been there to stop it before it got started. "So what if Wendler did try to get me to fight him? It doesn't change my crime."

"Crime! If there's been any real crime Wendler's done it. He's one sorry excuse for a man. They say he's forced himself on every peasant girl working in the castle. He's sick, I tell you. There are more than a few who wish you'd killed him instead of just putting a knot on his head."

"Enough. Commoners do not kill nobles."

"Then we ought to do away with nobility," mumbled Chamz.

Gant let it go. Instead he turned his thoughts to the coming night. Where were they going to sleep? There was a single inn on the road halfway between Netherdorf and Blasseldune. Soldiers would look for him there so better to camp in the woods. The old forest grew up so thick and close to the road that the tree trunks presented an impenetrable barrier. If they found any break in the trees, Gant decided they would stop.

Twilight fell. Rustling noises in the leaves followed them as they walked along the now deserted road. Other travelers had found shelter. Gant wondered where. They continued steadily east looking for anything that resembled a campsite. A light fog filtered onto the road. Eerie shadows played tricks with their eyes. Gant and Chamz moved more cautiously remembering stories about bandits on the road. There were no patrols here, which meant no soldiers to arrest Gant but no protection against thieves either.

From behind them they heard the growing sound of hoof beats. Gant turned. The riders were out of sight behind a bend in the road.

"Behind us," said Gant. "Soldiers, maybe."

"No, it's a lone rider," said Chamz peering back into the fog.

Around the bend came a single shadowy figure on horseback. As the rider thundered closer Gant's hand went to his sword. A horseman at this time of night was unlikely to be an innocent traveler. The figure moved closer and Gant recognized Wendler's shadowy outline. Approaching cautiously, Wendler slowed his gray warhorse and set it prancing sideways toward the pair. A great shield painted with King Tirmus' emblem hung from a loop at the rear of the saddle protecting Wendler's side. One arm was in a sling. The other held a heavy sword, one Gant recognized as his father's work. Wendler wore serviceable chain mail armor that showed signs of use. Wendler wasn't wearing a helm and Gant wondered if he would risk combat without it.

Nonetheless, Gant had his sword out. "Stay behind me," he whispered and shoved Chamz back with his free hand.

"Hey Wendler," shouted Chamz over Gant's shoulder, "come for the rest of the beating you should have gotten before?"

"Chamz, shut up," hissed Gant, staying focused on the advancing swordsman. "What do you want," he demanded, warily eyeing the horse. Fighting Wendler was one thing, bringing down a horse to do it another.

"Your head on a pike. The king's a gutless excuse for a ruler. His soldiers are slower than dead men. They should have run you down at a full gallop. And then beheaded you in front of your less-than noble mother and father."

"You think you can do it for him?" Adrenaline rushed through Gant until his fingers shook.

Chamz stepped back. Good, thought Gant, glad Chamz wouldn't get caught in the middle.

"Maybe. Maybe I just wanted to make sure you left town like a good little boy."

That stung. Wendler was two years older and had always gotten away with calling Gant "little boy" in Uric's classroom, though not when Uric could hear. Rage burned in Gant. He controlled it. Being an outlaw was bad enough. He did not want to add murder to the charges.

"I broke your arm with a stick and this isn't a stick," said Gant pointing his sword at Wendler.

"No, but it doesn't really matter. Netherdorf will soon have a new king and I'll be a knight. You'll be an outlaw with a price on your head and I'll come to collect."

With that Wendler reined his horse closer. He leaned forward and spit at Gant. Gant dodged it easily. Wendler circled, dug his spurs into his horse's flanks and galloped back toward Netherdorf.

Gant and Chamz watched him disappear into the swirling fog.

Chamz turned toward Gant. "What do you think he meant?"

"I don't know unless his father is stirring up the nobles against the king."

"Do you think he could get enough support to depose King Tirmus?"

Gant thought about it. "I don't know."

"Between your uncle and mother, don't they have enough noble friends to stop Wendler's father? I think the king should just recognize your nobility and be done with it."

"It's not that easy. There would be plenty of opposition to allowing every half-noble kid to have nobility status. Think about it."

A look of mischief crossed Chamz's face. "Yeah, every bastard in the castle is probably half noble. Too many of the nobles can't keep their hands off the maids."

"I hope this doesn't bring on a civil war," added Gant. The thought of the king replaced worried him. Not for his own sake but for what would happen to his parents, to his uncle.

They shuffled on in darkness. Without a torch they couldn't see their way but carrying one would be a beacon inviting bandits to attack. Gant touched Chamz' shoulder bringing them to a halt.

"Let's camp here," said Gant.

"Where? I can't see a thing."

"Me either, just push through the underbrush and we'll get under the big trees. Roll out your blanket on the first soft spot you find and we'll sleep right here."

"Aren't you going to build a fire?"

It would be easy for Gant to build a fire. He'd spent years starting forge fires for his father who had taught him all the tricks. But a fire was not a good idea.

"No fire."

"Okay," said Chamz glumly.

The two of them pushed through the roadside bushes, thorns stinging and pricking exposed skin. Once through the thicket, they found themselves in the old forest. Dead leaves cushioned their footsteps and they both managed to find an area free from sticks to spread out their bedrolls. Gant shared his food with Chamz and they both drank some water. They rolled up in their bedrolls and just before falling asleep they heard horses' hooves pound past at a full gallop. Soldiers, thought Gant. It's a good thing we got off the road. In the quiet that followed they both fell asleep.

     Gant dreamed of sword fights with Wendler, of the king's armies in battle and Gant a knight like his uncle. Overshadowing it all, he dreamed of an evil that pervaded everything.

Chapter 3

Gant woke tired and sore. The ground wasn't nearly as comfortable as dead leaves should be and strange dreams kept him tossing and turning all night. Streaks of sunlight filtered through the canopy of leaves. It was time to get up.

Chamz rolled out of his blanket and sat up. "What's for breakfast?"

"I still have some meat, bread and cheese."

"Good enough. You planning to share?"

"Sure," said Gant, rolling up his blanket and tying it to his backpack. "We can eat while we walk."

"Yes, the sooner we get to Blasseldune, the sooner we get jobs."

Finding a job in Blasseldune was not going to be easy, thought Gant. He wasn't going to work as a blacksmith or weapons maker. If he had wanted to make swords he would be at home working for his father instead of an outlaw.

Gant wrestled his pack up on his shoulders, fighting with the straps until the pack settled. Finally, he slung his sword over his shoulder and they started off. He pulled the last of the meat and cheese from his pack, tore the beef into two pieces, broke the cheese in half and shared with Chamz. He broke the last hunk of bread in two and handed a piece to Chamz.

They ate in silence, both still trying to wake up. The road wound through the forest, slanting rays of sunshine casting shadows that danced with them as they walked. Gant's thoughts turned to Blasseldune. He had the few coins in his pocket that should be enough for food and a room for a night or two. After that they would have to find work or stop eating.

He also thought about home. He wondered about his father. Was his father in trouble with the king because of Gant? That was the last thing he wanted. From now on Gant promised himself that he would make his father proud, even if his father never knew.

Finally, after what seemed an eternity, they passed the stone marker set at the eastern boundary of Netherdorf. It might be the border but he wasn't safe yet. There was no one to prevent the soldiers from chasing him all the way to Blasseldune. Gant picked up the pace.

Chamz finished his breakfast and said, "You know, if what Uric said is true you're going to be a hero."

"Some hero."

"Not now. But Uric thinks you are the one in the prophecy. If that's true, the king will have to pardon you. You'll have saved us all."

"Uric's a dreamer. He's filled us with ridiculous stories about dragons, knights and wizards. Fairy tales for children. And prophecies are nothing more than the wishful thinking of old, dead men."

"Then how do you explain Barlon Gorth taking over the Mountain Kingdom? That's in the prophecy."

"It is not. The prophecy doesn't say anything about Barlon."

Chamz took a drink from his water skin. "Not exactly. But you loved Uric's stories. You always said you'd grow up to be the best swordsman ever. That's why you trained so hard with your Uncle Jarlz. And you are good. You beat Wendler with a stick."

"I was a little boy listening to those stories. A lot has changed. I'm not a knight. I'm not even a decent commoner anymore. I'm a criminal. I have no family, no friends."

The look in Chamz's eyes stopped Gant.

"I'm your friend," mumbled Chamz.

"Yes, you are. And a good friend, too. I'm sorry."

Chamz clapped Gant on the back. "Okay. But don't ever say anything like that again."

"Okay."

They walked on. Morning turned into afternoon and the forest finally began to thin. Open spaces appeared, small fields with crops and farmers working to keep out the weeds. Farmhouses became more frequent and soon they were passing the large estates of wealthy merchants and tradesmen.

"It won't be long now," said Chamz as they passed another big stone house surrounded by stone walls with heavy iron gates. "Are you nervous?"

"Not exactly. Excited I think is more like it."

"I'm scared. Remember the stories your uncle told us about Blasseldune?"

Gant certainly remembered sitting in the smithy while his father repaired armor listening to Uncle Jarlz tell adventure stories. Often Chamz would be there too. They'd sit and listen instead of playing outside. Blasseldune had seemed like a fairy tale. Now those stories seemed more ominous. He remembered tales about inns that never closed where they served the best mead and ale, about the wild women (a fact Uncle Jarlz left out whenever Gant's mother was around). Mostly he remembered the street battles that left men dead.

"Mostly just stories, I expect," Gant finally answered.

"Maybe. But then why did so many travelers who stopped at your father's smithy tell the same stories?"

"Then maybe it is true. Either way there's no place else to go."

Chamz thought about that a moment, shrugged his shoulders and said, "So I guess I'm lucky I'm going with you."

Gant chuckled. Chamz always looked at the bright side. "How's going there with me lucky?"

"Because if there's any trouble, you'll take care of it."

"Let's hope there isn't any trouble. Instead let's hope we can find someone who will give us a job so we continue to eat."

"Jobs? Hmm, what kind of job can I get?" Chamz pursed his lips in serious thought. Then he said, "You hire on as a guard, soldier, city watch and I'll be your sword polisher."

"More likely we'll end up loading wagons or something."

"Hey look, there's Blasseldune," said Chamz as the pair rounded a bend in the dusty road.

Gant looked up. Just beyond the last few outlying homes stood the fortified wall surrounding the town proper. Gant noticed the wealthy homes outside the walls were more like fortresses with guards at the entrances. Maybe he could hire on as a guard.

They passed the last house outside the city and reached the archway through the walls. Hinged at either side were huge, wooden gates that stood open.

"Do you think someone will stop us?" asked Chamz.

Gant looked around. "I don't see any city watch. I guess this really is a wide open town."

They walked under the arch and for a moment the thick stone overhead blocked out the sun. No one challenged them. They entered through the moss-covered stone walls and got their first glimpse of the city. On the inside, tattered, little wooden hovels piled up against the wall, squeezed there by rough log huts that seemed to push out from the center of town. Each of the huts had straw-over-log roofs. Here and there dirty, half-naked children played in the street. Beside the front door of one of the huts an old woman sat on a tree stump. Her white hair was matted to her head and soot covered her face and her hair. She watched without expression as they passed, picking at an open sore on her leg.

"They certainly don't care who they let in, do they?" noted Chamz, glancing back over his shoulder.

"Uncle Jarlz said it was an open town. I guess he wasn't kidding."

They walked deeper into Blasseldune. The huts disappeared abruptly and shops took their place. Foodstuffs, armor, tools, weapons, clothing, leather goods, jewelry, furniture, everything could be bought, sold or bartered for in Blasseldune. In Netherdorf there were only a few craftsmen who plied their trades with the king's blessing. Here it seemed that anyone and everyone had a shop. Most of the commercial buildings were hand-hewn logs shaved to present a flat front. The sloped roofs had slate coverings. Occasionally a stone building rose massive and haughty over the squat log structures of the less prosperous.

The streets bustled with people. All kinds of people. Farmers, merchants, and armed men with grim faces. The heart of the city clamored with the noise of humanity going about their business. The few women were all escorted by gruff looking men.

"Hey, look at that bunch," said Chamz as they passed a grimy tavern.

Gant examined the tough-looking group of men huddled in front of the inn. They had wild, unkempt black hair down to their shoulders and bushy beards. All were armed with swords, axes, spiked maces or spears. Thick leather breastplates covered fur undergarments.

"Glad we don't need to ask directions," said Gant.

"We don't? Then where are we going?"

"The Drake."

"The Drake? What's that?"

Gant chuckled. He finally had one on Chamz. "An inn I heard my uncle talk about all the time. He used to stay there, if I remember right."

"So where is it?"

"In Blasseldune."

"You really don't know where we're going? We better ask for directions."

"You ask," said Gant and kept walking.

Chamz didn't stop. They passed several inns but none named the Drake. They also passed several side streets that were almost as busy as the main street.

Up ahead, from one of the busy side streets, came several dark skinned elves. The tightly bunched group hurried past the two young men. Gant eyed them curiously, noticing the upswept ears that ended in points and their reddish glowing eyes.

"Did you see that?" asked Chamz as the elves hurried through the crowd.

"How could I miss them?" Gant stopped to stare after the elves as they disappeared toward the gate where he and Chamz had entered. "I never saw a dark elf before."

"But you've heard the stories."

Gant turned and started walking again. "Which stories? The ones about how evil they are or the ones about how my great-great-great grandmother was Queen of the Dark Elves?"

"Well yeah, either story, I guess. Hey, maybe one of those elves is a long lost cousin or something. You should have asked them for directions."

"I'm not asking for directions. We'll find the Drake."

Gant tried to sound confident but he had doubts. They seemed to be near the center of town and there had been no sign of the Drake. Even so, he wasn't asking dark elves anything. He'd heard stories about them that included lots of reasons for them to dislike men. He'd even heard about vicious murders committed by dark elves, though he didn't know anyone who had actually known someone killed by a dark elf. Still he thought it better not to trouble them.

Now clearly past town center, the people on the streets began to thin out. The buildings appeared more run down, less prosperous, less likely to be some place Gant's uncle would stay. Finally he stopped.

"I think we must have passed the Drake," he admitted. "I guess we'll have to ask."

"Fine time to make that decision," said Chamz looking around at the rough bunch of men on the street. "Who are you going to ask?"

Gant looked from grim face to grim face. Nothing friendly about them. Then he saw a woman dressed in a dark cloak and gown escorted by two burly men-at-arms. The crest on their breastplates was unfamiliar to Gant but at least they belonged to some kingdom. He decided that they were the best choice.

As the threesome neared, Gant stepped in front of them. He bowed low trying to look harmless.

Immediately, both men-at-arms had their swords drawn.

"Stand aside," said the biggest.

Gant held his hands out front away from his sword. "Begging the lady's pardon, but we are trying to find an inn named the Drake. Can you tell us where it is?" He stepped back out of their path.

The woman started ahead, her guards cordoning her off from Gant and Chamz. She hurried ahead without a word. As the biggest guard turned to follow he whispered over his shoulder, "Two streets back turn left."

And they were gone.

"Well," said Gant, "I guess we'll go back two streets and turn left."

It didn't take long to find the Drake, a well-kept, two-story log establishment. They entered through the front door. The main room was full with men clamoring for food, ale or both. The patrons were a mixture of economic status and station. Some wore crests and some had no crest. All of them carried weapons and Gant guessed they could use them.

They found an empty table off to one side of the main aisle, seated themselves on the rough wooden stools and looked for a server. Their table was unfinished and stained by a multitude of spilled mugs of ale, more than a bit of food and perhaps even a blood stain or two.

Finally the serving girl made it to their table.

"What'll it be," she snapped.

"What do you have?" asked Chamz.

"Roast meat, ale, mead, and stew. Now hurry it up, I've got other customers."

"Roast meat?" asked Gant. "What kind of meat?"

"I don't know. I didn't kill it. It's meat, that's all. Now what do you want before I get in trouble for talking too long."

Gant wondered why she would get in trouble for talking, but didn't ask. "Meat," he said. "And ale."

"Me too," said Chamz. "And can we get some bread with it?"

"Yes. I'll be right back." She whirled around and was off across the room.

"Do you see those guys staring at us?" asked Chamz.

"They're not the only ones. I've a bad feeling about this."

"Ah, what could happen in the middle of a tavern? If there is trouble, you'll teach them a lesson or two."

"I wish you'd stop saying that."

The serving woman returned dropping two large bowls of shredded meat on the table. Brown gravy slopped over the edges onto the table. From under her arm she pulled two mugs of ale and set them down. "That'll be six pieces of silver."

Gant pulled out his coin purse and pulled out a single gold coin. "Here," he said handing the coin to her, "keep the rest."

For the first time the woman smiled. "Thank you, young sir. If there's anything else I can do for you, just ask."

She turned to leave.

"We need a room for the night," said Gant.

She turned back. "Sorry, the Drake is full. The best place for you two is the Hammond House. Respectable, for Blasseldune, and not too expensive. Go back to the main street, turn left, second street go right and you'll see it. It'll be safer for you than staying here. Tell 'em Anna sent you."

With that she hurried off.

"What do you think she meant by that?" asked Chamz, digging into the food with a wooden spoon he pulled out of his pack.

"I'd say this could be a rough place. I wonder why my uncle liked it here?" Getting to more immediate matters, Gant searched for something to eat with. He hadn't packed any utensils. And where was the bread? "What I really need right now is a spoon."

Chamz stuffed another bite into his mouth, chewed, swallowed, and said, "Why didn't you say so." He reached into his pack and pulled out another wooden spoon. "In case I broke one," he said and went back to eating.

"Always thinking of your stomach."

Gant took the spoon, filled it with the steaming, hot gravy, blew on it to cool it, and shoveled it in his mouth.

At that moment, the server dropped a loaf of bread on their table as she rushed past. "Enjoy," she whispered and was gone.

Gant tore off a chunk of the crusty brown bread and dipped it into the meat juices.

"Don't look now," said Chamz between mouthfuls, "but here comes trouble."

Gant glanced back over his shoulder. A large, scruffy man pushed his way through the crowd towards Gant and Chamz. He swayed slightly as he walked and Gant guessed he'd been drinking for some time. In one hand he carried a tankard that sloshed foam with each step. His other hand rested on the hilt of a sword hanging at his side.

Gant turned back to eating.

"Looks drunk to me. Those kind always caused trouble back home," said Chamz. "What do you think he wants?"

"Who knows? I hope he's looking for someone else."

"No such luck," said Chamz.

"You there," rumbled the man and poked Gant in the back with his metal tankard.

"Yes," said Gant, turning slightly to look over his right shoulder.

The man was taller and wider than Gant. His eyes were dark, blood shot, wild. He had a scraggly black beard that hadn't seen a comb or wash for a long time, bits of food perched there as witness. He wore rusty armor, inferior quality in Gant's mind. Whoever made the armor was a poor excuse for a craftsman.

"Stand up when I'm speaking."

He tossed the tankard aside, splashing those at the table next to Gant. None of them complained. The pewter mug clattered loudly in the silence that filled the room.

The stranger grabbed for Gant's shoulder. Gant easily brushed his hand aside.

"I said stand up," bellowed the stranger.

"What for?"

"So I can chop you down to size," he growled, pulling out his two-handed sword.

Chamz jumped to his feet taking his bowl with him. "You don't want to start trouble here. My friend is an accomplished swordsman. He's defeated tougher men than you."

"If you're his friend, then I'll take care of you when I'm finished with him. Draw your sword, if you know how, or die where you sit."

With that the stranger inched his sword back preparing to strike. As the two-handed sword started forward, Gant spun around, pulling his sword out as he turned. He parried the bigger man's sword off to the side. Before the stranger could recover, Gant sliced lightly into his exposed forearm. Next Gant spun his blade and struck the man with the flat on the side of the head. The big man staggered. Gant hit him under the chin with the pommel.

A glaze spread over the stranger's eyes. His sword slipped from his hand and clattered to the floor, followed a moment later by the resounding crash of his unconscious body. The room took a collective inhale. Then everyone turned back to important business they just remembered and the clamor of drinking men resumed.

Gant turned around and glared at Chamz. "What was that crack about me defeating tougher men? You trying to get us killed?"

Through a half smile Chamz said, "No, no. I just thought I'd get him to leave us alone."

"Worked well, didn't it."

Before Gant could sit back down, the serving woman was at their table. "You'd better get out of here. Talth isn't well liked but he has friends and no doubt they'll be here soon. Go to the Hammond House. Now."

Gant scooped in one more spoonful of the juicy meat and gravy, looked longingly at what was left, and decided it was best to avoid more trouble.

"Come on," he said and headed for the door.

Chamz was right behind him, clutching the remains of the loaf of bread.

Chapter 4

Miles from Blasseldune, up the mountain road west of Netherdorf, a massive stone castle sat glowering on a steep, barren hilltop. Bright orange fires made the narrow slit windows gleam in the darkness like great reptilian eyes. Neither moon was visible in the night sky and dark clouds hid whatever slivers there might have been.

In the castle, a foul group gathered in conference with the new Mountain Lord, Barlon Gorth. His dark, shaggy hair and thick black eyebrows framed a face that was even darker. His eyes were catlike, emotionless. He sat wrapped in heavy fur robes at the head of the rough-cut oak table. The cheery fire that blazed in the hearth did little to brighten the ominous mood that hung ugly as a night storm.

"Captains," growled Barlon, his voice deep and rasping like the sound of gravel grating on stone. "Report on the military training."

"First brigade is doing well. They are nearly ready. We will do m'Lord proud," answered the man seated to Barlon's left.

"The second brigade is ready, Sire," said the next man.

"And the third."

"The fourth also."

Around the table it went. Each of the 15 brigade captains reported that the training was on schedule. Then silence. Only three men had not spoken; the gray-haired general, the scar-faced spy and the knight in purple armor.

"Does General Ecker agree?" Barlon looked directly at the grizzled veteran commander. In Barlon's mind the general's opinion was more important than all the captains. The captains were untested in battle whereas the general knew the burdens war put on a man. "Are they ready?"

"Very soon. They will be molded into an effective unit in time for our attack." The general sat upright, proud, his gray hair a symbol of his wisdom. His spotless black and gold uniform sparkled with ribbons and medals on both sides of his broad chest. "By the time we hit Netherdorf, the men will be spoiling for a fight."

Barlon scratched his beard for a long moment. It was what he wanted to hear. Could he trust General Ecker to tell him the truth? If not, who could he trust? He decided to move on. "The spies, Shalmuthe, what do you report?"

The chief of Barlon's espionage corps was a short, stocky man with a livid scar from left cheek to left ear. He wore a tan calfskin tunic that concealed a deadly pair of daggers. On his right index finger a rune-covered ring flashed with a fire of its own. The man rose slowly from his wooden stool, and measured each man in the room. His hard eyes cut through them one at a time. Finally he fixed his gaze on Barlon.

"Netherdorf is a plum ripe for the picking." A sneer punctuated his words. "They suspect nothing. Their army is understaffed and the nobles are divided by silly squabbles over a blacksmith's son who escaped punishment for striking a noble's son. Some of the nobles may side with us. I've been discreet in my inquiries so as not to tip your hand, sire. We have the support of a young warrior named Wendler and likely his father as well. In the end, I doubt we'll need their help."

"What about the castle staff? And the gates?"

"The castle staff will be compromised as you wished. The gates will be opened when needed. Your plan to neutralize the only knight worthy of the title is brilliant. Everything progresses as planned." With that Shalmuthe settled back onto his stool.

Barlon's bushy eyebrows knotted in thought and he looked at the man seated immediately to his right. He was a blond-haired brute with black eyes that burned with an unbridled lust for death. His deep purple armor was unscarred from battle and sucked the light from the fireplace into a living darkness that surrounded the strange metal. A glinting silver triangle crisscrossed by black lightning bolts stood out on his breastplate.

"Are the Knights of Habichon ready?" asked Barlon.

"At your command." The voice was hollow, as if it came from another dimension.

"Excellent," Barlon said, nodding his approval. "Netherdorf will fall and the glory that should have been ours in the last war will follow. No one will betray us this time and those that pushed us into this dark corner of the world will pay. Carry out your preparations for the glory of the Mountain Kingdom. We move before the next turning of the Greater Moon." Barlon stood and waved them toward the door.

The men rose and the clatter of armor drowned out whatever whispered comments they exchanged. The vast chamber cleared to the ringing of mailed boots except for the massive blond giant in purple armor. He waited quietly at his liege's side. The reverberations of metal on stone died to a soft murmur and then fell silent. At last Barlon turned to the commander of the Knights of Habichon.

"Lom."

"Yes, m'Lord."

"You haven't forgotten my special instructions?"

"No. The king will die."

"And the others? The silversmith, the goldsmith, the sword-maker, the gem-cutter and the jeweler?"

"Will be brought to you as ordered."

"Good. Otherwise you may take such spoils as you can carry."

"Thank you, m'Lord."

It was all Barlon could do to look at those alien eyes, lifeless dots that burned with an animal lust for blood and death. Lom turned and started for the door. His armor soaked up the firelight leaving only darkness. Once Lom passed into the shadows he was virtually invisible.

Barlon returned to his chair and waited, drumming his fingers on the table. Over and over he reviewed the preparations, scrutinizing each detail for any flaw that would steal his victory.

Much was unfinished. One detail in particular held his attention and for that he had to wait on a midnight visitor.

Chapter 5

Gant and Chamz dashed into the street. Night had fallen and the streets were a murky sea of dark shadows sprinkled with splotches of yellow light from an occasional oil lamp. Here and there faint light shone through a dusty window. Gant turned toward the main street, warily checking for ambush. Chamz was so close behind he felt like an appendage.

They reached the main street. It too was sparsely lit.

"How come they keep it so dark?" asked Chamz. "Do they encourage muggings?"

"Shh," said Gant. "Listen."

They turned left and hurried along.

"Listen for what?"

They reached the second street on the right and turned in. It was so narrow that Gant and Chamz had to go single file.

"For the man tucked back in the doorway up ahead. I hear him breathing, but I can't see him. I'm sure he can see us."

"What'll we do?"

Gant started forward. He was tired. His only thought was to find a safe place to sleep. His hand went instinctively to his sword hilt.

"You there, in the doorway. Step out and show yourself."

Feet shuffled in the doorway but no one emerged.

Gant lurched to a stop, his heart racing. Chamz bumped into his back.

"Come out now or we will be forced to conclude that you mean us harm."

A frail, hunched shape emerged from the darker shadows into the faint light.

"I meant no harm. Just trying to find a place for the night. This street's usually deserted by this time." The figure bowed crudely and backed away.

"Okay, then be off," said Gant and waved the man down the street the way they'd come.

The dark figure slid by them, shuffled a little way, and then hunkered into another recessed doorway.

Gant hurried on. Chamz glanced over his shoulder nervously. Ahead weak light came through shuttered windows allowing them to read the weathered sign hanging in front of a two-story wood building: Hammond House.

"This is it," said Gant and turned in.

He pushed open the heavy door and entered a small, comfortably furnished common room. A heavyset man in a stained apron sat at a corner table. Next to him was a thin woman nearly his age. Both were eating a bowl of something brown, a half loaf of bread sat between them and each had a tankard near their elbow.

The man rose. "Can I help you?"

"We need a place to sleep."

"Anna sent us," added Chamz.

A smile spread over the man's features. "I am the innkeeper. A room you shall have. Upstairs or main floor?"

"Which is less?" asked Gant, mindful that his purse was already considerably lighter.

"Upstairs. It'll be eight silvers for the night, and for Anna's friends, I'll throw in breakfast in the morning."

Gant opened his purse, sorted through until he found eight silver pieces and handed them to the innkeeper. "We'll take it."

The innkeeper hefted the coins, and then dropped them in the front pocket of his apron. "Up the stairs," he said, pointing to a narrow set of wooden stairs that were so steep they were more like a ladder, "down the hall, second room on the left. Breakfast is soon after first light and lasts until the foods gone. And be quiet. I've got other guests already asleep."

"We're always quiet," whispered Chamz, "aren't we, Gant?"

Gant nodded and headed for the stairs. He heard the innkeeper lock the main door behind them.

They struggled up the steep stairs carrying their gear and soon were in their room. It was small, hardly large enough for one, let alone two, but the thick mattress was soft and wide enough for them both. Gant stacked his equipment in one corner near the door. Chamz put his gear in the opposite corner.

"Didn't it seem strange that the innkeeper would lock the door?" asked Chamz.

"I was wondering about that myself? How do they stay in business if they lock out potential customers?"

"Anna did say this is a more respectable place. Maybe they don't encourage late night visitors."

"I hope not. There's no lock on our door."

They looked at each other and immediately slid their gear in front of the door. Once that was done, they pulled off their garments, lay down and wrapped up in their trail blankets. Gant fell asleep dreaming about wild-eyed swordsmen attacking him.

#

A faint tap at the door disturbed Gant's sleep. Was it a dream?

"Gant," whispered Chamz from under his blanket, "someone's at the door."

It was pitch black. Gant couldn't tell how much of the night had passed but he was certain it was no honest citizen at the door.

The tap came again, a little louder. Gant slid off the mattress and fumbled for his sword, making a mental note to never let it out of reach again. His fingers found the hilt and as quietly as he could he withdrew it.

"Gant," came a soft voice from outside, "you don't need your sword, just open the door."

"Uric?" asked Chamz as surprised as Gant to recognize the voice.

"Correct," was the hushed response. "Now open the door before I wake up everyone in the inn."

Gant pulled the door open. Standing in the hall, holding a flickering candle, dressed in his usual, floor-length, thick purple robe, was King Tirmus' sage, Uric. The royal schoolmaster was tall, stately, with soft blond hair that hung to his shoulder. A powerful presence showed in green eyes so alive and strong that it was difficult to look directly into them. His face was devoid of facial hair and despite being older than anyone Gant knew, Uric showed no signs of age. Gant liked the sage and had marveled at the knowledge Uric willingly imparted to his students.

"May I come in?" Uric asked, his voice a low rumble in the quiet hallway.

"Yes, of course," said Gant, lowering his sword and backing up.

Uric stepped gingerly over the pile of equipment and pushed the door shut behind him.

"I'm sorry I could not come sooner but things are a bit troubled in Netherdorf."

"How'd you find us?" asked Chamz.

"I knew your uncle favored the Drake so I went there first. They're still buzzing about the way you stopped Talth. A pity you had such trouble on your first day here."

"Anna told you we came here," guessed Gant. "What about Netherdorf?"

"Political unrest. Your uncle Jarlz wanted to come himself, but the king needs all the support he can get right now. Some of nobles think the king is weak. They are using your fight with Wendler as an excuse to stir up trouble. Some have started rumors that the king and your mother have been lovers."

"That's a lie," snapped Gant.

"Of course. Castle rumors are hardly ever based on truth. People would rather hear ugly lies than the truth so rumors travel with a life of their own. In this case, nobles with their own agenda are looking to fuel their fires, doesn't matter where they get it. And worse is the new mountain king. He's using this to entice nobles to his cause, which is of course to conquer Netherdorf and use our resources to further his ambitions. In any case, the king needs all his loyal supporters around to pull things back together."

"If the king needs your support so much, what are you doing here?" asked Chamz.

"I needed to talk with Gant. There may be important things in your future. If I am reading the signs correctly, Gant, you will need to train with your sword like never before. When possible I'm sure your uncle will come to work with you but that won't be until things have calmed down in Netherdorf. Eventually, you must enter the Devonshield games. It is crucial."

"Crucial to what?"

"That doesn't matter. Just train hard."

"Okay, fine," said Gant. "What am I supposed to do for a job? We need to eat."

"I've taken care of that. Tomorrow, take this note," Uric handed Gant a small, neatly folded piece of parchment sealed with wax, "to the freightmaster at the Eagle Freight Company. His name is Brawnson. They are at the end of the North Road on the edge of Blasseldune. He is looking for trustworthy men-at-arms to help protect his wagons. My recommendation should be sufficient."

"Fine, now we eat," said Chamz. "How about a job for me?"

"That you will have to work out for yourself."

Gant took the parchment and carefully placed it atop his pack. "If things are so unsettled in Netherdorf, why are you here now? Even riding a fast horse it will take a full day to get back. Almost anything can happen in a day."

"Fortunately, I do not depend on horses. But you are correct. I need to go least I am missed. Remember what I said, keep up your training. Working as a guard will probably give you some experience though likely only against men of lesser ability so you will not improve other than tasting real combat. Jarlz will be here when he can. And Chamz, you see that Gant stays out of trouble."

"Yeah, sure," grumbled Chamz.

Uric turned and in a swirl of violet robes was gone down the hall. Gant closed the door and sat down on his bedroll.

"It would have been nice if he could have gotten me a job too," said Chamz.

"Shh."

"Shh, what?"

35

Gant held one finger up to his mouth for silence. Long minutes went by but he heard not the slightest sound.

"What are you listening for?" asked Chamz.

"I was waiting to hear how Uric got out of the inn. Did you hear a door open, a lock turn, anything?"

"No."

"So, how did he get in and out?"

"How should I know? He's a sage. He probably knows lots of tricks."

"I guess," said Gant and lay back down. "Let's get some sleep. I want to be up early and get over to the Eagle Freight Company."

#

Barlon sat alone in the main room. His mind wandered over his plans, searching for holes that would cost them their victory. He couldn't see any but he knew from experience that there were always unknowns that could not be prepared for and thus plans had to be flexible with options. And yet he saw no flaws.

Finally, in the darkness before the dawn, there came the soft rustle of robes. Barlon looked up from dozing. The newcomer stood at the end of the long table, twisting his boney fingers nervously in front of him. His sandy hair was wild, unkempt, and his gray eyes held a frightened sheen. Charcoal robes hung softly around him leaving only his hands and head exposed. He was young for a wizard, barely a wrinkle on his face. At times Barlon wished he could have found someone more experienced.

"Well, Razgoth," said Barlon. "Did the summoning work?"

"Yes, Master," said the wizard, shifting his gaze to the floor.

"Is something wrong?"

"Oh no, Lord. The spell went perfectly. It was just. . . a bit exhausting."

"And this lesser demon, the one you chose to test your spell on, what will keep it from running amuck and announcing to the world that someone is calling demons from the Dark Realms? What will keep it from giving away our plans before the next night of darkness when both moons are new and we can summon the Demon-Prince Varg?"

Here the wizard smiled for the first time, a half smile betraying his satisfaction. "Don't worry, sire. I have called up Egog, a minor demon of the night. He cannot enter daylight or even strong moonlight. The cave where I summoned him is his prison. Only on the darkest nights will he be able to venture out, and even then he won't be able to travel far before sunrise sends him scurrying back into hiding. I pity anyone who enters that cavern seeking shelter."

"Pity is for fools. You have done well."

Barlon rose and slapped the mage on the shoulder roughly, and then started for the door. "Sleep well. Soon we leave for Netherdorf."

"Yes, Master," said Razgoth. The wizard cleared his throat and stood unmoving.

"Is there something else?" asked Barlon, stopping after only a few steps.

"Sire, I wouldn't question your wisdom, but the smith's son, Gant. I am worried about him. What if he is the one of the prophecy? Even if I can summon Varg and the amulet controls him, this Gant may be able to destroy him."

"A worthy question but of no concern. The prophecy warns us of a warrior who has won at Devonshield. Has this Gant won anything?"

"No."

"Does it seem likely he will enter the games at Devonshield?"

"No."

"Rest assured we are watching him. If he enters the games, we may move to prevent it. Perhaps even this Egog you've summoned will be useful. Now off with you. We all have work to do."

"Yes, Master," said Razgoth and hurried out the door ahead of Barlon.

Barlon Gorth stood in the doorway and watched his wizard disappear down the hallway. Once Razgoth was out of sight, Barlon twisted the peculiar ring on his left hand. The magic in the ring bent the light unnaturally around the Mountain Lord and he became invisible. He passed unseen down the sparsely decorated halls, up the narrow tower steps to the uppermost room. There a bald, rotund little man sat morosely at a heavy wooden table. At the sound of the lock turning, the man slumped over the table as if a terrible weight pressed on his shoulders, shoulders ill suited for such a load.

Barlon entered the isolated tower chamber, twisted the ring until he was visible again and approached the trembling captive.

"Have you finished?" asked Barlon, a false sweetness in his voice.

The man shrank away from Barlon cradling a gold medallion in his soft, chubby hands.

"You will let us go once it's done?"

"Master Figgins, I've given my word. Once you provide me with the charm no more harm will come to you or your good wife. It is unfortunate that I had to demonstrate on her the consequences of disobeying my wishes. She waits for you now."

Figgins stared up at Barlon shaking with fear. Hesitantly, Figgins' trembling hand held out a blazing trinket. Barlon took it by the chain, inspected it, careful not to touch the medallion itself.

"You are sure it will bind Sir Jarlz' loyalties to me?"

"Of course. I'm a man of my word. Please don't handle it any more than necessary. Each touch uses a little of the magic. The amulet must examine the handler's identity, searching for the one who will trigger it. In this case, only Sir Jarlz will activate the charm. Still, it takes a bit of the power each time someone handles it."

Barlon twirled the round metal coin on its chain. A strange inscription glittered there and as Barlon swung the medallion, magical reflections twinkled across the stone walls seeking someone not present.

"Please, now can I rejoin my wife? You promised our freedom."

"And you shall have it."

Barlon Gorth yanked his sword from its scabbard beneath his fur robe. In one clean slice he severed the bald head from its pudgy body. A torrent of blood surged from the neck and the wizard fell with a thud.

"You have joined her as promised and I'm sure no more harm will befall either of you. Your weakness is intolerable," said Barlon. Without looking back he turned and left by the single door. There was a lot yet undone and time was running short. Now he had the medallion to give to his spy, Shalmuthe, who would see that it was presented as a gift to Sir Jarlz. Once around the knight's neck, it would guarantee Sir Jarlz' aid against King Tirmus.

Chapter 6

Gant and Chamz were up the next day before the sun. Hammond House was already astir with hot breakfast on the table. Guests were enjoying eggs, hash and bacon. As they entered the main room, the proprietor approached them.

"Will you be back tonight?" he asked.

"Maybe," said Gant. "I am going to see about a job at Eagle Freight. If that works out we would like to get a longer term arrangement."

"When will you know if you are staying?"

"Within the hour, I should think. I have a recommendation to Mr. Brawnson at the Freight Company."

"Good. Then I'll hold one of the better rooms for you as I have several being vacated this morning. What about your friend?"

"I'm going to get a job, too."

The innkeeper's brow wrinkled. "Do you have something lined up?"

"No."

The innkeeper smiled. "You look trustworthy," he said. "How about working here? I need someone to unload and stack supplies, clean stables, things like that. I can't pay much, but room and board is included."

"For both of us?" asked Chamz.

"That's not what I had in mind. But," and he looked at Gant again, "I suppose it might be handy to have a man staying here that can handle a sword and has the good judgment to use it wisely."

"What do you know about my swordsmanship?"

"Word gets around. Enjoy your breakfast," and he nodded at Chamz, "I've got work that needs done."

They finished breakfast and Chamz went to find the innkeeper. Gant hustled down the street to the Eagle Freight Company.

Soon Gant stood in front of the bustling warehouses, freight loading area and stables of the Eagle Freight Company. Crossing the dirt yard, Gant saw men loading, unloading or hitching horses to wagons. As he approached the log building that was the main office, a burly, armored man with dark eyes and a grim disposition held up one hand motioning Gant to halt.

"Stop. What do you want?" he asked Gant, his right hand on his sword.

"I've come to see Mr. Brawnson."

"Is he expecting you?"

"I don't know. I've a letter of recommendation and came to apply for a job."

"He's not hiring. Be on your way."

"Could you ask him first? I've come a long way and I really need a job."

"No, I won't ask him. We don't need troublemakers here."

"What does that mean? I didn't start any trouble."

"That's not the way I heard it. We all know what you did to Talth last night and we don't want trouble here."

"Did?" Gant's temper was rising. "He came over to my table. I didn't start anything."

Others were gathering around and Gant realized he was shouting. It rankled him to think people believed he'd been the instigator.

"Besides, I barely hurt him. If I wasn't such a nice guy, I would have killed him."

"Oh, now you're so good with your sword you could have killed Talth. Not likely. I think you're just another kid come to make a name for himself. Enough. Clear out."

Gant studied the men circled around him. They were burly, working men, anxious to see a fight. What could he do? He wasn't starting anything, that would only prove the idiot right, and then he probably would never get a job.

Gant turned toward the North Road gate when the main office door opened and a gangly man with light hair and flour-white skin stepped out.

"What's the ruckus?" asked the newcomer, staring at the guard who'd stopped Gant.

"Nothing, Mr. Brawnson. Nothing we can't handle."

"Mr. Brawnson," said Gant stepping closer, retrieving Uric's note from his belt. "I'm here to see about a job. I brought a note of recommendation from Uric of Netherdorf."

"Ah, Gant. I was wondering when you'd show up." Mr. Brawnson took the note, examined the wax seal, and then waved Gant into the office. "It's okay, Bork, I've been expecting him."

In the office, Mr. Brawnson read Uric's letter and explained to Gant that he was going to be working security in and around the freight yard. He had full authority to stop theft, break up arguments or remove undesirables from the property. After that, they went out into the freight yard and Mr. Brawnson introduced Gant to the others. When it became clear that Gant had been recommended by Uric and was also Jarlz's nephew Bork's attitude changed noticeably.

#

Gant began his duties as a freight company employee and the days passed quickly. During the day Gant guarded valuable goods for the freight company while Chamz worked at the Hammond House, which turned out to have more business interests than just the inn. Occasionally Gant was forced to use his sword, mostly against unskilled thugs and the confrontations were quick knockouts. Gant and Chamz began training behind the Hammond House in the evening. Though Chamz showed a natural ability with the sword he was no match for Gant. For safety, they trained with wooden sticks that approximated the length and heft of swords. Their swordplay, though rudimentary as far as Gant was concerned, was intense. Often inn patrons filed outside to watch as if it were a major sporting event. Chamz did his best but for Gant it was a step backward. Gant's father had promised to send Uncle Jarlz to

Blasseldune. Where was he? Gant needed coaching. He forgot about Talth and threats of revenge.

Chapter 7

The days passed quickly for Gant and Chamz. Gant's work at the freight company was uneventful except for an occasional troublemaker that Gant dispatched without bloodshed. The best part of each day was the evening sword practice with Chamz behind the stable. Chamz had improved enough to be a worthy sparring partner. For Gant's part he was determined to make the best of things.

One windy, cold evening with a hint of rain in the air, Gant left work and trudged toward the inn, his cloak flapping behind him like something alive. No sword practice tonight, he thought. Nothing to look forward to but a warm meal, a bit of idle talk by the fire and then off to bed. Dismal prospects.

He reached the Hammond House, pulled open the door and stepped inside, glad to be out of the wind. Shutting the door against the wind, Gant looked around. A fire roared in the hearth, the inn bustled with patrons and the warm cooking smells reminded him how hungry he was.

"Hey Gant," yelled Chamz from their usual table by the fire. "Look who's here."

Glancing toward their corner he recognized Uncle Jarlz.

Gant's face lit up. He hurried to greet his uncle. "Uncle Jarlz, where have you been?"

Jarlz stood up, rounded the table and gave Gant a warm hug and a clap on the back. "Great to see you," he said. "Some greeting."

Gant sat down overwhelmed to finally see his uncle. "Sorry," he mumbled. "I am glad you're here. I've been wasting away. I've done nothing to regain my good name or remove the blot on Father."

"On the contrary," said Jarlz, sitting back down. "Have some food."

Gant noticed the plate of roast meat, the fresh loaf of bread and a crock of butter in the center of the table. He pulled off his cloak, folded it and put it on the bench beside him. Waving for a pint of ale he said, "Will you be here long?"

"A while, I expect."

Chamz leaned over and said, "You should hear what's going on in Netherdorf. You're famous."

Jarlz laughed. "I wouldn't go that far. But people certainly are interested in you, Gant. It's hardly a day that someone from Blasseldune isn't interrogated in the inns about what you're up to and how you're doing. Your mother gets all the news straight away."

"And my father?"

"He is just as eager to hear about you and perks up every time they bring news."

"News of what? I haven't done anything."

"Well, stories do tend to grow in the telling." Jarlz took a bite of bread and chewed for a moment. "I came as soon as I could. You left things in quite a stir. Many of the nobles have set against the king for not pursuing you more vigorously. But their ill will has taken a back seat to other dangers, at least for now. So, I was allowed time off, so to speak, to see how my favorite nephew was doing."

Gant chuckled at the "favorite nephew." He was Jarlz's only nephew. "I'm doing all right, I suppose."

"What about your training with Chamz?"

"Yeah," shot Chamz, "what about that?"

"Well, yes there is that. He's improved a lot."

"And you haven't? Actually, I had hoped to test you tonight. With the wind, and rain, I think we'll put it off until tomorrow."

"I have to work tomorrow."

"Of course. We'll train in the freight yard. There's plenty of room and I'm sure Mr. Brawnson won't mind. Usually when I'm in Blasseldune, he's glad to have me hang around the yard, adds to the security, he tells me. For now, let's eat, drink and enjoy the fire. Time enough to be serious tomorrow."

They spent the rest of the evening at the table, talking about life in Netherdorf, about Gant's mother, Chamz' family and what was happening in the world. Some things were unsettling.

#

In the morning, they were up early and off to the Eagle Freight Company. As Jarlz suspected, Mr. Brawnson was more than happy to have them train in the main freight yard, a visual deterrent to thugs.

With a preliminary salute and Chamz as referee, they drew their swords and circled for a moment. Quickly, a crowd gathered, first freight company workmen and then townspeople and soon everyone who could crowd inside the fence.

Jarlz lunged in with a simple thrust. Gant turned it aside, circled and slashed down across the neck. Jarlz countered and redirected his sword in a lightning quick thrust. Jarlz stopped his sword point just in time to keep from piercing Gant's chest.

"One for me," said Jarlz, and pulled back.

A cheer went up from the crowd. The two combatants started again. Gant watched for an opening, saw one and rushed in. Jarlz turned it aside and circled into a thrust to the chest. Gant blocked it. Jarlz anticipated the move and countered with another attack. Gant sidestepped, went for a low slash and missed. Jarlz had him again. More cheers.

"Two to zero," said Jarlz.

It went on for nearly an hour. Gant kept seeing openings, openings he was sure he'd score on only to find he'd misjudged, or was countered at the last second. At thirty to zero, Jarlz called a halt to groans from the onlookers.

"You've improved a lot since our last workout," said Jarlz as they walked into the freight company office.

"I was terrible," grumbled Gant. "I'm worse."

Inside the freight company offices, Mr. Brawnson greeted them.

"Marvelous entertainment," he said, "but we aren't getting many wagons loaded."

"I'm sure," said Jarlz, clapping the freight company owner on the shoulder. "Don't worry, we'll leave you alone from here on."

"What do you mean?"

"I'm afraid Gant will be leaving your employ. He has more serious things to do and time is running out."

Gant noted the determination in his uncles' eyes. "What do you mean?"

"Training. That's what I mean. Chamz is a good friend and helped keep you from getting rusty. You need more intense training with a more advanced opponent."

"Who is that?"

"Me, of course."

"What will I do for money? For a room?"

"As long as I'm here you won't have to worry about money."

"And what about Chamz? Does he have to work while I play? He wants to learn swordsmanship as much as I do."

Jarlz took in a deep breath and let it out slowly. "Okay, I'll take Chamz as a student too but he will slow down your progress."

"No, he won't. And so what if he does."

"You won't be ready in time."

"In time for what?"

"For fate to catch up to you. Now come on, let's get back to the Hammond House. We'll have lunch and then go looking for a suitable practice field."

Jarlz pulled open the door to leave the freight office. "Thanks for keeping my nephew employed," he said to Mr. Brawnson.

Then he was out the door with Gant and Chamz running to catch up.

Chapter 8

Chamz was happy to be relieved of his chores at Hammond House. The proprietor was not so happy. Chamz was reliable and hard working and the owner counted on him for a number of things. Jarlz's offer of gold coins eased his pain and after a satisfying lunch, the three of them went searching for a training site. Gant wondered why they needed a new place, but Jarlz insisted they go away from town where there would be fewer distractions. By mid-afternoon they located a quiet hilltop meadow east of town overlooking the road to Maltic City. It was close enough to the road so they could reach it quickly but far enough away that they were not easily noticed. It was also the highest elevation around so people had to look up to spot them and, as Gant noted, travelers hardly ever looked up.

The grass was thick and lush making footwork more difficult. Training started with exercises and specific sword movements that Jarlz said were designed to increase the strength and flexibility of the wrist, arm and grip. Jarlz repeated them over and over for more than an hour. Gant and Chamz got so tired they nearly dropped their swords. After the exercises, Jarlz took out his sword and had each of his students attack him. Both Chamz and Gant were easy targets now, too tired to effectively defend themselves.

Finally Jarlz called an end to practice. Exhausted, Gant and Chamz dragged themselves back to Hammond House. They washed up and flopped onto a bench in the main room for dinner. Everything smelled extra delicious, though Gant was so tired he thought of skipping the meal. But the food came, the ale washed it down, and Gant was reenergized.

Chamz looked up from his meal and said, "Now that was a workout. Are we going to work that hard every day?"

Jarlz chuckled. "Are you ready to go back to work at Hammond House?"

"Well, no," said Chamz. "I just thought, well, we trained pretty hard before. Compared to today we were just playing."

"Combat training should be as tough as possible and still it won't be as tough as when it's for real. No matter how hard you push yourself now you'll still need to find unknown reserves when the time comes. And Gant doesn't have much time."

Gant lurched alert. "You keep saying that. What am I training for?"

"The world is changing. Evil grows and we'll need every available swordsman to defend against it. I think you will be an important part of that."

It was an answer without being an answer. Gant would have asked more questions but fatigue clouded his mind. "Okay," he said, "but right now I'm ready for some sleep."

"Yes, and sleep is what you should be doing," said Jarlz, rising from his bench and heading for their rooms.

They all went directly to bed. Gant was asleep instantly. His dreams were of sword fights, duels with evil men and then with a black, formless monster. In the morning he couldn't remember if he'd won or lost.

One day ran into another. The training was endless. At first a few curious onlookers came from Blasseldune to watch. But Jarlz made the boys work solo drills whenever anyone was watching. Eventually the curious left and then the sparring started again. Soon no one bothered to come.

Both swordsmen improved quickly. Gant began to score an occasional point on his uncle. And the fatigue they'd felt that first day faded. Now they trained even harder and still had energy at the end of the day to sit in the main room at Hammond House with an after-dinner pint and listen to the stories and gossip that circulated.

After barely a month Gant finally had a day when he scored more points than his uncle. And even Chamz scored twice on Uncle Jarlz.

The next day Gant faced his uncle. Gant tried to circle until he had his uncle facing the sun. Jarlz knew that trick and constantly maneuvered to get Gant facing the sun. As a result, neither ended up with the sun at their back. Gant measured the distance between them. Uncle Jarlz hefted his sword, smiling with the pride that comes when a pupil has learned their lessons.

"One more flurry," said Jarlz, "then we head back to Hammond House and talk about your future."

Gant nodded. It seemed early to be leaving the meadow. The sun was still high in the sky. But if Uncle Jarlz said it was enough, then it was enough.

Jarlz rushed in, his sword poised high for a down stroke. Gant parried deftly and counter-thrust to the ribs. Jarlz blocked but before he could attack again Gant arced his sword skillfully overhead and brought it to a stop with the softest touch at Jarlz's neck.

Uncle Jarlz grinned and said, "You've learned all I can teach you. Let's go get some lunch."

Jarlz clapped Gant on the back as they walked back to the road.

Chamz hustled along beside them. "Now are we going to start a real adventure?"

Jarlz laughed. "I think the adventure started a long time ago. For you, I think it's time you went home. Your father has his hands full and he's worried about you."

"When Gant can go home, I'll go home."

Gant turned to his friend. "Chamz, I'm the one exiled. No reason you couldn't go home for a bit."

Chamz ignored Gant. "Where is Gant going?" he asked Jarlz. "You seem to know and won't tell us."

"Wait until we're back at the inn. There'll be plenty of time for talking then."

Once they reached Hammond House they took their usual table. Today the inn was lightly attended. Gant knew everyone except for the stranger sitting at an empty table in the corner. His dress and the lute propped against the table suggested he was a traveling minstrel.

"Ale," shouted Jarlz once they were seated.

He leaned back slightly and rested one heavy boot on the unoccupied stool between himself and Chamz. He looked at Gant for a moment, considering, and then motioned with his big right hand for Gant to lean closer. Gant obediently leaned in. Jarlz smacked him hard on the ear.

"Never be so eager to obey another," instructed Jarlz through clenched teeth. "Follow your own mind else someone take advantage of your good nature."

Chamz tried to hide his laugh, but couldn't. Gant smacked him on the shoulder. "What are you laughing at?"

Jarlz frowned. "Both of you," he snapped. "This is no kid's game. You are men who will be counted on to do what is right despite our enemy's best efforts to deceive you. You must judge what you hear and see by your own yardstick. Not what someone else tells you." With that Jarlz leaned back and relaxed.

"I don't understand," said Gant, "I'd do anything you say."

"Me, too," added Chamz.

"I know, lad. It's best if you trust people less." A softness crept into Jarlz's voice. "You've been the best pupil ever, and Chamz, you've been a close second. But there is little more I can teach and you need to go your own way." He paused a moment. "I'm only holding you back."

The ale arrived. Gant grabbed his and took a sip. He'd forgotten how thirsty he was and the cool liquid felt good.

"How about something to eat?" asked Chamz, reaching for his mug.

Jarlz nodded. "Yes, a platter of the roast meat and bread will do."

Gant stared into his mug for a few moments. If training was over what was he going to do? Before he left Netherdorf he had worked in the smithy, regardless of his sword training. He wasn't going back to a smithy. And he didn't want a job in Blasseldune as a guard. He'd heard that the King of Mulldain was hiring troops but

Gant had no desire to be a foot soldier. He'd also heard of the free town of Kittenspenny's plea for help to fight off outlaws. The pay was small but the cause was just. Perhaps that dispute was already settled.

While Gant pondered his future, Jarlz serenely sipped his ale. A smile grew slowly on Jarlz's face, broadening with Gant's growing frustration.

Chamz finally couldn't take it. "All right. What is it Gant's supposed to do? You keep talking about our enemies, and the like. Let us in on it."

Gant looked up. "Yes, let us in on it."

Jarlz nearly choked on his ale. "Okay, okay. I had a feeling once I announced school was out you'd be at a loss for direction. And with the answer so obvious. You've got to think farther ahead, lad."

Chamz fidgeted with his mug. "Okay, Uncle Jarlz, quit stalling."

"You can only have one goal."

Chamz thumped his mug on the table. "Yes! The games of combat at Devonshield."

"By the Great Dragons' Fire, you're right," roared Jarlz, slamming his fist on the table so hard the mugs jumped with a spray of foam.

"Are you kidding? They're hardly games. People get killed. And only the very best even dare enter."

Chamz grabbed Gant by the shoulder. "Don't you see? If you win at Devonshield, it isn't just the prize. You're famous. Kings and nobles seek you out. You can choose your adventures. You're a hero."

"I'm not sure fate will allow Gant to choose his adventures, but otherwise Chamz's right. You need to enter."

"Who will sponsor me? I'm exiled and not even a noble."

"That doesn't matter. I'll post your entry fee and you can pay me back with your winnings."

"What makes you think I'll win?"

"You forget I fought there once. Almost won, except for the injury to my hand."

"Sorry. I didn't forget. It just seems impossible."

"Well, I say you're ready. For Devonshield or anywhere else."

"Then I'll go to Devonshield. But only if you go with me."

"And me, too," piped in Chamz.

"Try to keep me away," said Jarlz. "Chamz, I don't know. I promised your father that I would send you home."

"And you also just told us to think for ourselves. I'm going with you."

Gant grabbed Chamz's arm. "And I say he comes with us."

"Okay. Before we go I'll have to outfit you properly. You'll need a breastplate, helm and shield. It won't be fancy just serviceable."

"When do we leave?" asked Chamz.

"Tomorrow. Early. We'll get what we need this afternoon."

The food arrived and the three of them dug in. They didn't pay any attention to the dark-haired minstrel. They didn't notice him hurry off immediately after overhearing Jarlz say they would leave in the morning.

Gant thought about the games at Devonshield. It was unnerving. Fighting the best swordsmen was worrisome enough, but what if he killed someone? Not that he'd mean to, just that those things happened. He'd heard the stories. Maybe he shouldn't have agreed so quickly. Too late now.

Chapter 9

The next day dawned clear and wintry cold. Yellow and red leaves clung stubbornly to the trees. Gant, Jarlz and Chamz put on furs, heavy boots and pulled their hoods up to cover their ears. Gant wore the breastplate and mail shirt his uncle had purchased for him. It was uncomfortable and made carrying his pack harder. Jarlz led his horse, preferring to walk along with Gant and Chamz.

They said goodbye to the innkeeper and headed north. A stiff wind blew straight into their faces forcing them to keep their heads down. They marched briskly, the cold kept them moving. Despite the frigid air, despite the gray skies, they walked with buoyed spirits. Finally they had a goal and were doing something.

The wind made talking difficult and so the threesome tramped on in silence. It wasn't long before Gant's armor started to rub his chest raw under his light shirt. He endured it quietly for as long as he could.

Finally, he said, "Uncle Jarlz, this armor is cutting into me. Can't I take it off at least until we reach Devonshield?"

Jarlz chuckled to himself. "All the more reason to keep it on. That armor must become a part of you, as natural to wear as your pants. Otherwise it will hinder you in battle instead of protect. Better get used to it."

"Hey," said Chamz, a mischievous smile on his face, "if you don't want it, I'll take it."

"No doubt," said Jarlz, "but Gant is the one entering the games. Maybe you can have a go at it next year."

"Really? Do you think I'd be ready?"

"Probably as long as Gant doesn't decide to enter again."

"And Gant can sponsor me after he wins this year."

Gant said nothing. It was presumptuous to talk of winning when he'd never fought anyone except his uncle and his friend. And that was just practice. No, the tournament was going to be a lot different.

The trio continued steadily until midday when Jarlz pointed out a glade of young oak trees ringing an opening in the forest. A well-used fire pit sat in the middle of the clearing. Around it the trees formed a thick barrier and Gant couldn't see more than a few feet into the forest. At least the trees cut off the wind.

"I'll make a fire," said Chamz.

"Don't bother," said Jarlz. "We won't be staying long."

Gant slumped down on his pack. His legs were tired. More than that, he was cold through to his bones. "What's the hurry, Uncle?" he asked.

"I've a spot in mind for our evening camp and we are still a long way from it. There's no place worth staying between here and there so we need to keep moving."

Jarlz tied his horse to a sapling. Chamz sat down and started rummaging in his pack when the first volley of crossbow bolts struck. One hit Chamz in the chest, another deflected off Jarlz' mail shirt, another stuck in Gant's pack.

In one smooth motion, Jarlz pulled his sword, dashed to his horse and yanked his shield off the horse's back. Gant rolled over drawing his sword. Chamz fell backward blood flowing from his wound. He groaned and lay still.

A violent rage swept over Gant. He leaped up and dashed toward the unseen shooters. Jarlz advanced more cautiously, his shield up. Three more bolts flashed toward Gant. One went wide, one glanced off Gant's mailed sleeve, the third stuck in his breastplate just below the floating ribs. The tip poked through the layer of metal and leather and dug into Gant's skin.

"After them," shouted Jarlz, and sprinted headlong toward the attackers.

Gant grabbed the crossbow bolt lodged in his armor and, with a twist and tug, pulled it free. Tossing it aside, he ran forward and shouted "What about Chamz?"

"We'll tend to him after we've dealt with them," said Jarlz.

Jarlz disappeared into the thicket, forcing his way through the perimeter of oak saplings. He plunged in among the widely spaced trees of the older forest. Gant followed close behind using the path that his uncle had wedged open.

Another volley of iron-tipped bolts zipped at Gant. This time the bolts glanced off trees. Gant lunged ahead.

Moments later, Jarlz and Gant broke into a clearing in time to see three men on horses gallop away southward. In an instant, they were gone. Gant recognized one of them. Talth! He had finally made good on his vow of revenge.

"No use chasing them now," said Jarlz. "Let's get back to Chamz."

They hurried back to the campsite. As they ran, Gant said, "One of them was Talth. I tangled with him the first day we came to Blasseldune."

"Just like that coward to attack from ambush. We'll deal with him later."

Back at camp they found Chamz in a pool of blood. Gant fought back tears.

Jarlz leaned down, lightly touching the bolt in Chamz' chest. "I don't know if I should pull it out or leave it in. If only Uric was here."

Gant knelt beside his fallen friend. "I should have given him the armor," he muttered.

Bent over as he was, Gant didn't see Uric enter the clearing.

"Did someone call my name?" asked Uric, his soft voice filled with a strange power that gave Gant shivers. The sage stood tall, majestic in his amethyst robes. His eyes were two pools of green that hid many secrets.

Jarlz jumped up his hand going to his sword.

"No need for that," said Uric. "I reached Blasseldune only this day looking for you. They told me you'd left for the games at

Devonshield. I was worried that you weren't going to get there in time and so I followed up the north road."

"Can you do anything for Chamz?" asked Gant.

"Let me see," said Uric, bending down for a closer look. "He's taken a bad shot but I think I can put him right again."

Gant stepped back to give the sage room. "Can I get anything?"

"No," said Uric. "I have what I need in my cloak."

Uric wrapped his hand around the shaft of the crossbow bolt and eased it out. It popped out like a cork from a champagne bottle, blood spurting freely. Quickly, Uric placed a dressing of clean white cloth over the wound and pressed firmly. "Here," he said to Gant, "hold this in place while I prepare some medicine."

Gant knelt next to Chamz. His friend's face was ash gray, his breathing shallow. "You're going to be all right," Gant whispered as he placed his hand over the dressing and held it.

Uric retrieved a couple of bottles from pockets concealed within his robes along with another pad of soft cloth. For the next few minutes the sage mixed liquids from this bottle and that and blotted the cloth with the result.

"Okay," he said finally. "Let me in there."

Gant moved back.

Uric kneeled down, replacing the bloody dressing with the medicine soaked pad. He mumbled a few words that Gant couldn't quite make out, and then stood up. The medicine-soaked dressing stuck to Chamz.

"Now what?" asked Jarlz.

"I've got to get him back to Hammond House, a warm bed and some rest."

"Is he going to be all right?" asked Gant.

"He'll be okay. But it will take time." Uric's smile was reassuring.

"Okay, then let's get going," said Gant. "I'll help carry him."

"No," said Uric. "You and Jarlz must go on to the games. I'll see to Chamz."

"Don't worry, Gant," said Jarlz, "Uric will see that nothing happens to Chamz."

Gant's mind swirled. "He's my friend. I can't just leave him."

Uric put a hand on Gant's shoulder. "Gant, you must go to Devonshield. Chamz will be fine. I'll send him north as soon as he's well enough to travel."

Gant looked at his uncle for reassurance.

Jarlz nodded. "We need to go. And so does Uric."

"Okay," said Gant. He reached out, touched Chamz on the arm. "Get well," he said.

Jarlz untied his horse, slung his shield over the saddle and started toward the road. Uric lifted Chamz in his arms. Gant took one last look at his friend, shouldered his pack and followed his uncle. At the road, Uric turned south toward Blasseldune. Gant and Jarlz went north. Before he'd gone far, Gant looked back. The road was already empty as far as he could see. Uric must indeed be in a hurry.

Chapter 10

Gant and his uncle marched steadily all afternoon. Silently Gant worried about Chamz. As the day faded into dusk, a light mist began to fall. Jarlz guided Gant through the trees to the mouth of a shallow cave about a hundred yards from the road. Jarlz tethered his horse nearby and within a few minutes had a glowing fire perched in the cave opening. They sat, backs to the wall, in the dry cave. The fire warmed their spirits as well as their bones.

"How did you know about this cave?" asked Gant as the fire loosened his tongue.

"I found it years ago. An ambush drove me off the road and good luck led me through the trees to this hillside. The cave gave me a perfect fortress. Only one of the rogues could attack me at a time and the rabble that they were left them no match for me one-on-one. Several of the biggest fell before they got the idea they'd rather look for easier prey."

"Some people are born lucky," said Gant rubbing his hands in front of the fire.

Jarlz pulled a few pieces of firewood from a cache under a pile of stones and tossed them on the fire. "Sometimes you need a bit of luck," he said. "Sometimes you make your own luck. In the morning we'll restock the firewood."

He poked the hot coals with a long stick and continued, "Tomorrow night we'll sleep better. I know a wizard who lives within walking distance. Warm house, fine beds, and best of all, he'll know who to watch out for at the games."

"Good," said Gant and let the fire's warmth ease the tightness in his muscles. "Do you think Chamz is okay? It was a long way back to Blasseldune. It seems impossible for Uric to get Chamz there in time."

Jarlz smiled. "Don't worry about Chamz. Uric has his ways. Next time you see Chamz, he'll be fit as ever."

Gant still didn't see how, but his uncle's reassuring words put Gant temporarily at ease. His thoughts turned to his father. How was he doing in the smithy without Gant? He sat up. "Uncle, do you think my father is angry at me? I couldn't stand by and let Wendler do what he was about to do, noble or not."

"Gant," said Jarlz, putting one hand on Gant's shoulder, "your father loves you very much. He knows you did what's right. But he can't change the law. Often I think he felt inadequate marrying a noblewoman. But my sister loves your father and has never regretted the marriage. Somehow this will all work out."

"I hope you're right," said Gant.

Jarlz slapped him on the back. "Sleep now. I'll take the first watch."

"Okay," yawned Gant, "Wake me for my turn."

Jarlz nodded. Gant rolled over in his bedroll, his mind filled with questions about his father and mother and what was a real wizard like. And how could Uric just show up in the woods when Chamz was shot? Maybe Uric was a wizard. He fell asleep wondering.

#

Jarlz was still sitting in front of the fire like a fury statue when the morning sun woke Gant.

"Jarlz!" barked Gant.

"What?" Jarlz's head snapped around.

"You didn't wake me."

"Of course not. You needed your rest and I'm used to standing watch by myself. Now get up. It's time to be moving."

They wolfed down a cold breakfast bundled in their furs while the north wind whipped around the cave mouth. The small fire barely fought off the chill. Gant's feet were numb by the time they were ready to start the day's trek. He stamped heavily to bring them back to life.

They started off, keeping a fast pace all day. Except for bends in the road they walked straight into the wind. They pulled their furs around their faces and ears until only their eyes peeked out through slits. Gray clouds blotted out the sky making everything dull and lifeless. Occasionally a streak of sunlight burst through to lighten their mood. Neither of them cared to talk and they trudged on silently. Even lunch was on the move.

The quick pace not only kept them warm but also got them to their destination early. The sun was well above the horizon when Jarlz pointed to a narrow footpath leading off the road. They turned in and followed it until, through an opening in a wall of tall pines, Gant saw a stout log cabin. Amazingly, the windows were wide open. Flowers bloomed in well-tended beds up against the house.

Jarlz stopped at the edge of the ring of pine trees. Gant stopped behind him and only then noticed a shimmering wall that blocked their path.

Jarlz planted both feet, cupped his hands around his mouth and shouted, "Abadis." After a moment's pause he yelled louder. "Sir Jarlz of the Whispering Blade wishes to visit."

Whispering Blade, wondered Gant. What was that about? Must be another tale he hadn't heard. He made a mental note to ask about it the first chance he got. Just then a bearded face, wrinkled heavily around eyes that glowed, peered out one of the windows.

"Ah, Sir Jarlz, 'tis you. And with a young man. No doubt your nephew and new apprentice. Enter as you wish."

The old man mouthed a string of words that were strange to Gant and the shimmering wall faded. Jarlz stepped through with Gant close on his heels.

Once inside, the translucent barrier reappeared behind them. Gant noted that the air was warm, like a summer day. Jarlz dropped the lead line to his horse and the big chestnut mare lowered her head to taste the tender grass. Jarlz pulled off his furs and heavy breastplate and held them out at arm's length. Miraculously, a hand-shaped tree limb swayed down and scooped them up. The limb and its load disappeared back into the pine leaving no sign of the garments. Gant stepped back bewildered, a small knot growing in his gut.

Jarlz chuckled, motioned to the trees and said, "These are his servants. Enchanted to receive guests. They'll hold your bulky gear until we depart."

"But. . . it's warm, and. . ." Gant waved his hand around trying to formulate all the questions he had.

"Don't worry," laughed Jarlz, "Abadis' magic is powerful enough to control everything around this house, weather included. Come on, get your things off, lad, and let's get inside."

Gant obeyed. Warily he eyed the bough that took his furs and breastplate. And then the two men walked to the door.

The door opened as they approached. Inside, the main room was warm and cheery despite a cluttered of jars, boxes, sacks, bowls, and other paraphernalia. Shelves lined every wall and except for a small table with stools there was no furniture. The roaring fire in the fireplace on the far wall put a golden glow on everything. The old man Gant had seen at the window stood near the center of the room wrapped in dark robes, arms folded across his chest.

"Sir Jarlz," he said with a smile. "It's been long since we sat together. Welcome." He opened his arms and glided over to Jarlz, hugging him as a father would a son. Then turning to Gant, "And this must be the nephew you're always talking about. Grown up, is he?"

"Yes, this is Gant, my sister's son and the son of my sword maker, her husband. A fine man he's grown into wouldn't you say?"

Gant bowed stiffly from the waist not sure what the proper greeting for a wizard was. He said, "A pleasure to meet you, sir."

Jarlz turned back to Abadis. "Gant and I are going to Devonshield. Gant is entering. What can you tell us about other entrants?"

"There is time for serious talk later. First, let us dine. Surely you must be hungry from your long walk. I'm hungry myself and I hate to talk of important matters on an empty stomach."

Chapter 11

Meanwhile, Barlon Gorth sat at his table in the Mountain Castle, eating a meal of roast meat, crusty bread and an endless supply of ale. His wizard, Razgoth, sat with him.

"My Lord, are you certain we shall have the help of the craftsmen we capture?" asked Razgoth running his hand through his disheveled hair.

"Razgoth, you worry too much. We have ways to ensure they will give you all the help you need. The timeline has only moved up a little." Barlon worried that his masterstroke would be too late and not catch Netherdorf in turmoil. Already reports hinted that the nobles were less interested in the fate of the commoner, Gant, and more concerned about Barlon's growing armies. A unified enemy was not good. Perhaps his spies would yet be able to stir the pot a bit before the attack.

At that moment, Shalmuthe, Barlon's stocky master spy rushed in, stopped behind a chair, and stood motionless waiting for his ruler to speak.

"I hope you bring me good news," said Barlon between chewing. "Like maybe the Netherdorf nobles are going to revolt against their king."

"No. Nothing so important." His left hand went to the scar across his left cheek, rubbing it unconsciously. "I thought you'd want to know that our attempts to intercept Gant on his way to Devonshield failed."

Razgoth jumped up. "Failed. I told you Gant would be trouble."

Barlon waved Razgoth back into his seat. "Nothing has happened. So he goes to Devonshield. Until he wins there, it proves nothing. But," Barlon turned back to Shalmuthe, "how did you fail? I thought you had it all planned."

"Talth turned out to be less efficient in deed than in word. They did ambush Gant, as agreed, but shot only Gant's insignificant friend and when they saw Sir Jarlz, they turned and fled."

Barlon scowled. "Then Sir Jarlz is not in Netherdorf."

"True, Sire. He has gone with Gant to Devonshield."

Barlon rubbed his chin for a moment, thinking. "All is not lost. We may have to postpone our attack until after Devonshield."

"How's that, my Lord?" asked Razgoth.

"Fool. Capturing Netherdorf without capturing Sir Jarlz ruins the plan and the amulet becomes worthless. We'll wait until he returns. In the meantime, Shalmuthe, what about Talth?"

"I think he should be eliminated," growled the master spy. "Failure is not acceptable."

"Failure is not acceptable. Cowardice even less. We've no use for gutless vermin. See that he's taught a permanent lesson that others will not miss."

"Consider it done." Shalmuthe turned to go.

"Make sure you let me know when Sir Jarlz returns to Netherdorf."

"And make sure we know the results of Devonshield," added Razgoth.

Shalmuthe waved over his shoulder without turning and hurried off.

Razgoth leaned forward in his chair, took a drink of water. "Sire," he began, "what shall we do if Gant wins Devonshield?"

Barlon shook his head. "You are concerned about the prophecy. Are you familiar with the details?"

"I've heard it often enough."

"Let me refresh your memory. First a descendant of Bartholomew must win at Devonshield. After which he is supposed to receive a sword powerful enough to kill Varg. I'm guessing the dark elves have it hidden somewhere. We know Gant is such a descendant, so if he wins, he still must get this magic sword. If you think about it, the sword he carries is a nice piece of work but it is hardly the kind of weapon that would concern Varg. No, for now I don't see any reason to worry. We'll keep track of Gant and if he wins and suddenly has a new sword, then we will disarm him or kill him."

Razgoth thought about his liege lord's words and a plan took shape. A smile crossed his face. "That's when Egog will be of service. A service I did not foresee."

Barlon sighed. "There are lots of things you don't foresee. Sometimes I wonder if you are a wizard at all."

"But sire," choked Razgoth, "not all wizards are good at seeing the future."

"Obviously."

Chapter 12

Gant and Jarlz ate a hearty meal with Abadis. The food was delicious even though Gant couldn't identify anything on the table. It all seemed to be concoctions of ground and powdered vegetables, grains, and nuts. It was tastier than anything Gant could remember since his last meal at home. That reminded him of his mother and father. He wondered how they were and whether he would ever see them again.

While they ate, Abadis and Uncle Jarlz talked lightly of past events and of recent happenings. Finally Abadis cleared the table and gave them each a sparkling, crystal glass containing a translucent violet liquid. The aroma was euphoric. The flavor even better.

"So. Gant is to enter the competition?" started Abadis once they were all settled back around the table. "If Jarlz says you're ready, then I don't doubt it's true. I should warn you that Zeigone will be there to defend his crown. A nastier champion there has never been. Three times he's won and never left a man alive to fight another day. He's a scoundrel, a skillful one which makes him all the more dangerous."

"I'll wager Gant will show him a trick or two," said Jarlz winking at Gant.

"As for tricks, Zeigone has a few himself. He's won the last two titles by slashing his opponent's forearms. He uses a deft twist of the wrist that's very effective. No one's been able to defend against it and believe me they've tried."

"What about his weapons?" asked Sir Jarlz.

"Two-handed broadsword, light armor, no shield. Both sword and armor have a bit of magic in them, or I'm a blind old man. Zeigone was born evil and has only gotten nastier. He must be stopped."

"How can I defeat him? My sword has no magic, nor my armor."

Jarlz glanced at Abadis. A fresh gleam sparkled in the old man's eyes.

"Gant," said the wizard, winking secretively, "I must confess. I knew you would come, and in fact, knew your goal. Knowing Jarlz as I do, your training could be aimed at nothing else. So. . ." He rose and stepped lightly over to a small chest sitting unobtrusively next to a tall rack of powders, potions and books. Flipping open the lid he pulled out two silvery mail sleeves. "I wish it were more," Abadis said with a sigh, cradling the shimmering sleeves. "I made them for you. It took almost a month, but worth it if you can stop Zeigone."

The wizard stepped over to Gant with the sleeves laid across his outstretched forearms. The tiny metallic links intertwined in a pattern too intricate to follow, so perfect that they appeared solid. The firelight flashed and reflected off them in lively prismatic splashes of color. Gant had never seen anything so masterfully crafted in his life. How could he accept such a gift from a total stranger? "Take them," said Abadis. "They will only fit you."

"But, how can I repay you?"

"It is I who repay old debts," said Abadis and nodded to Jarlz.

Gant reached out and reverently cradled the brilliant chain mail sleeves. A strange warmth rushed up his palms, through his arms and spread through his body. An irresistible urge to wear the sleeves swept over him. Recklessly he pulled them on.

At first they felt awkward. They were too big, too vibrant, almost alive. Then they shrank, molding themselves to his forearms until they were like a second skin. The sensation faded and it was as if they weren't there at all. Gant had to concentrate to feel them. Every way he moved, they moved with him with an energy of their own. How much easier it would be to wield his sword, he thought.

"Wear them against Zeigone. They will deflect his attacks at your forearms and give you the speed to counterattack. No matter what, don't let him see you wearing them before your combat has begun, least he devise some new methods you are not armed against," warned Abadis sternly. "The others you fight, and there won't be many for Zeigone has scared off most men, will have little chance against you. Only Zeigone can test you and with these sleeves as a surprise, you can defeat him.

"Lastly, cruel as it sounds, do not spare him. If he lives I see only more evil."

"Kill in cold blood?" Gant was horrified. "I won't do it."

"You must," demanded Abadis.

"Evil men know no silence but the grave," broke in Jarlz. "And make no mistake, this Zeigone will kill you if he can. You will likely be forced to do him in first.

"Abadis, you've done us a great service," continued Jarlz, "for which Gant and I thank you. Our visit here has been more valuable than I had hoped. Gant will not betray your trust. He will dispatch Zeigone or I shall do it myself."

Abadis laid a gnarled hand on Jarlz' shoulder, "You know, old friend, that heroic deeds are for the young. Our time has passed. Be content to train those who carry on."

Jarlz nodded slowly. That over with, they all sat back around the table and sipped from refilled glasses. Talk turned to days past, old friendships, and the conversation carried long into the night. Gant sat quietly and listened. He wasn't going to kill Zeigone. If letting him live brought evil, then someone else would kill him later.

Soon though, he found himself caught up in the stories Jarlz and Abadis shared. It reminded Gant of Uric at the castle. Tall tales, fun to listen to. And all the while he soaked up a newfound warmth from the magic sleeves.

#

The next morning dawned clear and calm. The sun shone through scattered clouds. It was still cool, but comfortable for walking. Abadis fed them well before they left. Once more he wished Gant luck against Zeigone and reminded him to hide the sleeves until the last minute. And with that Gant and Jarlz started down the road to Devonshield.

Eventually they reached Devonshield. It was a quaint town built in the middle of a great forest. The buildings were almost exclusively wood. The lone exception was the king's towering stone castle. The shops were small and pushed together along narrow streets. The population swelled with the throngs who arrived for the games. Tents were packed together around the wide meadow that comprised the tournament field. Jarlz shed his distinctive armor and kept his face hidden to avoid being recognized, and Gant and Jarlz mingled with the crowds passing unnoticed into Devonshield.

Once in town Jarlz insisted they stay out of sight so that the other competitors would wonder who Gant was. Surprise could be the deciding factor, Jarlz explained and he planned to use it to their advantage. Jarlz knew an old stable master who put them up where they wouldn't be bothered and then he went alone to enter Gant's name in the competition so that up to the first match no one had yet seen Gant.

The next day was clear, sunny and a bit cool. When they reached the tournament site, Gant surveyed the vast expanse of meadow that served as the battlefield. He marveled at the number of tents surrounding the field sprouting dozens of colorful banners. At the end of the meadow, central to the combat area was the raised platform and tent of the King of Devonshield.

The splendor and majesty overwhelmed Gant. There was nothing like it in Netherdorf. King Tirmus forbid fighting for sport. For a moment Gant was filled with doubts. He'd only ever fought unskilled thugs.

"Are you sure I'm ready for this?" he asked his uncle.

Jarlz' reassuring pat on the back did little to calm Gant.

The draw for opponents put Gant in the opposite division from Zeigone. A good sign, his uncle assured Gant. There were only eight competitors registered. In the first match of the day, a wiry man named Evan bested a blocky man known simply as Tee by dodging, parrying and counter strokes. It was not a short match and Gant studied both men knowing that if he won his first match then the winner would be his next opponent.

The next match pitted Zeigone against the king's own entry, Sir Harold. Gant watched as the valiant knight attempted to avoid Zeigone's deadly slashes to the wrists and forearms, and failed. Bloody, and hardly able to hold his sword, Zeigone dispatched him with a thrust to the neck. Sir Harold died on the field.

Gant was up next. He swallowed back his fear and studied his first opponent. He was a huge bulk of a man named Brax. He carried a two-handed sword that matched his size. The king sounded the beginning and the two combatants advanced across the field. As they closed with each other, Brax pulled back his sword for a massive strike. Gant readied for it. Brax swung. Gant pushed it aside and countered with a cut to the head. Brax staggered for a moment, righted himself and swung again. Gant dodged it and swatted Brax on the side of the helm again. Before the bigger man could react, Gant hit him again, this time with the flat of the blade. Brax's head snapped back and Gant darted in and hit him with the pommel under the chin. Brax sank to his knees and fell forward. Gant sighed with relief, thankful it had been quick. Better yet, Brax soon would be fine.

The first round ended with a match between Argoll and Karnon. Gant barely paid attention, instead planning his strategy against Evan. It wouldn't be anything like his battle with Brax.

Karnon won and rested while Gant took on Evan. This time, Gant was up against a polished swordsman who was as quick as Gant and nearly as skilled. Back and forth they went, slash and parry, cut and counter. In the end, Evan yielded, totally worn out from two long drawn out contests. Gant was thankful he'd defeated Brax quickly.

While Gant rested, Zeigone took care of Karnon, slashing him to pieces until the loss of blood caused him to falter. Zeigone finished him with a cutting stroke to the neck.

The crowd loved a winner and after his first match, they cheered Gant even as they cheered Zeigone for his indefensible slashing attacks. Expectantly, the crowd waited as the two favorites worked their way toward the inevitable confrontation. Betting ran heavy on them both.

Finally it was time for the championship match. Behind the grandstand, Gant slipped on the magic sleeves and walked nervously out onto the field. He stopped at his designated spot. Across the way, Zeigone strode to his spot. The crowd quieted, breathlessly silent in anticipation. In his viewing stand the King of Devonshield stood up and paused at the railing, poised to signal the beginning of the final contest.

Gant stood on the grassy field studying his opponent. He hefted his sword in one hand and balanced his shield in the other. The magic sleeves warmed his forearms. Despite his earlier victories, Gant was less than confident. Not that he feared dying. It was more about letting down his uncle and Abadis. What if he failed?

Zeigone stared back haughtily, dripping confidence. His dark beard bristled from under his open faceplate; his heavy black helm seemed to suck the light from the air. The strange white, eye-shaped symbol on his breastplate stared hypnotically at Gant.

Now the king walked with measured steps to the large brass gong hanging on the front rail. With a slight rap he signaled for the contest to begin.

"Let the battle for the champion of the Devonshield Games begin," he said hoarsely and quickly returned to his seat.

Zeigone hefted his two-handed sword and strode boldly toward Gant. The mysterious white-eye emblem on his armor captivated Gant, forcing his attention to it. As Zeigone stalked closer, his sword cocked for the attack, Gant remained spellbound, his sword hanging at his side.

In an instant, Zeigone was within striking distance. A hush fell on the crowd. In the last possible moment, Gant snapped out of it and realized Zeigone was too close. Too late to wonder how he'd been tricked, Gant leaped backward, barely dodging Zeigone's first stroke. Gant circled to his right, raising his sword in defense. Zeigone pressed his advantage, lashing out again. Gant parried. Zeigone twisted at the last instant using the same ruse that had worked on the others. His sword flashed past the parry to slash at Gant's exposed forearms. There was an audible clang as metal slammed into metal and a blinding flash as the magic in Zeigone's sword clashed with the magic in the sleeves.

The stands erupted in a loud groan. Zeigone was already twisting for another slash when Gant's counterstroke caught him on the side of the helm.

Zeigone's head snapped back, his sword hand drooped. Gant rushed in with a straight thrust. Zeigone faltered only for an instant and blocked it. He countered with another twisting blow at Gant's forearms. Again there was the ring of metal and a flash of light. Gant ignored the attack, trusting the sleeves, and stabbed straight in. His sword point pinged heavily on Zeigone's breastplate, but the metal held and only a small dent showed that a hit had been scored. Zeigone slashed Gant a third time across the forearms and got a vicious backhand on the left shoulder for his trouble.

The two men slid away from each other, circling warily. Zeigone's confident air was gone replaced by a grim look of determination. Gant grew bolder sure that Abadis' gift would ward off Zeigone's favorite attacks. For each slash across the forearms, Gant dealt a smashing blow to Zeigone's black armor. Yet there was power in that armor and the best Gant could manage was a series of small dents.

Finally, Zeigone rushed in with another slash at the forearms. Gant ignored it and attacked. Too late. It was a fake. Zeigone twisted at the last minute just as he had done all day only this time he redirected his attack at Gant's head. It landed square on Gant's helm. The steel parted. The blade gashed an ugly wound along the side of Gant's head. A spurt of warm blood blurred one eye and an explosion of pain roared through him. Gant stumbled back. Zeigone dashed in. He stabbed at Gant's ribs. Gant blocked with his shield. Zeigone followed with a lightning two-handed swing at the head. Desperately, Gant parried, partially deflecting the blow. Before he could recover, a second slash rent Gant's helm.

Gant lurched backwards, staggered and went down on one knee. His mind whirled, bees buzzed in his brain. Zeigone snickered and moved in for the finishing strike, a two-handed, overhand blow.

But he savored the moment an instant too long. Through the haze, Gant saw the opening and his reflexes responded. Gant whisked the deathblow aside, and counterattacked in a blur of motion. His sword caught Zeigone at the joint between helm and body armor. A sickening, rending sound split the air. A gush of red spewed over the front of the black breastplate. Gant watched from a dazed stupor. The great sword slipped from Zeigone's hand and fell harmlessly to the ground. Zeigone tottered and fell with a crash of metal.

Pages rushed to remove the fallen man's helm and then bustled his body away to the medicine tent. Gant struggled to his feet. Statue-like he watched them clear the field. The taste of death gagged him. He turned to leave. He needed a place to retch. But arms were around him. Jarlz first, followed by the crowd. They shoved and jostled him to the king's stand.

Hardly able to stand, Gant stared up at the king, wobbling unsteadily.

"Oh Gant of the Ironlimbs," began the king, a smile on his thin lips, "Champion today. Come forward and claim your prize."

The king held up a small leather sack that clinked with gold coins.

"Well, 'Ironlimb,'" said Jarlz through a broad smile, clutching Gant around the shoulder to steady him, "I told you you were ready."

Gant sagged against his uncle. Someone lifted the sword from his stiff fingers. With Jarlz for support, Gant stumbled from the field, his body shaking from both fatigue and guilt. His uncle helped him to the combatants' tent and pulled off Gant's armor. A page brought warm water and rubbed Gant's aching muscles. A doctor followed the page and cleansed Gant's wounds. The head wounds caused considerable concern and the doctor suggested that Gant be taken someplace quiet to rest. With assurances from Jarlz, the doctor left.

Finally, once Gant had on clean clothes, Jarlz helped him to Jarlz' favorite inn. Amidst a torrent of well-wishers Jarlz rented a room upstairs near the back where they could have a semblance of quiet. It was all Gant could do to climb the stairs and trudge to the end of the hall. The day's events seemed like a dream. He flopped into bed without removing his clothes and immediately fell into a stupor-like sleep.

Chapter 13

The next morning a soft tap at the door woke Gant. He rubbed his eyes, stretched stiff shoulder muscles, and rolled from the straw-filled mattress. He felt his head and was surprised there was no ugly wound.

"Who's there?"

"Uric."

The sage is always near, thought Gant, and opened the door. Uric entered carrying a huge cloth sack bulging with lumpy objects. Today his amethyst robes hung from his shoulders wrinkled and dusty. Gant thought he looked as if he'd been rummaging in a closet.

Uric dropped the bag on the floor with a metallic thud.

Gant looked at the sack. Whatever it was it couldn't be that important. "How's Chamz?" he asked.

"Chamz is fine. Right now it's more important for you to know the truth," said Uric, straightening. "You are the one in the prophecy, the prophecy written by your great-great-great grandfather, Bartholomew. He was the greatest practitioner of magic that has ever been, unless you count the ancients at Tirumfall, though that was so long ago no one can separate truth and legend."

Uric paused, muttered, "But I digress." And then continued, "In Bartholomew's time, a demon lord named Varg ruled the dark elves. Varg had taken female slaves from the fair elves and from them he fathered the race of dark elves. He forced them to perform evil at his command. By chance, Bartholomew met and fell in love with the dark elf queen, Celestina. For a time they met in secret using Bartholomew's powerful magic to shield them from Varg's spies, cloaking them in invisibility. Eventually, through research in ancient magical tomes, Bartholomew gained sufficient knowledge to exile Varg back to the realms of darkness.

"Bartholomew knew that magic is ever changing and that somehow, sometime, Varg would be recalled by evil men who would attempt to use the demon's powers to rule the world. Looking into the future, his worst fears were confirmed. Varg would be recalled. And worse, Bartholomew saw that future wizards would not have the power to stop Varg. Therefore he made this magical armor and sword for his distant grandson who would win at the Devonshield games. For you. In your hands it can defeat Varg once and for all."

At this Uric flipped open the sack. Gant peered in at a beautiful set of silvery armor and the most magnificent sword he'd ever seen. The shiny hilt was engraved in the shape of a huge dragon standing beside a lone warrior. Slowly, Gant reached down and pulled the sword from the scabbard. As his hand withdrew the gleaming length of metal, a pulsing vibration tingled through his hand.

"May I present the sword Valorius Goodenkil," said Uric.

Gant examined the blade, marveling at the perfection, the flawless mastery of the smith's art. Yet there was more to this sword than any smith could have fabricated. The sword was without the tiniest mark, as if formed in an instant without the smith's hammer. He slid his thumb across her edge and the skin parted without pain. Gant looked in awe at the tiny drop of blood that oozed from the slit.

"What am I supposed to do with this?" he asked, holding it up.

"When the time comes, kill Varg. However, I must warn you that even this sword has been infused with only a limited, though very large, dose of positive magical energy and any time it meets negative magic it will be drained at least a little. Only Bartholomew himself was powerful enough to wield the level of magic held in this sword but it is not limitless. Don't waste it. Likely you'll need every bit of power in Valorius to put an end to Varg."

"Okay," said Gant. "When will that be? How will I know when it arrives?"

"I believe it may have already come. A night of darkness passed some time ago and only on such a night when neither moon is visible can Varg be summoned."

"I don't want to kill anymore. I'm not interested in prophecies or elves or demons. I want to go home."

"How will you do that?"

"I don't know." In his heart Gant knew that until something ended his exile he could not go home.

"Nonetheless these are for you," said Uric. "In the end you may find that some things are beyond your control. Beyond anyone's control."

Gant slid Valorius back into the scabbard. "How did you get these things if Bartholomew lived so long ago?"

"I also lived then. Bartholomew made them and entrusted them to me to give to his grandson when the time was right."

"How could you have been alive then? You must be more of a wizard than he was."

"I am not a wizard, in fact, not a man. But I knew your great-great grandfather well, maybe too well. I see a lot of the goodness that was in him in you. You do not wish to harm others even those who deserve it. But when the time comes you do what must be done."

"Not a man! Then who, what, are you?"

"It doesn't matter. I have fulfilled my promise to Bartholomew. Now I have to return to Netherdorf and settle a few details with King Tirmus. Then I shall be off to find out if Varg is in our world, and if so, where. I expected to see signs of his presence and so far there have been none."

"Maybe you are wrong. Maybe he hasn't come."

"Maybe he has not been summoned yet. There is another night of darkness in a few months but so much of the prophecy has come true I think Varg must be here."

Uric turned to go. Gant let his hand caress the fine, silvery armor and felt strange whispers calling to him. He didn't want it, didn't want to kill, not even Varg. He didn't want the responsibility.

He looked up and saw Uric's dusty back going out the door. "In the meantime, don't you think someone else should use the sword and armor, someone who would put it to better use?"

"No one else *can* use it. The sword and armor were given magical abilities to identify and imprint their one and only owner. They know you now and cannot be used by anyone else."

Gant hesitated. What did that mean? That he couldn't refuse them. Uric was nearly gone when Gant found his tongue. "Thanks. Thanks for everything. The sword is beautiful. Better than any I've ever seen, let alone hoped to make."

"Use it wisely. The sword's magic is not limitless."

With that Uric was gone. Gant stood staring at Valorius wondering what to do.

#

Gant sat on his mattress fretting over the turn of events. A piece of history had fallen on him and threatened to take over his life. Conquer Varg? What kind of courage would it take to face a demon? And even if he defeated Varg would King Tirmus pardon him and allow him to return home? Well, if it would get him home again, he'd like to get on with it right away. Not that that seemed likely. Uric didn't even know if Varg had come yet. What was Gant to do?

A loud knock interrupted his thoughts. "Open up," bellowed Jarlz.

Gant stood up, shuffled to the door and opened it. "What do you want?" he asked, stepping back to let Jarlz in.

"Lad, don't you know it is customary for the winner to buy the rest of the contenders a drink? You've slept the afternoon away and now the inn downstairs is full. They're waiting for you."

"So, you buy them a drink. Here's some money," said Gant pulling the coin purse from his belt and tossing it to Jarlz.

"By the Great Dragon's fire, lad, you can't keep all these people waiting. They want you. You're the champion."

Jarlz put one huge arm around Gant's shoulder and pulled him toward the door. "Come on. Worry about your troubles tomorrow. Tonight we honor the losers."

Gant pulled back.

"What's the matter with you?" asked his uncle.

"I may be a champion here but at home I'm an outlaw."

"Gant." Jarlz's smile faded. "Don't dwell on it. In time we may be able to reverse things. Heroes have become nobles before. And being glum the rest of your life isn't going to change it. Now come on, have a drink with those who think they have a new hero. Tomorrow you can have to yourself."

"All right. All right," said Gant, shaking his head. He might not feel like it, but the others who had fought in the games deserved better.

Together they trooped down to the large common room. A roar went up when the crowd caught sight of Gant. For a moment Gant's knees went weak. So many men cheering for him. Or were they just cheering for free ale? No matter. It felt strange. They praised him, yet he had let so many people down. If they only knew.

"Good show," said one rugged fellow as Gant passed on his way to the central table where a spot was held open for him.

"Right here," said Jarlz, pointing to a stool at the head of the table.

Gant sat and looked around at the throng gathered in the inn. He hardly recognized anyone. Who were all these people?

"What will you have, sir?" asked the serving maid who appeared at Gant's elbow.

"Ale." Gant looked at Uncle Jarlz who nodded with a sly wink. "And ale for everyone."

A cheer went up and the serving maid hustled off with her wooden tray to get mugs of ale. Gant fumbled with his purse, wishing to be ready with payment when the girl returned. Before he could get the purse from his belt, the huge man at his right reached over and laid a hairy hand on Gant's forearm.

"Good work," said the warrior. "You've rid us all of scum that deserved to die. Here's to your health." He gulped down the remains of whatever was in his mug, laughed and slapped Gant on the back. "Stuck him like the pig he was."

"Well. . ." Gant swallowed, wishing the ale would arrive. He eyed the man curiously. The black haired, black-skinned swordsman was dressed in strange animal skins. He wore silver jewelry inlaid with greenish-blue stones. Gant had seen a few others dressed similarly at his father's smithy and only remembered that they were from one of the southern lands.

"It was a lucky blow, hardly what you'd call skillful," he added looking down the table, not wishing to offend the stranger.

"Modest, too," said someone farther down the table.

With that the conversation rose to a level that made Gant's ears ring. All this commotion, especially about him, was unnerving. Again he fumbled with the purse, looking down to undo the thongs that held it to his belt. He hoped Uncle Jarlz would let him go back to his room soon. As he struggled with the purse, he spotted a familiar sword at the side of another stranger who had squeezed up next to the table. Gant recognized the sword as one his father had made, one of his better ones. He recognized the sword, but he did not recognize the man who carried it.

Gant tried to remember who had commissioned that particular sword. He could not. His father made too many to remember them all. Nevertheless, Gant was certain he'd never seen the man next to him. How did he get the sword?

An ale appeared in front of Gant and the server asked for three gold coins as payment. Gant counted out three pieces of gold, his mind still preoccupied by the mysterious appearance of his father's sword.

Jarlz nudged him as he was about to hand the girl the coins. "An extra coin is in order."

"Oh, yes, sorry," said Gant and added a fourth coin before handing them to her. "Thanks."

"Most generous, sir," she said with a twinkle in her eye as she turned and scurried off.

Gant leaned over and took a sip from his ale. Still curious, he turned to the stranger with his father's sword. "Excuse me for asking," he began, "but where did you get that weapon you carry?"

"Yes, it is a nice piece," said the stranger, "not magic or anything like that but she carries a good edge and holds it well. I found it a week or so ago. Quite a mess it was. I stumbled on it outside a cave near the trail from Falls Hill to Blasseldune. It's a well-known stopping place for travelers along that road. I dare say I won't be stopping there again."

Gant studied the man. Was he joking? Who left a perfectly good sword lying about? "You found it?"

"That's what I said. Never did find the owner or his body. Course I didn't look too hard either." At this he laughed, throwing his head back and roaring as if he'd told a great joke. Following the laughter he poured down the remains of his ale in one long gulp. "Whatever got 'em, I wasn't hanging around to tangle with it."

"Bandits?"

"No. I swear it was no man did this. A dragon more likely."

"A dragon? What makes you so sure?"

"I'm not sure. Like I said, I didn't see whatever it was. But there was a lot of soot, smoke-blackened stones and the like. And there were no bodies, though there was plenty of blood and some bits of skin and muscle. Maybe it wasn't a dragon. I suppose there are other things in this world that could have done it, but my guess is that it was a dragon."

"Where exactly was this?" Now Gant was intrigued whether the story was true or false.

"Like I said, I was traveling north along the road from Falls Hill on my way to Blasseldune. About half way between Falls Hill and the Rushon River there's a place where a little path goes off to the east through a grove of aspens. It leads to this cave. Lots of travelers use it, and I'm no different. So, I was looking forward to a good night's camp but when I got to the cave there's a mess around the opening. Lots of blackened stones, burned grass and trampled bushes. It's all torn up. And there amongst the mess is this sword lying on the ground, no scabbard mind you, like his owner dropped it in the midst of a fight. It had a couple of pretty big nicks in the edge, like maybe whoever was swinging it hit the rock around the cave mouth or something. I took one look around, grabbed it and rode out of there."

"Can I see the sword?"

"What for? I had a sword smith in Blasseldune refinish the edge. He said it was a good sword, so I kept it."

"Oh," said Gant, disappointed that he couldn't see the nicks, sure they would have told him what the sword had hit. "I'm sure it is a good sword. I hope it brings you luck."

"Yeah, more luck than the last owner."

With that, the stranger picked up his mug and ambled off to find other company. Gant nudged his uncle. "Did you hear that?"

"Some of it," said Jarlz, looking up from a crust of bread, roast meat and gravy he'd been eating. "Sounds strange to me. I know the cave he's talking about and travelers have been using it for years. No one's ever been killed there."

"Do you think he was lying?"

"No. He had an air of truth about him."

"Then it could have been a dragon?"

"I doubt that. Dragons are pretty scarce. There are other things it could be."

"That breathes fire?"

"A demon or bandits that use fire to hide their crimes. In any case, I wouldn't worry about it. It's a long way from here."

"But we are going back to Blasseldune, aren't we? I want to see Chamz again as soon as I can."

"We can leave tomorrow if you want."

Gant wished they could be going home tomorrow, the one place he couldn't go. He'd have to be satisfied seeing Chamz. Surely by now his friend was up and around and causing trouble. Gant sipped his ale, chatted with those who wanted a word with "the champion" and contemplated leaving in the morning.

He turned to his uncle. "I'm buying a horse in the morning and getting on the road as soon as possible after a livery stable opens. Are you okay with that?"

Jarlz looked up from his mug. "I'm as eager to get going as you are. If that's the plan then we should get to bed early. This party will go on all night whether we're still here or not."

They stayed at the party for what seemed like a long time to Gant but Jarlz insisted tradition demanded they not leave too early. As soon as possible they went to their rooms and turned in. As expected, the party went late into the night without them.

Chapter 14

The next morning Gant was up before sunrise while his uncle slept in. He went to the stables and bought a horse. She was unremarkable but serviceable and strong enough to carry Gant and his equipment.

When Jarlz did get up, Gant was ready to leave. Jarlz would have none of it. Breakfast first. And so they ate breakfast and talked. Jarlz talked about returning to Netherdorf, not only because the king required it but also because Jarlz wanted to see a certain jeweler's daughter, the Mistress Fallsworth. Gant chafed to be on the road. He couldn't wait to get back to Blasseldune to see Chamz.

It was mid-afternoon before they left. Once on the road, Jarlz hurried their pace, as anxious as Gant to be elsewhere. They talked sparingly, concentrating on the road ahead. They stopped the first night at Abadis' house for a hot meal and a night full of conversation. Abadis congratulated Gant on winning at Devonshield and on killing Zeigone. It was not something Gant wanted to discuss. What he did want to know was how Chamz was. Unfortunately, Abadis had no news about Chamz' health.

They left early the next morning and spent that night in the little cave off the road. This time Gant took the first watch.

#

While Gant and Jarlz traveled south, news reached Barlon Gorth that Gant had won at Devonshield and he summoned his wizard and master spy to another meeting. Barlon sat with his feet up on the table. His shaggy hair, matted and knotted from lack of combing, made a dark halo around his head. Razgoth paced the room, his charcoal robes flaring around his ankles with each turn. Shalmuthe sat stiffly across from Barlon, his red hair flaming in the firelight.

"I told you, sire," said Razgoth, turning once again, glancing at Barlon. "Gant must be stopped or plans to bring Varg back will come to nothing. The prophecy is clear. He will kill Varg and leave us without the aid we need to win a war with the Western Kings."

Barlon took a sip from the wine goblet at his elbow. "You worry too much, wizard. We will see to it that Gant does not interfere."

"But, my Lord, he has *the* sword," shot Razgoth.

"We know," said Barlon and turned to Shalmuthe. "Can your man get to Blasseldune in time to intercept Gant?"

"I have already dispatched him with orders to carry out our plan. The only thing in question is how long Gant remains in Blasseldune. If he stays more than two days, we'll catch him. If he's off right away, then we will have to track him down. Either way, it is only a matter of time before my man catches up to him and sets him down the wrong path."

Razgoth stopped, his arms folded across his chest. "And exactly what can you do to prevent Gant from fighting Varg once we've called him back?"

Shalmuthe glared back at Razgoth. "For a wizard you don't know much about magic."

Razgoth opened his mouth to reply but Barlon cut him off. "We all knew it might come to this and so we have a plan. Not to prevent Gant from fighting Varg, but to make sure the magic in his sword has been depleted enough that Varg will survive and the drained sword will be its owner's downfall instead."

Slowly a smile came across Razgoth's face. "Egog! You will get Gant to fight Egog. A fight he'll surely win but which will drain much of the magic from his sword. And with no wizards alive powerful enough to replenish that magic there won't be enough left for Gant to kill Varg. His weapon will be his own death."

Barlon chuckled, sipped his wine. "You do see. And so our plans do not go awry."

The smile left Razgoth's face. "How will you get Gant to fight Egog? Why would he waste his time?"

"Because he'll think he is fighting Varg," said Shalmuthe. "My man will make sure Gant thinks Varg is here and needs killing. The prophecy, you know, and all."

"Do-gooders are always easy to fool," added Barlon. "Everything will be fine and we will get on with the conquest of Netherdorf. Now, both of you get out." Barlon shouted to his guard, "Send for my generals. Get them in here now."

\#

When Gant and Jarlz reached Blasseldune, there was a happy reunion with Chamz at the Hammond House. He had healed and taken a job working as security for the freight company, his swordsmanship now somewhat of a legend in its own right. His first day on the job he'd stopped two disgruntled ex-employees in their tracks, barely harming either. Now he thanked Gant for teaching him how to disarm ruffians without cutting their arms off.

The reunion was short-lived as Jarlz was in a hurry to get back to Netherdorf, spurred by a messenger from the king calling all his knights back. Chamz likewise was eager to go back to Netherdorf to see his family. He was not looking forward to being considered a commoner once more and keeping his sword hidden. Somehow, he'd manage it for a while.

It was a sad parting the following morning as Jarlz and Chamz rode west toward Netherdorf. Chamz promised he'd be back in a week, ten days at the most, and Gant promised to wait. Gant rode with them a short way out of town before turning back for Blasseldune. Thanks to his tournament winnings he didn't need to work. But he wondered what he was going to do until Uric let him know that Varg had returned. He wouldn't have to wonder long.

Chapter 15

Three days later Gant sat in Hammond House's common room, picking disinterestedly at his bowl of porridge. He was bored. Yesterday he'd sat in the common room all day because the wind and rain made going outside miserable. Today the sun broke through the clouds and Gant itched to go out and do something. Half-heartedly he finished his porridge.

A group of road weary men sat at a corner table eating and talking low. As Gant was about to leave, one of them raised his voice and Gant heard him say, "I know it's Varg. And someone's got to do something about it before we all die."

"Shh," hissed one of his companions, grabbing him by the elbow.

Gant stopped, turned and walked to the table. The one who'd mentioned Varg had his back to Gant. He wore a long, dark cloak that disguised his physique. The man turned and stared at Gant. The stranger had a bony face with a sharp nose, brown eyes and high, pronounced cheekbones. He had black hair cut short and bushy eyebrows that vaulted over his eyes in a dark ridge.

As Gant reached their table, the man turned back to his companions.

"Excuse me," said Gant.

"No excuse for you," mumbled the stranger focusing on his bowl of porridge.

"Leave us alone," said one of the others.

Gant stayed where he was. "You've seen Varg?"

"I barely escaped death, youngster, and right now I just want to be left alone."

Gant retreated half a step. "But you said you'd seen Varg."

The man turned toward Gant and glared for a long minute. "Yes," he finally said, "I did escape Varg. Unfortunately, my partners weren't so lucky."

"How do you know it was Varg?" asked Gant, seating himself on the bench next to the stranger.

"Because the king sent us to kill him."

"The king? Which king?"

"King Tirmus, of course. He knew that Varg showing up spelled doom for all us good folks and what with his knights scattered round the countryside, he hired some of us independents with a reputation for accomplishing our mission."

"Where is Varg?" Gant's mind spun. If it was Varg, then it was his responsibility to kill the monster. And if the king wanted the demon vanquished, here was a way to redeem himself in the process. Perhaps he could go home.

"It was on the road south, almost to Falls Hill. There's a cave off the road used by lots of travelers for shelter. Or it used to be. Now, Varg's holed up there and kills anyone gets close."

"Can you show me where it is?" asked Gant.

"Show you? Are you crazy? I'm never going back there. Besides, I've got to get to Netherdorf to report to his Majesty. He's not going to like what I have to say, but it needs said."

"How will I recognize where to turn off the road?"

"It's not hard. The path is wide and plain enough. It leads east through a stand of aspens, the only aspens around, about half way between Falls Hill and the Rushon River ford. You do know where Falls Hill is, don't you?"

"Sort of," said Gant. He'd only heard of the Eastern Emperor's summer home in tales at his father's smithy.

"It's easy enough to find but you're a fool if you go there."

Gant got up and started for his room. "Maybe not," he said over his shoulder.

"Sure," said the stranger and went back to his companions.

Packing his belongings, Gant thought of the stranger in Devonshield who claimed he found the sword that Gant recognized outside a cave. It sounded like the same cave where this man claimed Varg was. Same cave, same demon. The two stories added up and Gant was sure he'd found the demon he was supposed to vanquish.

He finished packing in a hurry and settled with the innkeeper. Before he left Gant had the innkeeper promise that if Jarlz and Chamz returned to Blasseldune, he would tell them that he was going to kill Varg and let them know where. He loaded his horse and left before the noon meal, heading south on the road that led through the Great Forest to the Rushon River and then on to Falls Hill.

Chapter 16

Gant traveled south toward Falls Hill. The road led through the Great Forest and while less traveled than the northern roads, it was still wide and well maintained by the Eastern Empire. Gant knew little about the empire other than at present there was a boy emperor who hardly ever left his capital city.

Even during midday the road was shrouded in deep shade. Streams made fishing easy and Gant never lacked for food or water. The armor Uric gave him had a magical lightness to it that made traveling comfortable. The autumn days were still warm while the nights had a snap that made a fire a necessity for warmth as well as for cooking.

Gant hurried along, bent on finding and killing Varg not just to prevent the death of other innocent travelers, but he hoped that killing the demon would convince King Tirmus to pardon him. Though he harbored doubts that killing Varg would be enough.

On the ride south Gant thought about his father, his mother, Gwen and home. Gant wanted more than anything to go home and see his family. He wondered if Gwen had suffered. Stopping Wendler was worth it if she was safe. These worries ate at him like an open sore.

On the fifth day the road passed through a stretch of rolling hills, curved back and forth around huge rock outcroppings and came to the Rushon River. Gant forded it and continued south. He guessed that the cave wasn't much farther and he pushed ahead eagerly.

On the sixth morning, the road snaked through a brace of low hills, swung around a solid rock shoulder and ran through a grove of young aspens. A narrow path meandered off the road to the left. This was it.

Gant turned his horse onto the path and passed quickly through the aspen grove. On the other side of the trees a mountain meadow stretched off to a ridge of steep hills. The path continued over a shallow brook and went on to a dark cave entrance. The black opening stood out like an ominous mouth.

Gant halted, surveying the area. A horse with a leather hobble on its back legs grazed in the shade of the last aspens. Another horse roamed along near the cave entrance. Gant urged his horse forward. The nearest horse picked up its ears and eyed Gant suspiciously.

Where were the riders? Inside the cave? Gant listened for sounds that might provide a clue. Only the wind whispered in his ears. He nudged his horse with his knees toward the hobbled stray.

Climbing down from his horse he approached the stray. Laying a hand over the horse's neck, he said softly, "Easy there," like he'd done in his father's smithy. He circled the animal, looking for injuries. Other than a few minor scratches from thorns the horse was fine.

Gant examined the skin worn raw by the hobble. This horse had been unattended for some time. Gant reached down, loosened the hobble and pulled it off. No one would intentionally leave an animal that long. Something was wrong.

Gant straightened, looked for the rider, a body, or signs of a struggle and found no useful clues. Something had happened to the horse's rider. The cave loomed silent.

Gant hobbled his horse and walked to the cave mouth, cautiously scanning the ground as he approached. There was an old fire pit that hadn't been used recently. Ashes from past fires were scattered around in front of the cave. Gant searched them for tracks but found nothing distinguishable.

If Varg was in there, what would he look like? Gant didn't know. He should have waited for Chamz to come back to Blasseldune, or better yet Jarlz or Uric. He should have found out at least what Varg looked like. Too late.

Gant swallowed hard, his palms sweating. He reached for his sword and magically it leaped into his hand. Energy ran through his palm and up his arm strengthening his resolve.

He stepped gingerly into the dark cave. As his eyes adjusted, he could see that the cave opened into an oval room with a high ceiling. Numerous blackened fire pits ringed the entrance. Several of the fire's remains were scattered, pieces of charred wood lay around mixed with broken packs, torn bedrolls and miscellaneous equipment. In one corner an overturned stew pot lay with its rotten contents spilled out on the stone floor.

Cautiously Gant crossed the oval room, careful not to step on anything that would make noise. His eyes adjusted to the ever-dimmer light. His magical armor barely made a sound even on the hard stone floor.

The walls glistened with dampness. Gant heard the faint sound of water dripping in the distance. As the darkness closed in him, Valorius began to glow, a soft blue light that spread out in a circle. Handy, thought Gant, but hardly enough light to prevent him from walking into an ambush.

The room narrowed into a wide corridor that ran straight for a short distance and then turned to the right. At the corner Gant peered around it expectantly. Nothing. Only the distant pitter-patter of water drops hitting stone. The tunnel went straight off into the darkness. Gant worked his way forward, ever wary. His stomach twisted tighter. Where was Varg?

Holding Valorius high in front of him, Gant tried to see as far as possible. Water dropped from the ceiling and oozed down the walls. Now the wet floor sloped downward and Gant slipped once, nearly sliding downhill. He braced himself against the wall with one hand and gripped his sword with the other.

This wasn't good. How could he fight Varg when he could hardly stand up? Maybe he should turn back, try to lure Varg outside. Gant slid down the corridor and ended up in a larger cavern with a flat floor. The ceiling and walls arched away into the blackness. The rotten smell of death assaulted Gant's nose. His stomach churned and he nearly vomited.

Breathing through his mouth, Gant turned to his left and cautiously walked toward the smell. In a small rock alcove he found the remains of several bodies decayed beyond recognition. Bits of rotting flesh clung stubbornly to whitened bones.

Gant's hand shook. A chill in the air swept over him. He shivered. This was worse than he'd imagined. Gant listened intently for some sound but heard only the hammering of his own heart.

The loneliness struck him. What if he died here? No one would ever know. Not the king, not Jarlz, not Chamz, not his father. He took a deep breath. Uric claimed that Valorius had the power to kill this thing. What if he was wrong?

Something heavy scraped across the stone floor behind Gant. He whirled but Valorius' light didn't go far enough to see whatever was there. Gant froze, listening. Metallic claws clattered on the hard stone. Something scaly slithered toward him. Gant retreated. A monstrous beast crawled into the light blocking his exit. It towered over him on four massive legs. A broad, flat, armored head peered down at him, yellow, reptilian eyes glaring. The lower jaw hung open revealing a row of huge teeth.

Fear clutched Gant. He swallowed hard and took a deep breath.

"Varg," Gant managed in a shaky voice. "I've come to stop you here and now." Gant inched back as he spoke, putting more distance between him and the creature. He looked for a weakness, some spot that was unarmored, unprotected. He didn't see any.

"Varg?" rasped the monster, his voice like gravel rolling in a barrel. "You may praise whatever gods you worship that I am not Varg. I am Egog, called here from the realms of darkness by some insignificant wizard. Right now I am hungry."

Gant hesitated. Was this a trick? If this wasn't Varg, what was Gant doing here? It hardly mattered. Gant would either kill it or die trying. If he'd only waited for Jarlz. If only. That was fools talk. He was here, and so was this beast.

Egog slithered closer. "It has been several days since I've eaten. Your kind doesn't stop here anymore. I'll feed now. If you feel like screaming, please do so. It aids digestion."

Egog pounced, hitting Gant square in the chest, knocking him backward. Razor sharp teeth clamped shut around Gant's midsection. Here and there a tooth penetrated Gant's armor. Pain seared through him. But the armor held and Egog's teeth did not reach Gant's vitals.

Dazed from the initial impact, Gant barely managed to hang onto his sword. Slowly, Egog raised Gant off the floor until Gant was looking straight into one of Egog's huge eyes. Reflexively Gant swung Valorius. Just as he swung, Egog shook his head back and forth slamming Gant sideways. Valorius struck the rock-hard scales of Egog's eyebrow ridge. Sparks, a small explosion and a cloud of acrid smoke erupted. A numbing cold ran up Gant's arm. Egog shuddered.

The noise and smoke died away. Egog shook Gant again. Gant's armor protected his exterior, but now he was being whiplashed back and forth. His head buzzed. Desperately, Gant lashed out again. Another flash. Thunder rolled down the corridor. Again an unearthly cold tingled along Gant's arm. Ignoring the pain, Gant struck again and again. Each time the numbness grew and his grip on Valorius weakened. Smoke hung in the air burning Gant's eyes. Egog bit down harder, trying to crack Gant's armor.

Gant was on the verge of unconsciousness. He could not die here, not before he had a chance to right things in Netherdorf. He cocked his arm for one last thrust, his strength failing, he drove Valorius at Egog's eye. Somehow the sword struck true.

Above the thunder and flash, through the numbness that bit his hand, a scream of pain. It was so loud, so penetrating, it deafened Gant. Suddenly, he was falling. Dream like, the floor came at him until he landed with a crash. Jarred back to his senses, Gant rolled over and staggered to his feet.

He looked up through the smoke and saw green ooze dripping from one of Egog's eye sockets. The monster recoiled in pain, stunned.

"Praise be," said Gant, rejoicing.

"You miserable man-child," roared Egog, "I shall crush your bones."

Gathering his strength Gant rushed the monster. With two hands, he chopped at the pillar-like left leg. Valorius cut through the scales, biting into the soft flesh beneath. The cold came again, but less this time. Gant spun and sliced the other front leg. Egog screamed again and tried to back up.

Now Gant was underneath the beast and saw a crack in the belly scales, an ancient wound. With both hands he thrust straight up into it. Valorius plunged deep into the soft underbelly. Egog's death scream was lost in the explosion that brought stones crashing from the ceiling.

The shock wave drove Gant backward. He landed on the floor, fighting for breath. He peered out through the slits in his helm and watched the smoke drift lazily toward the roof. Finally, a gentle breeze blew from somewhere and through the wisps Gant saw Egog's shattered hulk collapsed against the wall. The beast was dead.

For a long time Gant lay still on the wet stone floor. He was too tired to feel joy, too hurt to move. A paralyzing cold gripped his hands. Eventually, he rolled over onto his back. Pain in his ribs reminded Gant of puncture wounds that dripped blood. He stared up at the lifeless gray stone ceiling dreaming of his father's smithy, of his mother's cooking, of Netherdorf. If only he could be there now. He didn't want to die alone.

Nausea clutched his stomach. He fought it down. Shivers ran through him. He took a breath, shook his head to clear it. He had to get out of there.

He saw his mother's face. She seemed to be calling him. How long had he been lying there? How foolish everything seemed. Wendler, Netherdorf, all so distant and so unimportant as he lay on the cold stone floor his life oozing away. He faded in and out of consciousness.

Eventually, he woke, remembered where he was and knew he had to get out of that stench-infested lair. If he was going to die, it would be in the open, where he would be found with the sky above him, not in this cave.

Hand over hand he crawled, driven by an iron will. A trail of red blotches on the wet stone marked his agonizing progress. Little by little he worked his way back toward the entrance. Finally, his strength gone, weakened by the loss of blood, he could go no farther.

Unconsciousness swept over him. He lay immobile, face down in the ash-covered dirt. Stars twinkled overhead. Gant didn't notice. He'd been so intent on crawling that he failed to realize that he was outside the cave. Night had fallen. The sparse forest shielded him from the cool night winds but not from the watchful eyes that lurked at the edge of the aspen grove.

Chapter 17

The autumn sun climbed slowly above the rugged mountain tops, kissing each with first a touch of pink, then gold, and finally full sunlight. Its rays illuminated a heavily armored column of horsemen riding from Barlon Gorth's castle. The cheery light contrasted with the grim faces.

Barlon surveyed his forces with red-rimmed, bloodshot eyes. He'd hardly slept last night. Less than 600 men, hardly enough to attack a castle, he thought. But his primary weapons were deceit and treachery. If his plan within the walls was thwarted, he'd never win regardless of how many men he had. With luck this would be simple. He did have the seventy-five Knights of Habichon, who fought like a thousand men.

No, his problem was not capturing Netherdorf Castle. His problem was capturing Uric alive. For that he trusted Razgoth. If anyone could contain that enigmatic sage, Razgoth could. Barlon's master plan was based on reports that Uric was really a dragon. What if he wasn't? That could be a problem.

And there were the craftsmen he needed alive: the blacksmith, goldsmith, jeweler and gem cutter, and their families. Capture should be easy if he could control his troops' bloodlust. Griffith's third brigade was the worst, little more than maniacs. He'd placed them in reserve. Hopefully they would not be committed until after the craftsmen were in custody.

Barlon urged his horse into a canter. In truth, his fear was that he'd be betrayed again. That core of doubt sat hard in his chest, even as he tried to shut it out. Early in his career he'd been betrayed just when the battle seemed to be turning in his favor. His king had sued for peace and left Barlon in defeat.

He forced aside his worries. Right now they had some distance to cover in a hurry. The thunder of hooves rose behind him as he moved down the road to Netherdorf. Soon he would complete the first stage of his plan. Revenge would be sweet.

#

Jarlz sat on his bed staring out the open window of his third story room in Netherdorf Castle. It was warm for this time of year and he watched the morning sun climb over the crags. He was up early out of habit. He'd taken a position teaching swordplay to the king's recruits and boredom settled heavily on his shoulders these days.

Once again he thought of Gant. He should have returned to Blasseldune by now. And if he had, someone would have gotten word back to Jarlz. He shouldn't have let Gant go off alone. He was too young, too inexperienced.

A cloud of dust along the west road caught Jarlz' eye. Funny, he thought, there rarely is traffic that way. Perhaps he would report it to the king before he went to breakfast.

A knock at the door caused Jarlz to turn from the window.

"Come in."

Timidly the door swung open. A slight, dark-eyed serving girl peeked in.

"Sir Jarlz?" It was not a question of his identity, but a request for permission to enter the room.

"Come in, come in." Jarlz recognized her from the kitchen staff. "What is it?" he asked when she hesitated in the doorway.

"I have been instructed to present you with a gift from Mistress Fallsworth." Her gaze remained fixed on the floor.

Alicia Fallsworth, thought Jarlz. Her beautiful face filled his mind. He'd always loved her but there had never been time. Since his return from Devonshield they'd spent a lot of time together. Maybe he should ask for her hand before something else happened.

"Well, let me see it."

Carefully the girl unwrapped a beautiful medallion. It glittered and winked at Jarlz. The girl held it up with the chain stretched between her two calloused hands. The pendant swung hypnotically. She stepped forward to place it over the knight's head. Something said no; Jarlz leaned back.

"Mistress Fallsworth said to put it on you myself and for you to wear it to breakfast. She'll come by and speak with you if you have it on." Again the girl's eyes shied away from his.

Jarlz hesitated. A gleam flashed off the medallion and caught his eye. He thought of the jeweler's daughter, of proper time spent with a proper lady. He bowed his head and the great gold medallion slipped neatly around his neck. The girl curtsied, turned and was gone.

Jarlz rose and looked out the window. The swirling dust cloud was a lot closer. It didn't matter. The medallion around his neck worked a parasitic magic that gnawed at his memories, rearranging them, twisting feelings and realigning his allegiance. Barlon now was his liege, King Tirmus the enemy. All that happened without Jarlz consciously aware of it. Without knowing why, Jarlz dressed in his battle armor and went down to breakfast.

#

Ralbert, Sergeant of the Watch, looked out from the gate tower at the rising sun. The beauty of a new day exhilarated him, so much so that he was a permanent volunteer for the last night watch. He endured the silent gloom each night with ever-growing expectations of the coming dawn. He was never disappointed.

He glanced again at the dust devil rolling over the nearest hill. He liked the playful winds that swirled through the mountains. Often sighting one was the only break to the night's boredom. Today, something was different. This dust cloud followed the west road straight for the castle. Perhaps a herd of wild animals, he thought. Still, he should call for the captain.

A giggle behind Ralbert made him start. He turned and melted in the deep brown eyes of Angelica. She offered him a cup of wine.

"You shouldn't be up here," said Ralbert. His smile said he didn't mind.

"I like bringing you a morning drink. It's so peaceful here before anyone is up."

She snuggled against his side and handed him the cup. He put one arm around her, feeling her warmth, and drank deeply of the fruity liquid. He enjoyed their little ritual, but in the back of his mind he knew they'd have to stop before they got caught. They'd ban him from service or worse.

He went to take another drink, but his throat muscles constricted involuntarily. He choked. A roaring fire burned in his guts, his eyes bulged. He looked accusatorily at Angelica. She pushed him away and stood up. His muscles, his heart and lungs ceased to function and in a moment he was dead. With no sign of remorse, Angelica rolled him against the outer wall where he couldn't be seen from below and headed for the gatehouse.

All along the west wall, other guards met a similar fate, dying without a whimper. As the telltale dust cloud transformed into a thundering column of armored horsemen, the great drawbridge and portcullis to Netherdorf Castle creaked open.

The horde forged into the town of Netherdorf and galloped up the hill toward the castle. Small groups fanned out with specific missions. They met little resistance, grabbing those targeted, killing any who opposed them and avoiding the rest. Barlon could not afford to waste time until Netherdorf Castle was his.

They passed through the village like a night mist. Up the road to the castle they went, their iron-shod horses beat a crescendo on the drawbridge and they were inside. There was no alarm.

#

On the far side of town, Gant's father was already up. The forge fire was hot and the ringing of his hammer drowned out the approaching horses' hooves. Suddenly the smithy door flew open and two hulking men in deep purple armor rushed in. A heavy mailed fist slammed into Gant's father's chin and he crumpled to the floor. They tied him, gagged him, carried him out, and tossed him into a prison wagon along with his wife.

Further down the road, Chamz sat eating his breakfast alone. His father had gone to tend to the livestock and his mother was out weeding the garden. The clank of armored horsemen aroused his curiosity and, thinking it was the king's men, he got up and went to the front door. Opening it, he stepped outside just in time to see Gant's parents wrestled into the prison wagon. Chamz saw Barlon's emblem on the warriors' shields and ducked back inside. Without thinking he snatched up his sword and ambushed the first intruder at the door. Caught by surprise, the soldier fell to a single blow. The next two fared no better. Chamz yanked the door shut and dashed out the back.

At the sound of the back door slamming his mother straightened up from weeding in the vegetable garden

"What's going on?" she asked, alarmed to see Chamz carrying his sword.

"Barlon's attacking Netherdorf. We've got to escape," hissed Chamz, grabbing his mother by the arm. "Where's father?"

Drug along behind her son, Chamz' mother could hardly catch her breath. "He's tending the livestock in the south field."

Into the trees they dashed, coming out at the edge of the south field. Chamz' father was working on the fence that ran along the edge of the forest. He turned, startled as Chamz and his mother burst from the tree line.

"What is it?"

"No time to explain," said Chamz, "Netherdorf is under attack and we must get to safety."

"If Netherdorf falls, where will we be safe?" asked Chamz' father, glancing around nervously.

"I don't know but we're going to Blasseldune."

A look of horror swept across his parents' faces.

"It's alright. I have friends there. Come on before they come looking for us."

At that moment, the clank of armored footsteps in the woods ended any resistance. Quickly Chamz led his parents to the woodland path that led east toward Blasseldune.

#

Barlon rode with General Ecker and Razgoth into the stadium-like courtyard of Netherdorf castle expecting the worst. His fears were unfounded. There were only two ceremonial guards at the interior castle doors. One fell to a crossbow bolt before he could move. The other ducked inside, screaming the alarm, slamming the massive doors shut. A heavy thud came from inside as the bolt locked the doors.

By now Barlon's men were in a frenzy. They wanted battle, and Barlon knew enough to give it to them. With a wave, he released the first brigade to attack those sleeping in the king's barracks. He sent the second brigade to the kitchen entrance, where he knew the door would be barred last. The fourth brigade leapt to the walls and secured them with light fighting. Things were going so smoothly, Barlon had General Ecker release the reserves of the third brigade to sack the town. A cheer went up as they wheeled and dashed back across the drawbridge. Barlon hoped he had not let them go too early.

Meanwhile, Razgoth dropped from his horse and ran to the castle doors. He knelt on the stoop and carefully inscribed a set of magic symbols sprinkling a glittering powder over the marks. At the same time, he mumbled arcane words and was back on his horse as the first screams came from the nearby barracks.

"We have but to wait," assured Razgoth.

Barlon eyed him coldly. His trust in magic had never been strong, and now that everything hinged on one man's spell, he liked it even less. "You're sure?"

"Of course."

"Remind me why we need to capture Uric, if indeed he is a dragon."

Razgoth sighed. "I told you. To make the amulet that will hold Varg you need a dragon's fire to fuse the metals. It's hotter and a trace of the dragon's magic will be infused into the work piece. Anything less and we'll never hold a demon unless of course we had the power of Tirumfall Tower."

Barlon grunted, still doubtful.

#

Jarlz sat in the dining hall, enjoying his breakfast. Through the window he saw the horsemen coming, but raised no alarm. Thoughts deep inside squirmed to break free, but the medallion's magic held them trapped. His new ego recognized his liege lord,

Barlon Gorth, leading his men into the courtyard. With the medallion in control of his mind, Jarlz was forced to believe that Barlon had come to reclaim him.

A scream echoed through the castle followed by shouts of alarm. Jarlz turned slowly from the window. His eyes locked with King Tirmus' steel gray eyes as the monarch entered the hall for breakfast.

"Jarlz, why do you sit idle?"

"My Master has returned." Jarlz did not get up, and something in his eyes said more to the king than his words.

The door opened again and a harried Captain rushed in.

"Your Majesty," he pleaded, "we are betrayed. The castle is lost. You must escape."

King Tirmus looked at Jarlz and saw the betrayal in the knight's eyes. Despair overwhelmed the king. There was no choice. "You'll go with me," he said to the captain.

"But my men. . ."

"No, you go with me. I am unarmed."

They left without a word. Slowly, almost reluctantly, Jarlz rose to join Barlon's forces. As Jarlz left the dining room, Uric, who had been upstairs in his room asleep, rushed past, his night robes streaming behind him. Jarlz moved like a sleepwalker to the kitchen where Barlon's troops poured into the castle. As Jarlz stepped into the kitchen, he saw the mangled body of the servant girl who had delivered the medallion. Remorse flickered through his mind and he wondered if Lady Fallsworth had truly sent the gift. He supposed it wouldn't matter; he knew he would be riding away. The medallion had won his mind.

Uric was furious. The treachery was obvious, guards dead at their posts, the gate opened without an alarm. Just before he reached the front doors he heard the ring of steel behind him. Turning, he saw the auxiliary guards being overwhelmed by troops in Barlon's black and gold surging out of the kitchen.

Instantly Uric assessed the situation. The guards were valiantly defending the entrance to the escape tunnel. The enemy was just as determined to gain it. How they knew where the tunnel was hinted at the depth of the treason. Uric guessed that the king had fled. And if they were to have any hope for the future, the king must not be captured.

Uric turned his attention to the intruders. The ceiling was too low to change into his real form and burn the lot of them, so instead, Uric recited the first verse of the spell that called lightning. A fuzziness buzzed in the air. Uric selected a target and unleashed a blue-white bolt that sizzled from his fingertip to metal armor. The metal heated like an oven. In a split second the man's blood boiled and he exploded. Most of his nose and pieces of skin shot out through the open faceplate.

Still holding back a reservoir of energy, Uric selected a second target, then a third and fourth before the full potential of the spell was drained. The remaining soldiers fell back, fear in their faces, their discipline shattered.

Rallied, the castle guards pressed their advantage and forced the insurgents into the kitchen. Uric turned his attention to the battle sounds coming from the courtyard, confident that the king would escape. He rushed through the halls to the main doors, anxious to join the king's troops outside. He slid back the bolt, yanked open the right-hand door and charged onto the stoop. Immediately he was seized by the titanic forces of Razgoth's spell. A magical sphere surrounded him, inside which time ceased. And then, as time stopped, Uric's body writhed under the magic, forced to revert to its true shape. Within minutes, instead of the robed sage, there stood a massive, gold-scaled dragon. For Uric, the world slowed to a timeless creep. He could neither move, nor fight the power that gripped him. His thoughts ceased. He became a gigantic reptilian statue.

The men in the courtyard froze in terror as the huge lizard formed in front of them. Silence settled over the battlefield.

Barlon's men regrouped first. They fell on the king's troops relentlessly, driving them back into a corner where the last one died defending the castle.

The noise of battle wafted away. Barlon looked around, anxious to claim the Kingdom. One of his soldiers came out through the main doors, slipped gingerly past the frozen dragon blocking his way, and approached Barlon.

"My Lord," he said now at attention, "the castle is ours."

"And the king?"

Hesitation. "Escaped."

"You failed!" Barren waved the subordinate away. With the king alive, there would be trouble from the populace. "Captain," he called to the nearest officer. "Take your brigade to scour the hills. Any men you suspect are fleeing this castle kill them and return with their heads. Hurry!"

The captain wheeled his horse, shouted to his men and within minutes they were gone.

"It won't matter," whispered General Ecker from his horse beside Barlon.

Barlon ignored him and glared at Uric. So Razgoth was right. The magic worked. Still, it was hard not to feel a glimmer of fear with the dragon towering over them, and though trapped in time, hatred burned fiercely in those vertical pupils. Barlon broke the stare, and turned to Razgoth.

"How do we get him to my castle?"

"The entire entryway stone must be raised with the dragon on it and the whole thing transported. The moment Uric is removed from the circle, he will return to life."

"You have made the preparations?"

Before the wizard could answer, a messenger in purple armor galloped into the courtyard, his horse's hooves reverberating hollowly as he crossed the plank drawbridge.

"My Lord," said the messenger as he neared Barlon.

"Speak."

"Lom sends word. The prisoners are ready for travel. All are accounted for."

"Then begin the march. I will follow soon."

Barlon turned back to Razgoth, but the middle-aged wizard was already directing a massive frame of timbers and pulleys up to the doorstep. Teams of heavy draft horses strained to pull the monstrous contraption to the door. More teams waited their turn in harness. Men with huge, stone cutting tools joined the work site.

Barlon said to General Ecker. "The castle is yours. Enjoy it. Send two messengers a day so I know how you fare. I will send word for you to join me when we are ready to attack the West."

The gray haired veteran smiled. "Thank you. I think I will enjoy a castle of my own."

Barlon shouted to Razgoth, trying to be heard over the din of iron biting stone. "See you at the castle. I'm returning with Lom and his knights."

"Yes, yes," said Razgoth, waving Barlon off without turning. "I'll be there soon enough."

"Sire," came a call from the kitchen entrance.

Barlon saw Sir Jarlz walking toward him. Instinctively Barlon's hand was on his sword. He steeled himself, not ready to trust in magic.

"My Lord," said Sir Jarlz. "Wait. I'll ride with you."

Within minutes, Jarlz was mounted on an impressive chestnut warhorse, and when the conquerors headed back to the Mountain Castle, Sir Jarlz rode with them.

Before long they caught up with Lom's prison column. The 75 knights in their purple armor rode guard on half a dozen ox-drawn wagons. Barlon eagerly eyed the craftsmen through the bars of the stout wagons. A good day, he thought. Even the family members had been captured. So much easier to deal with the craftsmen when he could threaten their families. And the troops hadn't gotten out of hand. The rape and slaughter of innocents never entered his mind.

Chapter 18

Dalphnia peered around the trunk of an aspen toward the dark opening to Egog's lair. She was tall and wiry. Her long brown hair floated in a gentle breeze like a halo around her head. She licked her sensuous lips and sighed. It was late and still there was no sign of the man who was supposed to be in that cave.

Maybe the trees were wrong. Maybe there was no one. And yet trees did not make up stories. Knowing Dalphnia sought a new mate the aspens had sent word from one tree to another. The leaves whispered of a young traveler who had entered the beast's cave with a sword of power and magical armor. Quickly that message reached Dalphnia's forest. She loved her forest and the trees loved her. They convinced Dalphnia to leave the safety of her forest and journey to the aspen grove. She had been without a husband for some time and thoughts of a suitable candidate made her heart seethe with dreams of a new romance, her kind of romance.

Finally, under the twinkling stars, Dalphnia saw a hunched form crawl from the cave, struggling to put one hand in front of the other. Her strange, brown eyes could see as well during the darkest night as they could in broad daylight and as she watched, the figure stopped.

For a long moment, she waited. The air sighed a funeral dirge. Dalphnia sprang forward, like a lioness after an antelope. In an instant she was beside the fallen figure. If this man could survive a fight with the monster in that cave, then surely he was intended to be her next husband.

She knelt beside him and touched his silvery armor. It resonated with a magic power that brought back memories of great wizards, of a past she had nearly forgotten. Even as she watched, the punctures in the armor healed. No one alive could make such armor and Dalphnia wondered how this man came to have it.

Gently she rolled him over. He groaned softly. Good, she thought, he's alive. Now, if I can only get him back to my wood, I can save him. And he's mine! She slid one hand under his head and the other under his legs. Expecting the armor to be heavy, she braced herself, and then heaved upward, practically leaping off the ground. The armor was as light as a feather, and though the man was heavily muscled, she lifted him easily. Her lithe frame held a magical strength that was a part of who she was, a magic of her own.

"Hold on precious man," she whispered and started across the meadow, vaulting the stream and dashing back through the aspens. "It won't take long and I'll have you home."

Instead of following the road, Dalphnia turned between the rolling hills into the deepest forest. She ran like a deer, as if unburdened, following animal trails through the forest. A few times the man in her arms sighed and twisted weakly against her grip.

Within a half hour they reached the huge ancient oak that held her tree house. A spiral staircase of intertwining roots and limbs twisted one over the other around the trunk. She carried the man up the stairs into the main room, which was nothing more than a myriad of intertwined limbs. The roof was a layer of leaves overlapped so tightly no rain could enter. She crossed the main room and went into a side room. Here she laid her precious burden on a bed formed by more thick branches with a fluffy leaf mattress.

It took her a few minutes to remove the armor. She tossed it on the floor. Now she examined the wounds left by Egog's slimy, poisonous teeth. She knew it was the poison that was killing Gant, not the actual punctures.

Dalphnia dashed back down the staircase, and ran through her garden until she found the herbs and roots she needed: crown root, sage flower, heart leaf, link wort, and feather thorn. Some were to counteract the poison. Some were for her own special potion, the one that captured the hearts of her husbands. Some of her husbands had to be tricked into drinking the potion. Others had been oh so willing. This time there would be no resistance and once the potion did the initial work, her own hypnotic talents would hold this man to her for a lifetime; his lifetime that is. Yes, she would save this man, save him for herself.

As soon as she'd collected everything she needed, she dashed back up into the tree house. A splash of water, some magical fire to heat the brew, and then to his bedside where she forced the dark liquid down his throat. He gagged and tried to push her away but she was too strong.

She studied his youthful face. He was beautiful. Finally she had a new companion, her sixth husband. She leaned over and gently kissed his forehead. A smile crossed her face. She backed up a step and sat on the bent limb that served as a chair.

Now she only had to wait. By morning, he would wake up. He would be hurting but the poison would be neutralized and the minute he woke and saw Dalphnia sitting there, his heart would belong to her. Maybe he would live a hundred years with her, others had. She looked forward to a future filled with love.

Chapter 19

Barlon paced around his chambers, his black mane sticking out wildly in all directions. Crisp fall winds cried at the shuttered windows, flapping the heavy tapestries hung to keep out the cold. Papers and maps cluttered the single large table; battle plans that went unused. The stools around the table were empty except for one. Razgoth sat pensively scratching the light colored stubble on his chin, listening to the thump of Barlon's heavy boots on the oak planking. The Mountain Lord, as Barlon demanded to be called, paused at the end of each leg, looked at the wizard, hesitated, and then resumed his march.

Things had gone smoothly except for the king's escape. Now, everything hinged on one insignificant blacksmith who refused to forge the links for the amulet's necklace chain. Without the chain, they could not make the medallion and without the medallion Barlon could not summon Varg. Without the demon prince, Barlon could do nothing. Despite torturing the fool and his wife, despite the whip and hot irons, despite Barlon's best efforts to *make* him do it, he refused. Meanwhile the Alliance of Western Kingdoms pompously thumbed their noses at the insignificant Mountain King. Barlon would show them.

Time was slipping away. Even with the medallion, Varg could only be summoned on a night of darkness; when both moons were missing from the sky. If Barlon wasn't ready before the next such night, he would have to wait almost two years.

Enough was enough. He stopped pacing. Razgoth looked up.

"My smith will make the necklace chain," said Barlon.

"He's not as good."

"Why do we need a blacksmith to make the chain anyway? Why not the jeweler?"

"This is no flimsy gold chain to dazzle the ladies. This needs to be strong enough to withstand the pressures that the magic will impose. It must be seamless with hefty links. It'll take a talented blacksmith. Yours isn't as good as the smith from Netherdorf."

"Good enough. The chain lends little to the magic."

"But any weak link may give Varg an escape point."

"I'll take the chance."

"As you wish," said Razgoth, then muttered, "We *all* take the risk."

"See to it."

"And the smith from Netherdorf?"

"Kill him."

Razgoth left the room and Barlon walked to the table. He rearranged the maps, examined his strategy and contemplated the defeat of those who had shamed him in the past. It seemed like only yesterday that he had been the commander of the former Mountain King's troops. That king, Micus, had assigned him the mission of capturing the western slopes from the tribesmen who swore allegiance to the Western Kings. It had been a hard-fought campaign and the troops under Barlon's superior guidance were on the verge of winning.

Victory! That's what should have happened. Instead, on the verge of glory, based only on reports that the Western Kings were massing their armies to counterattack, weak-willed King Micus gave up. Literally he begged the Western Kings for peace. The fool was replaced by Governor Sabbius and Barlon was discharged from service in disgrace. It was humiliating. The memory burned in his heart. Barlon could not allow his reputation to remain soiled. So Barlon had secretly gathered support from disenchanted military leaders and had eliminated the puppet governor.

Barlon had himself installed as the new king and now he controlled the Mountain Kingdom. Still, he knew he could have won that day, *knew* it. He'd been betrayed by a cowardly king. Barlon would never trust anyone again. Let others beware.

#

Razgoth went immediately to the smithy to fetch Barlon's blacksmith. He didn't like it. Barlon took Varg much too lightly, and now he wanted to have a lesser man fashion the necklace chain. It invited disaster. He'd take care of the Netherdorf smith later. Right now, there were more important things.

Razgoth led Barlon's smith down to the castle dungeon. In the first basement, a special forge and workshop had been constructed. On one side was a huge room whose roof was a massive set of doors that opened up into the courtyard. In that room sat Uric's motionless statue trapped in a magic sphere where time stood still. The great dragon's head gazed out through glassy eyes into the workshop where Razgoth led the blacksmith.

Otherwise the place was empty. On the walls sticks with magic light spells cast on them bathed the workshop in a brilliant glare. On the tables lay gems and lumps of precious metals ready for final assembly. The preparations for the amulet had been completed as far as possible without the chain. The jeweler, goldsmith and other craftsmen had been more than helpful. Now Razgoth showed the blacksmith his task. The thick-armed man looked up once at the massive dragon's head, gulped back his fear, and set to work.

Slowly, the chains took shape. Here and there, Razgoth made suggestions, minor improvements, not based on knowledge of the forge, but on his knowledge of the magical requirements that would pose unusual strains on these chains.

#

Two days later, the chains were ready and the other craftsmen assembled. Barlon met Razgoth in the dungeon ready to complete the amulet.

"Please," Razgoth said to Barlon, "you must stand around the corner, out of Uric's sight. I will create an illusion that looks exactly like you to fool him. Uric must not see two images or he will realize that he's being tricked."

"But I won't be able to see."

"There'll be nothing to see if you do not."

"Very well," said the Mountain King and stepped back out of sight.

Razgoth glared at his team. "Ready?"

They nodded. None spoke. Fear held their tongues.

"Make no mistakes," warned the wizard, and turned toward the shimmering sphere that held Uric captive in stasis.

Razgoth waved his hands, sprinkled some dust and quoted the verse for the spell that could create an illusion of life. The falling dust particles stopped in midair, congealing into a life-like Barlon Gorth. He followed that with another spell that would allow the illusion to speak when the time came.

Now, Razgoth's face darkened, carefully he quoted the verse and gestures that controlled time. Ever so slowly he evoked a weak spot in the sphere surrounding Uric. The weakness grew until it opened a hole exposing Uric's head. Razgoth allowed the weakness to spread back along the dragon's neck until breath again flared Uric's nostrils.

"You may surrender," said the illusion. "We will not harm you."

In Uric's mind he was still on the castle steps with the battle for Netherdorf Castle raging in front of him. The images that remained in his mind were of his enemy killing King Tirmus' troops. Before Uric could detect the illusion, a torrent of fire surged from Uric's mouth destroying the image of Barlon Gorth. Hotter than any mortal forge, the rushing flames flew past the illusion and struck the waiting metals on the stone table. The instant the metals softened, Razgoth reversed his incantation and the sphere of timelessness reformed around Uric. Once again time ceased for the dragon.

Razgoth turned away from Uric. The craftsmen were busy making the amulet. Fear slowed them and their fingers shook.

"Faster idiots. This trick will only work once. The amulet must be complete before the metals cool."

To speed them Razgoth rattled off a simple verse and tiny sparks appeared to tickle the hesitant craftsmen. They worked feverishly, disregarding the intense heat that burned careless fingers. Soon the gleaming product of their labors lay cooling on the blackened stone table.

It was large, half the size of a kitchen plate, and wrought with such intricate detail that it seemed alive. At the center was an ugly, semi-human caricature, four armed with claws instead of hands, and a face that swept upward and backward from the cheekbones into what seemed like miniature wings for ears. Around this miniature metallic beast was a twisting, interwoven myriad of inseparable, golden metal threads. Jewels encircled the rim, and they too seemed to be connected magically to the net of metal threads. The amulet seemed to be alive and the pattern ever-changing. The monster inside the woven net appeared to rip away at the mesh while the threads constantly reformed to block escape. And yet, if you looked away from the amulet and then looked back nothing had changed.

Barlon came out of his hiding place and stood beside his wizard. Side-by-side they admired the handiwork.

"Guards," commanded Barlon. "Take them back to their cells."

"But you said we'd go free," managed the jeweler before he was knocked to the ground.

"First we must see if your work was successful."

Barlon laughed as they dragged the helpless craftsmen from the workshop. His plan was unfolding perfectly. Doomsday would soon be upon his enemies.

"And now we are ready to summon Varg," said Barlon.

Razgoth gave him a sour look. "I have to complete the magic of the amulet. Ten days, maybe more. Then we must wait for the Night of Darkness."

"Yes, I know." Furrows of concentration wrinkled Barlon's forehead. "I'll be in the war room."

Barlon left the wizard to his task, hating delay, yet happy to be close to action again. Soon they would summon Varg and his invincible army would march. The three Western Kingdoms were doomed.

Chapter 20

Gant leaned against a black-skinned walnut tree. The day was peaceful. He enjoyed the soft breeze and the occasional patch of sunshine that slipped through the fluttering leaves high overhead. He couldn't remember ever feeling so good. The warm glow of ecstasy filled his veins. In fact he remembered very little prior to coming to Dalphnia's woods.

A butterfly flitted by lazily, working its wings in paired strokes. Lightly, the orange and black insect drifted in to land on a bright red flower. A hummingbird buzzed around Dalphnia's flower garden too. Gant watched it dart from flower to flower and then zip off to wherever it called home.

He twisted his head to watch Dalphnia's lithe form coming up the trail. Her long brown hair rippled lightly over her shoulders, her step was springy, almost as if her feet never touched the ground. She hummed softly to herself.

"How do you feel this morning?"

"Very well, thanks."

"Your wounds healed well." She smiled when she spoke and her words came out like tinkling chimes.

Gant thought only of her. Other memories were like distant dreams. She was tall and athletic. Gant had seen many women with fuller figures, but Dalphnia's beauty was in her slender, graceful strength. She moved as if floating. Her eyes were a deep brown, the color of polished walnut, and burned with intelligence. Gant had no idea how old Dalphnia was. She seemed younger than he was, but understood so much more than he did. She was patient and had a magical rapport with the trees. Her skin was soft, smooth as cream at the top of milk, but it seemed to change color from tan to dull green. She was beautiful. Gant felt his heart pound every time she came near.

"I guess so," he said finally, though he couldn't remember having any wounds.

"Today you should be ready for a walk. I'll show you my forest."

Gant rose slowly. His muscles responded stiffly, but without pain. Tightness persisted in several places along his back, but the euphoria he felt near Dalphnia eased even that.

"Come," she said, taking his arm.

Her skin felt electric. Gant's every nerve cried for her touch. Her fingertips against his upper arm sent shivers through him.

They walked along the winding path down the slope away from Dalphnia's treehouse. A blanket of brown needles marked the trail even though there were no pine trees in sight. She pointed out oaks, maples, beech, hickory and walnut trees. Once passed the hardwoods, they came to an intimate pine glade where it was easy to get lost in the thick evergreen boughs. Scattered clumps of wildflowers displayed her artistic handiwork.

Now and again, Dalphnia let her arm encircle Gant's waist. She hugged him lightly, like a parent does a child. Gant felt stirrings that were not new, but were different. Here was a woman that filled him not with a juvenile lust, but something fuller, stronger, more powerful. He longed to enfold her in his arms, but didn't. Somehow it didn't seem like the right time.

The trail circled around until they were heading back toward Dalphnia's home. All through her forest Gant noticed that the trees were taller and stronger than any others in the forest. Every variety was there even a grove of fruit trees: apple, cherry, pear, and peach, and each bore fruit, full and ripe.

Gant wondered how that could be since it was not the season for fruit.

"How can the trees have fruit?" he asked.

"They always have fruit," she laughed, as if that answered his question. Farther along, there was an open meadow in the midst of the towering trees. The grass was short, lush and green. In the middle was a row of five thin stone slabs set in the ground with names engraved on them. Gant saw them but only had eyes for Dalphnia and they passed by without comment.

Finally they strolled back up the gentle slope to Dalphnia's treehouse. As they walked she told him stories about the birds and little animals of the forest, calling them by names unfamiliar to Gant. She giggled between anecdotes, squeezing his arm, hugging him. Gant felt tired in a good way. Muscles that had gone unused felt warm and responsive again. Much of the tightness in his shoulders, chest, and legs had disappeared.

Again he wondered about his injuries. "Why do you ask me about my wounds? I don't remember any wounds."

"I found you wounded from a battle with a terrible beast. You were not far from here so I carried you home. It's probably just as well that you forget, the wounds were grievous."

Was she lying? He looked her up and down. She didn't look like she could carry him anywhere. Where did she get the strength?

She smiled. "I think you're ready. Tonight will be your first, I think."

"My first what?"

"You'll see," and she laughed, light and airy.

Gant followed her up the spiral staircase that wrapped around the massive oak into her treetop mansion. The floors were masses of intertwined branches. The leaves formed an impenetrable roof over their heads, and the walls were huge limbs that grew thicker than a man's chest. Gant noticed that the tree seemed to reposition its branches to suit Dalphnia. On hot nights, the branches unmeshed, allowing the cool night breeze to skip through and sweep away the pent-up heat. On blustery days, the branches tightened their maze to block out the tiniest draft. It was the most comfortable dwelling Gant had ever seen. He liked it here.

Once they reached the main room, Gant sat on a comfortable chair formed by two great limbs. "What's so special about tonight?"

Dalphnia turned from a storage sack made of dried leaves sewn together. "First, we eat. You'll need your strength. We'll watch the sunset together."

Gant looked to the west. The branches had parted to form a window through which he saw the huge orange ball sliding toward the horizon. Its fading rays painted the sky and treetops a glorious gold. It was a magnificent view.

Dalphnia brought a wooden platter loaded with fruits, nuts and golden grains. She sat next to Gant, so close their knees rubbed lightly. Gant felt the surging desire building again.

She leaned closer, lightly pressing a smooth purple grape to his lips. He took it, chewed it, savored the juice. Dutifully she fed him, satisfying his hunger. As he ate, the sun fell behind the distant treetops and darkness came. The branches gently closed the window. She turned aside and placed the tray on the floor. When she turned back, it was her lips she offered and Gant tasted them; tasted a new kind of sweetness that he thought would consume him. She broke off the kiss, took Gant's hand and led him up to her bedroom. Fireflies danced above them, giving them only enough light to appreciate each other.

#

Gant woke refreshed. He felt warm, his muscles strong and renewed. He couldn't remember ever sleeping that well. Then again, he couldn't remember much. His nerves pulsated with warm memories of the night before. Gant had never known the pleasure brought by the fusion of two people. He felt more whole than he imagined possible. Dalphnia had been gentle and patient with his naiveté. She coaxed him, teased him, caressed him, and all the while her musical laughter urged him on. Her deep throaty breathing brought them both to the final burst of delight.

He dozed for a time, woke up, stretched and ran his fingers through his disheveled hair. Scanning the bedroom he concluded that she was gone. He was still amazed at how sparsely the room was furnished. The tree probably provided what she needed, he thought. Slowly he got up, reluctant to leave their love nest. He rolled out of bed and went to the limb where his breeches hung. Leisurely, he pulled them on and then arranged his tunic.

On his way out of the bedroom, he noticed a tiny room tucked away on the left. Curious, Gant peeked inside. Hanging from a branch was an expertly crafted suit of armor. Next to the armor hung a belt, scabbard, and sword. Something about the armor and sword tugged at Gant's subconscious. He paused a moment to study them, to admire the superb craftsmanship. Whose were they? Maybe she was married. Or had been. Gant felt pangs of jealousy. Who was he? Was Gant the fool? He dashed from the room, down the stairs. He would demand answers.

He found her tending her flowers, happily caressing the delicate petals. A glow pervaded the garden and an aura surrounded her. Warm sunlight threw rivers of highlights off the wisps of her hair drifting in the light breeze.

She turned to look at Gant. Her smile softened his anger.

"Good morning," she said. "I thought you were going to sleep all day."

Gant almost smiled, but he couldn't put the thought of the other man out of his mind. "Whose armor?"

She stiffened. Her eyes gave away her uncertainty. Something cold passed between them and for a moment the harmony broke. But only for a split second. In that split second Gant was awash in a flood of memories, his memories. For an instant he knew who he was. And then the Dalphnia's harmonious charm swept over him again and his past vanished.

Dalphnia smiled a sad smile. "It is yours," she said kissing him lightly on the cheek. "I told you, I found you wounded wearing that armor. The sword was still in the lair, but I retrieved it. At first I thought you were dead." She stopped for a moment, her eyes looking somewhere far away. Her smile brightened and she laughed like dainty bells chiming a beautiful melody. "But you healed quickly, and strangely, so did the armor. You are a marvelous man, Gant."

She hugged him and kissed him again, this time on the forehead.

"But I don't remember being a warrior." As he said it glimpses of his memory flickered through his mind, but they were too faint, as if veiled behind a curtain and he let them slip away.

"It doesn't matter now," said Dalphnia, "we have each other."

She squeezed Gant so tight he thought she would never let go. Maybe she was afraid to let go, he thought, and hugged her back.

Holding her he wondered why he had doubted her? She had saved his life. She was beautiful, loving, and kind. He would think twice before he accused her again. He shouldn't have been prying anyway. "Sorry," was all he could say. He let go of her, turned and mounted the stairs.

She watched him go for a long moment before returning to her flowers. There would be many more warm nights.

Chapter 21

Snow swirled around the castle. Winter held on with a vengeance. Waiting for the Night of Darkness, Barlon harangued his captains on the glorious war they would wage. Silently, sullenly, they endured, waiting for action. Barlon, too, longed for battle, longed to see his enemies cringe before him and beg for mercy. Mercy he would never give. Only seeing them dead would satisfy his lust for revenge.

Finally, the Night of Darkness arrived. Barlon sat alone in the war room patiently waiting for his wizard.

The door opened and Razgoth slipped quietly into the room. "Sire," he said, "all is ready. After I form the portal to the Dark Realms, you must wield the amulet when Varg comes through."

"Good," replied Barlon, leaping from his chair. "I am anxious to meet my new ally."

Razgoth shook his head. "Do you realize the dangers? Demons are not want to serve man no matter how strong the magic that binds them. They pleasure only in suffering and pain."

"Then he'll enjoy his work." With that Barlon brushed past Razgoth and hurried down the gloomy hallways to Razgoth's workroom.

The wizard's chamber was deep in the bowels of the castle near the dungeons where Uric was held captive. As Barlon entered, having passed the bevy of guards and iron strapped doors, his eyes protested the smoky darkness. Scant light came from iron braziers full of glowing coals set regularly around a great magic circle drawn on the floor. Smokey candles sat in groups of nine at each corner of the room and on short, small tables placed at the midpoint of each wall. Their flames gave off more smoke than light. An acrid mist filled the room like wind-blown grit. It burned the nose and the back of the throat. Barlon forced himself inside and fought down a cough.

Razgoth entered beside him, surprisingly immune to the pungent cloud. "It is important to do exactly as I instruct."

Barlon looked reproachfully at his wizard. He hated being given orders. This time he excused Razgoth's rudeness. "Of course, I'm not stupid."

"You must stand exactly here." Razgoth gently moved Barlon into a small purple triangle that was drawn on the floor only inches from the great circle. Once inside, Barlon felt powerful magic vibrate through his boots.

"Do not move from this spot until I tell you to, no matter what you see or hear. When I nod, hold up the amulet so the demon can see it. I'll do the rest."

"Why all the warnings? Can't you make the demon respond?"

"No. I can produce the portal between dimensions and summon Varg to that opening but I cannot make him come over to our world. He must be lured here. My magic has no power in the realms of darkness. I only open the way. Once he steps through to our plane the spell will be completed and you will hold power over him."

Razgoth turned away from Barlon and walked around the great circle to a place directly opposite the Mountain Lord. The middle-aged necromancer weaved his spell, intricate hand motions and tracings in the air with his nimble fingers coupled with arcane chants. Lastly, he cast a dark powder into the middle of the great circle.

Slowly a deeper blackness grew in the smoky grayness at the center of the room. The darkness swelled, gaining size and shape until it became an opening into a hellish world. Flashes of red leapt from the void. A low wailing filtered into the room followed by a piercing shriek. Varg stood in the portal, broader and taller than a man and ugly as death. His skin was black, the total absence of light, his ears flared up away from his hard features like miniature charcoal wings. His red eyes flashed a blazing hatred.

"Who calls me to the world of my children?" His tone carried a false sweetness with an undercurrent of menace.

"I, Razgoth." The wizard raised both arms, muttered words of power known to few on Earth. "I have need of your power and you shall share the fruits of that power." More finger motions and an unintelligible arcane word.

"I see your power, wizard, but you interest me little."

"I will help you break the spell that keeps you from this world."

Varg turned his head, first to one side, then the other. Something stopped him before he could turn far enough to see Barlon Gorth. "And if I come, what will you do with me once I have completed your task?"

"You are free, of course."

"Name your task."

"The fall of the Western Kings."

Varg pondered, immobile. Then his body solidified, appearing like wrought iron. The portal closed silently behind him.

"Let's go. The Kings fall before the sun sets."

"No. We go with my Lord."

Razgoth nodded toward Barlon who gripped the medallion hanging around his neck and raised it to head level. He held it there waiting for the demon's eyes to fall on it.

Slowly, as if aware of someone else in the room for the first time, Varg turned toward the Mountain King. His sight swept around the circle until it reached the pulsating amulet. A flash of light flared as the demon's eyes came to rest on the magically wrought gold and jewels. The sparkle left Varg's eyes transferred to the image within the medallion. The demon's eyes became dull red and the tiny eyes of the likeness within the interwoven strands of gold flashed as if alive.

"He is yours to command," said Razgoth, dropping his arms. "Be careful what you say. He may interpret your words too literally."

"Fine. Will he stay somewhere until morning? I want to brief my commanders and then we'll need to know exactly what he can do for us."

"He'll do whatever you tell him, short of committing suicide."

"Go with Razgoth. He'll show you to your quarters. Stay there until we come to get you in the morning. Razgoth, take him to his chambers, then meet me in the war room."

"As you wish."

Varg trooped out on Razgoth's heels his face emotionless. Razgoth looked drawn and pale. Barlon Gorth smiled, satisfied with his plan's progress. It was going to take a while to figure out how best to use Varg but they had time. The snows would be gone soon and they would attack the West on the heels of the thaw. The first few skirmishes as they moved into the middle Western Kingdom of Chadmir would likely be only with border guards. Those could be overwhelmed by the Knights of Habichon while Barlon experimented with the demon's powers. It would not be long, and with Sir Jarlz enchanted to believe that Barlon was his liege the greatest living knight had taken one of the empty suits of purple armor. With all that in his favor, Barlon felt invincible.

Chapter 22

West of the Monolith Mountains were the three Western Kingdoms. The northern most was Scaltzland, a kingdom of warriors and warrior priests who lived in the great forests and mountains, hunting, fishing, battling the northern hordes, and mining and smelting ores.

To the south lay the farming kingdom of Dernium. It was a bountiful land of sunshine, fresh water and fertile soil. Hardworking farmers tilled vast fields that produced vegetables and grains. They herded cattle, sheep and goats. They were good at what they did, but they weren't soldiers.

Between these two kingdoms and on a direct line with the Great East-West road was Chadmir, a kingdom of merchants and traders who lived off the commerce that came through their lands.

With Barlon Gorth's conquest of Netherdorf, the three kings hurriedly arranged a meeting. As usual, the northern and southern kings traveled to Pogor, the capitol city of Chadmir. They met in the sandstone castle's light, airy council hall that towered over the thriving business district. Large windows opened to fresh spring breezes that whipped the countless colorful flags, pennants and banners marking the multitude of tents and shops in the streets below. Three chairs were arranged around an oblong table in the room's center.

King Petre of the nothern Kingdom of Scaltzland sat closest to the door. He was tall and muscular, his body honed by life spent as a warrior. He ruled over a populace of warriors and hunters. He arrived that day with a troop of his personal guard.

Seated mid-table was King Daggon from the southern farmlands of Dernium. He was a blocky man who tilled fields along with his people. He also brought a contingent of guards.

As host, King Fasoom sat at the head of the conference table. He was rotund with a disarmingly pleasant smile that hid a tough attitude for business.

"I say we teach this upstart a lesson," said Petre, scowling. He stretched his lean frame, slouching in his chair.

"You're always ready to fight," said Daggon, whose bulk hardly fit his ornately carved chair. "He's got what he wants."

"I'm not so sure," said Fasoom. "And there are problems other than with what he wants. Barlon Gorth now controls the only trade route between us and the Eastern Empire. Tariffs could become a problem, and even if not, trade will suffer if he doesn't keep the roads open. Perhaps Petre is right."

King Daggon scowled. "Trade, war, what talk is this? Peace is what we need, peace to grow our crops, peace for you to handle your trade and you to mine your metals. Peace is what I've sought, in our names."

Daggon pulled out a leather tube, uncapped it and withdrew a rolled sheet of vellum. He unrolled it and ceremoniously laid it on the table.

"Daggon, where did you get this?" asked Petre, craning his neck to get a good view of the document.

"An emissary of Lord Gorth, Shalmuthe, brought it in hopes we could strike a peace treaty before anyone did something rash. You see, this pact guarantees peace and is already signed by myself and Barlon Gorth. It has ample provisions for your signatures. Sign it. It guarantees peace for all. *And*, you'll note, it includes mutual defense provisions should the Northern Hordes attack us again."

"I don't know," said Fasoom, taking up the thin document in his chubby hands. "I'll have to read this carefully, have my advisors study it."

"Take your time."

Petre's frown deepened. "If Barlon is content with his little conquest, why didn't he set *himself* up as king in Netherdorf instead of that old soldier? What is Barlon saving for himself'?"

"He doesn't want power. He just needed the croplands to feed his people."

"Yes, you know about crops, Daggon. You and the people of Dernium are great farmers, but you know nothing of men. Barlon Gorth is not done. We should crush him now and restore King Tirmus to the throne in Netherdorf. Tirmus is an honest man."

The wiry leader of the northern kingdom locked eyes with the broad shouldered farmer. Each glared at the other stubbornly refusing to be the first to look away.

"I think we should wait a few days until I can dissect this treaty," said Fasoom. "Wars are costly. Inaction can cost more. Let us feast and enjoy each other's company for two days. On the third, we shall meet and discuss this until we reach a decision."

Petre nodded. "I can't go to war by myself."

"And I can't have peace if you do not," said Daggon.

"Done." said King Fasoom. He waved his hand for food, and the many rings on his hand flashed like twinkling stars.

#

On the third day, King Petre of Scaltzland paced the Council Hall impatiently. He was a head taller than most men but his lack of bulk belied an amazing strength and quickness. He was in extraordinary shape for one who did most of his work seated on a throne. He had renounced the easy life. He seldom over-ate and never drank to excess. Daily he honed his skill with arms, testing himself against his captains and officers. He took seriously his royal position as commander of the Scaltzlandian army. Often he led companies against the northern barbarians. Few knew the sword at his side still held a touch of ancient magic. He preferred to let his men think it was his skill that felled the enemy. Today he chafed at the tardiness of his fellow Kings. He had barely endured the wait imposed by King Fasoom while his advisors evaluated Gorth's treaty. As far as Petre was concerned, war was the only logical answer. Daggon was always slow to see the danger. His people were happy tilling their fields and milking their cows. Worse, they thought everyone else should be happy doing the same. Fasoom, on the other hand, was more pragmatic. His prosperity depended on trade and therefore he better understood relations between nations. Surely, he would not be fooled by Gorth's maneuver.

Footsteps sounded outside in the hall. Finally, Petre thought and walked to his seat. He sat down as the door opened and Fasoom entered with Daggon. The shorter merchant king had one arm around his bull-like companion, a bottle of wine swung loosely in his free hand.

"Ah." said Fasoom, raising the bottle in salute as he saw Petre. "You are already here."

"You're late."

"There's no hurry. Important decisions are best not rushed."

Fasoom crossed the narrow space between the door and the table, and went around to the head of the table to seat himself. Daggon worked his huge frame into his chair. He laid the treaty on the table.

"I have examined the document carefully," began Fasoom. "I believe Gorth is sincere in his attempt to make peace."

"Why?" demanded Petre.

"He is weak. His army is no match for ours. He has no political power, neither in the free cities nor within the Empire, and he does not have the resources to support a war against us on this side of the Monolith Mountains."

"So, you favor signing this."

"Yes. I have already done so. Only your signature is needed to make this binding."

Petre looked from Fasoom to Daggon. He hated it, hated turning on a friend like Tirmus. If things were reversed, Petre felt sure that Netherdorf would declare war on Gorth. And he would never trust a man who attacked one Kingdom without warning while seeking peace with those at his back.

"I won't sign."

"You'd wage war without us?" yelped Daggon. He nearly rose from his chair, his face reddening.

"No. My minister will sign in my absence. I will live by it unless Gorth gives me reason to do otherwise." Petre rose. "I'll send Durk up to sign it. I'm going back to Ferd."

"Give my regards to your Queen," nodded Fasoom

respectfully.

"Yes, from me too," added Daggon, heaving himself up to leave.

And so the peace treaty was signed and the kings returned home.

Chapter 23

Before King Petre returned to his capitol city, Barlon Gorth massed his troops, confident that the Western Kingdoms languished under a false sense of security. His men numbered only 15 brigades of 250 each. Along with them he had the 75 Knights of the Habichon under Lom's command, plus Razgoth and Varg. The rear column consisted of hundreds of smiths, armorers, men of medicine, cooks, butchers and porters. Cattle drivers drove the herds stripped from Netherdorf and wagons loaded to bursting with wheat, flour and rye. Ale was in short supply but hundreds of tiny streams flowed down from the Monolith Mountains and supplied water.

Varg strode beside Barlon's nervous horse. The demon's magical stride effortlessly covered the miles of road from Barlon's castle through Chamber Pass to Chadmir's border. Barlon rode proudly atop his beautiful warhorse at the head of the column. His thick hair streamed out from under his polished steel helm.

Razgoth rode at Barlon's immediate flank, along with Lom, whose dark purple armor dulled even the bright sunshine. Next to them rode General Ecker. Directly behind them were the brigade captains and Sir Jarlz who now wore the purple armor of the Knights of Habichon. Despite putting Jarlz in a suit of the Habichon armor, Barlon did not put Sir Jarlz under Lom's command instead keeping him as a personal bodyguard.

Barlon's army moved slowly. It took two days to get through Chamber pass. Finally, at sunset on the second day Barlon paused on a hilltop overlooking the Chadmirian border fortress of Bal. Its flag fluttered proudly in a light breeze. The last rays of the dying sun gave its colors a final burst of clarity.

"Camp tonight," he said turning in his saddle to address his captains. "No fires!"

The captains scurried away to get their troops bivouacked. Within minutes, a special crew pitched a large command tent. Smaller tents sprang up serving as quarters for the commanders.

A cook's tent appeared but the half dozen cooks milled around not sure what to do without a fire. Barlon gathered his leaders in the command tent. Razgoth, Varg, Barlon, Ecker, Lom, and Sir Jarlz crowded around a table covered with maps. Barlon stood at the head, Varg at his shoulder, the rest spread back away from the foul, ugly creature.

"The plan is simple," said Barlon. "In the morning, six supply wagons and 30 troopers from 1st Brigade will proceed to Fort Bal. General Ecker will lead them and request provisions and water from the fort's guard. The General will explain that you are enroute to Pogor with gifts for King Fasoom. They have no reason to suspect anything and courtesy demands they allow you in. Varg, Sir Jarlz and ten of Lom's men will be hidden in false bottoms in the wagons. Once inside, you will attack just before mid-watch ends. Take the gatehouse and hold the gate open until we arrive. Above all, let no one escape. We do not want to warn Fasoom."

"What of the troops inside Bal?" asked General Ecker.

"Kill them."

"And if they surrender?"

"Lock them in their own jails and we'll decide what to do with them later. Any other questions?" Barlon glared around the room.

The group dispersed. Each man retired to contemplate the coming action. Barlon left while a few were still looking at the detailed maps. Outside Razgoth was waiting. Varg was nowhere to be seen.

"Excuse the intrusion, sire," began the wizard, his hands clasp deferentially in front of his robes.

Barlon nodded for Razgoth to continue.

"I wonder about Varg. He accompanies you everywhere and seems content in your service. Why? It goes against all I've read about the entrapment of demons."

"He is our trusted ally."

"Ally? He is a Demon Prince. A thing of darkness. He cannot be trusted. He is probably feigning allegiance until such time as he can free himself from the amulet. Then we are doomed!"

Razgoth's face distorted with worry and terror. Barlon almost laughed. Magic was nothing compared to a mutual agreement.

"What have you done?" demanded the wizard.

"Promised Varg what he wants."

"And what is that?" Razgoth's furrows deepened.

"His freedom." Barlon chuckled, as if it were a terrific joke.

"His freedom." Razgoth visibly shrank from his ruler. "This is no defenseless peasant, sire. If you grant him his freedom, we'll be doomed. There is little magic left anywhere in this world that can stop him."

"Who said I'm going to give him his freedom? It is only one more ploy in my arsenal. He believes me, he trusts me." Barlon laughed.

"Sire, you endanger us all. When Varg realizes your lie." Razgoth looked around, suddenly wondering where the demon might be. "If he hears us talking. . ." he mumbled, and then to Barlon. "When does he expect you to release him?"

"After we conquer the Western Kingdoms. He knows that is my only interest."

"And when you don't free him, Varg will do his utmost to pervert your every command until he can get the amulet from you."

"Be still. You worry too much." Barlon's face darkened and Razgoth winced. Instead of a blistering harangue, Barlon smiled, patted his wizard on the shoulder and said, "We'll handle Varg when the time comes. Until then I have a devoted servant."

"Where is he now?"

"I sent him to intercept the night patrol from Fort Bal. He seemed to relish the idea of feasting on human flesh."

Barlon turned into his tent, leaving Razgoth alone in the darkness. The wizard stared blankly at the closed tent flap, his gray eyes wide. The idea of a struggle with Varg ate at his mind. Eventually, the mage returned to his tent but he did not sleep. Instead, he studied passages from the ancient tomes in his trunk. To call a demon was one thing, to return him, something else.

#

As the sun came up six supply wagons and accompanying troops ground their way toward Fort Bal. General Ecker rode tall and proud leading his modest force. Soon they reached the base of the stone walls of the Chadmirian outpost. The fort stood massive and imposing at the junction of the roads from Netherdorf, Zalmon, Pogor and Ferd. It had long guarded the entrance to the Western Kingdoms from the east through Chamber Pass. No wars had been fought in years and the legions stationed there had grown slack with inaction. Nonetheless, they stood their watches diligently.

"Who seeks entrance?" called the guard from above the gate as General Ecker brought his command to a halt.

"General Ecker, King of Netherdorf. I need water and rest before I continue to Pogor."

"What is your business in Pogor?"

"I bear gifts for the king to seal our treaty of peace."

"Wait," said the guard. He turned from the wall and scurried to a point on the inner wall where he could look down on the courtyard below.

"Sir," he called to an officer busy in conversation below. "General Ecker is here from Netherdorf. He seeks water and shelter. Shall we admit him?"

The officer glanced up. "Any sign of the night patrol?"

"No, sir." The guard waited for an answer, waited a moment more, and then asked again, "Sir, shall we admit General Ecker?"

"Yes, yes," waved the officer, already distracted by his fellow officers again.

Slowly the gates clanked open. General Ecker pranced in on his resplendent stallion followed by his troops and the squeaking wagons. They proceeded to a spot to the left of the gate near the outer wall. Once the party was inside, the huge iron gate clattered down.

General Ecker studied the interior defenses. The lookouts atop the walls were not armed with bows or crossbows. Those inside were in disarray. A moment's observation assured him that the nervous activity was due to their concern for the missing night patrol and not fear of treachery from his party.

Surprisingly no emissary came to the General to discuss provisions, water rights or quarters. The timing couldn't have been better.

General Ecker turned to his captain and whispered, "You may proceed. Notify those in the wagons to wait until your men are spread out and ready. You will strike the first blow."

The captain turned away and within moments his men began to casually disperse throughout the garrison, positioning themselves next to a Chadmirian soldier without drawing undue attention. A few more minutes and it would be too late for the fort's troops.

The captain returned to Ecker's side and was about to say something when the General saw the garrison commander and several of his lieutenants heading toward them. The General motioned his captain to silence.

"General Ecker," said the fort's commander, tossing a casual salute. "This is most inopportune. However perhaps you can do us a service."

"What is that?"

"Did you see any signs of a patrol? Our night patrol is missing. Twenty-five horses and riders without a trace."

The commander studied Ecker and his captain diligently. His lieutenants, likewise, craned their necks to check out the wagons, the few guards left near them and the soldiers fanning out through the courtyard.

The General feigned giving the question consideration while his sword hand inched toward the hilt at his hip. Imperceptibly, his captain also prepared for battle.

"No," said General Ecker. "We didn't see any signs of anyone in Chamber Pass. Perhaps they strayed up some side canyon."

As the fort's commander started to reply one of his lieutenants touched his elbow. The lieutenant's head was looking straight at one of Ecker's men mounting the stairs to the battlements. The General knew what was coming. He yanked out his sword and in one smooth motion slashed across the commander's neck, killing him where he stood. At the same time Ecker's captain had his sword out and chopped down on the nearest lieutenant.

The courtyard erupted. Each of Ecker's men lashed out at the nearest Chadmirian soldier. Cries filled the air. Twenty died in the first seconds. Troops from both sides rushed to join the fray. Hundreds of Chadmirian bordermen poured from their barracks where they had been on alert status. Quickly Ecker's men were outnumbered and overwhelmed by the enemy's fast response.

The remaining Chadmirian lieutenants pulled their swords and attacked General Ecker and his captain. To the general's left two of the Chadmirians pressured the captain, forcing him back and away from Ecker. In a moment these officers were joined by a handful of soldiers and the captain fell to a dozen sword blows. General Ecker retreated toward the wagons desperately parrying repeated thrusts.

At the wagon, the general's attackers faltered. Suddenly the general found himself disengaged as Varg stepped past him into the cluster of enemy soldiers. The Demon-prince had grown. He stood ten feet tall and sported two sets of vicious claw-tipped limbs. Their sinewy black muscles bulged like tree trunks. Without hesitation, Varg waded into the line of soldiers. Two of his arms tore the throats from the nearest two lieutenants. The rest of the soldiers hacked madly at this towering fiend. Their swords clattered uselessly off his rock-hard hide. Two more died without realizing their mistake, another fell wounded.

Now the Chadmirians backed away, stark terror in their faces. One or two swung again, half-heartedly, not believing the impotence of swords against this thing of darkness. They died for their hesitation.

General Ecker exhaled with relief. Free from battle he surveyed the situation looking for places to send his reserves. Varg quickly decimated the enemy ranks near the wagons. At the parapet stairs, the garrison troops momentarily held back Ecker's soldiers. But dark purple knights moved to the stairs, their armor unscathed by the defenders' swords. The darkness that followed them steadily advanced up the steps until soon they finished the last few men atop the wall.

Other purple clad warriors cleaved trails of blood and carnage through the massed troops in the courtyard. At the gate a handful of stubborn defenders worked valiantly to hold the gatehouse. Signals from the walls reported Barlon's arrival and the defenders redoubled their efforts to stem the inevitable.

Sir Jarlz moved to the head of Ecker's gatehouse contingent, his swordplay a symphony of destruction, his purple armor a breakwall against his enemies.

Just when Ecker thought all had gone perfectly, he saw a lone figure sneaking across the rooftops of the central building. The shadowy form was small, either a boy or woman. Ecker watched as the shape ran to a precarious ladder on the side of the west tower. There, hand over hand, the figure scrambled up toward the tower rooftop where Ecker saw a huge cage of homing birds.

"Archers!" he yelled.

Once the figure reached the top it would release dozens of messengers, all bearing a message of treachery.

"Archers," the general screamed again as the first bowmen ran up. "Shoot him," he snapped and pointed at the figure.

The first archer's bow twanged and a steel-tipped shaft clattered into the rock wall. The figure flinched sideways, almost losing his grip on the ladder. A second and third arrow launched. Both missed.

The slim figure reached the top of the ladder, ready to slip over onto the tower roof where he'd be safe from arrows.

"Hurry," snapped Ecker. "He must be stopped."

A chorus of bowstrings answered. A flurry of feathered shafts fell on the slim silhouette. The metallic clatter of near misses was drowned out by a woman's high-pitched scream. Two arrows sank into her flesh. General Ecker stood spellbound as he watched her grip weaken, sure that any minute she would fall. Instead, with a last surge of strength, she heaved herself over the top onto the tower roof and temporary safety.

General Ecker waited, expecting any minute to see the flock freed from the cage. A slim hand appeared, undid the cage door latch, and then retracted. The cage door fell open. Long seconds passed. Nothing happened. Meanwhile the fort's main gate rattled heavily behind Ecker as it opened on greased slides. Shouts sounded as Barlon's troops rushed in to aid their embattled comrades. Everywhere came cries for mercy as the remaining Chadmirians surrendered. Still the birds refused to fly.

From the tower rooftop, two bloodied arrows fluttered to the ground, tossed by an unseen hand. Seconds later, dozens of straining wings burst from the cage as the flock of pigeons exploded skyward. There were so many of them, it was pointless to waste arrows and Ecker held his archers from firing.

"Bring me the girl from the rooftop," he said to one of his men waiting nearby.

The soldier ran off, while the General watched the flock climb higher. Tightly packed, they flew, one swirling mass of wings. As they climbed higher, the flock thinned for an instant and Ecker caught sight of a single bird of prey flying at the center of the racing messengers. It was a fleeting glimpse. He wasn't sure. What would an eagle be doing with a flock of pigeons? Maybe it was only a trick of the sun or clouds. He turned and marched to the center of the courtyard where Barlon was instructing his men on the imprisonment of the captives.

"Well done," said Barlon, obviously pleased.

"Not as well done as I would have liked."

"What do you mean?"

"The birds were released. Fasoom will know of our attack all the way in Pogor."

"It is of no consequence. Did you see the way Varg cleared the field? He is unstoppable." Glee lit Barlon's face, but General Ecker also saw the disgruntled expression on Lom's face and the worry in Razgoth's eyes.

Barlon ordered the fort's stores plundered. He had his wagon masters take inventory and plan for operating a supply depot out of the fortress. Then he ordered unlimited drinking privileges for his troops until the stores were depleted. At the same time, others escorted the prisoners to the massive jails below the rearmost section of the fort.

While Barlon Gorth was busy given orders to his lesser aides, a runner approached General Ecker. "Sir," he reported, "there was no one on the roof."

"What?" The general looked up at the tall tower. Impossible. "Are you sure?"

"It's a flat roof with nowhere to hide. There's no one there."

The General made a mental note and said, "That will be all."

The soldier left.

"Let's find suitable quarters," said Barlon, returning his attention to General Ecker and the rest of his command staff.

It wasn't long before Ecker, Razgoth, Barlon and Lom were installed in the best of the Spartan quarters inside the main stronghold. Barlon's cooking staff went to work preparing a fine meal from the fort's provisions. Lom posted his men atop the walls and Sir Jarlz was placed in command of the watch. The rest of the troops camped on the plain around Fort Bal and the drunken revelry began almost as soon as the mead, ale and wine casks could be located.

Barlon was in an outstanding mood, joking and laughing with his men at the great table in the main dining hall. He ate his fill, mentioned an early morning staff meeting and retired for the evening, hinting he was not to be disturbed.

Before long the others drifted off and only Razgoth and General Ecker sat sipping their drinks.

"I don't like it," said the General, his hair flashing silver in the firelight. "Barlon takes this war too lightly. We have defeated only a tiny outpost and that full of Chadmirians. Wait until we face their combined armies, especially the battle-hardened legions of Scaltzland."

"Our Lord trusts too much in Varg's power," said Razgoth. Tonight the mage looked older than his years. Though barely into his forties, Razgoth looked ancient. His sandy hair was in disarray and his boney fingers trembled slightly as he held his wine glass.

"Varg is powerful, I'll vouch for that. The Chadmirian blades couldn't scratch his hide. And he certainly made short work of them, even those with armor."

"Varg is deadly," agreed the wizard. "But his power will as likely be against us as with us. Demons have little use for worldly goals. I fear our Lord may yet overplay his hand."

"We still have the Knights of Habichon. They have magic in their swords. They'll side with us if the time comes."

"Magic? Yes, a black and evil power. Have you noticed how their eyes turn deathly white if they wear the armor too long? More likely they would side with Varg if it came to it. If you remember, Habichon's knights turned on him when they went to the realms of darkness. The evil in that armor subverts them until they are loyal only to evil. I hope we don't have to find out."

"Speaking of that cursed demon, where is Varg? He hasn't been here all night. Usually, he won't leave Barlon's side."

"I'm not sure," confided the mage, "but I think our Lord has granted the demon use of the prisoners."

The general's expression showed his surprise and shock. Razgoth was correct. Screams, shrieks and wails from the cells persisted through the night. The bulk of Barlon's troops were past caring, drunk beyond comprehension, but those who remained awake that night were frozen with terror by morning. Even Lom's troops, who stood atop the walls, were touched by the rising horror though their tainted souls were beyond fear. Unlike the others, the knights of Habichon seemed to gain an eerie strength from the sounds of the dying.

As the camp began to stir the next morning, whispered rumors filtered through the ranks spread by those who remembered. Fear tainted every man's eye, and shadows darkened every mortal heart. All that is except two. Sir Jarlz was unmoved, his mind not his own, and Barlon saw only his victory, his mind burning with thoughts of revenge and conquest.

Chapter 24

In Pogor, capital city of Chadmir, King Fasoom received a battered and wounded visitor. She was petite and slender with close-cropped hair and great, round, brown eyes that seemed to see more than they should. She wore an ankle length gown of white muslin. Beneath it, a bandage was wrapped around the arrow wound to her right thigh. Another wrapping bound her left shoulder. As she entered King Fasoom's private chamber, she winced with each step, but her head remained high, her chin thrust out, her bearing proud and fierce.

"Amelia, what happened to you?" asked Fasoom with genuine concern. The chubby monarch motioned her closer.

"Barlon Gorth has taken Fort Bal. I am the only one who escaped."

"How? How so quickly?"

"A demon, a horrible beast that kills and cannot be killed, and the Knights of Habichon. We fought well, but Barlon has powers we cannot fight. I flew here as fast as I could."

"Damn, Petre was right," said the king with a scowl. "This treachery will not go unchecked. Rest for now. We will soon need you to watch Barlon's movements. In the meantime, I will inform Daggon and Petre. In a few days you'll be mended."

The king shook his head dismissing the girl. As she turned to go she heard Fasoom say to himself, "We get war even as we pray for peace, and Petre will tell us he told us so. What does Barlon Gorth hope to gain?"

Amelia left the king's chamber and limped to her quarters on the second floor. She ate sparingly from the food brought to her, and then slept from exhaustion.

When she woke, it was night. She felt better, but her shoulder and thigh were stiff and sore. She ate again, slowly. After she finished, she walked to the window, opened it and looked out. The smaller moon was only a thin sliver hanging low near the horizon. The larger moon was higher in the sky, but it too was only a thin crescent. Gently, so as not to hurt her shoulder, she dropped her gown and stood naked in the window for a moment contemplating the task she knew was ahead. And then resolved to go through with it, she whispered one of the spells that her grandfather had taught her. When she'd first learned them, it had been hard to stay focused and get the spell just right. After so many repetitions, she could cast either one, one for day, one for night, unconsciously. Now, her body took on a translucence, shimmering and transparent. Her limbs became great wings covered with powerful flight feathers and her body transformed into a great owl. She tested her wings against the cool night air. Satisfied, she picked up her gown in one talon, and then swooped off into the darkness.

She flew east along the road until she came to Fort Bal. Campfires dotted the terrain around the fort. Barlon's troops had not moved and didn't look ready to do so soon. She circled the sleeping army on silent wings, counting the tents, noting the numbers of supply wagons. And then she turned and flew off to the northeast.

She climbed steadily over the Monolith Mountains, crossing them near Barlon's mountain castle. Onward she flew making the best speed she could. Dawn brought daylight that bothered her eyes and she settled in a tall tree. Her shoulder ached, but she dare not rest. She whispered the words of the day spell and with a shudder of feathers, she changed into a large eagle. As always, she tested her new wings before she leaped into the air and flew off again, always northeast.

Now she could fly faster and at higher altitude. She climbed and sped on. The ground passed below and it wasn't long before she glided in to land before a stout log cabin ringed by tall pines. In a blink she was again Amelia. She pulled on the white thigh-length gown she'd carried with her, the soft white cloth covering her wounds.

"Grandfather," she called to the house from outside the ring of pine trees.

Abadis' face beamed from the window nearest the door. "Amelia," he answered, "come in, come in."

He rushed outside, waving her in, bubbling with laughter. "It's so good to see you. How is my favorite granddaughter? I wish I'd known, I could have had something ready to eat."

He threw his arms around her and hugged her. She winced, but it went unnoticed. Then he pushed her into the house still babbling his welcome.

He didn't stop until she was seated with a warm glass of his healing elixir. Finally he stopped talking and looked closely at her, his face turning grim.

"What's wrong?"

"I came to ask for help. King Fasoom is in deep trouble. Maybe worse than he'll admit."

"You're still working for that over-rich snob?"

"Yes, Grandpa. He's honest and he loves birds."

"Honest? I never met an honest merchant, king or commoner. Nevertheless, you didn't come all this way to hear an old man complain about merchants and their merchandise."

"No, I didn't. Barlon Gorth has taken Fort Bal. I'm sure he'll attack Pogor next. Fasoom thinks he can rally Petre and Daggon. He thinks their armies can defeat Gorth. Grandpa, they won't."

"Oh, come child. Barlon Gorth is hardly capable of raising an army large enough to threaten the Western Kings. I'm surprised he could muster enough force to take Fort Bal."

"You'd be right if it were a simple matter of numbers. Barlon can't have more than three thousand men. It's the demon. I saw him. I saw him laugh at sword strokes that would kill any man. And Gorth has recruited the Knights of Habichon."

151

"Hmm." The old man sat down heavily on one of the stools. "Habichon's evil returns to haunt us again. But a demon? What demon? Describe it."

"It was huge, ten feet tall at least. All black, with four arms that ended in claws and ears that swept back on the side of its head like wings."

The old wizard thought for several long minutes, his fingers tapping lightly on the tabletop. "I hope I'm wrong. I'll have to consult some of my records." He paused as if he'd thought of something else. "Probably should get in touch with Uric. The last I heard he was still with King Tirmus."

Amelia looked shocked. "Haven't you heard? Netherdorf fell to Barlon Gorth months ago. His General Ecker is the new king."

"Tirmus is dead?"

"They say he escaped, but the rest of the castle staff was killed."

"Impossible!" snapped Abadis gruffly.

"That's what we heard at Fort Bal. Grandfather." She looked sternly at his weathered face. "What's wrong with you? What have you been doing? You've lost touch with the world."

"Uh, well," a touch of color came to his checks. "I've been doing research."

"Research?"

"Forget that. What about Sir Jarlz? Uric? Have you heard anything about them?"

"All we heard was the castle staff was killed protecting Tirmus' escape. If they were in Netherdorf they're probably dead."

A deep sadness settled over Abadis. He conjured up warm memories of friendship.

"Grandpa," said Amelia softly.

The old man looked at her, his pain changing to anger.

"I could stay," she said and patted his gnarled hand with her soft delicate one.

"Surely you'll rest a while before you return. You'll need your strength."

"Yes," she admitted. "I am tired. If I can sleep a bit."

"Of course, of course."

He ushered her to his bed in the back room, kissed her lightly on the cheek and left. While she slept, he poured over three faded tomes filled with drawings, descriptions and legends of various demons, dark princes and creatures from the nether worlds. He stopped at one particular page, glaring over and over at the half page illustration.

After a time of pacing, scratching his chin and head, Abadis went to his shelves and pulled down another large encyclopedic volume. He opened it, thumbed a few pages, read carefully, and then slumped back on his stool. Amelia found him seated there when she woke. The look on his face chased the last touch of sleep from her.

"What is it, Grandpa?"

"Come here, child," he said softly. He pointed to the book open to an illustration. "Recognize this?"

She looked at the picture. "That's it."

"I was afraid of it. Uric was right. The prophecy is coming true." Abadis slammed the table with one fist. "Barlon is a madman! He doesn't know what he's doing."

Amelia turned the second volume around so she could read the text. It said:

"Varg, demon prince, true name unknown. Father of the dark elves, lord of suffering and torture, magically exiled to the realms of evil by the dark elves and Bartholomew. Confined there unless recalled. Sworn to vengeance against men and dark elves. Treacherous, evil, uncontrollable. NOT TO BE CONTACTED!"

She looked up at her grandfather. "If he was sent to the dark regions and confined there, how'd he get here?"

"The right summoning spell could break his restrictions."

"But who would do such a thing?"

"Probably that upstart, Razgoth. He's good, but impatient and reckless. Valdor taught him for a while, but the kid was too headstrong. Valdor eventually dismissed him for disobedience."

"If he was dismissed, how could he summon Varg?"

"He already knew too much. He's not stupid, just careless. For a time he studied under the black wizardess of Lost Mountain. That he is working for Gorth is not good. Razgoth always was impressionable, taking to causes without considering the ramifications. Poor Valdor is probably beside himself. He always takes his pupils to heart, even ex-pupils."

"Barlon must hold some power over Varg. The thing seemed anxious enough to do his bidding."

"A medallion, no doubt. Perhaps the kid's done it right. Then again, Varg may be just waiting for an opportunity to free himself." As an afterthought he added to himself, "I can't see how they could conjure up a magic fire strong enough to make the amulet unless Razgoth's progressed a lot since he left Valdor."

"What can we do?"

"You can go back to Fasoom. I'm not sure if we can do anything. Gant may be about to test his great-great-great grandfather's gift."

"Who?"

"Gant, Sir Jarlz' nephew. He's gone south chasing dragons. I need a few days of study and then I shall have to go find him. Maybe he's still in Falls Hill."

"Are you going to be gone long? What if I need to contact you?"

"Don't worry, I'll set the shield to recognize you. Enter and write your message on the mirror." Abadis pointed to an oblong reflecting glass on the wall half hidden behind a stack of jars, boxes and bottles. "I always carry this small mirror with me," he said, pulling out a miniature replica of the bigger mirror. "It shows me anything written on the larger mirror no matter where I am. I'll check for messages once a day."

"Okay, then I'll be off. King Fasoom probably wonders where I've gone." She rose and started for the door.

"Are you sure you feel up to flying? I could take you."

"I'm fine Grandpa. The flight will do me good. Besides, you have more important things to do."

She walked down the path past the pines, waved once to Abadis, turned the corner and lost sight of the house. She pulled off her gown, cast her day spell and transformed into an eagle. She tested her wings and took off, clutching her rolled-up dress in one mighty talon.

#

Miles to the west, away from men and their daily travels, there were others who watched events unfold. Deep in the Caverns of Darkness, the Dark Elf Queen, Sarona, sat upon her obsidian throne, caressing the carved devil heads that formed the arm rests. Her face was delicately thin with high cheekbones and ears that swept up and back to points. She had a sinister exotic beauty that frightened both men and elves. Her thin lips were pursed, her eyes serious, hard with black pupils that were so large they left almost no white. She could see perfectly well in the dim light given off by the faint patches of glowing red rock set in the walls and ceiling. The red hue cast multiple shadows and reflected off Sarona's dark skin, glistening from beads of nervous sweat.

Around the perimeter of her court chamber stood guards at ramrod attention, eyes fixed straight ahead. On either side of her, elder statesmen and women awaited the arrival of the latest messenger. On the raised dais with her were the Minister of State, Minister of War, Minister of the Hunt and the High Priest. Her personal guard stood like pillars, steadfast, loyal women-warriors who ensured others maintained their distance from the Queen.

Finally the doors at the end of the Great Cavern opened. In trotted a lean, dark elf dressed in light hunting garb with a bow slung over his shoulder. Two of the regular palace guards followed him in. The runner stopped at the foot of the five stone steps leading up to Sarona's dais.

"My Queen," began the runner with a bow.

"Yes, yes. You have word of Fort Bal?"

"Yes, Majesty. We watched Barlon Gorth march from his mountain castle, through Chamber Pass and take Fort Bal by ruse. The Chadmirians let Barlon's men inside and Barlon's troops killed them all."

Sarona motioned her Minister of State to her side. "Didn't our Ambassador to Dernium say they had a treaty with Gorth?"

"Yes."

She waved him back and returned her attention to the messenger. "How many soldiers does Barlon command?"

"Two thousand, three at most."

"Ridiculous!"

"Majesty, they were counted several times, and though strung out to give the impression of more, there are no more than three thousand."

"Are the purple knights with him?"

"Yes."

"Even so, he cannot hope to win a war with the West."

"It is the demon, Majesty. Varg is with them."

"So. Our father has returned as promised to wreak his vengeance on his 'naughty' children. You have done well. Rest and take food before you return to your duties."

She waved the messenger away.

"Get the sacred tome," she said, staring at the High Priest. "We meet in the War Hall as soon as you can get there."

Suddenly the Royal Hall was a flurry of activity. The High Priest stepped off with long strides on his way to get the requested volume. The royal guards huddled around the Queen as she rose. The other ministers scurried off with the news.

Sarona marched off surrounded by her personal guards. When she arrived at the War Hall she waved the guards to their customary positions, and discarded the long, showy gown she'd worn in court. Underneath she wore a light leather tunic and skirt. She carried a decorative dagger on her left hip and the royal scepter in her belt to the right.

As always, the world map lay open on the long table. Various figurines stood on the board, representing the units of other realms. No elf units were represented. Sarona went to a small flat box. She lifted the lid, reached in and pulled out the black miniature of Varg.

"Finally you come back for us," she said to the tiny statue, placing it next to the cast replica of Fort Pal. "After all these years, I hope Bartholomew's teachings are true, or we shall all perish."

The ministers began to file in followed closely by the High Priest. In his arms he carried a tremendous book with covers made of thin oak. Numerous runes were burned into the cover and though the book seemed ancient, a sulphurous odor clung to it. The High Priest set the massive tome on a pedestal designed to hold it at waist level. He mumbled a few words, nodded with his eyes closed and opened the front cover. Without hesitation, the High Priest flipped the yellowed pages to a well-worn spot in the text.

"Bartholomew writes," he read from the text. "Varg shall not stay imprisoned forever. Men of evil intent shall free him to do their foul deeds. Though their control seems perfect to their narrow sight, it is inevitable that Varg shall escape their power and seek the ruin of man and elf. Much cannot be seen about when, how, or why this will come to pass, but I fear that it will happen in a time when there is no magic strong enough to stop Varg once he is loosed upon my people."

The High Priest stopped. "And we have no wizards who can stop Varg." There was a plaintive note in his voice.

"I know that," said Sarona. "We all know he predicted Varg's return. Read the section that refers to ridding us of Varg, and stop talking as if we were doomed."

"Yes, Majesty." The priest flipped several pages, scanned until he found what he wanted, and then read aloud, "Though time holds many secrets, do not despair. There may be a warrior of your time mighty enough to kill Varg in this existence and send him back to his realm of darkness. It is less clear who this warrior may be. I can see battle, many battles and many will try and fail, but perhaps there is one who can succeed. Victory is not without sacrifice."

The priest flipped several more pages, and then read again. "I cannot discover the name of the warrior who can defeat Varg. Every attempt fails. Perhaps he does not exist."

"I cannot bear the thought of the carnage, the annihilation, of my beloved people. I have taken matters into my own hands as best I can. There will be a distant grandson of mine who will rise to the pinnacle of armed combat. I have seen this though I have no name to put to him either. I have fashioned a sword and magical armor like none elsewhere on this world. My sacrifice was great for it took almost a full year to accomplish, and in that time I missed my friends and lover grievously, as I know they did me. Yet, if it will save our races, I have no regrets."

"The sword and armor are entrusted to someone I know will deliver them at the proper time, someone who knows what clue to watch for. When Varg rises again, seek out my progeny, seek his aid, show him my words and pray that my powers are strong enough to last through the centuries. That is all I can do."

The priest closed the book.

"Well, where is Bartholomew's great-great grandson?"

The priest grunted.

"We know he won at Devonshield, Majesty," said the Minister of State. "He was with Sir Jarlz but went south alone. We lost him on the road through the Great Forest near Dalphnia's enchanted woods. He was headed for Falls Hill, but when we got there Gant never arrived."

Sarona glared at her minister. "Why was I not told of this immediately? Now our only hope is lost."

"We don't know that. Gant may live."

"Then where is he? Where did he go? Find him!"

She slammed her fist into her palm and stormed for the door.

"Priest," she shouted, pausing in the doorway, "look for another way to stop Varg. Don't stop until you have an answer."

Sarona left. The room fell silent. Eventually the ministers moved off to their daily tasks. Doom darkened their faces and wearied their bodies. The dark elves were preparing for their worst nightmare.

Chapter 25

Gant lay in bed and watched the sun rise through the opening between branches in Dalphnia's treehouse. He couldn't remember how many times he'd seen it rise from the treehouse. It didn't matter. The golden disc rose steadily higher as he watched. He was still aglow from her touch, happy for her, happy for himself.

From the garden he heard Dalphnia's silver voice singing. Birds whistled to her from the low branches of nearby trees. Everywhere within her influence there was harmony. Dalphnia brought him peace and everything around her.

Gant sat up. He wanted to go down to Dalphnia. Sometimes he helped her in the garden. Sometimes they walked in the woods. Always he was with her, every waking moment. He rolled out of bed, pulled on his breeches and peeked into the closet at the glimmering armor and sword that were supposed to be his. Every day he looked at the sword and longed to touch it. If only he could remember. But the memories were locked away. If it really was his, he should remember.

Today he stood a moment longer. Something about the sword held his attention. Hauntingly, it called to him. He started to turn away. The sword's lure strengthened.

He stepped toward the sword, still resisting the desire to touch it. The closer he got the stronger the feeling became until the lust to hold the sword burned in him. He struggled against it, reminding himself that the past was better off left buried. He was happy, content.

He inched closer. Emotions swept over him that he could no longer resist. As if sleep walking, he reached for the hilt. Almost before his hand moved, the sword leaped from its scabbard into his hand. The moment the hilt kissed his palm, his ancestor's incredible magic flooded his brain, sweeping away the cobwebs, dissolving Dalphnia's spell. Gant stood once more the son of the Joshua, Netherdorf smith. His memories rushed back like a tidal wave. He remembered everything.

He twisted Valorius this way and that, watching the sun flash off her blade. He marveled all over again at her perfection and power. The euphoria lasted only a minute.

Dalphnia's sweet song drifted up from the garden. He thought of her beautiful face, beaming up at him, as happy in his company as he was in hers. Now he knew what she was, knew the magic she had woven to keep him here. The spell was broken. And yet in his heart there was an attachment. Maybe it was love.

He was confused, hurt, embarrassed, all at once. He knew he should return to his own world and do whatever it took to erase the blemish from his name. To stay with Dalphnia was to join her other husbands in the quaint little graveyard.

And what of the armor, of Valorius? They might be needed. Uric had gone seeking Varg. How long ago had that been? Was he too late? He needed time to think. No, too much time had passed already. He had to get going.

The magic in Valorius called stronger than ever. Strange forces pulsed from the sword filling him with a foreboding that he'd never felt before. He recognized the sword's call to battle, knew that somewhere Varg waited, and he would have to answer. He owed it to Uric, and to Bartholomew. They had staked too much on Gant's ability to use Valorius against Varg.

He tried to remember the whole story Uric had told. About how Bartholomew had fallen in love with the Queen of the Dark Elves, and how they had eventually banished Varg back to the dark regions to save the elves and seal their marriage. He wished he'd paid more attention to the sage when he'd explained it.

Too late now, he thought, and resolutely donned his armor. Miraculously, he noted that the holes from Egog's bite were gone, not patched, more like healed.

What about Dalphnia? What could he say to her? His heart told him there was nothing that would ease her pain. He wished it wasn't necessary. Her spell was broken, but something lived in his heart, something born of a different kind of magic.

He went downstairs, Valorius at his side singing heroic songs in his mind. An old fire burned in Gant again, the same fire that had burned there since a boy on a school bench had listened to his first story of knighthood.

He strode to the garden. Dalphnia knelt with her back to him, glorious rays of sun reflecting off her hair. It almost made him take off the armor and hang it back in the closet.

"Dalphnia," he whispered.

"Oh, you're up," she said, turning. She froze the instant she saw him. The smile died on her lips. "You're going?" It was both a question and a plea.

"Yes, I. . ."

He took her in his arms and held her. It was a cold embrace. The hurt inside her came through.

"No one ever leaves," she whispered. "Gant," she pleaded, looking at him with wide brown pools that tried to pull him under, "I love you more than I've ever loved any man. Don't leave."

Her hurt was his hurt. The depth and breadth of it staggered him. "If only I could stay," he said finally. "But we'd never know happiness. Not with my family out there caught in the coming darkness or killed by it. I hate to leave, believe me. But I'm afraid I've been here too long already."

"Then I'll go with you."

"No. You belong here where there is love and life." Gant looked once more into those deep brown eyes. Pain flowed from them along with a flicker of understanding. "I'll come back to you," he said softly.

"No, no. Don't lie. You'll never come back." Tears followed. She turned and dashed up the steps into the treehouse.

Gant turned slowly to go. His heart ached. He *would* come back.

#

At first, Gant wasn't sure which direction to go and he wasn't going back to ask Dalphnia for directions. He moved generally eastward through the forest. Soon he crested a small hill and through the trees caught sight of the south branch of the Rushon River. He decided to make for that and gain passage on one of the boats that would pass on their way from Falls Hill to Malathon. From there, he'd buy a horse and travel to Blasseldune. Then he'd get word to his uncle.

#

Days later, Gant rode into Blasseldune. A river boat had picked him up and taken him swiftly down river to Malathon where he'd bought a horse and rode as fast as possible northwest, through Maltic City to Blasseldune. The city was much as Gant remembered, only this time as he rode into town, the tight groups of warriors and swordsmen nodded deferentially or stared tight-lipped and silent. A couple of men shouted "hello" and called him Ironlimb. He nodded, or waved politely, but without enthusiasm. The long trip had worn him down and while it felt good to be close to home, he knew this was as close as he could get.

Gant thought of Hammond House but instead went straight to the Drake hoping his uncle would be there. Jake came out from behind the bar as Gant made for his customary table. He sat down heavily, not from the weight of his armor, but from the weight of his travels. Dalphnia remained in his thoughts. He realized her hold on him was more than the magic she might have used on other men. He was determined to return to her one day.

Gant scanned the common room. Several patrons were dressed in working garb. Here and there sat armed men. In one corner, a lone dark elf sat with his feet on the table, sipping a mug of ale. There were no familiar faces and Gant was too tired to care. Jake set a large tankard of ale in front of Gant, and then leaned over to collect his fee.

"See the two in the corner," he said nodding toward the farthest corner. "They've been asking for you for the last week. Grim sort, they are, never speaking to anyone, except now and then when some new knight arrives. They'd ask if it was you. Next time I get to their table, they'll be asking who you are. What should I tell them?"

Gant studied Jake's chubby face. Fear erased the tavern owner's usual cheerful smile. And it was obvious that Jake did not want trouble. Nonetheless, Gant was not going to deny who he was.

"Tell them who I am," he said resolutely.

Jake started to say something and then silently picked up Gant's offered coin and turned back to other customers. Gant sipped his ale and watched the two strangers. They were bear-like men with shaggy, dark hair and wild unkempt beards. He wondered what they wanted. Huge broadswords hung at their sides and though they wore heavy fur garments Gant could tell they had breastplates beneath. He'd never seen either of them, though they reminded him of one of the warriors at Devonshield. Maybe they needed his help. After all, he was the Devonshield champion. He took another sip from the mug of ale. Curiosity got the better of him. He rose and went straight to their table.

"I'm Gant. I hear you're looking for me."

Both men looked up incredulously, their hands shifted to their swords.

The farthest from Gant said, "You're either a liar or you're crazy."

"Why is that?"

"Cause we've come to collect Lord Gorth's bounty. All former Knights of Netherdorf are worth one thousand gold coins."

"And you're worth three thousand, if you are who you say you are," said the second.

"What are you talking about? What do you mean, *former* Knights of Netherdorf?" Gant wondered what happened to King Tirmus' knights. Who was Lord Gorth? How could he put a bounty on Gant?

"Lord Gorth has taken Netherdorf. King Ecker now rules there, though he's gone to war in the West. The bounty will still be paid."

"Yes, we already collected five hundred for bringing in the head of one of the captains."

Gant's mind reeled. King Tirmus deposed! The knights hunted, and he along with them. "What about King Tirmus?" he demanded. His hands began to tremble.

"Escaped," said the first. "There's ten thousand gold on his head," he said tightening his grip on his sword.

Gant's eyes burned to pinpoints. A rage grew in him like nothing he'd ever felt. If Netherdorf had fallen, what of his father, mother, Uncle Jarlz, and Uric?

"What about Sir Jarlz? Have you taken him yet?"

"Sir Jarlz?" The first one laughed. "He was the only smart knight in all Netherdorf. He joined Lord Gorth at the outset."

"You're lying."

Gant's right hand moved toward Valorius and instantly she was in his hand. He leaped forward, Valorius whirling in short, practiced arcs. For big men, they were quick. Both rolled sideways from their stools, swords out, regaining their feet on either side of Gant.

"We may even have to earn the extra two thousand," joked the one to Gant's left.

"Doubt it," returned the other.

Gant stepped toward the man on his right. Nearby patrons scattered, leaving overturned stools in their wake. The bear-like figure held his ground. Valorius swung down, slicing the blade off the big man's sword as if it were soft brass. As the burly man stared at the stump of his sword, Gant lunged in with his right shoulder slamming into the man's breastplate and sent him sprawling backward.

The second man rushed Gant from behind. Gant heard his footsteps, spun, blocked with the flat of his blade, and then in one smooth motion chopped down on the bounty hunter's right arm. Gant stopped Valorius before she cut too deep. There was a rush of crimson and a grunt of pain. Gant stepped in for a backhand swing.

"Stop."

It came softly in Gant's ear, barely discernible, yet it echoed inside his mind with a strange power that demanded attention.

Gant stopped, turned. Behind him, dressed in full battle armor, stood the fairest warrior Gant had ever seen. The man was a full head taller than Gant. He had golden hair flowing out from under his sparkling helm. His eyes were the deepest blue but were tainted by a sadness that didn't belong. His face was square and lean with a strong, cleft chin. Even his teeth were white and perfect.

"You have attacked peaceful citizens unprovoked. I cannot allow it." Again the voice was soft, barely a whisper and yet it rang within Gant's mind loud and clear.

What could he say? To an outside observer it probably looked like he *had* attacked them. Yet they had come to kill him.

"It is not your business," Gant said finally.

"Right and wrong are always my business."

"Then you should learn which side is right."

"No. The sword shall decide."

With that, the stranger drew a beautiful, shimmering sword. Yellow rays glittered off the finely crafted length of steel. Faintly, here and there, a rune or marking shimmered as the stranger twisted it slowly left and right. Gant stepped back into a defensive posture with Valorius held ready. The newcomer's sword looked every bit as splendid, maybe more so. Gant realized this was not going to be easy.

"This is foolish," said Gant. The madness had left him and now the thought of more suffering revolted him.

The blond warrior did not answer. He darted in, his first move a straight lunging thrust at Gant's midsection. An easy snap of the wrists turned it aside. Gant slid backward another half step. The stranger wheeled his sword overhead, tracing an arc aimed at Gant's neck. The two blades met edge to edge with a fiery hiss of sparks. Gant noted with surprise that the other sword withdrew unmarked. So did Valorius.

Gant countered now, swinging low at the blond man's midsection. The stranger turned it aside. Gant followed that with another attack. That too was blocked. Now Gant had to block. The swords met again in a shower of sparks.

Gant thrust straight in, but was swept aside.

This time the stranger moved Valorius far enough to the side to create an opening on Gant's opposite side. The blond warrior struck like a snake. It was too fast. The magnificent sword slammed into Gant's armor, the force almost knocking Gant from his feet. There was a flash of white light and a loud crack. Gant's armor held. The stranger drew back leaving only a thin crease.

Gant staggered off balance, open to attack.

Instead of taking advantage, the stranger stared wide-eyed at Gant, his blue eyes riveted on the spot where his sword had landed. Gant righted himself. The stranger pulled himself up ramrod straight, his sword arm lowering ever so slowly until the tip rested on the floor.

"Excuse me, sir," he said, awe in his voice. "I've made a terrible mistake. I could not know you were The One."

Slowly, he lowered himself to one knee, laying his sword at Gant's feet. "If you'll have me, I seek only to serve you."

Bewildered, Gant returned Valorius to his scabbard.

"Rise. I am no lord to be served. I am a free man, like you. But why the sudden change?"

"Your armor. You have the armor that my sword cannot cut. That is the one I shall serve until death." He stood as he spoke, sheathing his weapon.

"I doubt if you're talking about me, though this is unique armor. How about an ale? Maybe you can tell me what is going on."

"As you wish, m'Lord."

"Stop calling me that," said Gant.

He glanced around and, assuring himself that the two bounty hunters were gone, turned and started back to his table. The stranger followed. The patrons had already forgotten the incident. Gant reseated himself and motioned for Jake. When the innkeeper arrived, the stranger ordered a glass of water. Jake left it on the table and went about his business.

"Who are you?" asked Gant as the inn returned to normalcy.

"I am Zandinar."

"I am Gant, formerly of Netherdorf. Today some call me Ironlimb."

"You were Champion at Devonshield."

"I was. Though more by chance than choice. But tell me, what has happened to the world? Those two I rousted from their table swore that Netherdorf has fallen and is at war with the Western Kings."

"Yes, that is the news these days. I just arrived from the north seeking m'Lord. The first part of my destiny is fulfilled. Now I need only follow you."

Gant studied Zandinar looking for any trace of mockery. There was none. "What do you mean, you've only got to follow me? I'm not sure where I'm going."

"It doesn't matter. You will lead me where I am supposed to be."

"How do you know?"

"It is foretold."

"By whom?"

"My mother."

"Oh." Gant examined Zandinar more closely. His armor had some strange power. It reminded Gant of the magic in his own armor but with a subtly different feel to the force emanating from it.

"What else do you know about the fall of Netherdorf?" asked Gant.

"Not much. There are few left who claim to be King Tirmus' men."

"Is it also true that Sir Jarlz has turned traitor?"

"That I could not say. I have heard this Barlon Gorth uses treachery and deceit as his first weapons and that a demon aids him."

"Jake may know more," said Gant and motioned for the innkeeper.

Leaving a table full of merchants, the chubby proprietor returned.

"Rooms for the two of us," said Gant as soon as the fat-cheeked innkeeper reached their table. He tossed Jake enough coins for the room and more. "What do you know of Barlon Gorth and Netherdorf?"

Jake looked at the floor. "Little enough. His agents spread the word that the peasants have been freed from an oppressive king. The few survivors that got this far told a grimmer tale. One I'd rather not repeat."

"And is he at war with the West?"

"I think that may be true. No merchants have come from the West in a month or more, and those that left for the West have not been seen again. Only evil men come from Netherdorf these days, and I begin to fear for Blasseldune."

"Can't you tell us more?"

"There's not much else to tell. Anyone who held a position in King Tirmus' court is wanted for crimes against the people, though the people were a lot happier when the king still ruled, and I dare say, they'd be more than willing to help him regain the throne, if he still lives."

"I see," said Gant, though he didn't really understand much. "What about my father, the smith? Or my mother?"

"I don't know," said Jake after a moment's thought. "With all the plunder, the killing I've heard about, I wouldn't want to guess."

"Thanks," said Gant and slipped an extra coin into the innkeeper's fingers.

Jake turned and hurried back to the merchants.

For a long time Gant was lost in thoughts of home, his father and mother, Uncle Jarlz and Chamz. And what about Dalphnia? He wondered why he had left the warm sanctuary of her treehouse. Then Uric's words would come back to him and he'd think about what must have happened to his family and that fueled his desire to do something about it. Who could help him? Only Abadis. Everyone else was gone.

Eventually Gant looked over at Zandinar who sat quietly, his plate empty. "Are you really going with me tomorrow?"

Zandinar nodded. "I am."

"Then we better get some sleep tonight," said Gant. "Tomorrow we leave for Abadis' house and it is a long way."

With that they both got up and went upstairs to their rooms. Gant did not fall asleep right away. The turmoil in his head kept him awake a long time.

Chapter 26

The next morning when Gant went for breakfast he found Chamz sitting at a table enjoying a bowl of porridge. The moment Gant entered the room Chamz spotted him and jumped up to welcome his friend.

"Great to see you, Gant of the Ironlimbs," said Chamz, throwing his arms around Gant. "When I heard you were in town and you didn't come to Hammond House I was pretty sure you'd be here at the Drake."

Gant hugged him back. "Am I glad to see you. But don't call me that."

"Hey, that's what everyone calls you now."

Gant shook his head. "Fine. How are you doing? Are the arrow wounds healed?"

"Completely. I never felt better."

"Great. At least there is some good news. I hear Barlon has taken Netherdorf."

"True enough."

"How'd you get away?"

"I grabbed my parents before Barlon's men saw us and brought them here. You should have seen the look on their faces when I said we were going to Blasseldune."

"I can imagine," said Gant, letting Chamz go. They sat down at the table across from each other. "What are you doing now?" asked Gant, waving to the server for a bowl of porridge.

"My parents and I are staying at Hammond House. I thought I'd get my old job back but it turned out that the City Council was worried about Barlon and decided to form a city militia. I got the job of leading it."

"So you're a general?"

"Hardly. We aren't that well organized. Or big. Wish I had known you were walking into trouble yesterday. We'd have stopped it. But I didn't find out until after things were settled. Not that you needed help."

Gant's porridge arrived. He took a few bites, and glanced around the room, assuring himself that he needn't worry about trouble from any of the other patrons.

"Nice sword and armor," said Chamz pointing with his spoon. "Just like the prophecy. I told you you're The One."

"I suppose. I'm on my way to Abadis' house looking for advice," he started, and then realized Chamz never made it there so added, "the wizard we were going to see when we were attacked. I am told that this sword was crafted specifically to defeat Varg but have no idea when, where or how that is supposed to happen."

"I can't help you with that. You could stay here and help me defend Blasseldune."

Gant sighed. "I wish I could."

Zandinar came in and sat down next to Gant. "Good morning," he said nodding to Chamz. "Who's your friend?"

While Gant made the introductions, Zandinar got a bowl of porridge. For a few minutes they ate in silence. As the bowls emptied, Gant said, "What about Gwen? Is she all right?"

"Nothing happened because of Wendler, if that's what you mean. The scum never said anything about Gwen. He claimed you ambushed him in the woods, that you had it in for him and jumped him from behind."

"I should have known he'd never bring her into it. Might lead to embarrassing questions. But I meant after Barlon's attack. Do you know what happened to her?"

Chamz shook his head. "Sorry, I don't know. And there's been little word out of Netherdorf since Barlon took over."

Gant pushed his porridge bowl away. "Great seeing you again. I wish I could stay longer but we've got to get going."

Chamz pursed his lips and said, "I'd go with you but I promised to take charge of the militia and protect the city, including my parents. You understand."

Gant clapped his friend on the shoulder. "Of course. Your duty is here now. Mine is elsewhere. We'll get together once this mess is put right."

After a short goodbye, Gant and Zandinar gathered their belongings, got their horses and headed for Abadis'.

#

While Gant and Zandinar rode north toward Abadis' house, Abadis traveled to Falls Hill. Abadis quickly learned that Gant had never reached Falls Hill and he took this for the worst. Determined to get to the bottom of Gant's disappearance, he backtracked up the road through Little Mountain Pass where he met four fur traders coming south. They had not seen anyone matching Gant's description. They did admit seeing a strange monster dead in the cavern in the hills where they stopped for an overnight. Along with it were the bodies of several men. Abadis hurried there, found Egog's dead bulk and guessed the truth. While this was not Varg it was a creature from the beyond and Abadis knew it would take a powerful sword to kill it. If Gant had used Valorius then some of the magic would have been drained. How much? And would whatever magic was left be enough to kill Varg? Abadis hoped so.

At the cave, Abadis' cast a spell that revealed signs of Gant's struggle but he could not find anything to indicate Gant's fate. As a last resort the aged wizard decided to visit the beautiful woodland nymph, Dalphnia, who lived nearby hoping that she could provide clues. To his surprise, he found her home empty. In the ninety-plus years he had known Dalphnia she had never been far from home. Something extraordinary must have happened to make her travel from her tree.

While he pondered her absence, he pulled out the small mirror he kept in one of the pockets in his robe. Through it he checked the mirror in his cabin and found it blank. He knew that things would soon reach a critical point and he had to locate Gant. He started the lonely trek through the forest, searching for either Gant or the missing nymph. His travels through the forest became a small tale of its own and it was several days before Abadis stood on the banks of the east branch of the Rushon River. He stared out at the slow-moving current, its brown eddies turning little pirouettes as the muddy water slid past. Patiently he waited for the next riverboat, all the while wondering how to find Gant.

#

At the same time, Gant and Zandinar reached Abadis' log home. The protective shield was there just as Gant remembered it with the sentinel pines inside. Though the shield was barely visible, Gant spotted it and drew his horse to a stop just before the magic barrier.

"Abadis," he called. "Abadis, it is Gant. Let us in."

Moments passed.

"Abadis. Please drop the shield and let us in."

Gant waited with fading hope. Abadis wasn't home. It was impossible to guess how long he would be gone. Perhaps there was a price on the wizard's head. Maybe he was already dead. Or if Sir Jarlz had joined Barlon Gorth, perhaps Abadis had too. Though such an idea might be possible, Gant refused to believe that Jarlz would have done so voluntarily.

"Why don't we go in?" asked Zandinar, his voice hardly audible.

"How?"

Instead of answering, Zandinar slipped off his horse. Snapping his visor shut he walked boldly to the shimmering barrier. Tentatively he reached out with one armored hand and touched the magical field. A faint blue aura grew around his fingertips and then Zandinar's hand penetrated harmlessly.

"We can walk through."

"What?" Gant watched the handsome knight step through the shield as if it were nonexistent. "How did you do that?"

Zandinar stepped back to Gant's side of the barrier. "Good magic never harms good magic. My armor lets me pass. Yours should too." Zandinar re-entered the wizard's grounds.

Still not exactly sure how it worked, Gant slid off his horse. He pulled his visor down and walked into the shimmering wall. A blue glow surrounded him filling his ears with a fuzzy noise and then he was through onto Abadis' climate controlled lawn. Gant glanced at the sentinel pines and was happy to see that they remained motionless.

A few running steps and Gant caught up with Zandinar. They walked to the front door. Gant knocked. As expected, they got no answer. They walked around the house and found no sign of Abadis.

"He's not home," said Gant. "We've come a long way. Perhaps we should go inside and leave a message."

"And where will we go then?"

"I don't know. Without Abadis, I guess my next choice would be to find King Tirmus, if I knew where to look. Or Sir Jarlz, if he hasn't really defected. Maybe Uric," said Gant. "Surely they wouldn't have killed Uric."

"Who's Uric?"

"Ah, my tutor. That is he used to be my tutor."

"Why not wait inside?"

"It isn't my house."

"Of course not, but maybe your friend is inside dead. We should check."

How stupid, thought Gant. It never occurred to him that anything could happen to Abadis in his own home. He opened the door and peered inside. The house was much as he remembered. They went in. The ever-present clutter of magical paraphernalia seemed to have grown since his last visit. The small table and stools were still the only furniture. The fireplace sat cold and black. Gant noticed an oblong mirror on the wall behind some shelves that he didn't remember seeing before. Someone had cleared out the bottles, jars and boxes to expose it. A colored grease stick lay by mirror.

"I wonder what this is for. And why is everything cleared away from in front of the mirror?" asked Gant. "Maybe someone is here, hiding, afraid to come out."

Gant ducked into the back room. It was empty except for a mattress that floated off the floor without benefit of a bed frame, and piles of written documents, many of which seemed like notebooks full of scribbling. There was no one there.

"No one," he said reemerging from the bedroom.

"We'll wait. Someone will come."

"Okay," agreed Gant. "For a day or two. But we'll camp outside the barrier with the horses."

Carefully they closed the cabin and exited out through the barrier. They settled into a little camp and built a small campfire for cooking and warmth. They both sat near it while their horses grazed over the tiny meadow outside Abadis' barrier.

Zandinar remained quiet, seemingly lost in his own thoughts. Even Gant's occasional mumblings brought no response. Gant couldn't help thinking about his mother and father. He wondered if they'd died quickly, mercifully. Probably not, he decided. And what about Jarlz? How could he betray King Tirmus? There were no answers and Gant continued to wrestle with the questions.

Eventually Gant slept and the night passed.

#

Earlier that day, on the hot plains that stretched out for miles from the gates of Pogor, two armies marched toward each other. The land was flat and now dusty as thousands of feet and hooves trampled the dry grasses. There was no high ground so Razgoth raised Barlon on a shimmering disc that held him above his horsemen; high enough to watch the formation of Fasoom's and Petre's foot soldiers as they moved to block Barlon's advance. A lone eagle soared high overhead and Barlon envied the bird its magnificent view of the battlefield.

Ahead and to Barlon's left were Fasoom's pikemen, dressed in scarlet and white. Their lines stretched straight as rays of sunshine across the battlefield, their long, steel-tipped poles held at the ready position forming a bristling thicket.

Against them, Barlon moved five brigades of foot soldiers. Behind them were Lom's knights, who had dismounted and were leading their horses so it would appear the footmen were unsupported. As soon as the battle started, the foot soldiers would mass near the center of the enemy line and open a hole. Then Lom's knights would mount and charge straight to the heart of Fasoom's headquarters. It would be short work.

Off to Barlon's right were Petre's foot soldiers. Armed with bows and short swords, they were more dangerous than the pikemen. Their weapons held an ancient magic, and though it was weak it might hold enough power to threaten Lom's purple armor. On that front, Barlon sent his massed infantry and Varg. The infantry out front to help obscure the demon's presence.

Barlon thought it was a good plan. King Daggon had not arrived in time to join the battle and would soon find himself without allies. Petre's handful of knights, at least those Barlon could see, were drawn back to protect their king. The only wizards present huddled around Fasoom and his aides. They held back their trump cards while Barlon played his. Soon it would be too late and Barlon would control the plain and the road to Pogor.

As Barlon watched, his foot soldiers reached the pikemen. Swords rang against shields and pikes. Barlon's men fought with a fierce determination. As planned, they massed at the center of the enemy line and quickly opened a gap. Immediately Lom's men were on their horses charging for the opening. Barlon's brigades scurried aside, disengaging the enemy in their haste to be out of the way of Lom's flying hooves. Surprisingly, Fasoom's pikemen hurried aside as well and the gap grew to a broad rift. The yells of men caught up with battle lust filled the air. Lom's purple clad Knights of Habichon stood out in a sea of red and white.

As the first of Lom's riders raced through the breach in the wall of iron-pointed pikes, they were met by a charging company of armor-clad cavalry wearing Petre's blue and gold. Barlon watched in horror as the two onrushing columns plowed into each other. The clang of steel sounded above the other battle noises, loud enough to be heard all the way back to Barlon's vantage point. The screams of the dying rose even higher. The purple line of horsemen slowed and finally ground to a halt as more and more of Petre's magically equipped horsemen joined the fray.

How had they known his plan? Barlon raged atop his floating platform. He forced his eyes to the other front. His troops, wearing their black and gold, clashed with the blue and gold of Petre's footmen. Slowly, Barlon's men moved aside and Varg's tall, black form surged ahead. In his four-armed version he snatched swordsmen from their feet, ripped them in chunks and tossed them aside. Petre's soldiers fought valiantly to prevent the giant demon from penetrating their lines but the weak magic in their blades was useless.

Varg ravaged their numbers for a few minutes, delighting in the slaughter. Then, the ranks thinned and, as if on command, the line of swordsmen parted, leaving a wide gap. Varg charged through until he was past the front line of the Western troops. The line fought its way back closed, cutting Varg off from the rest of Barlon's men.

From his raised position Barlon watched, intent on the slaughter of Petre and his aides. Varg charged them, filled with battle rage. When the demon was still fifty lengths from the command group, several of the servants in-waiting cast off their peasant garb and Barlon recognized Petre's most powerful wizards. They locked hands and let go a salvo of raging fire. For a moment, Varg was engulfed in the inferno. Calmly, he reappeared out the other side, laughing.

The wizards regrouped and cast another spell. This time a shimmering bubble materialized around Varg. He tried to step through it but a dazzling eruption of blue sparks stopped him. Varg raked at the bubble with his vicious talons producing another shower of sparks. Furiously, the demon lashed out again and again at the encapsulating globe. The sparks grew weaker and finally his talons cut slits down the front of the force field. Angrily Varg shredded a portal through the bubble and stepped back onto the plain.

By now Petre's command group had retreated. Varg sprinted after them. Before he could close with the circle of men another bubble formed around him. Again, he was held while he slashed and ripped at the trap. Eventually Varg opened a way through that force field and again the command group had retreated.

Barlon raged as the force bubble repeated a third cycle, frustrating Varg's attempts to gain on Petre's headquarters.

"Razgoth, get up here," Barlon yelled at his wizard.

"Sire, the disc will only support one man."

"Fine. Then you get up here and tell me what is going on."

Razgoth lowered the disc. Barlon got off, his face an insane scowl. Razgoth stepped onto the disc and raised it once more. He watched the cycle unfold yet another time. Their trick was easy to guess and Razgoth let himself down.

"Well, what is it? What are they doing?" demanded Barlon.

"It is a force field of positive energy, not strong enough to permanently capture or hurt Varg but enough to slow him down. It is lucky for them their wizards were in the right place."

"Luck!" screamed Barlon. "It was not luck. They met Lom's charge with Petre's cavalry. They *knew* what we were going to do. A spy! There's a spy in our midst. Recall the attack. Pull back. We must find the spy. Turn the camp inside out. Overlook no one. Bring me his head and then we'll attack and see if they can guess our plans."

"But, sire. . ." Razgoth started, but was waved away.

Barlon mounted his horse and without a word to his commanders, returned to his tent. He failed to notice the eagle soaring high above the battlefield. As the troops pulled back, it turned and winged its way toward the Monolith Mountains.

Chapter 27

In the middle of the night a great owl swooped low over Gant's campfire. It glided into the woods and settled on a thick branch. For a long time it sat there staring at Gant. Its great round eyes studied him, and then focused on the sleeping Zandinar. Watching the owl, an uneasy feeling grew in Gant. There was something different about the owl, a sense of intelligence in those great dark eyes.

Finally he couldn't stand it. "Zandinar, wake up," Gant said nudging his sleeping companion.

Instantly, Zandinar was awake, sword out, on his feet. "What is it?"

"That owl," said Gant, pointing.

"An owl?" Zandinar sheathed his sword. "Fight it yourself. I'm going back to sleep."

"No, you don't understand. It's watching us."

"So?" Zandinar rolled over in his bulky furs.

"Maybe it's a messenger from Abadis, a watch-owl or something. Maybe we can get it to come down and take a message to him."

"Goodnight."

Gant knew that there *was* something strange about that owl. Maybe it was an enemy sentinel watching for Abadis' return. Gant couldn't decide what to do. As he watched, the great bird spread its wings and sailed off between the trees toward the main road. Too late, thought Gant, and absentmindedly stirred the fire with a long stick. He tossed a couple of pieces of wood on the fire, and then sat back down as a shower of sparks rose skyward.

"I don't believe we've met," said a feminine voice from the shadows nearby.

Gant leaped to his feet, ready to pull out his sword. There, just inside the flickering circle of firelight stood a slim wisp of a girl dressed in a snow-white, knee-length gown. Her brown hair was cut short. A smile, half-formed, flickered on her lips.

"Gant, I'm Gant, recently of Netherdorf," he said, suddenly uncomfortable.

"Gant of the Ironlimbs?"

"Yes," he admitted, more than slightly flattered.

"Let me see the gauntlets."

"What gauntlets?"

"The ones you wore at Devonshield."

"How do you know about those?"

"I know everything my grandfather makes."

"Your grandfather? I didn't know Abadis was a grandfather."

"I'm sure there are a great many things you don't know. Now let me see the gauntlets."

"You'll have to help me off with my armor."

"No. I'm not accustomed to getting that close to strangers. Have your friend help you."

"What is this?" asked Zandinar, rising from his pile of furs.

"And you claim to be Zandinar," said Amelia. She dropped her pretext of wariness and walked boldly into camp, sitting lightly on a log that lay near the fire. "I've heard of you, too. Very noble and brave, you're supposed to be." Now she turned to Gant. "Show me the sleeves."

"Just a minute," he said sourly, motioning for Zandinar to help him remove his gauntlets.

There beneath his magic armor, Gant still wore the beautiful, silvery sleeves that had saved him at Devonshield.

"Satisfied?" he asked as Amelia inspected them.

"Yes, these are my grandfather's. But why aren't you waiting inside? He wouldn't mind."

"No way to get the horses through the screen," said Zandinar.

Amelia smiled.

"Now who are you and where's your grandfather?" asked Gant, more than a little indignant about being bossed around by such a wisp of a girl, even if she was Abadis' granddaughter.

"I am Amelia and my grandfather has gone looking for you. Come on, we'd all feel better inside. I don't have much time before I have to get back."

Without waiting for questions, the slender apparition in white walked to Abadis' protective force field and gingerly touched it with the tips of her fingers. The field slowly discolored to a pale blue and a large opening appeared.

"Hurry up, bring the horses."

She stood by the opening and waited while the two men gathered their belongings and horses. As soon as they were inside, she ducked through and the pale blue force field re-solidified. Quickly it faded to transparent until only a vague shimmer betrayed its presence.

They hurried inside, leaving the horses untethered on Abadis' grassy lawn.

"First, I've got to write a message," said Amelia and went to the mirror.

"So you're the one," said Gant and watched as she wiped the glass clean, and then started marking it with the colored grease stick.

Amelia's message read: War has begun. We are holding own for now. Gant is here.

She smiled, then went to the cupboard and brought three glasses. She poured from a dusty green glass decanter.

"Grandpa's elixir always makes me feel better," she said and drank heartily.

Gant sipped the dark liquid, noting that Zandinar avoided it. As the sweet fluid reached his stomach a warmth spread almost instantly through his entire body. The weariness and road-soreness disappeared. Gant felt totally refreshed.

"This is wonderful," he said.

"Yes, it helps fight the fatigue that flying brings on."

"Flying? What do you mean by that?" And how do you know so much about the war? Nobody else seems to know there even is a war," said Gant, studying Amelia. She was not a runner, her lower legs were smooth instead of lined with muscle.

"It only began this morning. Let's say a little bird told me."

Gant glared at her. Whatever her secret, she probably learned it from her grandfather. Magic was beyond Gant, except when it came to using his sword. "If you're Abadis' granddaughter, where are your mother and father?"

A new sadness overcame Amelia. "I never knew my father. He was a knight from the Eastern Empire who charmed mother on his way to war and she never saw him again. My mother died when I was young. My grandfather raised me."

"And your grandmother. Where is she?"

"You'll have to ask grandfather. Right now I have to leave," she said, and started for the door. "You two should wait here. Grandpa will be home soon. He'll know what's best. Tell him I'll be back tomorrow night to give him another report on the war."

"Fine," said Gant sarcastically. Inaction wore him down. It left too much time for thinking and worrying.

"We'll enjoy the rest," said Zandinar, sweeping one hand around the sparsely furnished room. And then he walked to his belongings, took out his water flask and drank deeply.

"Goodbye." And Amelia was out the door, through the shield and gone into the night.

Gant straightened up on his stool, his back arched to stretch stiff muscles. "We're stuck here. We can't get the horses out without her."

"Abadis better come home soon," said Zandinar.

The blond warrior threw down his furs and soon lay fast asleep on top of them. Gant was too tense to sleep. He paced around the table, worried about Sir Jarlz, his family and King Tirmus. And, as happened too often lately, his thoughts turned to Dalphnia. He wondered if she understood. Would she want him when he returned? Sometimes he wondered why he was doing what he was, but Uric's words rang in his ears, only Valorius could defeat Varg and only if Gant wielded the sword. Gant could not turn his back. Silently he vowed to go back to her when it was all over.

#

Meanwhile, miles to the south, on the Rushon River, a small sailing craft slid noiselessly toward shore. Abadis stood on the riverbank under a beacon of magic light that bobbed in the air out over the river where the approaching riverboat crew couldn't miss it. The old wizard waited as the captain guided his craft in dangerously close to shore.

"That's as close as I can get," hollered the captain, "you'll have to come out to us."

With a snort of disgust, Abadis thought about levitating to the boat but decided against it. Casting spells when he was this tired could lead to disaster. It wasn't worth it. Resigned, he stepped lightly into the cool, murky water and waded the few steps to the gunwale. The captain reached down a burly hand and helped the tired mage aboard.

"Welcome aboard, Abadis," said the captain.

"Thanks, Melvin, I presume the fare will be the usual."

"Of course, and this time, there's even a spare cabin. Yours without extra charge."

The captain led Abadis below decks through the fore hatch to a hallway lined with a dozen closely spaced doors, six on each side.

"Here you go," he said, pointing to the third one on the right. "The lock doesn't work too well, but I'm sure that won't bother you." There was a twinkle in the captain's eye as he turned to go.

"One question," said Abadis, lightly catching the captain's shoulder. "Have you had a young warrior aboard? With a magnificent set of armor?"

"No."

"Have you seen such a man on any of your trips? He probably would have been seeking passage from the bank near where you picked me up."

"No, but there are a lot of other boats, and the chance he'd find me are slim. Maybe some of the others in Malathon have seen him."

"A possibility. Thanks."

Abadis reached into a pocket in his robe and pulled out a few gold coins. Holding the stack between his thumb and first two fingers, he dropped them into Melvin's palm.

"There's a bit extra there so see that I'm not disturbed. I'm very tired, what with tramping around in the forest. It's not good for a man my age."

Melvin nodded and retraced his steps up the stairs through the fore hatch. Abadis entered the tiny cabin, shut the door and locked it with a quick spell. He cast a simple rejuvenation spell to help him sleep and recuperate and then, exhausted, he lay back on the straw-stuffed mattress, and fell asleep with his robes on.

Chapter 28

On the plains of Chadmir in Barlon's command tent, the Mountain Lord met with his staff. Scattered around the large folding table in the center of the tent were numerous chairs, some occupied, some empty. The lanterns set upon the table cast a warm light throughout the tent's interior that did little to change the gloomy mood. It would have been worse except Varg was absent.

"Have you caught the traitor?" yelled Barlon.

Blank faces told him "no." He surveyed the group, his captains and his trusted advisors. Only these men knew the plan well enough to have foiled it. It had to be one of them, but who? "Razgoth," he said, turning on the wizard. "What about their wizards' magic? How can we negate it? And Lom, you've got to do better against Petre's knights. You have magic armor. You're supposed to be invincible! What happened? What went wrong?"

Barlon went on ranting like a madman, stomping back and forth. He shouted question after question, never allowing anyone time enough to answer. Soon they had all ceased to listen. Finally Barlon ran out of words. He finished with, "Tomorrow we will clear the field of battle. Those inferior, soft, excuses for warriors will not stop us again."

The tent remained silent. Some of the men stirred as if to get up, others started toward the door. Barlon motioned for them to stay.

"Where is Varg?" asked Razgoth.

"Ah. I'm glad you asked," said Barlon, twisting his hands together, a hint of glee in his cat-like eyes. "While we sit here doing nothing my ally has forayed into the enemy camp. Darkness is his greatest friend. He will soon return to report our problems solved."

Everyone looked around the tent half expecting Varg to spring from the ground. Nothing happened.

"What is he up to?" asked Razgoth.

"He is delivering vengeance upon our enemies. Tomorrow Lom will accompany Varg and attack the northern front. Razgoth, you will soften the southern front and ten brigades under General Ecker will attack there. Five brigades will remain in reserve at my command."

"What of their magic?" asked Lom who knew he was attacking where Petre's wizards were strongest.

"Do not worry." It was a dark, gravelly voice from the back of the tent. Varg stood towering almost to the top of the sloping canvas roof. "Those wizards will cast no magic tomorrow because I've killed them tonight."

Silence.

Then Barlon smiled. "You were successful?"

"Yes. Individually, they had no protections strong enough to stop a Prince of Darkness."

"Then our victory is assured. That is all." Barlon waved them out.

The tent emptied except for Varg who stood impassive like some giant obsidian statue.

"You have done well. Your rewards will be great," said Barlon, clapping his hands together.

"Yes, master. My rewards are great."

"One day you and I will rule this world."

"And I shall have the realm of the Dark Elves."

"Yes, yes. Whatever you wish."

Barlon poured a cup of wine from the decanter on the table and passed it up to Varg. Then he refilled his own cup and both toasted to victory.

"Yes," Barlon mused, "as I have my revenge, so you too shall have yours. It is good we understand each other." Barlon cast his feet up on the table and leaned back.

He drank heavily, letting the wine take the edge off his tense muscles.

Varg stood silent. He drained the last of his wine and ate the bronze mug. "Good wine," he said and burped.

It wasn't long before one side of the tent opened without benefit of a flap. A secretive figure slipped in and the tent seemed to reseal itself. Shalmuthe stepped into the torchlight, his hard blue eyes glinting with menace.

"Shalmuthe," greeted Barlon, waving his mug to the newcomer. "Have you found our spy?"

"Perhaps."

"Well." Barlon poured more wine for himself and a mug for the master spy.

"Everyone returned to their tents and began immediately planning for tomorrow's battle. All except Griffith. He returned to his tent like the others but inside he has two women. Women I've never seen before. Instead of attending to business they attended to pleasure. Perhaps they are the link to the Western Kings."

Barlon sprang to his feet. "How did they get here?" he demanded. "Griffith's a madman. He's always been on the verge of rebellion. He loves women and blood more than our cause! He must be eliminated." Barlon shook an index finger in his spy's face.

Shalmuthe hesitated, and then spoke at the first lull in Barlon's rantings. "Lord, I'm sure you know best, but this is highly circumstantial evidence. Griffith may be. . ."

"No!" Barlon's fiery glare silenced the shorter man. "Griffith will be executed this night and the sluts that service him too. Sir Jarlz will take command of the 3rd Brigade and lead it tomorrow."

Shalmuthe clamped his lips shut.

"Varg, serve the sentence. Be quick. I don't want a lot of screaming. The men need what sleep they can get."

Varg nodded. A malicious smile twisted his lips. "With pleasure."

The demon left.

"Thank you, Master Spy," said Barlon. "What of our efforts in the Kingdom of Dernium?"

"All goes well. My man there is an expert in diplomatic maneuvering. King Daggon will never join this battle."

"Good. You may go. Or stay and share the rest of the wine."

"It is late, Lord," said Shalmuthe, gently placing his cup on the table. "I need some sleep too."

He left through the front tent flap. Barlon finished the wine, and another bottle besides, and then fell across the table and slept.

#

The next morning was cool with low hanging clouds that threatened rain. A few pockets of mist hung here and there in the slight depressions that dotted the broad plain. Barlon was in a black humor. His head pounded and he was struck with intermittent bouts of nausea. He summoned Razgoth early and then stalked around his tent waiting for his wizard to appear.

Finally, the weary, disheveled mage ducked in through the flap.

"Yes, sire," he said half-heartedly.

"About time," snapped Barlon. "I need something for my head. It's killing me this morning."

"I have little of the healing elixir left, sire."

"Give it to me and make some more."

"You know I'm no master of potions, especially healing. You may need what I have for something more serious."

"Shut-up and give it to me. Now!" Barlon held out his hand, demanding the potion.

"Very well," said the wizard, and reached into his robes to withdraw a small, almost empty, brown glass bottle.

Barlon took the tiny vial and eagerly gulped down the contents, tossing the empty container on the table.

"Let's go."

Barlon led the way to his command post and waited while Razgoth formed the disc. Then Barlon stood on the magic platform and was slowly raised about ten feet above the ground. General Ecker rode up and stopped before Barlon who looked down at the aging military professional.

"We're ready," said the General.

"Razgoth will open their ranks. You will break through and destroy them. Sir Jarlz will lead the 3rd Brigade. They will join Lom's troops against Petre's men. Everyone will wait for your first strike."

"I hope you enjoy the view, sire," Razgoth replied.

"I will."

Razgoth mounted his waiting horse. Nervously, he checked the paraphernalia and containers in the multitude of pockets in his robe. He joined General Ecker and together they rode toward the massed troops ahead and to Barlon's left. Barlon strained to see through the mist. Lom and Varg stood ready to the north. At the front of his new command Sir Jarlz wheeled his troops and started north to join Lom's purple clad warriors.

Across a narrow stretch of open plains, Barlon watched the armies of Petre and Fasoom mass in long lines of tightly formed foot soldiers. It won't be long, thought Barlon eagerly.

The opposing armies started toward each other like two massive lines of disciplined ants, their ranks holding a tight formation. When the two ranks to the south were almost to each other, Razgoth appeared at the front of Barlon's legions. Barlon could not make out the gestures, but suddenly a huge ball of fire burst in the middle of Fasoom's ranks. Even Barlon could hear the screams as men were charred to death.

A second ball of fire erupted. And a third. General Ecker's troops surged into the gap, forcing back the shoulders of the enemy column. Furious fighting tested men and metal, but Barlon's black and gold clad troops routed the shocked western foot soldiers.

To the north, Lom charged along with the 3rd Brigade. Petre's mounted troops met the charge with the clash of steel, and like the day before, the charge of the Knights of Habichon slowed. Petre's numbers clogged the path and it seemed a repeat of yesterday was upcoming.

But then, Varg appeared out of the packed formation, ripping and clawing both men and horses. The Western Knights' weak magic was useless against the demon. Their swords clanged impotently off his hard skin and he tore through their ranks thrilling to the slaughter of the brave, defenseless warriors.

Within minutes, the Western Armies were in complete disarray. The Kings and their staff fled, racing to gain the safety of the walled city of Pogor. Barlon's men chased the remnants of the army killing as many as possible.

The field became a sea of blood and bodies. Many of Petre's foot soldiers were trampled under the thundering hooves of Lom's knights. Varg reveled in dismembering and gutting every soldier he could catch. Barlon's triumph was complete.

#

Petre and Fasoom raced along the main road for Pogor. A few loyal men held with them, trying to cover their flanks, while Barlon's mounted troops picked away at the fleeing Westerners. The small group succeeded in leaving most of Barlon's men far to the rear. Only a handful of lightly armored cavalry kept pace. Along the way men fell, one here, one there, from each side, until, finally, now, the last of Barlon Gorth's fast troops was unseated and killed.

Petre looked back. "Slow down," he said, reining in his horse. "We've a long way to go and I don't want to walk."

The few remaining men slowed their horses to a trot.

"Where is that idiot, Daggon?" fumed Fasoom.

"Now he's the idiot," said Petre.

They rode a little farther. Up ahead a low grassy knell rose gently above the level of the plain.

"We'll ride to the top of that hill. From there we can see who's following us," said Petre.

Silently they rode to the top of the rise and halted. Turning, they saw the distant pursuit of heavily armored horsemen galloping down the road, a cloud of dust marking their progress.

"They're too far back," said Petre. "They'll never catch us."

Fasoom glared off to the south. "No sign of Daggon," he said coldly.

Suddenly, the small group was trapped in a shimmering force dome. One of Petre's men charged it, lance extended. The impact shattered his lance and sent him tumbling backward into the grass. The horse slammed into the invisible wall and went down stunned.

"What is it?" asked Fasoom.

"Some kind of magical cage," said Petre. "If we can't break out we'll suffocate."

As they studied the dome, trying to find an opening, a thin, sandy-haired figure materialized from behind the low edge of the rise. His robes fluttered in the light breeze. Beside the mage walked a tall black caricature of evil whose red eyes gleamed with a bloodlust.

One of Petre's men fired an arrow at the advancing pair. It ricocheted harmlessly off the inside of the force field. Already the air was getting stale, the horses were growing restless, men desperate. Another horseman leaped from his mount and hit the barrier with clenched fists. The two kings dismounted and let their riderless horses rear and kick. Lungs pumped harder, trying to get the last bit of oxygen. Hearts raced but the blackness came and one-by-one, they all fell unconscious. Inside the dome, nothing moved.

Only then did the barrier fade. Razgoth went immediately to the kings. Carefully examining their unconscious bodies, he revived them, administering the proper potion to each. At the same time he stripped them of swords, rings, jewelry and anything that might be used as a weapon. While Razgoth worked to keep the kings alive, Varg gleefully gutted the rest of the men and the horses, reveling in their slaughter.

Chapter 29

Barlon's troops massed before the locked gates of Pogor's massive walls. They did not set up siege engines or catapults. Instead Barlon, Varg, Razgoth and a contingent of Lom's men marched up to the gates. In front of the procession, heavily shackled and guarded by purple clad knights, were King Fasoom and King Petre.

"You, on the wall," shouted Barlon from horseback. "Tell your city leaders to come forth and bargain for the life of your king."

A guard raced from the wall to deliver the message. It wasn't long before the great gates inched open and a sullen group shuffled out to meet with Barlon. Two grizzled, stoop-shouldered old men led the way. A short, fat middle-aged man dressed in thick velvety robes followed them. Next came an honor guard and finally Barlon's spy, Shalmuthe.

"Gersh, who are these men?" blurted King Fasoom when he saw who came to bargain for his life. He was clubbed into silence by the guards.

"My Lord Gorth," began the nearest elder statesman. "We want no more war. The good people of Pogor seek only peace, prosperity and freedom to carry on trade."

"Then surrender the city and there will be no need for more bloodshed."

"Will you guarantee the safety of our citizens?"

"Of course. This war is foolish. Throw open your city and peace will return."

"And the king?"

"He will stand trial for acts of war. Most likely the good citizens of Pogor will find him guilty of a great many crimes and he will be forced to spend the rest of his life in the dungeons."

"He won't be killed?"

"Whatever the citizens decide." Barlon smiled sweetly, waiting for Pogor's leaders to take the bait.

"What citizens will try our king?" questioned the second statesman.

"Whomever you choose. Yourselves if you wish."

The men put their heads together, a short exchange followed, and then they separated.

"It is done. The city surrenders with peace guaranteed for all citizens and the king to stand trial with the elders as judge."

"Fine. We enter the city in three hours."

Barlon turned back to his waiting army and the city leaders returned through Pogor's gates, which remained open.

At his command tent, Barlon ordered a great carriage be readied for his triumphant entrance into Pogor and all the troops dressed in their finest. A huge feast was to be prepared and served once inside the city. Everywhere there was hustle and bustle. With the mundane chores handled, he called a staff meeting.

Varg arrived first. He stood black as night, waiting.

"I'm glad you're here first. I have an errand for you. Kill Petre and Fasoom."

Varg's eyes glittered like rubies. He nodded and was gone.

Soon the others trickled in. Lom and Ecker came together, the general remarking on the good fortune of Pogor falling without a long and costly siege. Lom remained silent, his white eyes unblinking. Razgoth entered the tent alone, stoic and silent. Shalmuthe simply appeared and as usual, no one saw him enter.

"Thank you for coming," beamed Barlon when they were all seated. "This day seals our triumph over the West. We will soon march victoriously into Pogor and her riches will be ours."

"And what of Daggon?" asked Lom. "Will he come to be cut down like the others?"

Barlon pointed to Shalmuthe. "While we fought the battle with steel, he's fought with weapons of a different sort."

Shalmuthe rose to speak. "King Daggon is returning to his farmlands. I made sure accurate reports of your sweeping victory reached him as he marched north. Included in those reports was the assurance that resistance was hopeless. Daggon is a sensible man. He has retired from the battle, swearing allegiance to Lord Gorth."

"Ha! Well done," said Barlon, clapping his hands together with glee.

"And what of the wizards of Scaltzland, and their home front armies?" asked Razgoth.

"Ah, there too Shalmuthe has prepared well," said Barlon.

The master spy looked to Barlon before speaking again. Barlon smiled and nodded. Shalmuthe said, "There will not be any reinforcements coming from Scaltzland. A few weaker wizards and a sizable guard force loyal to the king remained in Ferd, their capitol. Once news of the war reached them the wizards wanted to go south immediately to help King Petre, and would have been here by now except for the High Priest of Zor. We have been grooming him for this chance to overthrow the king and turn Scaltzland into a theocracy. He denounced the king, swore allegiance to Lord Gorth and is setting up Scaltzland as a religious state. His followers along with troops from our legions are swiftly taking control from the king's followers. Soon our ally, the High Priest, will rule in Ferd and the fight will be over."

Razgoth gulped down an outburst against religious rulers and sat stone silent waiting for the meeting to end. He wondered about Varg's absence.

The meeting ended with enthusiastic exchanges about the merriment waiting inside Pogor. As soon as everyone else had gone, Varg entered the tent. He opened a leather sack and dumped the heads of King Fasoom and King Petre on the table. Their dead eyes still carried the torment and pain of their violent deaths.

Barlon uncorked a bottle of wine, tipped it up and drank heavily. "You've done well," he said to Varg, drinking between words.

"Yes, you've won your empire," said Varg. "Now I want my freedom." The demon prince's eyes burned brighter than a hot fire.

"No," snapped Barlon. "My enemies are not yet defeated."

"They are. All are dead or subservient to you." Varg reached for the medallion around Barlon's neck.

"Stop," shouted Barlon, clutching the magic talisman.

The fine-spun gold threads of the amulet that controlled Varg tightened around the demonic figurine locked within. Varg stopped, his hand still outstretched.

"I will give you your freedom after Daggon lies dead at my feet, and the people of Scaltzland call me ruler."

Barlon drank another long draught from the bottle.

"Soon," he said. "Soon you will go free but not until I'm done with you."

Varg backed away slowly. Hate filled his eyes but Barlon was too drunk to notice.

"You will walk at my side into Pogor," Barlon told the demon. "If anyone tries to harm me, kill them!"

"As you wish."

Barlon left the command tent and went to his personal quarters. He pulled out his black and gold dress uniform, the one he'd had years before when he was only a captain. The same one he wore the day he had been forced to surrender by his treasonous king. He donned it now. With added embellishments and a few alterations, it looked more stunning, more regal than it had in the lost days of Barlon's youth. Now he was Ruler, not just an officer of the line. Now he commanded all. He admired his trim military image in the looking glass. Splendid, he thought. The people of Pogor will be grateful for my rule.

Soon thereafter, Barlon Gorth's forces marched pompously into Pogor. Barlon rode in the lead. A small band of drummers hammered out the beat to announce their coming. The streets were lined with dutifully respectful merchants who had temporarily closed their shops. There was no cheering, no flag waving. Here and there a tear fell. Stout men-at-arms stood their posts on either side of the main boulevard. Many a loyal guardsman had trouble keeping a dry eye as well. There were no attempts at violence on

Gorth's person and Varg strode dark and forebodingly silent at his side through the gathered throng.

Finally, they entered the interior courtyard of King Fasoom's castle. The two gray-haired elders, who had earlier met Barlon at the city gates, stood perched atop the long tier of broad steps, waiting for Barlon to arrive.

Both men stood stiffly, unmoved by the pomp and military ceremony. As the entourage approached the bottom of the stairs, one of the elders shifted from one foot to the other, craning his neck as if trying to locate someone or something.

Barlon reached the bottom of the stairs, leaped from his horse and dashed up the wide stone steps two at a time, Varg on his heels. He stopped before the elders.

"Are you ready to turn over the royal scepter?"

"Where is King Fasoom?" demanded the second elder.

"He is king no longer. Why do you care?" Barlon's voice was a harsh rumble.

"You said he would be brought to trial," reminded the first.

"He was killed trying to escape," said Barlon reaching for the scepter.

"No, you lied."

Both elders stepped back, motioning for the guards. Barlon's sword flashed once, twice, and both men fell dead. Varg stepped between the guards and Barlon. His cold, soul-piercing glare stopped them. Barlon leaned down and picked up the city scepter.

"I am the new king," he proclaimed, turning to the assemblage. "Tonight there will be feasting in my honor."

A roar of approval went up from Barlon's troops. The city dwellers turned glumly from the scene. Slowly, the gathering broke up, leaving the soldiers to find refuge where they could. Barlon spent his first hours strolling through the marvelous sandstone castle, admiring the craftsmanship and architecture of the massive, lavishly appointed structure, with its high ceilings, wide windows and intricate carvings.

That evening Barlon's supply master put forth an elegant banquet prepared from the best of the castle's provisions. Wine flowed into the streets and before the night was done, his army fell into a drunken slumber. In the city streets, Barlon's drunken troops looted and pillaged unhindered. Barlon, too, drank heavily and was carried to bed by Lom in the wee hours of the morning. Only Varg and a few others refrained from over indulgence.

At dawn's light, an exhausted serving girl set her tray down in the kitchen. She had seen a night full of drunken revelry and she was tired. She mounted the stairs past sleeping soldiers and entered her second story room. There she slipped out of her coarse rags, fit only for a scullery maid, and carefully removed the wax scar that had turned her pretty face into a horrible apparition. She picked up the knee-length white gown that lay over the bed and walked to the window. With one hand she threw it open and watched the new dawn.

Her heavy sigh broke the silence. Fatigue bore crushingly on her. There was no rest. She cast her spell of change and became a great eagle, tested her wings, and launched into the growing light.

#

The same night Barlon's troops enjoyed the splendor of Pogor, a small sailing craft glided silently down the Rushon River. Abadis stood at the rail, his robes fluttering gently in the stiff breeze. He peered intently at the forest slipping past, hoping to catch a sign of Gant. Occasionally he saw the luminous, green eyes of some wild animal, but there was no sign of the young warrior.

The smaller moon sent fingers of light dancing across the wavelets, but Abadis paid no attention. War was pending, and somehow he had to find Gant. The boat was still a day away from Malathon and Abadis had hoped to find Gant before he reached the city. What happened to Gant after he vanquished Egog? He had to be somewhere between the cavern and Blasseldune. Maybe he had not gone to the river. Maybe the foolish boy had struck off overland to Netherdorf. Maybe he had been killed in the wild. There were still many powerful creatures roaming the wilderness, even a few that Valorius might have trouble with.

Abadis scanned back along the boat. It wasn't large and probably could carry a dozen passengers. He'd only seen one since boarding late yesterday evening, and that was an elderly merchant from Falls Hill. Abadis had seen him before and from what little he knew, the man was moderately successful and totally dull. By this late hour, the decks were clear except for the bow watch and helmsman.

At that moment, a lithe, feminine shape approached Abadis hesitantly. In the relative dark it was hard to see her features, yet there was something vaguely familiar about her.

"Abadis," said the woman, half questioning, half greeting, her voice light and musical.

"Yes," he said, his mind struggling to identify the voice.

"It is you," she said and stepped up next to him.

"Dalphnia," the wizard said, finally able to see her face. "You are a long way from home. Don't tell me no men come to your forest anymore."

"Oh no," she laughed. "I found the finest man I've ever known. But he left me. Can you believe it? Left me to go to war. I decided too late that I needed him. I love him too much to say goodbye. I'm going to find him. And that thanks to the stone of freedom you gave me."

"That trinket? Never did me much good. But how could a man leave *you*? I thought your magic bound men to you until death."

"Not this one. I think it was the armor, or maybe the sword. It really doesn't matter. I can only love one man, and as long as Gant lives, I'll find him."

"Gant!" The wrinkles froze on Abadis' weathered face. "You found him near the cave in Little Mountain Pass."

"Yes, near death. I nursed him back to health. And he was mine, until the day he touched his sword. It broke my spell. After all I've been through, all the men, you'd think I could handle one rejection." Her face saddened. "I can't. He's special. There's something about him. . ."

"There certainly is. How long ago did he leave?"

"A few days. I went to Falls Hill and booked passage on the first boat."

"And I've forgotten the mirror." The wizard turned and, with a rustle of robes, started for his cabin.

"Abadis, you know him," she said, grabbing his sleeve. "Help me find him."

"I can't. Forget him. He's not like any other man alive. He'll never come back. I'm sorry, but I must go."

He rushed to his room, never looking back, never seeing the tears streaming from her delicate cheeks into the dark river water.

He made a sign at the door to undo the lock, hurried in, signed the door locked again and pulled a small, oblong mirror from deep in the folds of his robe. It looked exactly like the one in his cabin except it was only a few inches long. The message on it in tiny red letters read: "War has begun. We are holding own for now. Gant is here."

He cursed, loud and long. Then, quickly he recited the words of travel, threw a dash of dust into the air along with a few hand signs, and the wizard vanished from his cabin.

Chapter 30

Gant paced restlessly around the small room that served as Abadis' kitchen and living area. He had too much idle time to think. He couldn't sleep. As soon as he lay down, his head raged with problems, mostly about things beyond his control; his family, his uncle, King Tirmus, Dalphnia. Especially Dalphnia. Would she be there when he got back? If he ever got back. Where was King Tirmus? Questions without answers.

Zandinar, for his part, said little. He seemed content to let fate choose his path. Most of the time he either slept or sat wrapped in his furs even though the house was warm.

Gant paced back and forth across the room as he'd done a hundred times already. Zandinar slept quietly against the far wall. There was a faint hiss in the air and there stood Abadis, his bearded face contorted in a grimace, deep furrows across his forehead.

"Abadis. It's about time."

"Way past time," said the mage. "Who's your friend?" he asked pointing to the ball of furs.

"Zandinar."

"Oh?" Abadis paused a moment, his expression thoughtful. Finally he mumbled, "Maybe he's found his destiny." Then to Gant he said, "Has my granddaughter been back?"

"No. She said she'd be back as soon as she could."

"Tonight, I hope. Meanwhile, I've got things to do."

"What about us?"

"Wait here."

Abadis turned and started for his workshop. He stopped, turned back. "Almost forgot. The sword. What about the sword?" he asked, holding his hand out for it.

"What about it?"

"Let me see it," said Abadis shaking his hand impatiently.

Gant pulled Valorius from her scabbard. "What do you want Valorius for?"

"To see how much magic was sucked out of her by Egog. You don't think the magic in an object is unlimited, do you?"

Gant handed the sword to Abadis and watched the wizard turn the sword over slowly in one hand, his eyes half closed as if sensing its magical energy.

"Well?" asked Gant.

"Hard for me to tell. There's still more magic in her than I can gauge. But will it be enough to stop Varg?" He handed the sword back to Gant. "I wish Uric was here," he muttered entering his workshop and closing the door behind him.

Gant felt Valorius. He felt the tingle of magical energy. He couldn't remember what she'd felt like when Uric had given her to him. Was she weaker now? Maybe. He wasn't sure. He returned Valorius to her scabbard.

Sitting down at the table Gant eyed a strip of dried beef. His stomach churned. Maybe a little food would help. The dry stringy meat went down hard. He chewed more to relieve the tension than for sustenance.

Hours passed and Gant fidgeted with his equipment noting that his armor had healed from the dent Zandinar had put in it. He went outside and worked sword exercises on the grassy area in front of the house, slashing and parrying imaginary opponents until arm weary.

Finally he went back inside. Zandinar sat at the table polishing his sword.

"Abadis come out yet?"

"No."

"How long have you been awake?"

"A little while."

Gant admired Zandinar's sword. "Where did you get such a magnificent weapon?"

"My mother."

"Yes, you told me that. Is she a wizard?"

"You might call her that."

"Was your father a wizard?"

"No, he wasn't. He probably died a long time ago."

"You don't know if he's alive?"

"No. I never met him."

Strange, thought Gant. If Zandinar never met his father it seemed unlikely he could know whether he was a wizard or not. And what kind of a wizardess was Zandinar's mother?

After a moment of silence, Gant walked to a cabinet and helped himself to a small glass of Abadis' elixir. He swallowed the smooth liquid quickly and then turned back to Zandinar. "Where are you from?"

"North."

"Where north? Penton? Kittenspenny?"

"I'm not from any town."

"What made you come here?"

"I seek only my destiny, which was first to find you."

Before Gant could say anything else, Abadis shuffled somberly out of his workshop. Both swordsmen looked up and waited for the old man to speak. Clearly something was on the wizard's mind.

Abadis stopped at the table, dropping heavily onto one of the stools.

"I don't understand," he said. "I can't locate Uric. Usually the magic flux near him makes it easy for me to find him." Abadis looked up, fixing his gaze on Gant. "Uric was still at Netherdorf Castle, wasn't he?"

"Last I knew."

"Then he should have been there when Gorth attacked. Even if they succeeded in killing him, his body would still hold enough magic to pinpoint it. But there's no trace. It's as if he vanished."

"Maybe he's taken King Tirmus somewhere safe."

203

"And not told me?"

"Maybe he tried. You've been gone a lot."

Abadis scratched his gray beard thoughtfully. "Yes, I had to hunt you down. We must have your sword if there's to be any chance of defeating Varg."

"And maybe mine as well," added Zandinar, still polishing it.

"Right now," said Abadis, "I think we're going to need an army to stop Gorth. We'll need enough troops to tie up his soldiers so we can corner Varg, otherwise it's hopeless." He stopped, thought of something else, and then added, "I wonder where Uric is."

"What about the Eastern Empire?" asked Zandinar. "Maybe they would help. They're supposed to have the largest army anywhere."

"Perhaps. But they have a boy emperor who listens too much to old ministers and they want little or nothing to do with the West unless there's money or power in it for them. Maybe Gant could ask. I'm not well thought of in Malathon." Abadis' voice took on a deep note of sarcasm. "The ministers fear anyone with power. They're afraid I'll catch the emperor's ear."

"Then we need to get going," said Gant. "It's a long ride."

"I can take you," said Abadis. "It's near my limit for distance and while there are no wizard's circles in Malathon that I know of, I do know a place where it should be safe to take you."

"What's a wizard's circle?" asked Gant.

"A guaranteed safe spot. It is a magically protected zone that prevents change within that location. We put them in strategic spots where we expect to travel regularly. Magical transport can be very dangerous. Buildings get built, furniture and walls get built or moved and when that happens you can easily appear within something solid. The end."

"So you know somewhere in Malathon that hasn't changed?"

"Yes. It'll be okay. I can take you there but you'll have to go to the emperor's court and present our case. While you do that, I think I'll do a bit of exploring in Netherdorf Castle."

"Let me go with you."

"Some other time. Right now we each have a task that must be done."

"Okay," said Gant, biting his lip. "While you're in Netherdorf look for my mother and father."

The thin spark of hope that glimmered in his heart burst into flame. Maybe his parents were all right and he would see them again.

"I'll do my best. You just make sure you see the emperor."

"How will we get in to see the emperor? Walk up and ask to see him?" Gant tried to imagine how one gained an audience with an emperor. He couldn't think of anything short of charging in at sword point and he was sure that wouldn't work.

"That's pretty close. All you'll need is a little gold."

"I haven't got any gold."

"Yes, you will need gold." Abadis waved his hands in the air, mumbled a few strange words and suddenly a large iron ring appeared in the floor attached to a trapdoor that hadn't been there a moment ago. "Help yourself," he said.

Gant grabbed the iron ring and though the trap door looked like it was made of hardwood planking, by himself he couldn't budge it. Zandinar lent his strength to lifting the ring and they succeeded in pulling aside the three-foot square cover.

Inside was a huge chest buried beneath the floor. Gant eagerly flipped back the lid to reveal a fortune in gold, silver and gems. He stared in disbelief, never dreaming such wealth existed, let alone under Abadis' floor.

"Well, go ahead. Take a few handfuls of gold coins." The graying wizard motioned Gant to move, a laugh in his gray eyes.

Gant took out his nearly empty coin purse and stuffed it with coins. He closed the chest and with Zandinar's help, replaced the trapdoor. Another spell and the ring and trap door disappeared.

"Now, take my hands, form a circle and be very still," said Abadis, holding out a gnarled hand to each of them. "Moving during casting can break down the spell and then who knows where we'd end up or whether we'd live through it." Once he had a firm grip on the younger men and the circle was complete, he mumbled, "Let me see, the exact location for Sylvia's is. . ."

Abadis recited a barely audible verse and a whispered location. A fuzzy luminescence surrounded the group and Abadis' room vanished. They were swept along a featureless tunnel through some unimaginable dimension and then in a rush they materialized in a sparsely decorated bedroom. Gant steadied himself as a wave of nausea swept over him. It passed and he looked around. A large mirror hung on the ceiling looking down on the single occupied bed. The moaning from beneath the thrashing covers made Gant queasy all over again. Abadis hustled them out the door into the hall before those in bed noticed they had visitors.

Abadis pulled the two warriors down a flight of stairs into a lavishly furnished sitting room on the ground floor. The walls were light colored wood that shone in the bright sunlight streaming through wide windows. Paintings of scantily clad women hung strategically around the room along with a large, exquisitely framed mirror. Four beautiful young women sat in various stages of undress that brought a flush to Gant's ears. An elderly woman stood behind one of the younger women, meticulously combing the younger woman's shoulder length shiny hair.

"Sylvia," said Abadis as they entered the room.

The older woman turned, startled at first, but then a smile smoothed away the surprise.

"Abadis," she called, running to him, throwing her arms around his neck and kissing him. "I certainly wasn't expecting to see you. You were just here and I thought you had important business that was going to keep you away for a while." She elbowed him playfully and now it was the wizard's turn to redden.

She looked at Zandinar and Gant. "And you've brought friends. Are they in need of a good time? You know we'll take real good care of them, you scoundrel." Sylvia hugged Abadis again.

"No, actually your place is the only one I could remember well enough to use. This is Gant and Zandinar," he pointed to each in turn. "They have to see the emperor this afternoon. I thought you could give them a good meal and let them stay here until I get back to pick them up, probably later tonight." Abadis pressed a small stack of coins into Sylvia's hand.

She looked at the money and started to give it back. "I don't want this," she said with mock sternness. "I'd much rather you stayed for a while instead of running off again."

"Keep it." said Abadis. "I'll be back soon."

"Are you sure all they need is a meal?"

"You could help them get in to see the emperor. Otherwise, yes, all they need is a meal. Now, I *must* go."

Abadis bent and gently kissed Sylvia's cheek. Before he could pull back she grabbed his head in both hands and kissed him on the mouth. Abadis' ears turned crimson, but he kissed her back before pulling away.

"Hurry back," Sylvia said with a wink as the wizard began his chant.

A fuzziness grew in the air and the wizard vanished. Sylvia ushered Gant and Zandinar into a combination kitchen-dining room off the main reception area.

Several of the girls followed them gleefully and quickly put together a wonderful meal of roast beef, fresh bread and baked apples.

"What kind of place is this?" asked Gant, savoring a bite of baked apple.

Sylvia laughed. "You don't get out much, do you? I run the finest, most exquisite brothel in all the Eastern Empire. Are you sure you don't need something more than a bite to eat?"

Gant choked. "Really?" he sputtered and then thought of Dalphnia. "No, thank you. Maybe Zandinar?"

The knight shook his head no and Sylvia returned to the reception parlor. Gant and Zandinar ate in silence ever conscious of the surrounding femininity and though one girl would flash a bit too much leg, and another might bend over a tad too far, both men's eyes remained fixed on their food.

Finally when they finished, Sylvia returned with a huge bull of a man. He stood taller even than Zandinar and so wide he had to slip sideways through the door. He was dressed in a loose-fitting silk shirt and pants that helped hide his bulk, but the tree-trunk arms hanging from the short sleeves were impossible to miss.

"Gant, Zandinar," said Sylvia, touching each on the shoulder as she introduced them, "this is Rolaf. He will take you to the Imperial Palace and see that you talk to the right people."

"Just exactly what reason do we have to gain a hearing with the emperor?" asked Gant, not sure what he was supposed to do.

"It doesn't matter," answered Sylvia. "Every afternoon, except Holy Days, the emperor receives complaints and petitions from the populace, at least in theory. Actually, he only hears those with enough gold to pay off the court secretaries and sub-ministers in charge of arranging his schedule. With a few coins in the right palms, you will be at the top of the list."

Gant patted the plump purse at his belt, and nodded, "We brought gold."

"Good. But you better hurry. It won't be long before the emperor begins today's sessions."

At that, Rolaf said, "This way," and led them out the back door, around the corner, up a short alley and into a broad busy street. People in all manner of dress rushed this way and that. Some had carts loaded with merchandise, others hawked what they carried in their arms, and some seemed to wander without purpose. Men-at-arms moved up and down the streets, some dressed in the red and gold uniform of the Eastern Empire instead of the brown of the city guard.

By the time they got to the Palace, Gant was lost. They'd turned up so many streets, none of which ran straight for more than a block, that he'd soon forgotten where they'd come from. They entered the beautiful, grass courtyard of the Royal Palace and ran into a throng of men dressed in the most expensive clothing Gant had ever seen.

Rolaf swerved around the noisy crowd and slipped behind a large, well-tended flower garden. They went down a winding maze of color and fragrances eventually arriving at a small metal door set in the weathered stonewall of the palace. Rolaf knocked three times.

The door opened a crack. A soldier in full dress uniform peered out, his uniform spotless and pressed so every crease stood out razor sharp. Each gold button and the gold epaulets flashed in the dim sunlight.

"Rolaf," grunted the soldier and swung the door open.

"We need to see His Imperial Highness." Rolaf pointed to Gant's coin purse and motioned that a coin should be given to the guard. Gant did so and they were escorted quickly to a desk in the hallway immediately behind the door. Here a man in red robes sat reading from a parchment list. The guard stopped before the table, saluted, and then turned and went back to his post.

The official looked up. "Rolaf," he said. "Who is your 'client' today?"

"Gant," said Rolaf and motioned for Gant's purse again.

Another gold coin changed hands and they were led a short distance down another hall to another man at another table. The first man nodded and returned the way they had come.

"Mr. Vice-Secretary," began Rolaf. "Sir Gant needs to meet with his Imperial Highness today. Is that possible?"

The man looked coldly at Rolaf. "His Diviness is very busy today. Perhaps?" He waited.

Rolaf held up four fingers and Gant quickly laid four coins on the table.

"Ah, yes. There is one opening left. Follow me."

They went up a flight of stairs, down another hallway into a small room with soldiers at the door. They were presented to a robust man at a tiny desk.

"Rolaf," he said glancing up. "Important business today?"

"Yes, very important, Mr. Under-Secretary."

"Well, let me see. I suppose you'd like an appointment near the beginning."

"Yes. First if possible."

"It'll be very costly for his Majesty."

Rolaf held up ten fingers and immediately Gant had ten coins on the desk.

"Very good," said the Under-Secretary and scraped the gold into his pouch. "Follow me."

They walked quickly down the hall to another, larger office, again guarded by troops wearing the red and gold uniform of the

Eastern Empire. The Under-Secretary knocked on the door, and then left them. A guard opened the door from the inside and escorted them into a lavish office.

"Mr. Secretary," said Rolaf stopping before the massive desk, bowing deferentially. "These honorable men *must* see his Divine Highness as soon as possible." He waved for Gant to put ten gold pieces on the desk.

The white haired secretary looked blankly at the stack of coins. "Maybe tomorrow," he said.

Rolaf waved for ten more coins.

"Later today?"

Another ten and the coin purse was nearly empty.

"Ah, yes. I can see you *are* in a hurry. I think now will be fine. Captain!" he called and one of the guards took a step forward. "Take these men to the Imperial Chamber. See that they are first to see the emperor."

They followed the officer until they came to a short line of men waiting in front of a thick red tapestry hung between two ornately carved marble pillars. The small gathering buzzed with trivial talk of wealth, road conditions, prices and taxes, each man dressed in finery unknown in Netherdorf.

The Captain shoved his way to the front of the pack. There two guards stood preventing entry past the curtain. "These men are next," said the Captain. A groan went up from those already waiting.

The two soldiers nodded. "There is someone before the emperor now," said one of the guards, "but it won't take long. He's made his contribution to the Church."

A knowing look passed between Rolaf and the guard, and Rolaf, Gant and Zandinar were given space at the head of the haphazard line. The Captain left.

"Now, if we get in before someone else pays more," whispered Rolaf. Then he added, "Give me your swords. No weapons are allowed in the emperor's presence."

Reluctantly Gant handed Valorius to Rolaf.

Zandinar refused. "I'll wait here."

"Okay, then Gant will have to present your case alone."

Minutes later, a fat, heavily-jowled merchant was led from the room behind the curtain. Perspiration covered his shiny forehead, but he smiled and muttered something about the divine wisdom of the emperor. One of the guards ushered Gant in past the curtain almost as soon as the other man was gone.

A stooped old man dressed in white linen met Gant on the inside of the red curtain. He led the young warrior to a spot before a huge raised dais where the emperor sat on his throne. Behind him stood four old men. Heavily muscled servants waved broadleaf fans and a cluster of guards stood in a semi-circle around the throne. Several strange blue and orange birds fluttered in polished brass cages hanging near the emperor.

The rest of the room was empty. No one stood witness to the emperor's justice. There were other doorways but they were all curtained off and heavily guarded.

In the dim light Gant examined His Majesty. A forlorn boy of thirteen or so slouched on the throne, apparently disinterested in the proceedings. His face was pale from lack of sun and his regal robes hung sloppily from his gangly frame. A heavy gold crown rested slightly askew atop thick, brown hair that was trimmed bowl-fashion. The boy emperor barely looked up.

"Sir Gant of Netherdorf, Your Majesty," announced the frail man who'd escorted Gant into the chamber. With that the guide turned and left.

"I am Gant of Netherdorf, sire," began Gant. "I have come to ask the emperor's help. Netherdorf has been conquered by the Mountain-Lord Barlon Gorth who now makes war on the Western Kings. We need military support to stop him. It is said your army is the finest in the world, which is why I have come to you."

Gant noticed grave expressions exchanged between the emperor's ministers, while the young boy perked up and seemed to hang on every word.

Gant continued. "King Tirmus has been a true friend of the Empire and now hides in exile. He should be returned to the throne. Even now, the Western Kings may have fallen. Once that happens, how long before Barlon Gorth turns on the Empire?"

The emperor sat up straight, suddenly alert, a new sparkle in his eyes. He started to speak, but one of the ministers hurriedly whispered in his ear. The boy slumped back. The ministers huddled. Gant could barely make out their hushed voices. Again, one of the ministers spoke to the emperor.

This time the boy gesticulated excitedly but quieted as the ministers crowded around. Finally, the group separated.

The emperor looked sadly at Gant. "Request denied," he said.

Guards hustled Gant back to the red curtain.

"But, your Highness. Many will die needlessly if you don't. . ."

"Silence," roared the foremost minister. "The emperor has spoken."

Guards led Gant away. Zandinar and Rolaf waited with expectant faces as Gant was shoved back through the curtain.

"He won't help," said Gant. He looked at Rolaf. "Isn't there anything else we can do?"

"Not unless you want to fight the Imperial Army and all of the City Watch."

Dejectedly, the three of them returned through the maze of streets to Sylvia's. The women there tried to cheer Gant, but he wanted no part of it. Failure was not something he took lightly. There was nothing left to do but wait for Abadis.

Chapter 31

Abadis appeared in Uric's third floor room in Netherdorf Castle, a place he'd visited many times and knew almost as well as his own home. He chanted softly the incantations for invisibility and his image disappeared from the mirror on the wall attesting to the spell's success. He searched Uric's room thoroughly for a clue to his friend's whereabouts. There were none.

When he was satisfied there was nothing to find, the aged wizard tiptoed down the narrow stone steps to the ground floor. He slunk through the kitchen past the busy staff and went out the small door at the back. He made his way around to the front of the castle, noting the stonecutters working on a new front stoop. Silently he moved out past the black and gold uniformed gate guards and left the castle unnoticed.

He followed the main street down the hill through Netherdorf. He was careful not to bump into anyone on the streets. He turned at the first street on the left, walked a half a block, slipped into an alley where he made sure no one was watching and reappeared. Visible once again, he strode to the next cross street and went into the third shop on the left.

It was a dark hovel, crammed full of jars, bottles, potions, powders, herbs, and exotic chemicals. Abadis walked purposefully to the back and rapped his knuckles on a rickety old table that doubled as a sales counter.

"Yes," came a faint, high-pitched voice from behind a stack of goods.

"Stop sleeping and come out here," demanded Abadis.

A shriveled, old man stepped from behind the piles of merchandise. His eyes sparkled with life.

"Abadis," he cackled. "I thought I had seen the last of you years ago."

"Ha! Elan, I keep telling you, you can't outlive me. I'm a wizard. You're a mere sage and alchemist. It's inevitable."

"We shall see, we shall see. What do you want anyway? Nothing is on special and I will not quibble over price."

"Too bad. I love to haggle, but today I haven't got time."

"Oh my, in too much of a hurry to try to cheat me out of my profit? You are in a hurry."

"Do you know Uric, King Tirmus' sage?"

"Of course. He bought a thing or two, but I never saw any real talent in that youngster. I heard he died in the castle. Lots of people died. Me, they did not seem to notice." Elan winked.

"Hmm," Abadis thought for a few minutes. He found it hard to believe that Uric had been killed. His body would be almost impossible to dispose of unnoticed, and even if Uric was dead Abadis should still be able to locate the body.

"What about a dragon? Did you see a dragon after the battle?"

"Dragon? Well sort of. They hauled a dragon out of town the day after Gorth took over. Or at least it was a life size statue of one. I think they took it to Gorth's castle though I cannot imagine why."

Abadis looked sternly at Elan. "Are you making this up?"

"Of course not. They packed up a big stone slab with a dragon on it and wheeled the whole thing out of town. There were a bunch of horses straining to keep it moving."

"And took it to the Mountain Castle?"

"Well now, I do not know that for sure, but that is what I heard."

"This is going to be harder than I thought."

"What is?"

"Nothing. Forget you saw me."

"Yes, of course, anything you say, but where are you going?"

"Gorth's castle. I'll be back later. I'll probably need to pick up a few things."

With that Abadis left the dingy store and headed back through town, eventually walking west down the road toward the Monolith Mountains. He walked briskly, his robes flapping behind him in the freshening westerly breeze. He held a steady pace until a bend in the road and a low rise hid him from the view of other travelers.

Quickly he recited the words of travel and zipped instantly to a wizard's circle he knew near a familiar fork far up the road. Here a less-traveled road led up to the Mountain Castle. It had once belonged to the line of Mountain Kings until they tired of their meager kingdoms and tried to conquer lands to the west. Now it seemed another lord ruled there who wanted to conquer the West. The trouble was it looked as if he might succeed.

Abadis turned up the gravel road that snaked toward the black stone fortification atop the distant hillside. The castle glared down at the weary wizard as he wound his way up the dusty switchbacks. There was something ominous in the dark arrow slits that peered out from rough walls.

The first time Abadis went behind a shoulder of the mountain that blocked the view from the castle, he cast his invisibility spell. Then, cautious not to make a noise, he worked his way up the steep slope until he confronted the massive iron gates. They were locked tight, and the guards on the wall gave no indication that they would be opened soon.

I guess I'll have to fly, he thought, and opened a loose pocket in his robe. He took out a small metal box no bigger than his thumbnail and removed a delicate pair of fly's wings. He recited the few words to the spell, gripped the wings gently and made the correct gestures, and Abadis lifted smoothly off the ground. He flew over the towering wall, landing gently in the inner courtyard.

"Perfect," he muttered, and walked to the inner keep's door, which stood open, and slipped inside.

After several false turns Abadis located the stairs that led down to the dungeons. As he started down the worn stone steps where the light was dimmest, he stopped and recast his invisibility spell to be sure it wouldn't fade at the wrong time.

At the bottom of the stairs, Abadis paused. Several sets of iron doors blocked the way. The old wizard peered through the small, barred windows into the hallways beyond. Which way should he go? The first two halls were totally dark and didn't look promising.

The third was sparsely lit by smoky torches in iron braziers. Abadis noticed a collection of instruments of torture in the central room just beyond the doors. Off the main room were a couple of holding cells.

Cautiously he slid the door open, glancing around to be sure there were no guards around. Inside he closed the door and stepped out into a large chamber. Not only were there machines of torture, but also a large blackened stone table, sputtered with the remains of the goldsmith's art. Finally, his eyes adjusted to the dim light and he saw that the back of the room had been tunneled out to form a massive cave-like chamber.

There, trapped in a sphere of timelessness, was Uric. His huge, lifeless eyes skinned over by the magic that held him.

Abadis approached carefully, wary of magic traps. Finding none, he tiptoed to the outer edge of the translucent sphere surrounding his friend. He studied it, first visually, then with a series of magical probes. Soft green light flashed each time a spell touched the sphere. Nothing penetrated the bubble surrounding the dragon.

"Hmm, yes," said Abadis finally. "We'll have to get you out of there, old friend."

The gray wizard threw open his robe and searched through the multiple pockets and pouches inside. Within a few minutes he found what he needed but before he could begin the spell that would neutralize Razgoth's trap, something hit him from behind and knocked him down. His head slammed into the cold stone floor and darkness overwhelmed him.

It took only a few seconds, but when he regained consciousness, Abadis stared into the face of a huge, black mastiff that held him pinned under massive paws. The dog's fangs gleamed only inches from the wizard's face. A second dog circled behind the first, thick saliva dripping from its curled lips. In the doorway behind them both stood an ugly brute of a man wearing a studded leather breastplate. He brandished a short sword in his right hand.

"Good boys," rasped the guard. "Whoever you are, don't move or the dogs'll tear yer heart out."

Abadis lay motionless, partially stunned by the fall. His head swam in a fog and it was hard to think clearly.

The guard advanced, sword ready.

"Some kinda wizard, are ya?"

He pushed the dogs back and grabbed Abadis by the collar. With a twist and spin he yanked the old man to his feet.

"Take off your clothes," said the guard, pressing the sword tip to Abadis' throat.

The dogs inched closer. Abadis tried to think. He had no choice. He took off his clothes, his ancient body thin and wrinkled beneath.

The guard laughed. "Ain't much to ya, is there?"

The guard tossed the clothes into the corner. And then he grabbed Abadis by the shoulder and shoved him naked into a cold, damp cell next to Uric. The door clanged shut with the ominous ring of cold iron.

"Here you'll stay, 'til Lord Gorth returns. He'll know what to do with ya."

The guard left. Abadis shivered. The straw on the floor was covered with fungus. The bed was bare, made of half-rotten planks. He tried to remember where he was, why he'd come here, but his mind was blank.

Chapter 32

Gant waited impatiently for Abadis' return. He tried to stay out of the way, but the girls fussed over him despite his protestations. Afternoon dragged into sunset. The evening meal came and went, almost untouched by Gant. Night fell over Malathon. Sylvia's became noticeably busier. Gant and Zandinar opted to stay in the kitchen out of sight of the steady flow of customers.

Hours passed. Gant dozed uncomfortably in a hard-backed chair, his head lolled back at an odd angle. The clientele dwindled until finally the house was practically empty except for the girls who straggled upstairs to go to sleep. Zandinar slipped out to the sitting room and went to sleep on a couch.

Heavy footsteps startled Gant from his slumber. Before he could get up, three armed men wearing the emperor's red and gold surrounded him, swords drawn. Gant sat up alert but motionless.

"Who are you?" he asked. Was this a raid on Sylvia's? He kept his right hand near Valorius, ready if needed.

For a tense moment nobody moved. More booted footsteps and a second group hustled in through the back door. Gant twisted his head to see the newcomers. A broad shouldered man who Gant guessed to be slightly older than himself entered first. He wore the polished, scroll-worked silver parade armor of an officer in the emperor's guard. Half hidden behind him strode the boy emperor, dressed in nondescript armor and the common uniform of the Empire's lowest troops.

Behind the emperor came an old man. He had dark hair shot with streaks of white and a wrinkled brown face with heavy furrows star-bursting from the corners of stern brown eyes. The old man paused in the doorway, looked nervously around outside, and then slipped in and closed the door.

"Your Highness," stammered Gant, dropping his hand away from his sword. "What are you doing here?"

"Looking for you, Gant of the Ironlimbs," said the boy emperor, a mischievous glint in his eyes. "Let me introduce Kalmine," he said, pointing to the old man who'd entered last, "my one trusted advisor. And Captain Hesh and soldiers Krist, Patt and Faltern. Also loyal to me."

Gant nodded to each. "I would have returned to the palace if you wanted to see me. How did you know where to find me?"

"An emperor has ways." The boy chuckled as if that were a joke. "If I wanted you to come to the palace I would have sent for you. Instead, I wish to join you. I am smothered in the palace by controlling ministers. I have no power. I am going with you to search for and recover the Sword of Emperors. When I come back, no one will deny me my birthright. With Thantalmos, I will *be* emperor. Then I'll get rid of the idiots who suffocate me day after day."

Gant saw the fierce determination grow in the emperor's blue eyes and the set of his chin.

"I think that's impossible, your highness."

"Then you can go to jail. I'll claim you kidnapped me. If I go back to the palace you'll go with me."

"But it's dangerous out there."

"No worse than in my palace. Boy rulers don't live long, and anyway, my ministers keep me under thumb. I spend each day forced into the same dull palace routine. I am nothing but a title they use. I have to get away and you are my only chance."

"I can't take you with me."

"You must. I have to get out of here."

"Let them come along," said Zandinar who had entered the kitchen unnoticed.

"It's dangerous. He'll get killed."

"So. Everybody dies. You and I may die. Has your spirit died? Aren't you filled with a sense of adventure, of wonder?"

Gant paused. It did seem strange for him to be telling others to avoid danger.

"Okay," he conceded, and then to the emperor, "but you are *not* in charge. You will follow orders, and no one is to address you as 'Your Highness' or 'Majesty'. What's your name?"

"Pristum."

"Then Pristum it is, or better yet, just Pris."

The boy nodded and Gant read his dreams in his eyes.

"You might as well make yourself comfortable, Pris," said Gant, motioning to the chairs in the kitchen. "We're waiting for someone else, and we don't know when he'll return."

The boy emperor glanced over his shoulder at Kalmine. A trapped look crossed his face. "We can't wait long. Chantel will send out troops once he discovers I'm gone. If we don't leave now, you'll have to fight the entire City Watch."

"That shouldn't be too hard," laughed Zandinar, and the soldiers tensed. "However, I think Abadis has been detained, else he would have returned by now."

Gant nodded agreement. Anything was better than sitting around doing nothing. "Under the circumstances, we'd better put some distance between us and Malathon. Let's go to Abadis' house. We can wait there and it should be safe."

"As good a plan as any," said Zandinar.

"I'll tell Sylvia we'll meet Abadis at his house," said Gant and started out of the kitchen. He paused and then turned back. "Pris, can you find horses for all of us? We'll need them."

Pris nodded and sent Captain Hesh out while Gant went to talk to Sylvia. Gently knocking on her door soon had her up. She promised to relay the message when Abadis returned, but insisted they not leave until she could pack them something to eat. By the time she had everything ready, Captain Hesh was back with eight splendid horses requisitioned from the Emperor's First Horse Legion by order of Captain Hesh. Gant was last out the door. He mounted the horse waiting for him, thanked Sylvia for the food and drink, and the party started off down the dimly-lit alleyway.

The steady clatter of the horse's hooves echoed between the close-packed buildings as they moved down the narrow twisting streets. Once they passed a duo of City Watch on foot patrol. They passed quickly and did their best to conceal their identity from the men. Everywhere along their course, the windows remained shuttered and they passed unseen out through the western gate.

Once out of Malathon, they increased the pace to a canter. Gant rode beside Zandinar where he could talk without being overheard. "What do you know of this sword the emperor is looking for?"

"Only the legend everyone knows," said Zandinar, keeping his eyes on the road.

"What's that?"

"Thantalmos. Screaming Death, The Sword of Emperors, given to the First Emperor by the High Elves when elves and men were friends. It was lost by the 7th Emperor, Maxidim, during the First Forest War. The elves recaptured it and vowed never to return it. It is said that no man except the emperor can pick it up and live."

"Does it exist?"

"Probably. Who knows? Most legends have at least a fragment of truth."

They rode on through the dark countryside in silence. Before long, the walls of Maltic City loomed in front of them. Here they detoured off the road, passing through the woods on the south side of the city to avoid detection. Shortly after dawn they regained the road west of Maltic City and headed for Blasseldune.

They rode steadily the rest of the day occasionally passing a caravan with its brace of wagons and accompanying mercenaries. The caravan masters nodded and politely moved aside, respecting the uniform of the Empire. Just before nightfall they left the territory claimed by the Empire. They camped for the night in the wilderness, choosing to avoid the large campgrounds or inns regularly used by the caravans. Instead they found a small clearing off the road and camped there.

The fire burned cheerfully in the little stone pit. They tied the horses nearby and set watches. Gant and Krist took the first turn. Zandinar and Patt volunteered for second watch, and last would be

Captain Hesh and Faltern. Pris demanded a turn. Gant refused and the emperor sulked away but was soon fast asleep.

Gant settled down in a spot out of the firelight where he had a view of everything that happened in the camp without being seen. For a while, Krist sat hunkered beside a bush on the opposite edge of camp. As time passed, Krist became restless, shifting from one foot to the other, standing, stretching, and then crouching back down.

Finally, near the end of their watch, Krist crept over beside Gant. He cleared his throat, looked around nervously, and then asked, "Were you really the winner at Devonshield?"

"Yes," said Gant quietly, a bit flattered.

"Have you killed many men?"

"No, not many." A trace of nausea reminded him of those he'd had to kill. "None that I could avoid."

They sat in silence for a few minutes listening to the fire crackle. When Krist spoke next his voice quivered. "I've been wondering. Is it true, the enemy we go to fight is led by a demon?"

Gant stared into the soldier's face; the orange glow of the firelight highlighted the fear there. "Yes, there is a demon among their forces. Do you want to go back?"

Krist straightened. "No, sir. I'm sworn to his Highness and I'll be with him unless they kill me."

"I wouldn't worry about it. Who knows if and when we will meet our enemies? I doubt we will be killed tonight."

Zandinar rolled over in his furs. "Don't be too sure about death. She's a warrior's companion."

A rustle in the leaves some distance from the campsite halted the conversation. Gant reached for Valorius and immediately she was in his hand. The three of them listened, eager to catch any sound, but the woods remained silent as a tomb. Slowly, Zandinar got to his feet and slipped out between the dark tree trunks. Gant grabbed a brand from the fire and followed with Krist on his heels. They found nothing and returned to camp.

"It was probably just an animal. It's my turn, so you two get some sleep," said Zandinar, and woke the second guardsman.

Gant lay down on his bedroll and was soon fast asleep.

Morning dawned and the party pushed on after a cold breakfast. The road became a winding streak of dust flowing between towering oaks and maples. They moved swiftly, but boredom set in and their movements became mechanical. Gant had a gnawing feeling that they were being followed, that eyes watched from the deep shadows of the wood. He saw nothing though and the day stretched on.

By early evening, they approached the outskirts of Blasseldune. They'd seen several farmers returning from the market. Unless a farmer could contract for deliveries with one of the major inns there was little chance for a decent profit. It seemed these were less fortunate men as their wagons were empty except for a few staples.

Before they could see the buildings of town, Zandinar pulled his horse to a stop. The blond warrior turned to the rest of the party. "I don't think we should go through Blasseldune. Gorth has agents there, and these uniforms will bring a lot of questions."

"We could cut between fields," said Gant indicating a set of wagon tracks that turned north off the road and ran between cultivated fields toward a distant tree line. "Somewhere up that way we can strike out through the woods and join the Devonshield Road north of Blasseldune."

Zandinar turned his horse onto the wagon track and the group followed. They passed endless rows of well-tended vegetables and an occasional farmhouse set back from the dirt wagon trace. Here and there stands of trees served as windbreaks or woodlots. Slowly they worked their way northwest, circumnavigating Blasseldune.

Eventually, they passed the last farmhouse. The wagon trace ended and they entered the forest. Tall trees arched overhead blocking out the low sun. The party closed ranks and slowed to let the horses pick their way over tangled roots.

Gant guided them toward the last faint rays of the dying sun. He wanted to reach the Devonshield Road before nightfall. In the growing twilight, his peripheral vision caught a shadowy movement slipping from tree to tree. But when he looked in that direction there was nothing there.

"Stop," said Gant, pulling his horse to a halt. "Someone's out there," he said pointing in the direction he'd seen movement.

The column halted, all eyes focused on the woods. The forest remained still and unmoving. The fading sunlight cast thick shadows and only the faintest rays of light filtered to the forest floor. They waited a minute. Still nothing. Gant kicked his horse and galloped to the spot where he thought he'd seen the shadow. There was nothing except a twisted, man-sized stump of a long dead tree. He wheeled his horse around.

"Nothing there," he said rejoining the party and starting forward again.

"It would do well to keep a sharp lookout," noted Zandinar.

As the sun set, the group came out on the road to Devonshield. Immediately, Gant turned north up the wheel-scarred trace.

Blasseldune was somewhere to the south, too far away even to see the lights.

"Master Gant," whispered Captain Hesh. "Wouldn't it be best if we camped here rather than travel in the dark?"

"Yes," added the aged Kalmine. "And the Emp -- I mean Pris is a bit tired and needs rest."

Gant stopped, looked at the sagging youth, and contemplated the dark expanse of road winding ahead in the blackness. "You're right. Let's move back into the trees far enough so as not to be seen."

Eagerly the party pushed into the forest and set up a hasty camp. They built a small fire carefully shielded from the road. Again Gant stood first watch with Krist. The night huddled black and quiet outside the little circle of firelight. Gant had an uneasy feeling that they were being watched. Now and then, he thought he heard a stick crack, but the cheery fire masked the noises from the forest. Occasionally, he caught a glimpse of something moving just outside the limit of his vision.

Eventually he woke Zandinar. "Your watch," he said. "There's something not right about the woods tonight. I hear noises and think I see something, but there's never anything there."

"Nerves," said Zandinar flatly. "Get some sleep."

Gant nodded and slipped into his blankets but sleep took a while coming as he imagined all sorts of terrors lurking around their camp. Finally, with a stern effort he forced himself to think of Dalphnia, about her warmth and the peace he'd felt near her. He fell asleep.

Zandinar woke Captain Hesh and Faltern for the final watch. While the rest slept, the Captain and Faltern sat comfortably around the fire and nodded off to sleep. The fire burned down to coals. The absolute blackness before dawn stole over the camp hiding the growing band of shadowy figures watching from cover. With the darkness, the intruders moved stealthily into the camp. Quietly they surrounded each slumbering figure with a bristling wall of spears. At a nod from their leader they prodded the sleepers with razor-sharp spearheads.

Gant came fully awake. Valorius leaped into his groping fingers. The steel tipped spear nudged his unprotected neck and he glared up into half dozen sets of cold, dark eyes.

"No one move, or you'll all die," barked the leader from beside the fire pit.

Gant saw that everyone was surrounded. Even if he escaped, the others would pay the price. He fought to control his burning rage, forced himself to remain motionless.

Chapter 33

In Pogor, Barlon Gorth wrestled with the everyday problems of wielding power. His "people" were uneasy, merchants demanded justice for breached contracts, thieves stole, and new conscripts turned up daily seeking to join his ever-swelling army. Success bred success. He hated dealing with mundane problems preferring to strut along the battlements viewing his city, reminding himself how masterful he was. He loved power and wanted more.

But Barlon knew that power could just as easily be lost. So even on his best days he felt a sense of dread. He was wary of a populace unenthusiastic about his rule. He never left the castle grounds and all the castle servants were trusted staff who came with him from the Mountain Castle. He did not permit locals inside unless they were heavily guarded. He worried about revolt and with these thoughts in mind he had sent for Shalmuthe, Sir Jarlz and General Eckert.

The scarred master spy relaxed in his customary chair in the tower chamber facing the others.

"These people are more interested in their profit than who runs the city. There are few left who would openly oppose you. Some thought of stirring up resistance, but we've ferreted them out and their heads line the streets," reported the spy.

"Then any that remain have gone underground," said General Eckert.

"Yes, and my men are after them."

"Good," said Barlon nodding his approval. "Never let up. There are too many ignorant peasants who know nothing of justice. Do whatever you have to and get rid of anyone who opposes us."

"Don't worry." The look in Shalmuthe's eyes signaled that the peasants were the ones who should beware.

Barlon smiled, stood, and paced a few steps toward the window. Turning, he asked, "Are the plans complete for taking Blasseldune?"

General Ecker nodded, half-heartedly. "Yes, we are ready. A poorly defended city is an easy mark, but shouldn't we consolidate our power here before extending our forces to the east?"

"General Ecker, you surprise me. Don't you want a larger kingdom?"

"I've had little enough time to enjoy the kingdom I already have. It won't be long before I'm too old to enjoy anything."

After a moment's silence the gray haired warrior added, "There's too much trouble here to start another campaign. You say it's about finished, but what about the underground here in Pogor? What about Daggon?"

Barlon's smile widened. "Yes, what about Daggon?" He turned to look at Shalmuthe. "Have you invited the king here?"

"Yes, he will arrive day after tomorrow."

"You see, General, there are no problems here. The Farmer King is a fool. I've sent Varg and Lom's knights to 'escort' the good king to Pogor. A pity I can't be there to see it. Soon his head will adorn my palace. He is the last. After he's dead, I've repaid the treachery of the Western Kings."

Barlon finished his walk to the window. He gazed out, hands together behind his back. For a few minutes, the room was silent.

Finally, Sir Jarlz spoke. "Sir, do you trust the Scaltzland Priests?"

Barlon whirled. "Not in the least, and Shalmuthe has a plan for them, too, though we won't discuss it here. Yes, things are going perfectly. Superior men attract power. The rest remain peasants where they belong."

"Is that all, my lord?" asked Shalmuthe, rising from his chair.

"Yes, of course, you've better things to do."

As Shalmuthe left, General Ecker and Sir Jarlz rose. With a nod from Barlon, they too left. As soon as they were gone, Barlon yelled for the guard. A stern-faced young soldier entered.

"Have the kitchen send up a bottle of wine," ordered Barlon. "And be quick about it."

The guard disappeared and Barlon slumped into a chair, throwing his feet up onto the table.

Barlon closed his eyes and dozed. He snapped awake at the sound of the door opening. A girl dressed in the coarse garb of the kitchen servants stepped timidly into the room carrying a tray with two bottles of wine and several cut crystal goblets. Her face was an ugly mass of scar tissue. She set the tray lightly on the table before Barlon and stepped back with a hint of a bow, her eyes on the floor.

"Wait," said Barlon, before she could leave. "Come here," and he motioned her back.

Obediently she took a step toward him. His eyes ran up and down her body, a hunger there that seldom colored Barlon's face.

"Do you like your new king?" he asked, his voice husky with desire.

"Yes, m'Lord," she said without emotion.

"Then you'll wish to stay with him."

She looked up, revulsion in her eyes that she covered before Barlon noticed.

"The kitchen master said I was to come right back."

"So, I'm the king."

"Yes, m'Lord, but I'm sure there are nicer women than I."

Barlon poured a goblet of wine and drank deeply, draining the glass in one mouthful. His eyes cleared and he looked up again at the frail girl with her horrible face. Barlon laughed, throwing his head back, and then poured another glass of the deep red wine.

"Yes," he said finally. "There are more beautiful women than you. Back to the kitchen." He drained the glass a second time.

The serving girl curtsied, retrieved her tray and slipped out into the hall. She passed several guards on her way to the narrow stairwell. As soon as she'd gone down the first few stairs, Amelia slumped against the sandstone wall, the tray dangling from her hand. She wasn't cut out for this. She liked open air, freedom, not secret, covert spying within constricting castle walls. She took a few deep breaths and let her heart slow.

Heavy footsteps sounded on the winding staircase and immediately she was up, moving down the stairs. She hoped it was not Varg. She'd seen the monstrous demon more than once. So far she had always managed to keep her distance. His insatiable lust for blood and death gave her chills.

She rounded the curvature of the staircase and almost dropped her tray. Sir Jarlz, long-time friend of her grandfather, plodded steadily up the steps, his head hung down. He wore the exoskeletal purple armor of Barlon's knights.

For an instant, Amelia panicked. She started to turn, thought of running back up the stairs. That wouldn't help. She'd only be running to Barlon's guards. Worse, she'd be drawing attention to herself. Steeling her screaming nerves, she went down; step-by-step nearer to being exposed. She glared down at the worn stone steps hoping to make her face invisible, hoping the wax scars on her face would hide her identity.

Nearer, they drew, and finally, as they passed, she couldn't help glancing up to catch a look at his face. The wax scar tissue worked. There was no recognition. Sir Jarlz' eyes stared straight ahead, lifeless, covered by a shadow. And in that instant, Amelia saw the thick medallion around his neck. Magic, she thought. That medallion is a mind trap. Somehow she had to get the medallion off of him.

She hurried back to the kitchen and sped through the endless list of chores. She cleaned, she scrubbed, she made countless deliveries of food, wine, cheese, whatever the nobles wanted. No one came down for their meals anymore and Amelia ran endlessly, hoping for a delivery to Sir Jarlz.

Finally, she got an order for a tray of cheese, bread and ale for Sir Jarlz. The head cook told her which room was his and she hurried off. Fear sent her pulse racing. Somehow she had to get the amulet from Sir Jarlz.

She knocked lightly on his door. No answer. She slipped inside and looked around. No one was there. She placed the tray on the small table and left.

Back in the kitchen she went to the cook. "I went to the room you told me, but Sir Jarlz was not there. I left the tray. Are you sure that was his room?"

"Yes," said the cook busy with other preparations. "Sir Jarlz is seldom in his room at the evening meal but we have orders to leave food anyway. Now, get this plate of beef to the barracks."

Amelia took the platter and hustled along. She worked long into the night as she'd done every night as serving wench. While she made her deliveries, she worked on a plan to free Sir Jarlz from the medallion. Finally the nobles began to go to sleep, the castle quieted and the cook told her to go to bed. Making sure no one was looking, she took a small block of cheese, a bit of bread and a tray, and ducked out into the hall.

Quickly she sped to the nobles' wing, carrying the tray. She passed two guards at the entrance to the nobles' hallway. Neither bothered to ask the pathetic serving girl where she was going. She skipped up the steps to the second floor, nearly tripping over the drunken form of one of the Brigade Captains asleep on the stairs.

She rounded the top of the stairs, turned right, and entered a long, dimly lit hallway. In a moment she was at Sir Jarlz' room. Delicately she tapped on the door, hoping the knight was asleep. No answer.

She reached for the catch when a voice behind her growled, "You there, what're you doing?"

She froze. Slowly, she turned and stared up into a pair of battle-hardened eyes. The man was huge, dressed in the uniform of the castle guard. His sword was out and ready.

"I-I'm to bring a bit of food to Sir Jarlz," she said fighting to hold her tray steady.

"He's been asleep for hours. Take it back." He waved her away with his sword point.

"I can't do that. The cook'll have my hide if I don't make the delivery."

"Then eat it yourself. You look like you could use it."

Again he waved her away.

"But what if Sir Jarlz awakens and finds his snack missing? Then I'll be in worse trouble. Let me put the tray in his room. It'll only take a moment."

The guard hesitated. His sword point sagged. "Okay, just be quick about it."

Silently, she opened the door just enough to slip into the room. Sir Jarlz lay on his back, his thickly muscled chest bare above his breeches. The heavy amulet hung off one side of his chest like a mountain climber scaling his side. The bread and cheese she'd brought earlier was almost gone. She put the second tray of bread and cheese on the table beside the first.

She noticed the ale had disappeared and hoped that deepened the knight's slumber. Hurrying, she slipped the medallion up over his head so only the chain under the back of his head kept her from taking it. Gently she pulled on the chain, steadily increasing the force until the chain slid between his hair and the pillow. He mumbled in his sleep and rolled to one side. The medallion came free.

She froze, holding her breath. Sir Jarlz' eyes never flickered.

Running lightly on the balls of her feet to the door, she stuffed the medallion up under her sack-like dress so it caught in the belt she wore underneath. Now, slowing, she snuck out the door. The guard was at his post at the end of the hall near the stairs. She felt the amulet swing with each step, like a pendulum. She kept her strides small, hoping to avoid having the amulet raise a bulge in her dress.

The guard glared at her, but said nothing as she reached the stairwell. She hurried down through the dark, back to the room that had been hers when Fasoom was king. No one used the rooms in the older hall and her things remained untouched. She hid the medallion, and then, exhausted, lay down to sleep. In the morning she would fly with the medallion to the forest in the foothills and hide it in an abandoned eagle's nest.

#

The sun flowed in through the slit windows on the second floor of the nobles' wing. Sir Jarlz woke feeling fresh, revitalized, like a heavy weight had been lifted from his shoulders. He swung his feet to the floor and looked at the evil purple armor against the wall. A flood of memories washed over him, memories of Netherdorf Castle, of dead friends, of Uric hauled away, of battle against the Western Kings and through it all, his sword killing people he knew.

"How? Am I mad?" he grumbled. He got up, kicked the armor and watched it tumble over. "Why would I wear that cursed armor?" he asked but got no answer. He looked around for a clue, his hands trembling. "I've killed them!" He slammed his fist into the purple breastplate. "Killed them all, gone crazy listening to Barlon Gorth," he screamed. He kicked the armor again.

Hot tears blurred his vision. With one swipe, he slung the food off the table. Spinning, he lashed out in every direction, swinging wildly, smashing the stools, overturning the table. And then, when there was nothing left to hit, he fell on the bed and cried bitter tears that did nothing to wash away the horrible guilt.

When he could neither cry nor rage anymore, he got up, pulled on his traveling shirt and went out. He walked like a man in a trance, stumbling blindly out of the castle to the first inn he found. There he sat and drank until afternoon. When he fell from his stool, the innkeeper had him dragged outside and laid under a parked hay wagon to sleep it off.

Chapter 34

The afternoon sun brightened the topmost tower chamber. Barlon Gorth slept in one of the chairs, a spilled wine goblet on the floor beside him. Empty wine bottles stood like soldiers at attention in staggered rows across the tabletop. Barlon's alcoholic stupor persisted despite the bright daylight. At the door to his back, two knights stood stiffly at attention in purple armor. They both stared ahead, their pure white eyes seemingly blind. Wendler was one of them. Barlon had paid them no attention all day.

Unnoticed by the unconscious Mountain Lord, a pinpoint of blackness formed in the shadows in the far corner of the room. Slowly it grew until it was a pulsating sphere of darkness that filled the entire corner. And then Varg stepped out of the void, a brown leather sack clutched in one massive claw. He looked over at the sleeping figure. Smiling, he set the sack on the table and slowly unfolded the stained leather to reveal the bloody head of the Farmer King, the last of the Western Kings.

"Your enemies are dead," he whispered to deaf ears.

He went to Barlon and deftly slipped the medallion from his neck without waking him. In his eagerness Varg let the chain rub against the man's ears, but it didn't register on Barlon's numbed senses. Triumphantly, Varg placed the medallion around his own neck. Immediately, the gold threads in the medallion released their hold on the demon's likeness that was in the middle. As the medallion loosened its grip on the molded image, the miniature's eyes went completely dull while Varg's eyes shown brighter than ever.

"Barlon," he roared, his voice thundering through the stillness.

Barlon snapped awake. His bloodshot eyes focused on the creature before him.

"How did you get in here?" he demanded. "Guards!"

The two Knights of Habichon stood unmoving, their white eyes unblinking.

"They are with me," hissed Varg. "The armor has converted their souls to my cause."

"But how did you get in here? My men outside the door were told not to let anyone enter."

"I came a different way."

"Magic? I didn't know you knew such tricks."

"There are many things you'll never know." The Demon-Prince's voice dripped with contempt. "I know a little magic, though I'd never qualify as a wizard. My strength, my power, my invulnerability make all that unnecessary. I have brought you your enemy's head." He pointed to the bulging-eyed, bloody head resting on the table. "Now, you promised my freedom."

Barlon glanced back at the monster. "Not yet. Not until the Priests of Scaltzland are humbled before me."

"It is as I thought." Varg touched the medallion now hanging on his chest.

Barlon's eyes widened as he clutched his own bare chest in despair. He started to scream, tried to turn the ring on his left hand, but faster than he could have imagined, one clawed hand clamped around his throat stifling his sound to a choking gasp.

"But we had a bargain," rasped Barlon through a half-crushed windpipe. "You can't break a bargain."

"My part is done."

Varg squeezed and his hand crushed tighter than a vise. The pressure built in the squashing arteries and veins of Barlon's neck until his head popped off like a thumb-shot grape. His dead eyes reflected the same terror that was still visible in King Daggon's head. Hot blood pumped in waves over the chair onto the floor. Varg released his grip and Gorth's body collapsed to the floor.

Varg went to the window and pulled the thick curtain over it to shut off the sunlight. Then he went to the growing pool of crimson and dipped one claw into the warm blood. Slowly, meticulously, he drew a large circle on the floor in the darkest corner. After the circle was complete, he filled in around it with a multitude of symbols, runes and signs of power, re-dipping the claw regularly, until the circle was finished and surrounded by runes. He sprinkled a few drops of blood in the center and began a dark, evil chant. Blackness grew in the center of the circle, swelling to fill the area inside until an arched portal opened forming a doorway into a foul landscape. Visible through the blackness was the fiery nether planes of Varg's home. The land seen through the portal was cracked and barren, tortured beyond recognition. Flames shot skyward, if there was a sky. The land burst open in a crazy spurt of molten lava and clouds of inky smoke obscured the landscape.

The Demon-Prince waited a few moments. There was a flapping of great leathery wings and through the opening shot a large, bat-like creature with a twisted, skull face. It landed on strong hind legs that resembled a man's yet ended in a goat's hooves.

"Lord Master, you have freed us."

"Yes, Grapus, fetch my army. Guide them to the bridge and lead them through."

The great winged monstrosity spread its wings and dived back into the blackness. It soon disappeared across the broken landscape.

Chapter 35

Amelia woke later than she'd planned. The sun was already well above the horizon. Quickly she recited the spell for changing and became a great eagle. She tested her wings, and with Sir Jarlz' medallion clutched tightly in one talon, she flew through the window out across the bustling city of Pogor. As fast as she could, she headed east for the Monolith Mountains.

The sky was clear, with only occasional high white puffs of cotton, and she made good time. The sun had not reached midday when she glided in to land in the massive jumble of sticks that formed an abandoned eagle's aerie atop a mighty redwood. She rested only a moment after hiding the medallion deep in the nesting material, and then soared back into the sky.

She was already late for her duties in the kitchen, and knew the cook would be furious. She sped on trying to think of a suitable excuse to blunt the cook's wrath. Another day or two and she'd have to leave anyway to report to her grandfather. After which she wouldn't be able to return.

The plains passed swiftly below, and soon she glided over the sprawling outskirts of Pogor. If she'd been watching, instead of thinking, she would have noticed the masses of people racing from the city, or, as she neared the castle, she might have seen several black creatures flying around the tower.

She started her final glide toward her window, when a huge, dark shadow fell across her. She turned her head to see what was coming. Too late. She only caught a glimpse of the fanged skull before a talon ripped into her right wing, bowling her over in midair.

She fell, curled in a fetal position, trailing a plume of feathers, a ball of broken, flightless pain. The black creature flapped wildly to a halt and hovered, trying to follow her crash. However the trail of feathers obscured Amelia's plummet, and the nightmarish monster didn't see her plop into the mound of hay in the wagon. It merely turned and flapped noisily back to join the others circling the tower.

#

Razgoth stood in his room, lost in thought. Perhaps things would work out all right after all. The people of Pogor seemed willing to accept Gorth's rule, Varg had been docile enough, and if Razgoth got enough time to study, maybe the demon could be re-exiled.

A vast black shadow sailed across Razgoth's window, interrupting his thoughts. What was that? And then the monstrous flying demon circled past the wizard's window. Razgoth knew what it was. Fear trickled across his gray eyes. Something had gone wrong.

Immediately the mage was out of his room and into the hall. His first thought was to get to the tower room and find out what was happening. On the stairs above him he heard heavy, hooved feet stomping downward. Without thinking, Razgoth recited the teleportation spell he knew so well and his body vanished, only to reappear in the top tower room.

With a tiny burst of light, Razgoth materialized in Barlon's tower sanctuary. His eyes swept over the carnage. King Daggon's head remained on the table near where Barlon's headless body had fallen. A great pulsating blackness filled the air within a magic circle drawn in blood on the floor and through it stepped nameless, horrible things. Varg stood before the gaping portal and accepted each of his minions' sworn fidelity as they entered the world of man. A massive hole had been blown outward through the thick walls of the tower. Through it, flying things launched and landed. Several other black humanoid monsters stood around Varg.

All this Razgoth took in in a split second. He knew the danger and prepared to teleport back to the Mountain Castle, where he'd be safe, at least temporarily. Before he could begin his incantation, a stubby, barrel-like thing scuttled at him from behind and ripped into the wizard's right leg with sharp claws.

Razgoth screamed, that spell forgotten. In his anger he automatically went on the offensive. A quick word and gesture and flames leaped from his fingertips burning the stumpy creature. The beast collapsed, a charred lump.

Varg looked up at this intrusion.

"Kill him," rasped the Demon-Prince, and motioned to two towering, four-armed guardians at his side.

Razgoth fired a blast of blue-white electricity at the nearest creature. It shriveled before the sizzling bolt and fell dead at the wizard's feet. Without pausing, Razgoth unleashed another bolt that forked and slammed into the pair of assassins moving toward him.

To Razgoth's surprise, the two beasts fought frantically with their four hideous arms to deflect the bolt. Most of the magic dissipated without visible effect. Immediately Razgoth fired another bolt.

Before he had time to gauge the effect of his second blast, a heavy blow landed on the base of his skull. The room spun. His knees buckled and he fell. Desperately Razgoth fought to remain conscious. By sheer will power, he managed to ward off the growing curtain of blackness.

Instinctively, he rolled aside, dodging for the moment the growing numbers of pursuers. His head ached fiercely. He couldn't concentrate. All around him, claws flashed, reaching to carve up his flesh. His spells were a jumble inside his brain. One mistake and he'd kill himself with a failed spell. He must think clearly or die.

Just when it seemed he could not escape, his mind grasp the only spell it seemed capable of remembering. It was a quick, simple distance translation that could take him outside the castle. He snapped off the verse and the simple finger motions, and just as the talons came down to rend him, he was gone.

For a moment, Razgoth lay on the cobblestone street where he appeared. He knew it wasn't safe and with supreme effort, he dragged his battered body to a hiding place beneath some trash piled haphazardly against a nearby building.

Chapter 36

Abadis wrinkled his nose at the disgusting mixture of mashed vegetables, gravy and beef that was supposed to pass for stew. He bit into the dried bread crust and considered his miserable existence. Naked, locked in a damp cell. He remembered the dogs, remembered the jailor, but he could not remember how he got there in the first place.

He pushed the bread around in the goo, let it soften, and then ate the dripping chunk. Lousy, he thought. Now and then glimpses of his life whisked through his mind only to slip away like the mist that disappears before the morning sun.

He had sopped up about half the gravy when he heard the keys clink in the lock at the end of the corridor. The hallway door opened and the squat jailer and his two brutish mastiffs entered.

The jailor peered in through Abadis' cell bars and grunted. "Not done yet?"

Abadis stared back blankly.

"Too bad. Give me the dish. I ain't comin' back down here tonight."

Tonight? Days and nights were passing without a clue. How long had he been locked up?

"How long have I been here?" Abadis asked, only half expecting an answer.

"What d'you care? You and the dragon ain't goin' nowhere 'til His Majesty returns."

Abadis slid the metal dish under the door. Dragon! Lost memories rushed back. Uric. Yes, that was why he'd come here.

Uric was trapped here and Abadis had come to free him. Suddenly Abadis was filled with dread. What a fool he had been, overlooking the possibility that there would be guard dogs whose sense of smell would not be fooled by a simple invisibility spell. How long had he been a prisoner? How long had Barlon been free to make war unchecked? Worse, would Gant still be waiting for him at Sylvia's?

By now the jailor had retrieved the dish, checked Abadis' water bucket and left. Abadis stared out into the hall and noticed his robes and undergarments heaped in a pile outside the cell. He needed what was in that robe.

Several spells came to mind that required things in the pockets of his robes. But first he had to get out of the cell. Without his robe spells couldn't be anything complex. He strained his memory, back to his earliest days as an apprentice. Yes, there were spells requiring little or nothing except a word and a gesture, but he needed something to get him out of the cell, not something to make a stone laugh, or silence a fly's buzzing.

He sorted through the seldom-used beginner's spells one by one. Finally he came to one that had promise. Searching the cell for but a moment yielded the pinch of dust required. Then carefully, straining to remember each word exactly correct, each gesture, he recited the spell.

It was a distance translation, good for traveling a few yards. He only needed to move a few feet. He recited the spell and his body dispersed into energy, slipped through the iron bars and reformed outside.

Abadis checked his hands and feet, his bony legs, his scrawny arms. He was all there and functioning. By the gods, he thought. I'm lucky I remembered it right. He dressed quickly. Several of his pockets had emptied their contents onto the floor. He carefully returned everything to their correct locations.

Picking up a small mirror, he paused, gazing at his reflection. "Damn," he muttered, grasping his left ear where the ear lobe should have been. "I didn't quite get it exact after all."

Having no time to consider the consequences, Abadis secured the proper powders and dusts and stepped over in front of Uric. "I'll have you out of there soon," he whispered.

And then Abadis began the complex spell to release Uric. After nearly half an hour of exact recitation and complex motions with fingers, hands and arms, Abadis produced a globe of golden energy that hovered between him and the gigantic dragon's head.

A wave of his hands sent the globe gently drifting into the sphere surrounding Uric. Energies clashed. The golden sphere nibbled away at the magic globe that held Uric trapped, like ants stripping a carcass. As Abadis' sphere moved slowly forward engulfing the dragon, the giant reptile's eyes cleared, then his forelimbs twitched and flexed, and finally the tip of his tail returned to life.

Uric took a deep breath, blinked and stepped cautiously into the room, his massive body crammed into the tight quarters.

"Abadis, what are you doing here? Where is everyone?" asked Uric, looking around the room, a puzzled expression on his face. "Where are we?"

"Barlon's Mountain Castle. You were caught in a time trap, and I've been stuck in prison. Barlon's called forth Varg and who knows what else by now."

Uric's body began to shimmer and twist, shrinking and distorting until within a moment, the amethyst robed sage stood in its place.

"How do you do that?" asked Abadis. "It's a spell I'd like to know."

"It is no spell," said Uric. "Dragons have some magic that is innate in our nature. Changing shapes is one. But if Varg has been recalled then we've already lost too much time. We need to be on our way."

"To my place," said Abadis.

They linked hands and Abadis cast the spell for travel. Instantly they disappeared from Barlon's dungeon, traveled down the magical corridor in a plane were distance did not exist and reappeared in Abadis' home.

"Wait a minute, I'm overdue on a pickup."

Again Abadis completed the spell and was gone. Moments later he returned, a frown crinkling his face and accentuating the wrinkles.

"Something wrong?" asked Uric as soon as Abadis reappeared.

"Yes. Gant left Sylvia's several days ago, bound here. He and Zandinar should be here by now."

"Zandinar?"

"Yes, do you know him? I've seen him a few times over the years, sometimes years apart, and he never seems to age. He's always seeking his destiny."

"I know something of him," said Uric, a far-away look in his eyes, "but I wonder what part he will play in this." He refocused on Abadis. "What were they doing at Sylvia's?"

"It's a long story. They were supposed to wait there for me. For some reason they didn't, and worse, they left in the company of the emperor and a handful of his guards. We'll have to find them. If the emperor is captured by Barlon's agents it will not be good."

Uric held up a confused hand, shaking his head. "Before we run off, I think you'd better tell me what has happened while I was trapped."

"You're right." Abadis related all that he knew while Uric listened silently.

"The world is changing rapidly," said Uric. "I think we should hurry to Blasseldune and see if our young friends made it that far."

"Agreed," said Abadis. "Unfortunately, I don't know anyplace there well enough to take us by spell."

"I do," said Uric and this time it was the dragon that voiced the words for the spell and transferred them to Blasseldune.

#

Bitterly disappointed, Abadis and Uric returned to the wizard's house. Despite the picturesque setting, gloom settled in. After discreetly questioning every trustworthy man either of them knew in Blasseldune, the only possible conclusion they could come up with was that Gant had never reached the city.

"They must have been attacked on the road," suggested Uric, now seated stiff-backed on a stool.

"Attacked maybe, but not stopped. Who could defeat Gant in his armor? No brigands that I know."

"Not brigands, but what of magic? Even Razgoth, who is far from a master, trapped me. And what of the Dark Elves? Both the miller and two of the fur traders said they'd seen several of them in Blasseldune. Are they in league with their old master, Varg?"

Abadis scratched his beard. "I cannot believe the elves would join Varg. Sarona fears Varg as much as any. And she more than anyone would realize Gant's value as Bartholomew's heir."

Uric considered that and then said, "Too bad her mother didn't live a bit longer. Perhaps we should visit the elves. Sarona may have a hand in this, and if she doesn't already, she should. Her armies will be needed, since it looks unlikely that men will align to stop Gorth."

"Yes, Sarona and the Dark Elves are an important force. Let's not waste time. Do you know a spot well enough to transfer to? I used to but I haven't been there in a long time and probably wouldn't get it right."

"No, the closest I can go is Netherdorf, and I don't really want to go there. We'll have to fly."

Without waiting, Uric was out in the yard, his body shimmering and twisting, changing into his massive reptilian self. Without a word, Abadis climbed on his back. The wizard settled into a comfortable spot between the multiple ridges of golden scales and hung on. With a rush of wind, Uric was airborne and they were on their way to the Caverns of Darkness, home of the Dark Elves.

#

Gant sat up and returned Valorius to her scabbard. Despite the spear at his throat, he felt no fear for himself. It was the others who were vulnerable. Gant rubbed his eyes with the backs of his knuckles and studied his captors. Even in the faint glow from the fire's coals, he knew they were a Dark Elf patrol. Their slit eyes, swept-back pointed ears and slender, shorter stature were unmistakable.

Zandinar, Pris and the others scrambled to their feet, cautious of the spear points bristling around them. Gant got slowly to his feet, scrutinizing the leader who was taller than the others, though barely to Gant's shoulder. His hands were large, the left one missing the two smaller fingers. His nose had been broken and was twisted off-center to the right. He held a scaled-to-size broadsword in his right hand. It was the only sword among them. Unlike the other elves, Gant caught the occasional glint from a black breastplate on the leader's chest. He continually scanned Gant's party, surveying the entire camp.

"What do you want?" asked Gant, once he was on his feet.

"I'll ask the questions," snapped the leader. Gant waited and the leader went on. "Are you Gant of the Ironlimbs?"

"Yes."

"Then you will go with us." The leader motioned to his men who prodded them toward the forest.

Gant balked. "Where are you taking us?"

"It's not yours to ask."

Zandinar stepped next to Gant. "We're not going anywhere until we know what this is about."

Gant glared at the elf leader, their eyes locked. Captain Hesh and the three guardsmen encircled Pris defensively.

"You'll kill a few of us but Gant and I will kill your whole party. Why risk it?" asked Zandinar.

The elves inched forward with their spears only to have the elf leader motion them back. "You are right," he said. "There is no need for violence. I am Forest Lord Barkmar. Queen Sarona sent word to all patrols to find Gant and bring him to the Caverns of Darkness. Rumors of war in the West trouble her. She seeks counsel with Bartholomew's descendant."

The tension eased on both sides and the spear points inched lower.

"Then why the show of force?" asked Gant.

"Gorth's men are everywhere. We weren't sure who you were," answered Barkmar. "We should be moving." He motioned toward the forest.

"In the dark?" asked Pris. "Through the woods?"

"Yes," said Barkmar sternly. "The daylight is not far away and Gorth's agents comb the woods by day looking for refugees from Netherdorf. There is an elf trail only a little way ahead. We must be off. We've wasted too much time already."

"We are going to Abadis' house first, aren't we?" suggested Kalmine from his position beside Pris.

"There's no time," said Barkmar. "It's too far north."

Before Gant could disagree Zandinar said, "It won't matter. Abadis has missed our rendezvous already. He's better equipped to find us than we are him."

"You'll have to leave the horses," said the Elf Lord as several of the men started to load their bedrolls onto the animals. "Where we're going the forest is too thick for them."

"What will happen to them?" asked Pris.

"Don't worry," said the elf, "they'll be found soon and as valuable as a good horse is, they aren't likely to be mistreated."

Without further discourse the party started off through the woods. The elves set a lopping pace that was easy for them to maintain but was too fast for the men. Soon the party slowed to a moderate walk. Still, the miles dropped behind them and by sunrise they'd left the road to Devonshield far behind.

All morning they moved along a trail so ill defined that often Gant wasn't sure they were on a path. The massive trees slowly thinned to scrawny, low bushes and the soil turned rocky. Before long they were on a graded gravel trail through the rugged foothills of the Misery Mountains.

The afternoon sun beat down and Gant found himself drinking frequently from his water skin. Pris was having his troubles. His thin, boyish legs weren't used to heavy exertion and he sagged under the burning sun. There were no clouds to block the blazing heat and before long they were stopping frequently to rest and let Pris' tired muscles recover.

Shortly after one of these rest stops, as they marched down the gravel trail, a flurry of arrows rained down on them. The elf to Gant's left went down with an arrow in his thigh. Another elf was hit in the chest and fell.

Before anyone could react, a second flight of arrows whistled in from the other side of the road. Three more elves were hit. Gant's armor shed one of the feathered shafts as if it was nothing more than a bothersome insect. Zandinar's armor turned aside more.

"They're in the rocks on both sides of the road," yelled Zandinar.

The elves dove for cover. A third volley of arrows clanked harmlessly on stone. With a cry, Zandinar charged the rocks above the trail to the left. Gant took the cue, dropped his visor and rushed the attackers hiding in the rocky cover to the right.

Arrows glanced harmlessly from their armor and quickly the two of them were amongst the assassins.

The instant Gant reached the rocks, a bullish warrior leaped out from behind a large boulder, an axe held overhead. Before the man could bring down the axe Valorius flashed once and severed the man's arm. Gant reversed his swing and cut into the man's guts. He fell dead. Gant whirled to meet a second brigand rushing at him. A short parry moved the man's sword aside and Gant cut him down like a scythe fells wheat. Across the road, Zandinar slashed away with his massive sword and brought down another man.

Now, Barkmar charged the men on Gant's side of the road. Captain Hesh, Krist, Patt and Faltern dashed to help Zandinar. Pris leaped to his feet, but was pulled down by the ever-present Kalmine.

Bows were forgotten and steel rang on steel. The brigands not engaged immediately broke and ran. At this, the elves rose from cover with their spears ready. As the each fleeing man became visible between the rocks, spears flew unerringly. Most fell where hit. A few struggled on. Some of those were stopped by other spears. Few escaped. Within moments it was over.

"Who were they?" asked Pris, wide-eyed, once the combatants had rejoined him on the road.

"I remember one of them from Blasseldune," spat Zandinar. "He was one of those spreading stories of treason about Gant. Undoubtedly Gorth's men."

Barkmar returned to the road, a look of awe replacing his usual stern expression. "Fought like a true Champion," he said, admiring Valorius.

"Yeah," mumbled Gant, not comfortable thinking of his victory at Devonshield. It still bothered him that he'd had to kill to win.

"We should be going," Kalmine reminded them, and set off down the road, pushing Pris ahead of him.

The elves regained their spears and soon the entire party was moving along the road again. Shortly after they'd resumed their march, Pris worked his way alongside Gant.

"You certainly can fight," he said. "I think you and Zandinar could defeat an army single-handedly."

Gant glanced at the young emperor. He saw the heroic dreams in Pris' eyes. "I'm not so sure about that. We're well trained and have the best weapons, but even we wear down."

"I'll bet Gorth has no chance," continued Pris undaunted. "You are invincible."

Zandinar stepped beside them. "No man is invincible," he said sadly.

"Will you teach me to fight?" asked the emperor glancing from one to the other.

"We'll see," said Gant and clapped him on the back. "Maybe when there's time. Now save your strength for walking."

They continued walking along the graded, rocky trail the rest of the day stopping frequently in the shade of large boulders or rock outcroppings. By late afternoon they began encountering elf patrols from the Caverns of Darkness. These hurried off after exchanging information with Lord Barkmar.

Whatever news he got Barkmar kept to himself. He pushed ahead with renewed vigor testing the limits of Pris' endurance. Gant was proud to see that the emperor went on without complaint.

Even when the sun dropped below the horizon, they continued. At one point Kalmine insisted they make camp, saying Pris could go no farther. But Barkmar overruled the old man, promising Pris a bed when they reached the elves' stronghold. Still Barkmar gave no reason for the haste. Gant suspected something bad had happened or was about to.

Just after midnight, Gant saw the huge, black opening of a mammoth cave. There were no lights, no visible guards, no gates, drawbridges or portcullises, but Gant knew he was about to enter the Caverns of Darkness.

#

The woodland nymph Dalphnia raced effortlessly through the woods alongside the road. She had been to Malathon but no one had seen Gant. She'd wasted more time there than she'd meant to and finally gave up and left the city. Once in the forest her magical empathy with the trees let her communicate with them through a primitive telepathy. So she'd questioned the trees. While they weren't very good at distinguishing one man from another, they knew magic. And yes, they'd felt the passage of not one, but two men carrying swords of great power, traveling with several others. And they had ridden toward Blasseldune not long ago, although she knew "not long ago" to a tree might be a day, a month or anything in between. Trees just didn't keep track of dates.

She headed for Blasseldune, running tirelessly through the woods, faster than the swiftest horse. The miles fell away. All around the trees whispered to her about the animals nearby, about what was ahead and to the sides. Trees were enchanted by her presence no matter where she went. Even in the dark she felt safe.

She wasn't far from Blasseldune when the trees brought a different message, of men camped beside the road, several of them, with a campfire (trees always took note of fires) and horses tied nearby.

Gant, thought Dalphnia, and in her excitement, she rushed headlong into the camp without asking the trees if these men carried swords of power. She stopped in the dim circle of light from the dwindling campfire, having run so swiftly and silently she'd passed the lone sentry without an alarm. One look around and she realized her mistake.

There were six large, bushy bearded, armed men cast around the fire like sticks dropped by high winds. Before she could duck back into the forest, the guard shouted a warning. Several of them leaped to their feet, coming immediately to a half-crouch, swords drawn. They had her surrounded.

"What 'ave we got here?" roared the largest one, brandishing his sword.

"Looks like just what we was lookin' for," said another, and lunged at her, his thick fingers eagerly grasping for her arm.

There was no time to exert her influence on these men. She dodged the initial rush and tried to push off a second attacker. Before she could escape she was tackled from behind. The force slammed her to the ground, knocking the wind out of her. She fought to get a breath.

"I'm first," growled the leader, and he shoved the other man off of her. Roughly he clawed at her shoulder, rolling her over to face him. Her knees came up reflexively, but he thrust his hairy arms between them forcing her legs apart.

"Stop," she hissed, "or else!"

"Or else what?" laughed one of the men in the circle.

Trees, she thought. I need help. She reached out using the empathy she had with trees to the nearest oak and the 80-foot tall tree responded. A three-inch thick limb swooped down shattering the skull of the man on top of Dalphnia. Blood and brains splashed across the carpet of dead leaves beside Dalphnia. He was dead before he fell over.

Another limb caught the man next to him in the chest knocking him over backwards. He yelped in pain and rolled away from the tree.

"What the 'ell's happenin'," snapped one of the assailants.

"Th-the tree hit 'em," managed another.

Dalphnia was on her feet. The remaining men cowered away, their eyes glued to the trees.

"Hey, didn't mean no harm, just 'avin' a little fun," said one, his forced smile ripe with fear.

"Fun for whom?" she growled. "I suggest you learn how to treat a lady."

"Yes, m'm. We'll be rememberin' that."

"I'm sure you will."

With that Dalphnia raced back into the woods, remembering to ask the trees specifically about swords with strong magic.

Chapter 37

Amelia woke slowly. It was dark. The stiff scratchy hay itched her bare skin. Why was her bed so uncomfortable? Slowly, the burning fire in her shoulder brought her back to reality. She lay buried deep in hay piled atop a wagon.

Around her she heard sobbing and wailing and an occasional scream. She remembered the terrible black creature and its attack. Barlon must have called forth more hellish spawn.

Cautiously she clawed her way up through the hay until her head poked out. Peering through a thin veil of the stalks, she noticed the light from a hooded lantern moving furtively around inside the tavern next to the wagon. Here and there, dim lights flickered on and off in other buildings. Almost everywhere it was dark. Down the street thick flames licked up the side of an old, wooden church. Heavy black smoke rolled away into the night sky. An occasional breeze blew her the nauseous stench of burning flesh.

For a moment she lay still, collecting her wits. What happened to Pogor? Overhead she heard the sound of leathery wings. Amelia froze, fearing detection, remembering her nightmare attacker. She lay perfectly still until whatever it was passed overhead.

Slowly, she got up on her hands and knees and inched toward the back of the wagon. As she neared the open back end, the hay thinned and she realized she was naked. Somewhere in the castle her white gown lay where she'd left it. It never occurred to her that she wouldn't be back to retrieve it. Now she looked with new interest at the light moving inside the tavern.

Maybe there were clothes inside that she could get to without being seen. She hunkered down in the hay, burrowing deeper into the thin layer near the back of the wagon.

A rasping cough from beneath the wagon made Amelia go rigid, afraid even to breathe. Another cough, a heavy throat clearing and then a loud spit. She heard cloth rustling as someone struggled to sit up followed by distinctive noises from someone large trying to stand up. A loud crack resounded as their skull bumped the bottom of the wagon.

"By the Great Dragon's Fire," grumbled a familiar voice.

More rustling and a dark figure with broad shoulders rose from under the wagon. The man rubbed his head and looked around as if perplexed. He turned toward the inn, seemed to make up his mind, and headed for the steps. As his head turned to the right, Amelia caught his full profile silhouetted against the light from the burning church. It was Sir Jarlz!

"Sir Jarlz," she rasped through pain-clenched teeth, but the big man lurched up the stone steps. "Sir Jarlz," she said louder. "In the wagon."

He stopped, glanced behind him, and then peered through the darkness at the wagon. Unsteadily he retraced his steps. Amelia hastily brushed aside the thin layer of hay covering her face.

"Amelia," said Sir Jarlz, reaching the back of the wagon. "What are you doing here?"

"I need a dress. Or breeches and a shirt that fit," she said, ignoring his question.

"What?" A startled look came over his rugged face. "Has some evil befallen you? Ruffians accosted your womanhood?"

"Nothing like that. I crashed here. My dress is in the castle somewhere, but I'm not going back to get it."

Understanding surged through Jarlz' eyes. "Wait here. I'll fetch something from the tavern."

Happily she retreated into the hay burying her head once more.

Sir Jarlz shook his head to clear away the last of his nagging hangover, the reasons for it forgotten in favor of more important matters. He turned and mounted the stairs to the main tavern door. He pulled on the handle. It was locked.

"Open up in there," he shouted, thumping his fist on the doorframe.

There was a scurrying inside, the door swished open and a large pair of hands snatched Sir Jarlz off the stoop into the common room. A hooded lantern sat on one table blocked off so only a thin pencil of light showed. The plump mistress of the inn and her rotund husband stared wild-eyed at the weaponless knight.

"Are you trying to get us killed?" asked the innkeeper gruffly.

Jarlz looked around again. The inn was empty except for the couple in front of him. No lights, no fire in the hearth. The windows were tightly closed and shuttered.

"Where is everyone?"

"Gone," was the innkeeper's answer. "Left town, or trying to. Now, what do you want?"

"I need a dress."

The tavern owner took half a step back. His wife covered her open mouth with one hand.

"It's not for me. My friend in the alley lost hers and needs something to wear."

The couple relaxed noticeably. "How big is she?" asked the woman, her face taking on a gossip's knowing smile.

"Just a wisp of a thing," said Jarlz, holding up his hand to indicate her height, and then spreading his hands to show her approximate size.

"We've got nothing," said the man, beads of sweat on his wrinkled forehead.

"No, I don't, but one of the serving girls is sure to have left something," added the woman and before either of the men could react she grabbed the lantern and ducked into the kitchen, leaving them in darkness.

For a few minutes Jarlz stood patiently listening to the soft click of the cupboard doors opening and closing. Curious, he asked the innkeeper, "What has happened? This afternoon a man could buy a mug of ale and rest here. Now, you say everyone is fleeing

Pogor. There are fires down the street and I see no one fighting them. And your tavern is dark."

The chubby man wiped his forehead with the back of one hand.

"It's Gorth," he said. "He's brought more demons and turned them loose. This afternoon, shortly after, eh, shortly after we escorted you out, they started coming from the castle. Big black, evil, lawless things. They killed anyone on the street. Then came the men and they killed more. People ran, everyone ran.

"Well, almost everyone. Martha, she's my wife, and I couldn't run," he let his hands sweep down over his bulk to indicate why. "So we hid in the secret cellar we built years ago when we were outside the wall before the new wall was built. They came, stomping around upstairs. We stayed down there and just came up a little while ago. We thought we could sneak away tonight."

Jarlz remained quiet, thinking. Something was wrong. Barlon had never mentioned razing Pogor, and though now with his mind his own again Jarlz knew him for what he was, Jarlz doubted Gorth would allow this. With the town destroyed, it left his army without supplies.

As far as bringing in more demons, if they brought one they could bring more. And more demons meant more fighting and Jarlz was totally unarmed and helpless.

"Do you have any weapons? Anything we could use to defend ourselves?"

"Only the axe over the hearth. It's old. My grandfather brought it back with him from the dwarfen wars. It's still in good shape. Shiny as the day it was made. Take it if it'll help. It's yours."

"Well it's not my first choice in weapons, but it'll have to do," said Jarlz, noticing that the light was returning from the kitchen.

"Here you are," said Martha, holding out a plain brown dress of coarse cloth that appeared only slightly too large for Amelia.

Jarlz took it, flipped it over his shoulder and went to the mantle. Above the broad fire pit, a beautiful, short-handled forester's axe hung in iron cleats sunk into the stone chimney.

Jarlz took it down and hefted it. It was perfectly balanced and the edge glittered razor sharp in the dim light. A set of strange runes adorned the head. To test its edge, he ran the cutting surface along his hairy left forearm. A soft sigh escaped involuntarily as his forearm was shaved smooth as a newborn's behind.

"You certainly must have gone to a lot of work to keep this in such good shape."

"No," said the innkeeper, "I've never taken it from the hooks."

Jarlz hefted the axe and tried to think of a way to repay them for such a gift. "Pogor isn't safe anymore. We need to get out of the city. I think it'll be better if we go together."

The innkeeper and his wife exchanged fearful looks.

"I'm Sir Jarlz, late of Netherdorf Castle. You know the city and I can protect you. It'll be best for us both."

Still the two did not seem convinced.

"I've been working in secret for the true king," the knight added, trying to cover his own guilt as well as ease their fears. "Looks like you'll need help and I could use someone who knows the city."

Still the couple hesitated.

"Well, if I wanted to kill you, I'd do it now."

A curt nod passed between them. Martha picked up the lantern and slipped away into the kitchen.

"I'm Jonathan Stonethumb. Martha's gone to get our son, Ratheyon. He's our last. Plague got the other two, and we won't be havin' any more. He's all we've got."

"We'll make it," said Jarlz. "Hurry and make sure you've got enough food and drink. I've got to go out for a moment. I'll be right back."

The innkeeper nodded, but Jarlz was already out the door. He went to the wagon and tossed Amelia the dress.

"Took long enough," she snapped, wriggling into the simple gown while trying to stay concealed under the hay.

"We're leaving Pogor. The innkeeper and his family are going with us. I don't know what's happened, how Barlon could allow this. Everything's gone crazy. I think I've gone crazy, too."

Amelia crawled out of the wagon. Her shoulder oozed blood where the black thing's talons had ripped her open. The blood refused to clot and already, a tiny spot moistened her dress.

"You're hurt," said Jarlz, reaching gently for the wounded shoulder. Just then the rustle of dry wings sent them both diving beneath the wagon.

Long minutes passed in silence. Amelia peeked out from under the wagon. It was too dark to see anything overhead. They waited a few minutes more, and then slipped into the tavern, where Martha, Jonathan and a young boy sat huddled around the lantern as if somehow its light could protect them.

The boy was thin, unlike his parents, and sat stone-like, his hands folded in his lap. He looked to be no more than eight or nine years old with a straw-like shock of hair bristling from his head. He flinched as Jarlz and Amelia entered.

Quickly Jarlz introduced Amelia, and then asked, "What's the best way out?"

"This way," said Jonathan, taking the lantern and heading out through the ransacked cooking area.

Martha and Ratheyon followed closely behind the innkeeper. Jarlz hefted the axe in his right hand, helped Amelia with the other, and went out the back door, following the bobbing light. They went down a narrow, twisting alley to the left, at every step imagining that they'd be attacked by monsters.

At each turn they stopped and peered cautiously around the corner before proceeding. Jarlz kept a lookout behind them and was soon satisfied they weren't being followed. They moved through a maze of back streets, avoiding the main thoroughfares. It wasn't long before Jarlz saw the outer wall rising over the top of the clustered houses. Here the innkeeper stopped, staring out across a wide street.

Up and down on both sides of the street buildings were burning, filling the street with a hellish glow.

"We have to cross here." Jonathan pointed to a narrow opening between buildings on the opposite side of the street.

Jarlz peeked out around the corner of the buildings and noted that the street ran straight to a gate less than a hundred yards farther. "Why? We could make a run for that gate from here."

"Maybe you," said the stout innkeeper, "but not us. In any case, the main gate will be guarded. Where I'm going, there's a narrow gate used by some of the merchants to avoid the taxes at the main gates. We've a better chance there."

Jarlz looked to Amelia who nodded her approval. They were just about to cross the street when two men dashed around a corner farther up the main street followed by a young girl. One of the men carried a blacksmith's hammer clenched tight in his right hand.

In hot pursuit were two gigantic black monsters with burning red eyes. Each stood a good deal taller than Jarlz and much broader. In their hands were short, curved knives that glinted menacingly in the red flames from nearby buildings.

As they watched, the closest beast tackled the girl, pinned her to the street and with one powerful stroke, severed her head with the razor-like knife. The men never faltered, running for their lives with the second beast close behind.

"Cowards," spat Sir Jarlz through clenched teeth, and tensed as if ready to attack.

"No," came Amelia's soft voice at his shoulder. Her fragile hand gripped tightly around his bicep. "You can't help them, and it would doom us."

Jarlz nodded sadly. Inside more guilt piled atop the mound already there. He vowed silently that somehow he would wreak revenge for these atrocities.

The first monster finished with the girl and lurched upright, looking first one way and then the other. Flaring red nostrils sucked in the air, sniffing for new victims. The group in the alley huddled back in the darkness. Minutes passed like hours until finally the hulking slasher lumbered off down the street. A horrible scream echoed down the rows of once prosperous buildings. Another victim had been caught.

They waited only a few minutes more, and then one-by-one dashed across the street to the alley beyond. Jarlz went first, the axe ready, while the others waited. The alley was empty and dark. Jarlz motioned for the others to follow. Amelia, Martha, Ratheyon and finally Jonathan made it across as fast as they could.

"Which way?" asked Jarlz once they'd all reached the alley's relative safety.

"That way," said Jonathan and pointed up the alley. He scurried ahead, turning down another alley that branched off to the right. A couple of more turns and twists and they saw the small, wooden door set in the thick sandstone outer wall.

Jarlz called a halt and the tired bunch slipped into the deep shadows of an overhanging balcony. Nothing moved. The darkness surrounding the doorway was so deep that a dozen men could have hidden there. Off to the left, someone screamed. Everyone tensed.

Then, they saw it. One of the black slashers stood motionless in the shadow of the recess around the door. His nostrils flared at the sound of the screams and that tiny movement gave away his position. Knowing where it was they could also make out the knives it held in each hand.

"Wait here," said Sir Jarlz. Hefting the axe he stepped into the open and started walking toward the door as if unaware it was guarded.

Boldly the beast stepped from its hiding place, the two wicked knives flashing. Jarlz hefted the axe and braced for the beast's charge. Instead, the creature stomped deliberately up to the knight. When Jarlz swung his first stroke, it ignored the attack. The axe head bit deep into the creature's neck. A howling scream ripped from it and reverberated down the narrow corridor. The scream turned into a long wailing note, and with it the world seemed to fall silent. Goose bumps tingled along the skin on Jarlz' muscular forearms. Jarlz pulled the axe out of its neck and chopped again. The axe sliced the rest of the way through the neck and the ugly head bounced to the ground. Its lifeless husk slumped over backward.

The world stood silent for only a moment before the air burst into a flurry of activity. Leathery wings flapped madly to reach their fallen comrade. From a few blocks away, the tramp of heavy feet signaled more killers were coming.

"Hurry, through the door," yelled Jarlz and waved for the others.

The door opened easily and Jarlz held it as the others dashed for it. Amelia led the way. When she reached the monster's carcass she reached down and grabbed one of the wicked curved knives that lay on the ground. It felt warm to the touch, warmer than the air in the burning city, but not enough to burn.

By the time she'd retrieved the knife, the others had passed her, and she ran through the door last. There was a short passageway through the thick fortress wall, and then they reached another thicker door of iron bolted from the inside. Jonathan burrowed his way to the front, and fumbled only a minute before he had the bolts open. The door swung outward quietly.

Jarlz stepped out into the night. Only a few stars struggled through the combination of natural clouds and billowing smoke that rose over the city. A breeze stirred the air, fanning the flames inside the walls. Without hesitation, Jarlz pulled the others through, knowing the enemy would soon be at the door in force.

There was a narrow path leading from the door, evidence of the heavy illicit traffic that had passed through the walls. It curved out into the darkness to the right where Jarlz guessed it met the main road somewhere ahead. The party hustled down the path as fast as they could, ever aware of the soft rustle of leathery wings. The tavern owner and his wife quickly fell behind. Jarlz dropped back with them.

"Off the path," snapped Amelia, once they were away from the door.

She dove into a shallow ditch that ran beside the path and pressed herself into the wet slime at the bottom. The others did the same. The last one reached hiding only a moment before they heard a flyer sail overhead with a soft whoosh. Two more soared by and for a while the air above was filled with their raucous cries. No one dared look up. Jarlz knew they couldn't stay there long. Dawn was coming.

Chapter 38

Lord Barkmar led the tired group of elves and men into the cave. The cool, damp air refreshed them as they marched down the gentle slope into the bowels of the earth. A hundred yards into the cave, the chamber T-ed into two smaller tunnels. They went left. Once around the corner, rows of torches filled the corridor with a comforting yellow glow. Here the walls were smooth, cut-stone. Gant marveled at the construction done in solid rock.

The Forest Lord hurried along forcing Gant to jog to keep up. Pris was barely able to stay within sight of the group. At the next branch, Lord Barkmar stopped.

"Gant, you come with me," he said motioning down the right tunnel. "The rest go with Stork. He'll take you to your rooms."

A tall, lean elf from Lord Barkmar's band stepped forward and started off down the left branch. The others followed, too tired to argue and anxious to get to the promised beds.

"Where are we going?" asked Gant, as he watched the others disappear.

"Your friends want to see you immediately," said Lord Barkmar starting off faster than ever.

Gant ran to keep up, dodging other elves in the tunnel. What friends, he wondered. They made several more turns, went down two sets of steps, twisting and turning. Finally they stopped before a gray metal door set in black rock. Lord Barkmar touched the small green square next to it and the door slid open.

"In there," he said.

Gant stepped into an empty room. He turned around but the Forest Lord was already gone. The door slid shut in Gant's face. Turning back to the room, Gant noted a small table, a bench, two chairs and a short squat bookcase that held half a dozen volumes. The unique thing was that the furniture was carved from living rock. Seemed more like the work of dwarves, thought Gant.

The chairs and bench had thick, furry animal hide covers that provided more than ample cushion. Gant sank into one of the chairs. He threw back his head, closed his eyes, and rolled his neck to get the kinks out of tired muscles.

Another metal door whooshed open to Gant's left startling him. Abadis and Uric entered, smiling.

"Gant," said Abadis, rushing to the young man.

Gant hugged the old wizard fiercely. He saw tiny droplets form at the corners of his wrinkled, gray eyes. Then he noticed Abadis' left ear.

"What happened to your ear?"

"Oh, nothing." Abadis waved away the question. "Where have you been?" The worried look on his face reminded Gant of his father whenever he came home late.

"Where have I been?" Gant almost laughed at the ridiculous question. "I should be asking you. You were supposed to be back the same night. You left us at Sylvia's. We had to ride through the woods while you zipped around with your magic."

The gray wizard chuckled. "It took a little longer to free Uric," he thumbed over his shoulder to the robed sage standing behind him, "than I thought. I got a little careless."

"Easy to do," said Uric. "Though I'm still curious why you were meeting them at Sylvia's?"

Abadis folded his arms across his chest. "Because no one would think of looking for us there."

Uric stepped forward, extending one hand to Gant. "You look well after such a strenuous journey."

"I'm okay," said Gant, his fatigue momentarily forgotten. He shook his former teacher's hand, glad to see familiar faces again. "What are you doing here? I thought you'd be at Abadis' house waiting for us or Amelia."

A dark expression crossed both faces. Abadis said, "Amelia hasn't returned for several days." He swallowed hard and Gant saw a deep sadness cloud the old man's eyes. "She may not be able to come back."

"Resistance to Gorth centers around the Dark Elves now," said Uric. "We assume the Eastern Empire has refused aid."

Gant nodded and Abadis spat. "Stupid men. They don't realize where their best interests lie."

Uric went on as if uninterrupted. "It is up to the Dark Elves and the King of Mulldain, and neither have large armies. Sarona has sent out runners to ask for the king's help. Rumor has it that King Tirmus is hiding there. If that's true, Mulldain will help, and Tirmus may have gathered his knights, those that escaped. Still, it won't be much. Of course Abadis and I will do what we can, but you must defeat Varg if we are to have a chance."

"I hope I can," said Gant.

"You will. Believe in yourself. We will do what we can when the time comes, but even our magic can only slow a Demon-Prince, and not for long. Valorius is our only hope. As for the sword, Abadis says you used it against Egog. Let me see the sword." Uric held out one hand.

Gant pulled Valorius from its scabbard and handed it to Uric. The sage held it lightly, as if measuring something about the sword. For a moment his eyes narrowed to slits, his stare intent on the blade. "Yes, some of the magic is gone."

"How much?" asked Abadis. "Is it still strong enough to stop Varg?"

"Who can say? I have never done battle with Varg. Only Bartholomew knows what strength Varg possesses. But have hope. Bartholomew may have seen this turn of events. And who knows what help the elves may be." Uric returned the sword to Gant.

Gant fondled Valorius. Uric's words resurfaced in his mind. Yes, it had come to this. He had hoped it wouldn't, had wished the killing would stop. But it hadn't. And whether he liked it or not, it wasn't going to stop unless they did something about it. He had defeated Egog. Varg might be a different matter. He'd have to trust

Bartholomew and do whatever he could. At least when it was over, he could go back to Dalphnia and set things right with her.

"I brought help, too," said Gant, snapping out of his reverie. "A great warrior named Zandinar, the Emperor Pris and four of his soldiers."

Uric nodded. "Zandinar will indeed be a force in this," he said, "and any soldiers will help."

"Enough," said Abadis, stepping between the two. "Sarona has requested our presence in the morning, and you should sleep."

"What does she want of me?" asked Gant.

"She wants to meet Bartholomew's descendant. And I would guess, she'll let us in on her plan to keep Gorth west of the Monoliths. We'll know soon enough." He clapped Gant on the shoulder and led him down a short hall off the sitting room. At the first doorway they turned into a luxurious suite.

Gant noticed two other bedrooms sprouted off the hall like leaves from a clover stem. Uric and Abadis' rooms guessed Gant. He followed the wizard into the room.

"This is your room," said Abadis. "Get some sleep."

Abadis left, closing the door behind him and within minutes Gant had his armor off and was fast asleep on a strange floating bed that supported his weight without touching the floor.

#

Gant woke up sometime later, rested and refreshed except for a gnawing hunger. He rose, eager for breakfast. He washed his face and hands in the silver water bowl someone had left on a table against the wall. Then he dressed, donned his armor, buckled on Valorius, and went back up the short hall to the sitting room.

Uric and Abadis sat at the table, a bowl of fruit, nuts and sweet breads in front of them.

"Good morning," said Uric, looking up as Gant walked to the table. "You look better this morning than last night."

"Feel better, too," said Gant, biting into a crisp red apple.

Abadis and Uric got up and went to another table where they spread out a small map. Gant wolfed down several more pieces of fruit and two of the tasty sweet breads. He washed it down with a glass of the purest, most refreshing water he'd ever tasted. His hunger blunted, Gant went to look at the map with Abadis and Uric.

"Blasseldune will be his next target," said Uric, flatly. "To do that he'll have to come through Chamber Pass. With the confidence he's built during the last campaign, he won't believe we can stop him. That is his weakness."

"Perhaps," said Abadis, "but maybe he'll be satisfied being Lord of the West. What can he gain by attacking Blasseldune?"

"Men of power are never satisfied. The power he gains only feeds his lust for more."

Abadis grimaced. "Yes. I suspect you are right. In any case we'll need to prepare for the worst. We should talk this over with Lord Barkmar before the Queen holds her meeting."

Hastily, Abadis folded the parchment map and put it in a pocket in his robes. The pair stood, and turning, walked to the door.

Gant followed them. "I'll go with you."

"No need," said Abadis over his shoulder. "This won't take long. Relax, enjoy the food."

Gant sat down, wondering what the Queen was like. He munched on some of the nutmeats and for the first time in a long time he relaxed.

The door opened behind him and an elf entered.

"Are you Gant?" asked the elf, bowing slightly from the waist.

"Yes."

"Follow me please. Your friends wish you to join them."

So soon, he wondered, but got up and followed the elf down a long twisting corridor. They went down several more sets of winding stairs and Gant guessed they must be near the heart of the mountain.

Eventually they entered a large domed, chamber. The central portion of the room was empty, only a smooth stone floor. Around the sides, in raised sections, were rows of stone chairs, many with animal furs draped over them. The seats were empty and the room was ominously silent. The escort led Gant to the middle of the vast circular arena and stopped.

"Give me your sword. No weapons are allowed beyond this point."

Gant started to reach for Valorius. "Where is everyone? Where is Uric and Abadis?"

The elf lunged for Valorius. Gant jerked back. The elf reached again for Gant's sword. Gant hit the elf under the chin with his right mailed fist, knocking him to the floor. The elf lay still.

What was going on? Gant glanced around. Entrances ringed the central arena about every thirty feet. Which way had they come in? That one, he thought. How was he going to get back to his room? He hadn't seen a single elf during the last ten minutes. He couldn't possibly remember all the twists and turns.

With an audible swish, a door opened behind Gant. He turned to face it. A tall figure stepped into the arena wearing black armor that flickered with a light of its own. The high crested helm was curved to deflect sword blows. In the stranger's left hand was a sword, not unlike Valorius. On his right arm was a golden shield.

The warrior walked to the center of the chamber, stopped, bowed to Gant and then, without a word, charged. His long, leaping strides covered the distance between them with amazing speed, the slivery sword held ready to attack or defend.

What was happening? The Dark Elves were friends. Surely this was a mistake. The mysterious warrior reached Gant and slashed viciously at Gant's neck. At the last instant, Gant dodged and the sword smashed down on Gant's shoulder.

There was an explosion of light and thunder. The pressure of the blow raced through Gant's nerves but the sword failed to cut through Gant's armor.

"What do you want?" yelled Gant.

Even as he spoke, Valorius sprang into Gant's hand. His attacker lashed out with a flurry of slashes. Gant turned aside each attack with an effortless parry, smoothly deflecting with the flat of Valorius' blade. Like fireworks, brilliant light flared each time the swords touched.

Still, Gant struck no offensive blow. He could not bring himself to attack without knowing why.

As the battle wore on, the black figure began to tire. Now an inky darkness began to form around the black armor. It clung to the air like an impenetrable thunderhead, surging, billowing until it blinded Gant. Twice in quick succession blows rang off Gant's head and breast.

Still Gant's armor held. Each contact brought a flash like lightning in a midnight storm. In desperation Gant held Valorius out in front of him, gripping her hilt with both hands. The sword began to vibrate, humming at an ever-increasing pitch until the sound passed out of Gant's hearing range. Whatever the effect, there were no more attacks. Gant just wanted to end this combat and get out of the darkness. And then Valorius began to glow, brighter and brighter, eating away the darkness. Soon Gant stood in the center of a blazing nova.

In a fury, Gant swung a two-handed stroke at his opponent's sword. There was a flash of light indistinguishable from Valorius' fiery radiance and Valorius cut through the other blade as if it were paper.

With a dull clatter, the blade fell to the floor leaving the black figure holding a useless hilt. Then with a deft down stroke, Gant split the black breastplate like opening a clam and brought Valorius' razor tip to rest against the exposed throat.

"Yield, warrior," yelled Gant, the blood rushing in his temples.

Instead, the black clad figure twisted, trying to pull Valorius from Gant's hands. Gant lunged. The blade sank into the flesh at the base of the throat. The warrior went down in a heap, blood gushing like a fountain.

Gant sheathed Valorius. "Now what?" he asked himself.

He went to the unconscious form of the elf who had brought him to the cavern. A slap to the cheek brought him around. Gant pulled Valorius and pushed the point under the dark chin.

"You're going to lead me back out of here, understand?"

The elf rose, shaking, his knees wobbly. Gant grabbed his arm and started for the opening he thought they'd come through. There would be time for questions when he was back to safety.

Chapter 39

The flyers soon gave up and the sound of their wings faded in the distance as they retreated back to the city. Jarlz scrambled up onto his hands and knees in the damp, weed-infested ditch. He crawled to the top of the ditch and pushed aside the vegetation, checking for pursuit. To his right, in the distance, the city's outer walls were silhouetted against a backdrop of red glare from the fires that still burned inside. The path was deserted in that direction.

To his left, the path stretched away into the empty darkness. Directly opposite where Jarlz knelt, on the other side of the path, a thick grove of trees stood ominously close to their exit route. The perfect ambush site, thought Jarlz, and considered the options. They could not go back toward the city and they couldn't stay where they were for long. With the innkeeper and his family and Amelia's injuries, they wouldn't get far cutting across country. No, the only option was to spring the trap if indeed there was one.

"Stay down," he said over his shoulder.

Amelia and the others hunkered down, staying as still as possible. The festering wound in Amelia's shoulder was bleeding again and she bit her lip to keep from screaming.

Poised at the edge of the path, Jarlz paused on his hands and knees. He looked left and right. Nothing moved. He stood up, cautiously balancing the axe. He waited a moment. When nothing sprang from behind the trees he turned and walked away from the city.

As soon as Jarlz turned his back, a demonic creature launched at him from the cover of the tree trunks. It was a head taller than Jarlz, and unlike the slashers they'd seen before, it had four arms that ended in hooked claws instead of hands. Its long, strong legs thrust it forward in a frog-like leap. Its first bound took it halfway to Jarlz. It landed heavily and coiled for its next leap. Jarlz heard the thud and tensed. In one smooth motion the beast launched again and landed only a few feet behind the knight.

Jarlz had been expecting an attack but he hadn't anticipated how quickly his attacker would overtake him. He spun around, the beast nearly upon him, the right pair of claws drawing back to strike. In one smooth motion Jarlz sank the axe deep into its chest. It crumpled backward, gurgling and coughing through the hole in its chest.

Jarlz pulled the axe free, and swung again, hitting it at the base of the neck. It recoiled, trying to strike back. Jarlz brought the axe down again, splitting its chest wide open. It stumbled, dark blood gushing from the wound, and fell over backward, dead.

Jarlz stood poised, ready to defend against another attack. Nothing else appeared. No flyers returned. He waited a moment longer, and then whirled and dashed to the ditch.

"Up," he hissed through clenched teeth, "up and run. We've got to be away from here before the sun rises."

Those in the ditch clambered up onto the path and started off, hampered by fatigue and injury. Amelia faltered, her right arm hanging like a dead weight.

"I can't run," she said, struggling to stay on her feet.

"Then I'll carry you," said Jarlz and swept her up in his powerful arms. He was surprised how light she was, and glad of it.

They managed to run for a short spurt and then fatigue forced them to walk. Soon they were reduced to a shuffle, fighting to put one foot in front of the other. Slowly, the city fell behind as they moved out onto the plains. The path they were on joined the main road, but they elected to stay on the flat grasslands off to the side of the road. Far to the east where the sky met the Monolith Mountains, the horizon began to brighten. Jarlz looked for a place to hide as the thin vale of gold grew into a new day. To their left, they found a small streambed whose banks were choked with overhanging willows. Thankfully they slipped in under the whip-like branches.

With first light, they finally got a good look at each other.

Raytheon's eyes were wide with fear, yet even fear couldn't hide the exhaustion. Jonathan's rotund chest heaved as he fought for breath. The tavern owner's wife, Martha, who was almost as large as he, wheezed uncontrollably. Jarlz knew he must look grim. But it was Amelia that drew his attention. The wound on her shoulder oozed blood and the front of her brown dress was stained almost to the waist. Jarlz pulled aside the garment and winced. The ugly, festering gash was turning black at the edges.

"It must have been an evil thing to cause this," he said gritting his teeth. "We need to get you to a healer."

"Not much chance of that," Amelia said, trying to smile. She leaned back against the trunk of a willow.

"Here, let me have a look," said Martha, scurrying to Amelia's side. "I nursed my boys when they were young. . ." She trailed off. A sad, dreamy look filled her eyes. She pulled aside the shoulder of the dress and after one look at the nasty gouge said, "It needs to be cleaned."

She went to the stream, tore a corner from her dress and dipped it in the fresh trickle of water. She took it back to Amelia and scrubbed the wound hard, making Amelia wince.

Mumbling to herself, Martha went back to the watercourse and searched until she found a slick patch of blue-gray mud. Scooping up a small handful she knelt next to Amelia and expertly plastered the mud over the wound, her chubby fingers working the mud with practiced precision.

"There. That should stop the bleeding if you don't move too much." She smiled, and then gently pulled the shoulder of Amelia's dress over the wound. "Sleep now," she added and went over to sit by Jonathan.

"What do you think?" asked Jarlz, sitting down against the tree next to the innkeeper and his wife.

"It's a bad wound. It doesn't look that deep, but something is rotting the tissue around it." Martha wrung her hands, the remorse clear in her thick-jowled face.

Jarlz closed his eyes for a moment. "Do you know where this stream goes?" he asked, laying the axe beside him and folding his hands in his lap.

"It goes under the road a bit farther ahead and then runs on to the mountains. Although it's not much of a stream."

"Do the trees grow all along it?"

"They do, as far as I've ever been," said the innkeeper, throwing one arm around his boy who had seated himself beside his father.

"Somehow we've got to get word to Blasseldune," said Jarlz, almost in a whisper, half dozing against the tree.

"Why?" asked Amelia.

"Barlon's going to attack there next and with these monsters at his command, I don't think he'll wait long."

"I could fly there," offered Amelia, drawing suspicious glances from the innkeeper and his family.

"No," snapped Jarlz. "We'll find another way."

The morning passed. Each dozed fitfully, afraid to fall completely asleep, yet too tired to stay completely awake. By midday, their stomachs grumbling in symphony, the innkeeper's wife produced a small leather sack filled with bread and dried meat. They ate and drank from the cold, clear brook where it bubbled over some stones. The food and water seemed to refresh them despite the lack of sleep.

Midafternoon Jarlz got them up and going again, always careful to stay under the willows.

From under the cover of the thick undergrowth near the stream, they watched scores of refugees fleeing across the plains or along the road. Most ran out in the open. A few drove wagons loaded with valuables they could not bear to leave.

Flocks of black flyers wheeled overhead like giant vultures. Several times Jarlz' group watched helplessly as the flying demons descended on helpless refugees. Screams filled the air as the dancing winged beasts cavorted over their prey. In addition to the flyers, marauding packs of evil beasts patrolled the road. Like a crazed wolf pack they ripped and tore into shrieking groups of fleeing men, women, and children.

As the party neared the bridge where the stream went under the road, they saw a pack of slashers armed with their long knives surround three men on the road. Silently, the party huddled among the willows and watched. The three men formed a circle, back-to-back, with their swords bristling outward. As the first monster moved in, one man slashed at it but his blade rang uselessly off its hide. Unfazed the monster cut open the man's right arm with a single slash. The other creatures waded into the trio impervious to the sword stokes, killing them slowly, slashing at arms and legs until the three men bled to death. Finally, the creatures ripped open their guts and ate lustfully of the entrails.

Jarlz hustled the party away from the gruesome sight. They followed the stream under the road, steadily moving toward the Monolith Mountains.

For the rest of the afternoon, the party moved cautiously along under cover of the thick willows. Occasionally, they saw others slipping along the stream. Jarlz' party avoided them, not willing to trust strangers. Everywhere there was danger and death. They moved on grimly intent only on escape.

The sun dropped low in the sky, and with the coming darkness came more dangers. Shadows could hide Barlon's creatures waiting in ambush. Jarlz hurried them on, hoping to reach the foothills before it grew completely dark. They were tired, their legs ached, but they kept moving.

Shortly after sundown, they heard loud noises directly ahead. Jarlz halted the party. In the twilight, Jarlz peered through a curtain of willow branches. Just ahead in the streambed he saw a lone figure fending off a slasher armed with twin curved knives. The man wore tattered, soot-covered robes that were singed black around the edges. He carried a crude, carved staff. Jarlz watched as he whirled the staff at the monster and landed a solid blow to the beast's head. The thing ignored the impact and drove forward.

The man back-pedaled, dodging one slash after another. He swung the staff again. It broke across the thing's shoulder. The man stumbled backward and fell. He lay flat on his back mumbling incoherently. The thing crouched over him, knives drawn back for the killing stroke.

277

Jarlz watched in horror. The man had fallen only a few feet away. He raised the axe, coiled his legs and lunged. Before the beast could strike its first blow, Jarlz brought the axe down hard on its neck. The razor sharp blade sliced through its exposed neck sending the head tumbling off into the underbrush. A geyser of inky blood spouted from the severed stump and the slasher toppled headlong into the stream. An expanding cloud of darkness flowed away, polluting the clear water.

"Are you all right?" asked Jarlz, scrambling over to the fallen man.

The stranger tried to find words but none came. Jarlz reached down and with one powerful hand, pulled the struggling refugee to his feet. The man's once exquisite robes were torn and burned, his face covered with soot and sweat. His sandy hair, like a shock of straw, stood out at all angles. His gray eyes held fear and confusion.

Despite his rag-tag appearance, the man looked vaguely familiar. But recognition seemed tied to the worst parts of a nightmare that swirled in Jarlz' mind. The sun was gone and the growing darkness obscured the stranger's features. Jarlz let it pass. The rest of the party gathered together, huddled against the night, worried what other monsters lurked in the brush.

"Thanks," muttered the battered newcomer, his voice a thin whistle through cracked lips.

"It's okay," said Jarlz, and then turned to the others. "We have to keep moving. I don't want to be near this dead thing at night. Others may follow its blood trail upstream."

"You're right," added Amelia. "We're almost to the foothills. We'd be safer there."

Before they began the innkeeper reached down and took the two long knives from the dead beast. He kept one and gave the other to Raytheon.

Reluctantly the party stumbled forward, still following the stream. Jarlz led the way, his axe ready. Amelia struggled along behind him, her shoulder throbbing but no longer bleeding, her strength almost gone. Martha and Raytheon came next, and then the stranger, whose blood-caked right eyebrow made it difficult for him to see and he stumbled often. Jonathan brought up the rear, and was soon helping the shattered refugee. The roly-poly innkeeper bent to his new task without a whimper.

It took several hours to escape the hot, grassy plains. The larger moon rose, a full round ball of gleaming silver. The smaller moon was only a faint crescent on the western horizon. Now the little stream bubbled over sheets of bedrock, splashing and gurgling through a narrow, natural sluice in the rugged hillsides. The willows disappeared and only chest-high brush clung to the wet banks.

Once into the foothills, they climbed out of the stream and went uphill, moving back away from the stream, searching in the moonlight for a safe shelter among the boulders.

They found a spot among jagged slabs of upturned rock and settled down in a hollow between a massive boulder and a vertical cliff face.

One by one exhaustion overtook them and they dropped into a troubled sleep. Jarlz, steadfast in his duty and determined to redeem himself for past transgressions, remained awake long into the night.

Clouds covered the moon and the darkness deepened. The distant splashing of the brook and a slight breeze muffled the high whoosh of leathery wings. Jarlz heard the flyers, but could not see them. He hoped they could not see the poorly armed group huddled behind the boulder.

Night thickened and still Jarlz forced his eyes to stay open. The others slept. Jarlz watched them toss fitfully. He wondered what dreams troubled them. The innkeeper snored from time to time, and then he'd start at something and roll over.

Once the stranger gave an outburst of strange verse. Jarlz thought it was the language of magic, but it was too garbled to tell.

Eventually Jarlz's eyelids flickered closed. His head nodded forward, his chin resting on his chest. Reflex snapped his head back as he fought to stay awake. The night can't last much longer, he told himself, and tried to force his exhausted mind alert. His head bobbed forward again, and once more he fought off sleep.

Suddenly he was wide awake. The rattle of small stones dislodged by heavy feet brought him to a crouch. It was close. His ears strained to catch any sound. Pebbles rattled behind him, and more not far to his left.

    Quickly Jarlz slithered to the others, shaking each, whispering for them to get up. Slowly each rose to a crouch with whatever weapon they had. The darkness closed in. They saw nothing, but the noise of crunching gravel left no doubt. They were surrounded.

Chapter 40

Gant kept a firm grip on his reluctant guide knowing that if the elf got loose he could easily outrun Gant. They exited the arena, turned left and followed the tunnel past two side branches until it dead ended at a cross tunnel. The elf went right without hesitation, Gant hanging on to him. They ascended a set of stairs, went right around a corner and down a short hall to another set of stairs. Gant remembered these stairs. Maybe.

At the top was a double set of narrow doors. If Gant was right there would be two guards on the other side. The elf opened the door and stepped through, Gant at his heels. There were no guards where he'd expected them. Gant pulled the elf up short.

"Where are the guards that were here before?"

"How should I know? The Queen sets the guard as she wishes and she doesn't consult me."

Gant pushed his sword point into the elf's skin until a drop of blood oozed out.

"Killing me won't help."

Gant pushed him forward. Several more turns, another set of stairs and they ended up on a broad landing that branched into half a dozen passages. From the passage on the far right three elf soldiers emerged, saw Gant, and stopped. There was a brief outburst in elfish, and then all three drew their short swords. The tallest stepped forward.

"You, take your sword from the elf."

Gant considered the three elves and what might happen if he let his prisoner go. "Take us to Lord Barkmar's quarters," he said.

A buzz of elfish. Gant's captive tried to pull free. Gant jerked him back.

The tallest elf soldier waved his sword at Gant. "Let him go."

"Okay. Keep your swords on me, but take me to Lord Barkmar."

More elfin discussion and then, "Follow us."

The tallest elf led off, Gant and his prisoner right behind him. The other two elves fell in behind. Within a few minutes the whole nervous procession stopped at a door. The lead elf knocked and Forest Lord Barkmar answered.

"Gant, come in," he said, stepping back to let Gant inside. "What's this all about?"

The elf soldiers shuffled sheepishly. Gant shoved his prisoner into Barkmar's living room. Abadis and Uric were there sitting around a table, half empty glasses in front of them. Lord Barkmar said something to the soldiers in elfish and they left. Lord Barkmar shut the door and Gant related his story.

"I'm afraid you've met members of the Watchers For Darkness. Fanatics who pray for Varg's return. They wanted to take Valorius," said the Forest Lord.

"What about this one?" asked Gant, nodding to his prisoner.

"Let the authorities take care of him. We've been called to the War Hall. The Queen is waiting."

Gant turned his prisoner over to other soldiers and then Lord Barkmar led them to the War Hall. On the way Gant and Lord Barkmar were joined by other elves and soon had quite a procession. The group entered the War Hall through a pair of massive, ornate doors that stood open. It was a huge circular, domed room with a raised central section. A large table sat in the middle of the platform. There were so many elves clustered around that Gant could not actually see what was on the table.

Gant followed Lord Barkmar across the wide expanse of open floor at the back of the room and approached the raised section. As they approached, Gant caught a glimpse of the elf queen. She stood near the middle of the table, surrounded by elves in military uniform. She spoke first with one, then another, always gesturing toward the table. Her dark pointed ears swept up past black hair that was pulled back into a single braid that coiled around her neck and looped over her left shoulder until it hung down over a small, silvery, rune-encrusted breastplate. In her right hand she held a short, black stone scepter. Her eyes were narrow cold slits close together around a thin, angular nose. Her lips were thin and blacker even than her hair. There was no hint of warmth in her stare. Yet in her iciness was a pure beauty like that of great sculptures.

In attendance on the main floor were a host of elves dressed in fine cloaks, breeches and shirts. Like peacocks showing off, most wore gaudy gold and silver jewelry. The glitter of gems sparkled from luxurious pendants. So this was elf nobility, thought Gant.

Lord Barkmar led them up onto the platform to join the huddled council. Finally Gant could see the huge tapestry draped over the table. The cloth was a masterfully sewn map of the world with little metal figures and intricately carved miniatures of cities and towns placed on it.

"Here is Barlon's main force," said the Elf Queen, pointing with the scepter to the carved miniature Pogor. "New recruits swell his battalions daily as the scum of our time rally to his promise of easy spoils and plunder."

She continued, "In addition he has garrisons here, here and here," she pointed to the outpost at Bal, Barlon's Mountain Castle, and Netherdorf. "He controls all three Western Kingdoms, thanks to the idiot farmers in Dernium and the evil priests in Scaltzland, and he has a foothold this side of the Monoliths. We expect Blasseldune will be his next target, and then the Eastern Empire. We do not know how soon he plans to attack. We must see that his troops do not get through Chamber Pass. Our main force will travel through the wilderness to the Pass. If they arrive in time, we'll fortify the ridges, trap the pass and the plains before it, and ambush his forces when they arrive."

"What about his forces at Netherdorf Castle? They'll be at our backs," said an elf near the front of the throng on the main floor.

"Good question, Lord Mesthane, and for that we trust to aid from Mulldain. As I said, Barlon's garrisons on our side of the

Monoliths are small. King Herzolt has enough troops to defeat them, especially if King Tirmus and his knights ride with them."

"Will they come?" asked several of the elves in the crowd.

Sarona looked coolly from face to face. "Who knows if any human will ever side with a Dark Elf? We will know soon. Our runners should have made it to Mull City by now, and our answer may already be on its way back."

A murmur of questions and supposition ran through the crowd, only to be quieted as the Queen motioned for silence. "What of the dragons, Dragon King?" she asked, staring at Uric.

Uric spoke without apology, considering each word carefully. "I won't ask their assistance. This is a matter of men, not dragons. I stay involved myself only out of love for my long departed friend, Bartholomew. I vowed to see this finished, and I will."

Another murmur passed through the crowd. When things quieted, Abadis cleared his throat loudly. All eyes turned to him. "What of the High Elves? Will your cousins help?"

Sarona's mood darkened. "As you know, there is no love lost between us. We will not humble ourselves before *them*. In any case, they are not eager to meddle in the affairs of men either." She paused and then added, "Any suggestions, or questions?"

Uric stepped forward. "Pardon my question," he said deferentially, "but how old is your intelligence on Gorth's positions?"

"Runners arrive each morning and each afternoon."

"The messenger never came this morning, Your Majesty," said one sheepish noble.

"Perhaps it is time I went to see for myself," suggested Uric.

"I agree, Queen Sarona," added Abadis. "Your scout is long overdue. Perhaps Barlon has caught some of them."

"Maybe," said Sarona coldly, "and I appreciate your concern for your granddaughter, but let us see what the afternoon runners bring. Until then, rest, eat and prepare for the battle that cannot be far away."

Uric nodded agreement. Slowly the group disbanded. Several elves stayed to suggest alternate attack and defense strategies. That soon broke down to telling stories of ancient wars and glorious victories.

Gant, Uric and Abadis were escorted out of the War Hall by a young Dark Elf. As they walked, Gant asked, "Why don't they get along with the High Elves?"

Uric answered. "Long ago, there was only one race of elves. But in those times, Varg and his kind were free to enter this world as they chose. In time he seduced a number of the elfin maids to his evil ways. Their offspring became the Dark Elves."

"But Batholomew freed them from Varg," interjected Gant.

"True. Their hearts are no darker than yours or mine but their cousins still see only their black skin."

"That's stupid," said Gant.

"No more so than a hundred other prejudices," said Abadis.

At that point they were ushered into a large banquet hall where Zandinar, Pris and the other Easterners waited impatiently.

"Where've you been?" shouted Pris, bouncing from his chair to greet them.

"Discussing strategy with the Queen," said Gant, smiling at the emperor's boyish energy.

"Then we'll be going to war soon?"

"Probably."

"Great. I'll get to go west of the Monoliths, finally."

"Probably not," said Gant.

"Why not?" Pris' smile faded. "The Mountain Lord has taken the Western Kingdoms. Won't we be attacking him?"

"Pris," snapped Gant, "this is not a game. Gorth will probably attack us. First Blasseldune, then your Empire."

"Yes, of course," said Pris, now dead serious.

Gant saw Captain Hesh and Kalmine exchange whispered comments. Before Pris could ask any more questions, Gant walked over to where Uric and Abadis were talking softly. At the same time, two elf maids brought in heaping platters of food, roast venison, steaming and dripping in its natural juices, and piles of steamed vegetables. The succulent aroma made Gant's mouth water. The rest of the group headed for places at the table as another elf maid brought in a tray laden with fine wines.

Gant touched Uric's arm to gain his attention. "What did she mean when she called you the Dragon King?"

"Just what she said."

"Are you a dragon? If so, how come I've have never seen you except as the castle sage?"

"I never intended anyone to know. Now it seems everyone does."

"There are more of you? I mean more dragons?"

"Yes, there are still a few dozen of us left, but only two mated pairs. We reproduce so slowly it may be a hundred years before there is another birth."

"Then why won't you help us?"

"Hatred dies hard. Long ago there were a lot of dragons. Men feared us, hated us, mostly without reason, though there were some dragons who deserved that hatred. Heroes sought out dragons to kill often without thought as to whether the dragon they killed was evil or good. And though we are powerful, we are not invincible. Many of us were killed by men. We moved far from men, living in self-imposed exile. Most of those alive today had loved ones killed by men. Hatred fills their hearts. I feel for them and understand why they will not help men, even good men."

Gant thought about it. Strange how complex good and bad could become. He would try to remember how easy it was to confuse the two and never to take up Valorius against an enemy until there was proof of his evil. A shame that such noble creatures as dragons could be forever alienated from humans because of a few misguided men. But now, the smell of delicious food and the busy sounds of others already at the table overwhelmed Gant, and he headed for a seat at the table.

Chapter 41

After eating there was little to do but wait for the afternoon runner. Uric and Abadis left with a craggy ancient elf to discuss some obscure principle of magic. Pris and his entourage went on a tour of the elf stronghold led by a young, 72-year-old elf that Pris had met the night before. That left only Gant and Zandinar in the dining area.

Sitting across the table from Zandinar, Gant wondered what the enigmatic warrior was really like. For all the time they'd spent together, Gant knew hardly anything about him except that he claimed to have a destiny tied to Gant. Maybe they were more alike than Gant wanted to admit. Gant had a destiny, one he didn't want but couldn't seem to escape.

"What's this destiny you talk about?" asked Gant.

A deep sadness filled Zandinar's blue eyes. "It is what I must do."

"Must do? Who makes you do it?"

Zandinar didn't answer.

"Surely you've been doing other things before you met me."

"Yes. I've championed the rights of the oppressed. But that was only to pass the time until I met you. Now I need to do what must be done."

Gant pursed his lips at the cryptic answer. "Then you see the future?"

"No. Only my fate."

Gant saw that Zandinar was becoming uncomfortable. He felt guilty prying into Zandinar's life. But still, Gant wanted to know the man, know who he was. He told himself to let it be and set aside the other questions on his mind. Zandinar rose and left the room.

Gant sat for a while thinking about his own future. He thought about Dalphnia and her woods. If he ever got through this he would go back. He hoped she would be waiting. As far as he was concerned, he'd had enough adventure to last a lifetime.

And then Gant thought about his parents. They might be alive. Probably not. Why would Barlon spare them? He hoped they hadn't suffered. Silently he cursed having been away from Netherdorf that day. And what about Uncle Jarlz? And Abadis' granddaughter? The price of war came high.

Eventually he left the banquet hall and returned to their quarters. Once there the door hissed open and Gant slipped into the sitting room. The door hissed shut behind him. A muffled cough from the corner startled Gant. He spun toward the sound but no one was there.

Immediately Valorius was in his hand. He'd heard of people being invisible. Had Barlon's men penetrated the Caverns of Darkness? Was this another trick to get Valorius? Tentatively Gant probed the air in front of him with the tip of his sword, feeling for anything solid.

A hushed snicker sputtered from the hallway behind him. Gant glanced over his shoulder and saw Pris, hand clapped over his mouth fighting laughter. An elf crouched behind the emperor, grinning mischievously. Gant lowered his sword and turned on them.

"What's so funny?"

"You," answered Pris making jabbing motions with his hand.

Both of them snickered again.

"I thought I heard someone in the room," said Gant gruffly and returned Valorius to her scabbard.

The elf and emperor laughed louder.

"You heard something like this?" asked Pris, mumbling an arcane phrase with a twist of his fingers and then pointing to the corner.

A loud cough burst from the spot where he'd pointed.

Reflexively Gant spun toward the noise. Now Pris and the elf burst out laughing. Gant stomped over to them, hands on hips, glaring.

"What's this all about?"

Pris forced back more laughter and tried to explain between gasps for breath. "Oakentile is teaching me magic," he answered. He got control of his spasms. "He says I've got a natural ability and could someday become a great mage. Like Abadis."

"So, what's the cough?" Gant asked, still unamused.

"It's really harmless," said Oakentile, defensively.

"And simple, too," added Pris, rattling off the words and finger movements again. Another loud cough came from the corner.

Gant ignored it. "If you've a talent for it, it's good that you get the chance to learn but isn't it dangerous? I've heard of wizards self-destructing. Blowing themselves up with a failed spell. Maybe you should ask Abadis' advice."

"It's true that messing up a spell can be dangerous," said Oakentile. "But I only know a few simple spell exercises that don't call up enough energy to do any real harm. Even messed up they aren't very dangerous. The worst might be a slight shock. These are really just mental exercises. A wizard has to have total control of his own mind first, you know. But Pris already has better mental control than I do so I thought I'd show him a little."

That's good," said Gant, pushing past towards his bedroom, "but could you practice somewhere else?"

"Sure," said Pris and they scampered off.

Gant entered his bedroom and started going through his equipment. If they were going to battle, he wanted to be sure everything was ready. He took his time unpacking everything, laying it out, cleaning and repairing or replacing things.

By the time Uric and Abadis returned, Gant had finished with his equipment and was back in the sitting room.

"Back so soon?" asked Gant jokingly.

"I eventually get hungry," said Abadis, eyeing Uric.

"Then go eat," suggested Uric, "I have better things to do."

"I thought we were waiting for the afternoon runner," said Gant, suddenly aware of the tension.

"He never made it," said Uric flatly. "I'm going to see why."

"Gorth may have already marched," added Abadis. "Many of the elves think it is too late to cut him off at Chamber Pass."

"Then we should be marching to meet him," said Gant.

"As soon as I return. Eat while you can," replied Uric.

Abadis nodded and motioned Gant out the door. "We'll see you soon," Abadis said to Uric as he and Gant headed for the dining hall.

As soon as the others were gone, Uric's body shimmered and reformed into a small, intensely yellow canary. Then, with a dainty sweep of his wings, like a specter, he flitted through the passages and out of the Caverns of Darkness. He flew westward, following the broken ridge of the Misery Mountains.

He raced along the south foothills as the sun sank behind the horizon. When darkness covered the world, and men's eyes could no longer see what passed overhead, the tiny canary lengthened, its wingspan stretched until finally Uric resumed his natural form. As a dragon he winged westward covering the miles effortlessly. His gleaming reptilian eyes seeing more than any human eyes could.

Uric followed the Misery Mountains west until they butted up against the towering Monoliths. Here he wheeled to the left and headed south. He passed high over the Mountain Castle of Barlon Gorth and flew on toward Chamber Pass. At the pass he peeled off to the right and followed the Great East-West road, sure that somewhere along this route he'd find Barlon Gorth's armies camped.

Instead, he saw a dozen wheeling, flapping black shapes, squawking at each other in an alien tongue. It was a language unfamiliar to Uric and instantly he was on alert. Uric had spent eight centuries in this world and here was a creature he had never encountered. He needed an explanation.

As the dragon sped toward the flyers, they squawked and whirled toward Uric, intent on guarding their territory. At first, they flew directly toward the dragon. As the flyers neared Uric and realized what they faced their orderly pattern broke. Panic stricken they turned and fled for Pogor, shrieking like a flock of blue jays.

Uric considered chasing them, sure that he could catch one of the obnoxious things and find out where they'd come from. Suddenly, a blaze of light erupted in the hills to his right. He banked and gave up the pursuit to investigate this unexplainable beacon.

#

Among the boulders, Sir Jarlz glared into the engulfing darkness. Any moment the demons would rush them, tearing into his party. Unable to see the enemy, he felt helpless.

"Amelia," whispered Jarlz in the direction where he'd last seen the frail girl, "can you light a fire? Quickly! If we can see these monsters, we'll have a chance."

"Don't bother with a fire," said the robed stranger in a rasping voice, "I'll give you light."

Jarlz heard the man scramble atop a large flat rock. The stranger mumbled arcane words, made intricate motions, and with the last pinch of mage's powder left to him, produced a dazzling sphere of intense white light. He cradled the glowing globe in his cupped hands and held it high overhead illuminating the area around them.

In the brilliant light Jarlz recognized the face, though the features had aged tremendously in such short a time. It was Barlon's personal wizard, Razgoth. What was he doing here? There was no time to think about it. In the glaring light a dozen of the monstrous assassins were visible. There were slashers and the four-armed, sickle-clawed slayers that leaped like frogs. Stunned by the sudden burst of light they held up a hand or claw to shield their eyes.

Jarlz leaped at the nearest creature, bringing the axe down solidly on its neck. There was a sharp crack as the dwarven axe bit through the spine and severed the head.

Immediately the circle of beasts went on the attack. Two of the monsters rushed Jarlz, their knives flashing. Another attacked Amelia. Three more surged around the innkeeper's family while others encircled Razgoth.

Jarlz retreated until his back was against a tall stone slab. The two creatures in front of him feinted, slashed and dodged, but Jarlz kept them at bay with the longer reach of the axe. But his strength ebbed quickly. Lack of sleep took its toll. He knew he couldn't hold out for long.

Amelia rolled away from her attacker into a crevice between two boulders. She pressed herself down as small as possible and slithered into the narrow opening just ahead of razor-sharp claws. Pain flared in her shoulder. She ignored it, bent on escaping the death that now dug frantically at the rock opening.

Jonathan and Ratheyon, armed with the hooked knives they'd picked up earlier, formed a protective shield around Martha. The closest monster slashed out with hooked claws. Ratheyon chopped down on the creature's exposed forearm, cutting deeply. The arm jerked back.

Another slayer rushed in, slashed twice at Jonathan and pushed past, groping for Martha.

Pain burned the innkeeper's ribs where one of the claws ripped into his chest. He ignored it, his wife's danger fueling his frenzy. He leaped on the beast from behind throwing one arm around its neck. Stinging cold surged through his body. Jonathan slashed into its back with the knife. Blood and gore spewed like a fountain. The two of them went down in a heap at Martha's feet. The third beast leaped for Jonathan's back but Ratheyon intercepted it with a quick upward thrust to the ribs. The first monster shook off the wound in his forearm and scrambled back into the battle.

Meanwhile, Razgoth held the ball of light as high as he could with one hand. Deftly he reached into his robes with the other and brought out a small green dart. With a flick of the wrist he cast it at the nearest attacker. True to the target the little dart sped. It struck the monster square in the chest, penetrated only slightly, and then erupted in a fiery blast that opened the black chest cavity like a broken pumpkin.

Enraged, three more beasts rushed Razgoth. They swarmed over him slashing and cutting with talons and knives. Valiantly the mage held the light aloft until he was crushed under by the weight of his adversaries. The light bounced once and went out.

Darkness flooded the camp. The demon-beasts howled with delight, leaping and cavorting, slashing wildly in the darkness.

Suddenly a buffeting hurricane blasted across the rocks from a mighty pair of wings. A massive shape hovered only a few feet overhead. Glinting reptilian eyes searched for prey, and faster than the eye could follow, the great dragon's head shot out. Huge fangs snapped closed on the slayer bearing down on Ratheyon.

With one claw Uric fired glowing bolts of green that struck with unerring accuracy. Beasts fell like dead leaves. Suddenly the cramped hollow between the giant rocks became a death pit for Varg's minions. Within seconds they lay dead at Uric's feet and he settled gently to the ground.

Martha cried softly, holding her husband's head in her arms. Jarlz staggered away from the protective rocks, bleeding from several wounds. Amelia crawled out from her hiding place. She slumped against the boulder, her shoulder on fire.

"Thank God," whispered Amelia. "It is you, isn't it, Uric?"

"Yes," said Uric reassuringly. "What happened? I've never seen creatures like these. They have a deep evil about them. Is Barlon calling more creatures from Varg's domain?"

"Uric!" blurted Jarlz. "By the Great Dragon's Fire, I mean, is that really you? All these years, you never told me you were a shape-changer."

"Actually, I am a dragon. Some things are better left secret, even among friends. Many times I've thought to tell you, old friend, but never found the right time." Uric sang a short arcane verse and another ball of light sprang into being in the air above them.

Jarlz checked his party. Amelia held her shoulder but otherwise seemed okay. Jonathan stirred softly in Martha's lap and appeared to be holding on despite the gash in his ribs. Ratheyon stood, knife in hand staring at the massive gold dragon that had just plunked down among them.

Jarlz walked to the rock where Razgoth's body lay. He shoved away the black carcasses atop the downed wizard. "Here's the man we needed to talk to," he said, "but I'm afraid it's too late."

"Who is he?" asked Uric, examining the mangled corpse.

"Razgoth, High Wizard for Barlon Gorth. I don't know why he's here, but something has changed in Pogor."

Uric gingerly inched up to the fallen mage. He chanted a long verse and an unearthly chill coalesced above the dead man, sending shivers through the party. A musty, dead smell rose from the corpse. When Uric finished, the eyes in Razgoth's head rolled wildly for a minute, and then focused on the dragon.

"Why do you call me?" came the hollow voice from Razgoth's unmoving lips, a voice from far away.

"You must help us," said Uric softly. "Why were you here? Why not in Pogor? And what are these demonic creatures?" Uric pointed at Varg's dead minions.

"They are the advance units of Varg's army."

"Varg's army? Has Barlon called on them too?"

"Barlon is dead. He was a fool, and I as well. Varg opened a gate to the dark regions. His evil subjects are pouring through. They come to devastate all life, as they have done in Pogor. I barely managed to escape. Soon all the land west of the Monoliths will be barren and dead. Then they will come for you."

Uric's eyes clouded in thought. No one moved, waiting. Then Uric's eyes hardened with a hatred not for the dead man at his feet but for the evil loosed upon the world.

"Where is the gate? The exact location."

"It's in the top room of the tallest tower in Pogor Castle at the northeast corner."

Uric thought for a few minutes more. Finally he spoke again. "Thank you. Go now in peace to your final resting. Fear not, your body will be buried here."

"One thing you must do for me. Tell Valdor I am sorry. He was right. I wanted to tell him myself. Ask him to forgive me."

"It will be done," said Uric and Razgoth's eyes went lifeless once more.

Uric scooped a deep grave with his sharp talons, cutting through solid rock as if it were fresh tilled soil. They laid Razgoth's body in the pit, and then Uric fused a solid slab of stone with his breath sealing the tomb airtight. With one claw he carefully scratched "Razgoth" on the surface near where the head of the wizard lay.

"Now let us return to the elves. They can treat your wounds," and Uric motioned the five survivors onto his back.

Numbly they clambered aboard, finding more than ample room on the wide expanse of Uric's back. Each rider settled securely into a spot between raised scales where they could hang on and soon the great dragon flew swiftly toward the Caverns of Darkness.

Chapter 42

The sun was coming up before Uric glided in to land at the Caverns of Darkness carrying his wounded and exhausted cargo. As soon as he landed, Uric became the familiar sage in purple robes. Dark elves swarmed out and hustled the injured to medical help.

"Tell the Queen we must meet at once," said Uric to the nearest elf.

The elf nodded and dashed back into the cave. Uric followed at a brisk walk, heading straight for Abadis and Gant's bedrooms. He woke them, dodged their questions, and told them to get dressed and meet him in the Council Chambers as soon as they could.

It wasn't long before the Great Council Chamber was a mass of elfin nobility. Uric, Gant and Abadis were given places at the table. Pris tagged along, but was relegated to a back seat. The elves did not take him seriously because he was so young. Rumors buzzed around the room with the conjecture that Barlon's army had already reached Chamber Pass. Some thought Barlon was now unstoppable.

Uric waited patiently until Sarona brought the room to order. As soon as the room fell silent, she turned to Uric sleepily, "You called for a meeting. Now you have it."

"Barlon Gorth is dead." Uric's words fell like lead. All the guessing of a few minutes before was forgotten. Several among the crowd gasped, then smiled. Many laughed, assuming the war was over. Uric let their hopes soar only a moment. "Varg has taken control."

This announcement swept the room like the scythe of death. The elves shrank in terror. Their worst nightmare had come true. Their mortal enemy was free to ravage them once more.

Before the news had fully settled in, Uric continued. "He has opened a gate to his realm and is calling an army from the Beyond. I met some of his weakest minions and even these are formidable butchers. Neither man nor elf can stand against them without a magic weapon, and against some undoubtedly only the strongest magic will have any effect.

"Everything is changed. This is no longer a war of men; it is a war for life itself. Sarona, you must beg the High Elves for help, beg for their stores of ancient weapons, retrieved and guarded for just such a time. What magic you have will be needed. If there are not enough elves to carry the weapons you have, then men must take them. We either fight together or life on this world will cease."

"And what of the dragons?" shot Sarona, an accusing glint in her eye.

"I will seek their aid, though there are some I fear will never help. Those that will, I will bring as soon as possible."

An undercurrent of speculation flashed through the room.

Finally, one Elf Lord from the middle of the throng parted those in front of him. "How do you know this? Have you been to Castle Pogor?"

"No," said Uric calmly, "but in the hills last night I spoke to Razgoth, Barlon's personal wizard. He was dying of wounds inflicted by Varg's demons. He told me what happened, admitted his own folly in Barlon's plan.

"As soon as we can rally our forces we will have to strike Castle Pogor. The magical gate must be closed at all costs. Every minute it remains open, our enemy gains strength."

Forest Lord Barkmar stood up near Sarona's right elbow. He spoke loud and clear. "Queen Sarona, allow me to go to the High Elves as your ambassador. I will do everything possible to win their support."

The Queen considered for a moment, and then nodded her approval. "As you wish. Is there anything else?"

"That is all, Majesty," said Uric with a deferential bow.

The meeting broke up. Uric stopped Lord Barkmar as he was leaving the Chamber.

"Lord Barkmar, I will fly you to the land of your cousins. It is on the way, and I can get you there much faster than on foot."

"Thank you, Dragon King, but Alnefer, the royal wizard, says he can still remember the High Elves halls. He will transfer me there this morning."

"Risky. The buildings may have changed. I'll fly you and Alnefer. He can bring you back, and once he sees how things are now he can take you there next time."

The Elf Lord thought for a moment, his eyes searching the walls as if hoping to see the answer written there. Finally he said, "Thank you. Alnefer and I will be ready within the hour. Where shall we meet?"

"At the entrance to the Caverns."

Uric hurried off, as did the elf.

Meanwhile, in another part of the caverns, Gant and Abadis walked back to their chambers.

"Is there enough magic to stop these creatures?" asked Gant.

"We'll gather the five Grand Wizards. Valdor, myself, Waltern, Nicotir, and Franathar. Each is a teacher and the highest authority on his particular specialty. The lesser wizards will be called, too, but first the Council of Five."

"Speaking of teaching someone magic, have you talked to Pris lately?"

"Yes, I spent most of yesterday afternoon with him." Abadis smiled. "I'm going to take him on as an apprentice. Haven't had an apprentice in years." He chuckled softly to himself. "And never an emperor."

"Then he's doing well?"

"Well? He's phenomenal. His mental discipline already surpasses many journeyman wizards. His mind is uncanny. He reads a spell, runs through the motions once and in a moment he's casting it. I can't believe it. If he weren't set on returning to rule the Empire, he has the potential to be the greatest mage since Bartholomew. Don't tell him I said that."

Gant wrestled with that idea. Pris a wizard? And no one was ever compared to Bartholomew. Not even the greatest living mages. Maybe the kid had hidden talents.

"Isn't it dangerous? I mean, I've heard of wizards loosing control of a spell and exploding or disintegrating."

"Of course, it is dangerous. If a wizard looses focus and let's his mind wander, then the energy summoned for a spell can run wild, out of control. And if that power is strong enough, it can be fatal. That's why it'll be a while before Pris is taught anything really powerful. For now, he's doing fine despite being impulsive. And he lacks experience in selecting the right spell for the task, but it'll come, and mark my words, Gant, he'll be a great one. Probably sit on the Council of Five one day. Maybe take my spot when I retire."

While Gant considered that news, they reached the door to their bedrooms. Abadis went through the door to their chambers while Gant continued on down the hall toward the surface. Once outside Gant found a place to sit in the sun and collected his thoughts. He knew it wouldn't be long before the biggest battle in history began. He would have to shoulder his part. What was his part? Was it just to kill Varg? There were so many things yet undone, so many things unsaid. Burning foremost in his mind was Dalphnia. What if he died? He'd never get to put things right with her.

As Gant sat in contemplation, Uric, Lord Barkmar and an ancient, shriveled elf in funny, patchwork robes came out of the Caverns. Uric changed from the sage in purple robes that Gant knew so well into a huge dragon. Gant sat stunned. Before he could catch his breath, the two elves climbed aboard and with one mighty sweep of Uric's vast wings, they were airborne. In minutes, they were tiny specks in the blue sky and then they were gone.

Uric flew north over the Misty Mountains straight for the vast forests ruled by the High Elves. He streaked over mountains, forests, plains and rivers. Soon they could see the magnificent towers that marked the High Elf capitol. Uric plummeted into the city square. He landed gently as graceful elves flocked from nearby buildings to witness the rare arrival of a dragon. As the High Elves recognized the two dark elves dismounting from Uric's golden-scaled back, their expressions soured.

"Listen to your cousins," boomed Uric, loud enough to be heard throughout the city. "If not to save yourselves, then because I, King of Dragons, request it."

Uric hated pompous displays, but this was no time for quibbling. As soon as Barkmar and Alnefer disembarked, Uric was again airborne. "I'll be back to see if you need any help," he called over his shoulder.

He soared higher and higher, rising into a fast moving river of air that rushed past his face like a tornado. He followed it, back toward the river's source, twisting and turning until he faced due west. Here he slowed until his strokes held him steady. It was only then that he sang the spellsong of home known only to dragons, a song he had waited a long time to sing again. As the spell was completed, Uric disappeared from the world of men and entered the Land of Dragons.

The instant Uric materialized in his homeland he was greeted by a shrill whistle of steam from one of the lookouts. He answered with a booming rumble and glided down into the massive, mile wide canyon that was home. His eyes soaked up the natural beauty of the cliffs, the rock faces of red, orange, brown and gold. It was gorgeous; so long only a memory that the king felt tiny droplets form at the corners of his eyes. He blinked once and reminded himself of the urgency of his business.

He glided steadily downward passing numerous ominously dark caves in the rock. Occasionally a dragon's head peeked out to see who flew past.

As he neared the great, central cavern that was the lawful home of the Dragon King, there was a snort from below and a huge golden dragon launched from the rock ledge protruding below the cave mouth. Glittering and blazing with the afternoon sun, she spiraled higher, crooning a welcome.

"Uricimalidmus," she shouted, using Uric's full name, a name shared only with family, as she climbed to greet him. "It has been a long time since you were home. I missed you, as did our sons."

"Mallamenatta," Uric replied, barrel-rolling with joy. "It has been too long, and yet I'm afraid I will go again. Perhaps you'll go too."

She swooped to him, caressing his back with her wingtips as she curled around him in midair. Together they banked and dove in to land gracefully on the wide, sandstone ledge at the entrance to their home. For a long moment they intertwined their supple bodies in silence. No words were necessary.

Slowly she separated from him.

"What are you talking about, returning to the world of men?" she asked, stepping back to study his face.

"They need our help. Varg has opened a path to the dark realms and his evil spawn are coming through bent on consuming all life."

"Can't they help themselves?"

"Maybe, but I think not. I've come to call a Council."

A great sadness filled his eyes, a sadness she could read easily.

"And what of Bazdentanfel? You'll never convince him to go."

"Then I'll take those who will go. I will not force anyone but time is our enemy. We must meet now. Where are our sons?"

"Pith is with Valmie, and Hamiz is racing the gorge. They'll be back soon. You rest, I'll call the others."

Uric nodded, then nipped playfully at Mall's ear. She ignored it and launched herself from the ledge, banking away to the left.

Uric slipped into his home. The cool stone so familiar, yet after years of absence, there was a strangeness about it. The central corridor ran slightly downhill, and then opened out into a huge, domed amphitheater hundreds of feet across with a raised rock plateau fifty feet high at the far end. Almost reluctantly, Uric stretched his wings and flew to perch atop the plateau where he could be seen by all the dragons that would soon arrive. Centuries past, the Council Theater would have been packed with hundreds of dragons. Today, Uric knew there would be few indeed.

Silently he waited. His thoughts focused on his promise to Bartholomew, powerful wizard and true dragon friend. He weighed that promise against family responsibilities. Yes, he'd promised to see this through to its end, see Varg defeated once more. But in some ways Uric wondered if men were better left to their fate. Too often he'd seen friends turn on one another over matters of honor. What honor came from killing friends? It didn't matter, he'd given his word and he would not go back on it.

The sound of leathery wings interrupted his thoughts. A silvery head poked into the chamber followed by a slim, silver body.

"Father," came his son's loud whistle. "You've returned at last. I thought I would molt to gold before you returned."

"Yes, Pith. By your size, I'd say you are about ready. I'm glad I waited no longer. You look splendid. How's Valmie?"

"She's fine. She'll be here soon. Mom says you've come to call a Dragon Council."

"Yes. Times are not well in the outer world. I hope this business can soon be ended."

Before they could say anything else, there was a rustle of wings and two more dragons, a great red and a great black, rumbled into the massive chamber.

"Bazdentanfel, welcome," said Uric, "and to you, too, Mizradefindis."

"Thank you. Mizradefindis and I are glad to see you," said the massive black, seating himself.

Other dragons trooped in and found room near the base of Uric's raised plateau. Uric's wife returned and took her spot beside him. His two sons were given honored spots at the foot of the plateau.

Slowly Uric related the events from the outside world, as accurately as he could. When he finished, the assemblage remained silent for long moments, each dragon revisiting their memories of men and their world.

Finally it was Bazdentanfel who spoke. "I will not help. I would rather aid Varg and his demons. I lost two sons to men and my father died at the hands of the demented mage Amodeus, Slayer of Dragons. I said I would never return to their world and I will not, unless it is to seek revenge."

Others murmured agreement. Uric knew that within minutes all would be lost; that none would come. "It is true, many of us have reason to hate humans. I, too, have lost ancestors at their hands. Yet there are many dragon friends among them. Many of them cherish things of beauty as we do. And love binds them in its purest forms, as we too love. Can we let them die? Are there none amongst them worth saving? And what of the elves?"

"It doesn't matter," said the black dragon, rising. "They have tormented and hated our kind for eons. Now they get their just reward."

"Wait," shouted Uric. The assemblage stopped, some halfway up. "Think what you are doing. All life will die! Are we as callous as the worst men?"

A faint murmur rustled through the assembly but none voiced support.

"If we turn our backs now, who will come to help us when Varg needs more victims to fuel his lust for death? What will stop him from killing us, too?"

Again there were hushed whispers of agreement, nods of approval.

"I'll stop him," snapped Bazdentanfel. "We are dragons, you know, not men." Bitter contempt resounded as he spat the last word.

With that, Bazdentanfel stretched, turned and stalked proudly from the chamber, Mizradefindis behind him. About half the others filed out with them. Those remaining whispered among themselves, the current of conversation running sympathetic to the old black dragon.

"It is as I feared," said Uric softly, bending near his wife. "Where has our sense of morality gone?"

"Taken by men's magic," she hissed. "Only you have seen good in their hearts."

"Would you turn against them, too?"

"No, my husband, but I ask you not to think poorly of the others."

Uric turned back to those still seated in the room.

"Who will follow me?" he asked.

Only his two sons spoke up, their voices brimming with an enthusiasm born of Uric's many stories of the outer world, a world they'd longed to see but had been forbidden.

And then, hesitantly, Valmie added her voice to that of Uric's sons. And Ferthanzama, Valmie's gold-scaled mother, nodded her ascent.

"It is but we six, then," said Uric to those remaining. "I had hoped for more. What of you Veeverfisma?" Uric pointed to an ancient red dragon, turned orange with age who sat near the plateau.

"No," she shook her head. "I am too old for it."

"Are there no others?"

None answered.

"If that's all the help I bring, so be it. I hope it is enough. We can't wait any longer. Follow me."

Uric launched himself from the towering rock platform and soared straight across the vast chamber. Folding his wings, he shot through the connecting tunnel and burst from the cave entrance into the bright blue sky like a golden streak.

The two large golden females followed. Behind them came the three younger silver shapes, straining their wings to keep up. When they reached the magical aura of the transfer zone they chanted the verse of passage like a choir on their best night.

Suddenly they were over a vast ocean, winging their way to the dark land mass ahead. Swiftly Uric led them over the looming cliffs where waves burst on a jagged shoreline, across pine forests and sweeping meadows, until at last they settled in the center of the dazzling city of the High Elves.

It only took a few moments for a large crowd of elves to gather. The young silver dragons were awed. It was their first sight of creatures they'd only heard about in stories. Immediately they started a buzz of childish small talk behind their parents' backs. Likewise, the elves gathered to admire the beauty and power of the dragons. For many this was their first dragon sighting.

As the crowd milled around the huge reptiles, many of the elves hesitantly touched the great, scaled sides. Uric sat motionless until he sighted Forest Lord Barkmar pushing his way through his massed cousins carrying a package wrapped in heavy cloth. Behind Barkmar came several less enthusiastic, gray haired elders.

"Dragon King," Barkmar addressed Uric. "My cousins have reluctantly agreed to lend us their magical weaponry. And they will lend us one company of their finest archers equipped with arrows of power. That's it."

"You have done better than I, but no use quibbling. While we talk, our enemy grows more numerous."

"Yes. Alnefer and the High Elf mage Hawthorne have already begun transfer of the equipment and archers. I'll return with you, if you don't mind."

"My pleasure. Climb aboard."

The dark elf stepped on Uric's forearm and then vaulted to a place upon his broad back and seated himself where he could hold onto a raised scale with one hand and cradle the bundled present with the other. As Uric spread his wings to leave, the nearest silver-haired elf elder stepped forward.

"Lord Barkmar," he said in a voice stronger than his frail, old body seemed capable of producing. "Tell your Queen we will come to negotiate peace when this is done. Perhaps the dark and fair skinned elves can overcome their differences."

"I look forward to the meeting of our peoples," said the Forest Lord, as his dragon mount leaped to the skies.

"Don't forget the emperor's gift," yelled the High Elf leader at the departing silhouette.

The six mighty dragons soared gracefully into the cloud-flecked sky.

"What gift?" asked Uric, turning his head around on his long muscular neck so he could talk to his passenger face-to-face.

"This," said Lord Barkmar, holding up a cloth-wrapped parcel. "It is Thantalmos. Screaming Death. Gift of the High Elves to the first Emperor, Kristoph. Lost in the First Forest War when the elves fought the 7th Emperor, Maxidim, for control of the vast central forest before the High Elves moved north. The High Elves vowed it would never fall into human hands again. Now there is hope that peace will return between peoples, and this is a sign to the emperor that the High Elves are ready to pursue that peace."

"I've heard the legend of Thantalmos, though that is one story from before my time. I only hope Pris lives to regain his Empire so the hope planted this day will see fruit."

The Dark Elf sat still for a moment, staring off into space, a blank look on his face. "The same could be said of my people and my cousins," he said. "I also wish reason could overcome mindless hatred, ancient prejudice, but time will tell."

They flew on, faster with each stroke of mighty wings. The wind rushed past trying to blow the elf lord from Uric's back but Lord Barkmar held tightly to the package even as he clung to Uric's back.

Chapter 43

When Uric, Lord Barkmar and the dragons arrived at the Caverns of Darkness, they found an army camped in the surrounding foothills. King Tirmus and his few surviving knights had arrived along with King Herzolt of Mulldain and his thousand-man army. Their tents spread out around the cave mouth, their pennants flapping in the breeze.

The moment Uric touched down, an elf dashed up. "Dragon King," he said, "Sarona asks that you and Lord Barkmar join her in the War Hall for a meeting immediately."

Uric transformed into the purple robed sage and the other dragons used their natural shape-changing talent to become men and women dressed in long robes. The elves watched in silence, many of them old enough to remember when dragons were commonly seen doing just that. Once changed, Uric followed Lord Barkmar to the War Hall while the others found an unobtrusive place to wait. By the time Uric and Barkmar got there, the hall was packed. The lower level was jammed with lesser elfin nobles and unit commanders from the armies of men. On the raised central section, Sarona stood at the head of the map table along with Abadis, both of the Kings, Gant, and a host of elfin lords and military commanders.

"Welcome, Dragon King," said Sarona, catching sight of Uric. "What news do you bring?"

"The high elves have promised to dispatch a company of their best archers under the command of the High Elf Lord

Hawthorne to support our defense and they are willing to lend us what magical weapons they have."

Lord Barkmar, still holding onto the package he'd brought with him spoke up. "It is little enough, your majesty. I did my best but our cousins are less than enthusiastic about helping us."

"You did well, Lord Barkmar," said the queen. "See that the magical weapons are dispersed as evenly as possible between men and elves."

"It won't be enough," said Uric. "The creatures that Varg calls from his plane are impervious to normal weapons of any kind and some of the most powerful can only be harmed by weapons equally powerful. Any concerted attack by them will be our ruin."

"What do you suggest?" asked Sarona.

Abadis leaned forward. "Perhaps we should capture the Mountain Castle. There are magic weapons in Barlon's armory and I do not think there is a strong contingent guarding it."

After a moment of whispers throughout the gathering, Queen Sarona stood. "Then it shall be done. Lord Barkmar, take the Forest Division and assist the armies of men to retake the Mountain Castle. At the same time we need to defend Chamber Pass least our enemies overrun us on our side of the Monoliths. Lord Malimir," she said looking at an elf standing next to Lord Barkmar, "the Mountain Division will fortify and hold the pass along with the High Elfin archers. Lord Hawthorne will report to you. You must hold Chamber Pass at all costs."

"As you wish," said Lord Malimir.

"Majesty," said Uric. "Dragons can open the gates to the Mountain Castle."

"Yes, that would speed things and time is of the essence. Go with Lord Barkmar and retrieve what magic weapons can be recovered as fast as possible."

"If you have no task for me," said Abadis, "I'll track down the members of the Council of Five and bring them here. I think we will need all the support we can muster if we are going to close Varg's portal."

"Go with our blessings," said the queen. "King Tirmus and King Herzolt will remain here with me until you return. Then we will plan our assault on Pogor and figure out how to close that portal."

"I had planned to go with my army," said King Herzolt.

"I also," added King Tirmus.

"You have capable leaders who can handle the attack on the castle. More important will be our quest to close that portal and for that we must be in total agreement. I cannot plan such an operation without you."

After a moment of strained silence, both kings nodded agreement.

"If King Tirmus is in agreement, my eldest son, Prince Theodore, will command the combined armies of Mulldain and Netherdorf," added King Herzolt. "He is a capable leader and has lead my armies before in border clashes in the northern forests."

"Agreed," said King Tirmus.

"Then we are agreed," said Sarona. "Any questions?"

The room remained silent, everyone contemplating their assigned task.

"Then be off," she said and the meeting was over.

What magic weapons they had were distributed immediately following the meeting. It didn't take long.

By late afternoon the combined armies of Mulldain and Netherdorf were ready to begin the march to Barlon's castle. Before the armies set off, Gant was called to a meeting with King Tirmus. With a lump in his throat he entered the king's tent and found it crowded with nobles and knights. Gant knew many of them including his Uncle Jarlz.

Sheepishly Gant approached the table set up near the back of the tent where King Tirmus huddled with his commanders. The king looked up and spied Gant.

"Come on in," he said, motioning Gant to the table. "I've been waiting to see you."

"If it's about Wendler," started Gant.

The king cut him off with a wave of his hand. "Wendler and his father have shown their true colors. You have committed no crime that I can see, and more so, have exhibited courage and duty that are befitting of knights. Therefore, kneel, Gant of the Ironlimbs."

Gant shivered, his stomach rolled over and he swallowed hard. "Sire?"

"Kneel," said the king and withdrew his sword.

Gant knelt, his heart pounding.

Touching Gant's shoulder lightly with his sword, King Tirmus announced, "I dub thee, Sir Gant of the Ironlimbs, knight of the realm of Netherdorf. Rise and be recognized."

Gant managed to get up hardly aware of the cheers from those gathered in the tent.

"Further more," continued the king, "I place you in command of the Knights of Netherdorf."

To Gant's surprise, the knights cheered and shouted, "Hail the Devonshield Champion."

Uncle Jarlz approached Gant, a serious expression on his face. He clapped Gant on the back and said, "Congratulations. You've earned your place as knight and leader. I'll be proud to serve under you."

Gant studied his uncle for a moment. There was something different about him, something lost. "You look sad. What happened?"

"Not now," said Jarlz, the melancholy in his eyes deepening. "We have more important things to do. Someday I'll tell you what I remember. Maybe."

It made Gant uncomfortable. In an instant he'd gone from outlawed blacksmith's son to knight and commander. Even more bothersome was the fact that something had changed with his uncle.

Trumpets sounded assembly and Gant joined his new unit only to find Zandinar, Pris, Kalmine, Captain Hesh and his three soldiers waiting with the knights.

"Hey Gant, we've been assigned as your personal guards," said Pris. "This is going to be great."

Captain Hesh frowned. Kalmine nudged the emperor. Zandinar scowled.

"Probably not," said Gant and surveyed his line of knights.

At that moment, Lord Barkmar approached Pris carrying the package he'd brought from the High Elves.

"A gift for you," said the elfin lord and handed the package to Pris.

Gant watched the boy's eyes bulge as he unwrapped a magnificent sword recognizable to anyone who knew the legend of the sword of emperors.

"Wow. Thantalmos," exclaimed Pris, reverently cradling the sword in both hands. "I can't wait to get back to the capitol with this."

"Time for that later," said Kalmine and ushered the emperor to a waiting horse.

Gant could only shake his head. He knew the legend of Thantalmos, sword of Emperors. Only one man could hold it, the true emperor. Pris! Noting the gleam in the emperor's eye as he strapped on the sword Gant wondered what mischief the emperor planned.

And then, with high hopes, the armies moved out. Gant's squad of knights fell in behind Lord Barkmar and Prince Theodore.

By nightfall, they had barely gone five miles. At dusk the foot-weary men set up camp. Strict discipline and a routine practiced many times made it a simple matter. The elves established perimeter guard positions and since they were still a long way from the Mountain Castle, campfires were lit to fight the chill night air.

They pitched a headquarters tent and next to it set the banners of Mulldain, Netherdorf, Lord Barkmar and the Eastern Empire. Uric and the accompanying dragons took human form and spent the night in camp, except for one who flew patrol over the camp in case any of the black flyers crossed the Monoliths.

After a short review of the plans for the next day, the command tent emptied. As the meeting broke up Pris looked for a chance to talk to Uric or Lord Barkmar about the sword from the High Elves. The Dragon King slipped away and spent the evening with his family. Lord Barkmar and Prince Theodore went to their tents immediately after the meeting and did not take visitors.

Gant alone stayed in the tent. His new leadership position worried him. It was one thing to be responsible for your own actions, another to have responsibility for others. Between that and thoughts of the coming battle he knew he'd never sleep. He went over the strategy. The plan was simple enough. Maybe that's what bothered him. It was too simple. The dragons would crash the gates. The army would pour in and overwhelm the defenders.

He, Zandinar and the Netherdorf Knights would lead the charge. He wasn't sure what he'd do with Pris. He couldn't have the emperor up front.

Gant studied the maps. As the night dragged on, he thought more and more about their real foe waiting in Pogor. What would it take to reach Pogor and close the gate?

Shortly after mid-watch, a dark skinned elf runner entered the command tent.

"Where is Lord Barkmar?" he asked, looking around the tent.

"Gone to bed," said Gant, looking up from the maps. "What is it?"

"A spy."

"In camp?"

"No, sir." Gant found it funny to hear the elf address him as "sir." "They got past the first two outposts. I shot at him with my bow and he ran. We found two guards on the outer perimeter fast asleep."

"How many intruders were there?"

"Only one as best I could tell."

"Then I don't think it's too important. A single spy who never even reached the camp's interior can't have done much harm. By afternoon, our coming won't be a secret anymore anyway."

"Sir, you don't understand. Elves do *not* fall asleep on duty. They've had a spell put on them. There may be magic traps laid in our midst."

Gant considered that possibility and decided at least some investigation was warranted. "I'll have Uric check," he said. "You may return to your post. I'll tell Lord Barkmar when he awakens."

"As you wish, sir."

The elf retired from the tent. Gant hesitated a moment. Had he been too hasty? Perhaps it was a harmless incident, perhaps not. He'd get Uric to check for magical mischief and if anything was amiss, he'd find it.

Gant strode to the dragons' tent, happy to have a simple problem to occupy his mind. When he got there, he found Hamiz, one of Uric's sons, preparing to take over aerial patrol. Gant explained his dilemma and the silver dragon insisted on carrying out the investigation so his father could sleep. Within minutes Hamiz was back, reporting that there were no magic traps anywhere in camp.

Relieved, Gant returned to the command tent. Eventually he fell asleep in a chair. In the morning, Gant woke sputtering, drenched in a cold splash of water. He lurched awake ready to thrash someone. Pris stood alone in the tent, a smirk on his face. One look at Pris' boyish face and Gant's anger evaporated. Gant laughed and wiped his face with his hands. Pris laughed, too. The emperor was a likeable rascal and Gant hoped nothing would happen to him before they returned to Malathon.

"What is with you and these practical jokes?" asked Gant, wiping off with a towel he found near the washbasin.

"I'm just practicing my magic," said Pris. "Now come on, let's get some breakfast before it's all gone."

Off they went to the mess tent where breakfast was being served by the experienced supply personnel from Mulldain who didn't seem to mind the extra mouths. An hour after sunrise, the army marched on through the mountains, winding their way between the steep, impassable crags. The sun shone down through sparse white puffs scattered across the blue dome of the sky. The air was cool and the column made good speed.

Chapter 44

By noon, the forward scouts encountered the outlying posts of the Mountain Castle. There was only marginal resistance from the few soldiers manning the outposts. The elves quickly neutralized them and tried to seal off all routes back to the castle but several of Barlon's messengers got through. Steadily the army moved forward.

After several more hours of hard marching the ominous black stone fortification rose ahead, standing out against the light browns and grays of the surrounding rock. The castle stood near the top of a rocky peak with the mountainside sloping steeply downward from it. A single gravel and rock road led up to the main gates. It was an imposing sight, designed for easy defense.

Undaunted, the army marched on, the men in high spirits now that their target was in sight. On command from Prince Theodore, the army spread out and ringed the downslope side of the castle well out of arrow range. He arranged his cavalry near the road, ready to charge to the castle once the gates were opened.

The younger dragons wheeled overhead, while Uric, in sage form, walked with the command group. Gant waited with his knights. At any moment the dragons would crash through the Mountain Castle's heavy iron bound gates. Gant felt his pulse quicken.

Suddenly, against the blue sky, he saw a dark speck flying toward them at incredible speed from the northwest. One of Uric's sons flew to intercept it while it was still a long way off. As Gant watched, the much smaller silver dragon escorted a huge dragon in to land near the Dragon King. The new arrival bowed her head as she landed, her red scales faded to orange, her eyes soft and mellow, the years having taken their toll.

"Dragon King," she addressed Uric with soft deference.

"Yes, Vee," said Uric, "have you come to join us?"

"No, as I told you, I am too old for such nonsense but I owe you debts of honor from years past so I came to warn you. Bat is going to lead the others against you. He made a pact with the Demon-Prince to assure his position when the forces of darkness come to power. The others are silly youngsters who will not listen to me. I fear it will be dragon against dragon. If it must be, I stand with my king."

Uric bowed low. Vee was the oldest living dragon. She had survived more battles with men and beasts than most could remember. In her time she had been a power unto herself. Now, her time ran short but her mind was filled with an ancient wisdom.

"Thank you for coming. We must go and stop Bat before it is too late. If dragons help guard the portal it will be nearly impossible to close." Uric turned to the others. Fear registered in the faces of many of the elves. Whispers of dragons fighting alongside the horrible forces from the dark realms spread like a cancer.

Uric knew there was no time for talk. "You'll have to manage the castle," he said. "I'll be back when I can. If I can."

Without another word Uric leaped into the air, changing shape as he rose. In an instant all of the dragons were airborne. Lord Barkmar, Gant, Prince Theodore and the other commanders stared after them. For long moments they remained silent, watching the rapidly diminishing dots on the horizon. Soon all seven dragons were gone.

"Now what?" demanded Prince Theodore, glaring at those around him.

"You heard him," said Lord Barkmar, "we'll have to take the castle ourselves. Have the men form siege lines with grappling hooks."

"Are you crazy?" shot back the Prince. "It'll be hard enough to climb up the mountain side much less reach the walls. Even if we had a battering ram, preferably one with overhead cover to shield the troops, how would we get it to the gates?"

"Well we don't have any of it. There aren't even any trees to build a battering ram," said Lord Barkmar hotly. "And we can't just stand here doing nothing."

Gant stepped between them. "It's plain we don't have the siege equipment we need, and that we don't have time to starve them out. But we can't be throwing away men's lives either. We'll have to come up with another plan."

"Like what?" asked both of them.

"I don't know. Maybe Zandinar and I can climb the ropes and gain a foothold on the wall. Think! Between us we've got to be able to come up with something better than rushing up the side of a mountain to attack a castle."

For a moment they did stop to think but before anyone could offer another plan, an elf runner raced up.

"Lord Barkmar," said the runner, stopping at rigid attention.

"What?" Barkmar asked, scowling at the intrusion.

"Sir, we are being attacked by an army of trees."

"Trees? What are you talking about, elf?" snapped Prince Theodore.

The elf turned and pointed to the rocky canyon that extended away to the east. Gant shaded his eyes from the sun with one hand and looked in the direction the elf pointed. At the far end of the canyon stood a solid green forest that hadn't been there earlier. Closer, a groove of tall hickory trees had detached itself from the main forest and slowly, like a herd of ponderous beasts, advanced upon the rear of the siege army.

"Evil magic," stomped Prince Theodore.

"It must be an illusion," said Lord Barkmar.

"Perhaps," said Gant, "but we'd better find out before it reaches our troops. Zandinar and I'll go."

"Me, too," added Pris.

Gant glared at the young emperor.

"We'll all go," said the Elf Lord, starting off with springy strides toward the advancing wall of trees. "There are many possible explanations, some good, some evil, but we'd better find out which it is quickly."

Gant whirled to follow along with the rest of the command staff. They rushed past the troops waiting for the call to battle. Rumors flashed through the camp and soon every officer along their path fell in behind them in an ever-growing military parade. Down the draw they went, picking up speed as they neared the lumbering trees. About a hundred yards from them, Lord Barkmar halted the procession. Those at the rear spread out until the entire canyon width was four or five deep in soldiers, all buzzing with questions.

"Now what?" asked Prince Theodore, watching the trees advance unchecked.

Lord Barkmar studied the trees for a minute, and then turned back to the Prince. "What if they're peaceful?"

Without another word, Prince Theodore turned and strutted three steps ahead of the soldiers massed at their back. "Stop," he yelled at the top of his lungs, holding up one hand to signal a halt, "and state your business."

Behind them Pris giggled until Kalmine hushed him.

"Perhaps you could do better," snapped Prince Theodore turning on the boy.

"Yeah," shot back Pris, undaunted. "Like a fireball in their midst."

"Enough," snapped Lord Barkmar.

"Look, they've stopped," cried several voices from the crowd.

Indeed the front line of thick-trunked hickories had halted, each tree settling to earth with a thunderous rumble.

From within the line of trees a loud voice boomed toward the men. "I seek audience with Gant of the Ironlimbs. Send him forth, alone."

"What is this?" mumbled a startled Lord Barkmar.

"Friends of yours?" Pris asked Gant with a wink.

"You can't go," said Prince Theodore. "It's a trap."

"And we can't stand around gawking at each other," said Gant. "I fought Egog. I'm not running from a dozen trees."

Gant started resolutely toward the cluster of trees. The instant he reached for his sword, Valorius magically left its scabbard and flew into his beckoning hand. "Wait here. If I'm not back soon, burn them to their roots."

Gant walked warily toward the somber, leafy hardwoods. As he approached, the nearest trees heaved themselves up and moved aside, using their thick roots like crabs scurrying across the sand. The second row of trees did likewise and Gant stepped gingerly into the aisle formed for him.

At any moment he expected an ambush, creatures of darkness to sweep him under. He'd never seen a tree walk. How could anything less than a god or devil be responsible?

He followed the open trail into their midst. Over his shoulder he noticed the trees closed in behind him cutting off the view of his comrades. The only noise was the sound of his own soft footfalls on the loose rocks of the canyon floor.

Finally the trail ended in a small, sunlit glade. He stepped to the center, peering into the shadows surrounding him. There were no sounds, no movements. For a moment he began to think he was alone.

"Gant?" came a soft, musical voice that was sweetly familiar. "Is that you?"

"Yes," he said. "Is it. . . ?"

Dalphnia stepped out from between protective trunks, her long brown hair sweeping down over her shoulders like a royal train. Her walnut brown eyes sparkled as she stepped into the sunlight. Her smile challenged the daylight.

"I have looked so long for you."

Gant lowered Valorius. "Dalphnia," he choked.

It was all he could get out before she wrapped her arms around him, kissing him with a burning fire. Together they stood in a shaft of sunlight, embracing, the rest of the world forgotten.

Gant pulled back. "What are you doing here?" he asked softly, holding her at arm's length.

"I came for you. I love you."

"And my thoughts have been on you ever since I left. I told you I would return as soon as the war is over; as soon as Varg is defeated."

"Varg?" she spat.

"Yes, he has returned, and brought creatures of darkness with him." Gant explained briefly all that had happened since he'd left Dalphnia's peaceful gardens. By the time he finished, her mouth stood open.

"You should go home. Wait for me there. It'll be safer," he said.

Her face remained cold and stern.

Finally her features softened. "I'll go with you," she said. "There's a lot I can do."

Gant was about to say no when a roaring blast of fire ripped through the trees, scorching trunks, crumpling leaves and catching several of them on fire.

"Stop! Stop!" yelled Gant, racing back toward his friends.

He ran through the trees heedless of the heat and flames. Here and there some of the trees smoldered. Gant burst out of the grove. Several of his companions had moved closer, including Lord Barkmar, Pris, Zandinar and Prince Theodore.

"What's going on?" yelled Gant, running up to them.

"Oh," said Pris sheepishly, "you're all right."

"Did you do that?"

"Yes," said Pris, eyes lowering. "You said if you weren't back soon to. . ."

Gant cut him off. "Forget that, we've got to put out the fire. Quick!"

"No problem," beamed Pris amid stern stares from the others.

Before anyone could object, Pris poured a thimbleful of water into one palm, recited a magical verse, contorted his fingers just so, and threw the water into the air. Instantly a sheet of water formed in midair above the smoldering trees. It fell heavily, dousing the hungry flames amid a sizzle of protest. Little wisps of steam hissed up from blackened trunks, but the fire was out.

Then, from the shadows of the trunks stomped a tall woman, her hair hung in wet, matted tangles. She shook the water off her arms, sputtering as she walked toward them. Behind him Gant heard the soft rustling as arrows were fitted to bow strings.

"Put them down," shouted Gant, turning to the archers behind him. "She's a friend."

Hesitantly the bows sagged. Arrows were returned to their quivers. Gant turned and ran down to take Dalphnia's arm.

"Some welcome," she snapped.

"Sorry," was all he could manage.

But the light was back in her eyes. She smiled and hugged Gant. By then they'd reached the command group and Gant quickly introduced Dalphnia to the enraptured men and elves. Introductions finished, Gant turned back to Dalphnia. "What are you doing here with an army of trees?"

"Trying to get close to you without getting stuck by an arrow. Last night I tried to sneak into camp. I got past the first two sentries, but the third shot an arrow at me. The trees were to make sure it didn't happen again."

"Well you've come just in time," said Lord Barkmar. "Do you think your trees could break down the castle gates?"

Dalphnia thought for a moment. "Probably as long as I remained close enough. Trees do not handle complicated tasks without constant encouragement."

Lord Barkmar smiled. "Wonderful. Likely the castle defenders will shoot a lot of arrows at them if they advance on the gates. Do you think they will be able to withstand such an attack?"

"Arrows are not much concern," said Dalphnia. "Fire is another matter."

Lord Barkmar turned to Pris. "Can you repeat any of the spells you just cast? If so, maybe between them and our archers we can keep those on the walls from trying to burn the trees."

Pris smiled. "I've got enough of Abadis' powder to cast the ball of fire once more though I'm not so sure about the water spell."

"Fine," said Prince Theodore, "let's get on with it."

Lord Barkmar turned to his archer captains. "Move into range of the castle parapets and stay under cover. I don't want anyone wasting arrows until we see the first sign of flames. The instant it is clear that they are going to try to burn the trees, I want everyone to shower them with arrows as fast as you can."

With that, the archer captains moved their troops into position.

"I'm going with Dalphnia," said Gant. "Sir Jarlz will take command of the Netherdorf Knights."

"Okay," said Prince Theodore. "I want all the mounted units at the ready on the road out of arrow range under my command. The instant the gates are opened, we will charge straight into the castle. The foot soldiers will follow. Lord Barkmar you have command of the remaining units."

"Let's move," said Barkmar and everyone hurried to their assigned positions.

Dalphnia and Gant walked down into the grove of hickory trees. Once in the middle Dalphnia used her extraordinary ability to connect with the trees urging them into movement toward the castle gates. They trees obediently lurched up and lumbered to the road. Once on the road they turned and headed toward the castle. Dalphnia and Gant walked along staying in the midst of the clustered hickories.

"You're amazing," said Gant. "How do you do it?"

Dalphnia laughed. "It's what all woodland nymphs can do. We not only enchant men, we enchant trees as well. Now let me concentrate. This isn't easy for me or the trees. It's more complicated than the kinds of things trees usually do."

Onward toward the castle they went, being careful to stay within the protective grove. The trees ambled slowly uphill toward the castle gates. Heads appeared over the battlements, faces that stared down in disbelief. Then a smattering of arrows arced down, thunking into the hardwood trunks or glancing harmlessly off the branches.

Gant pulled Dalphnia behind him. "Stay behind me. My armor will stop any arrows and I don't want you getting hurt."

Soon the arrows flew thicker and thicker until the air was nearly filled with shafts. Several glanced off Gant's armor, nearly missing Dalphnia.

"Are you sure you have to be with the trees?"

She huddled behind Gant. "It's the only way this will work."

They kept moving slowly forward and the arrows continued to rain down on them. It hardly bothered the trees. From their ordered positions, the elves and men watched, holding their fire, content to let those in the castle waste their arrows.

It wasn't long before the men on the parapets realized their folly and the arrow storm abated. As the trees surrounding Gant and Dalphnia reached the gates, the first flask of burning oil appeared on the wall. The bright orange flames stood out like a beacon. It was the signal the elves had been waiting for. A flurry of arrows whistled toward the top of the castle walls, bringing cries and angry shouts from behind the merlons. A single burning flask fell harmlessly to the ground away from the trees. Before more oil could appear, a huge ball of fire flashed through the air and splattered on the upper edge of the wall sending the defenders scurrying for cover.

"Now's our chance," said Dalphnia and the trees went to work.

As Gant watched, Dalphnia guided them skillfully up against the castle gates. First the trees sent thick, braided roots burrowing into the rocky soil. The ground cracked and heaved as the root system swelled the earth out of its natural bed. Once anchored, the hickories forced their strongest limbs against the massive gates. Several of the largest trees leaned in applying pressure with their trunks. There was a tremendous grating sound followed by tortuous creaks, moans and snaps.

All other noise stopped. Everyone watched spellbound, waiting to see if the trees could force open the iron strapped doors. From above, dozens of eyes peered over the top of the wall. Suddenly, with a tremendous boom, the gates splintered, sagging open on bent and twisted hinges.

A fierce battle cry sounded behind Gant followed by the thunder of charging horses. The trees parted and Prince Theodore and Sir Jarlz galloped past at the head of the column of knights. Zandinar tossed Gant a sword salute as he rode by.

Gant kissed Dalphnia hard. "Retreat, you've done your job, we'll take care of the rest. Wait for me at the command tent, I'll be there soon."

Their eyes locked for one long moment. In her eyes was the quiet peace Gant dreamed of. For now it had to wait. Gant spun and ran toward the courtyard. Reaching for Valorius brought the sword instantly into his right hand. He pulled down his visor with the other hand and rushed into battle. Already, the trees were uprooting and retreating.

Immediately inside the castle, Gant found chaos. Men wearing Barlon's black and gold ran down the stairs from the battlements brandishing axes and maces. Almost before Gant was inside the gate he was attacked by a brutish man swinging an axe. Gant ducked and sliced underneath cutting through the man's chest.

A clang rang from Gant's back plate, the force knocking him a step forward. He wheeled to find a swarthy, bearded mercenary staring dumbfounded at the splintered knob of an axe handle still in his hand. Gant severed his throat before he could draw another weapon.

To Gant's right was one of King Tirmus' knights, Sir Ragula, besieged by a mob of chain-mailed swordsmen who threatened to pull him off his horse. Gant hacked down the only man between him and the knight, and then he was at the back of the nearest of Ragula's attackers. Gant swung Valorius back and forth like cutting wheat; the magic in her blade severed the hard iron links like so much straw, cleaving through the man's backbone. Gant waded into the midst of the group, swinging Valorius over and over, felling one after another.

Within minutes, Sir Ragula was riding to catch up with Prince Theodore, Sir Jarlz and Zandinar, who had cleared a swathe through the undermanned ranks of the castle defenders. By then the castle was in full rout and those trying to flee through the gates fell to the foot soldiers pouring in from outside. It wasn't long before the Mountain Castle was entirely in friendly hands. Gant saw Lord Barkmar enter with a squad of bowmen. The dark elf began issuing orders, supervising the orderly search and liberation of the castle.

Prince Theodore rejoined Lord Barkmar, while the knights encircled the few prisoners.

Gant caught up with Lord Barkmar as the elf was about to enter the main stronghold.

"If you don't need me for anything further," said Gant, "I'll be back at my tent."

The elf nodded without turning and Gant was off at a run.

He could hardly contain himself. He rushed to Dalphnia. And she, just as eager for their reunion, greeted him warmly. She hugged and kissed him. They slipped away to Gant's tent to spend what time they could alone.

Chapter 45

In his private tent, Gant and Dalphnia shared the evening meal and a glass of wine. Their hands touched lightly while they ate, letting their fingers tell what their words didn't have to, absorbed in each other.

Eventually Gant told Dalphnia about his travels, about meeting Zandinar, Abadis, Amelia and Emperor Pris. After which Dalphnia explained her decision to search for Gant and, as a woodland nymph, why that was such a difficult decision to make. She told about traveling to Falls Hill and the riverboat voyage where she ran into Abadis. Finally she told him about her near disaster with the woodsmen. Gant still found it hard to believe her unique abilities to both charm men and bond with the trees and forest animals. He knew that she had originally used her powers of enchantment to capture his heart but now it was her warmth, honesty and beauty that fueled the genuine love he had for her. There was no more need for enchantments.

Pris interrupted them with a shout from outside the tent flap. "Gant, come quick. There's someone in the castle that you need to see."

Gant slid his hand from Dalphnia's. "I'm coming, Pris," he said, and then added to Dalphnia, "Come with me."

"Sure," she said standing, wrapping one arm around his waist.

They exited through the flap and found Patt and Faltern waiting with the grim-faced emperor.

"Lead the way," said Gant, waving for Pris to guide them. And then noticing Krist's absence, asked, "Where's Krist?"

Pris struggled to speak, a watery shine in his eyes. His two guards maintained a military brace, but their red eyes forewarned of the tragedy Gant guessed was coming.

The emperor choked. "H-he took an arrow." He paused to take in a breath and regain his voice. "He's dead."

It was like a stab in the gut. Gant liked the soldier, admired his loyalty to Pris, and remembered his naïve hero worship. A tear stung Gant's eye. He fought to keep back a flood.

Dalphnia's empathetic nature sensed the others' deep sadness. She said, "I'm so sorry. He must have been someone special."

Gant clenched his teeth, fought to steady his breathing and started toward the castle. "Let's go," he said, forcing his thoughts to Pris' insistence that he go to the castle. "Who's here that I need to see?"

The group lurched forward.

Pris' mood lightened ever so slightly. "Just wait, you'll see."

He darted ahead, hurrying in through the castle gates. Once inside the walls they crossed the courtyard where Gant noticed the Netherdorf knights staged near a long, low building. Without stopping Pris went straight to the massive central keep. Out front a ring of banners flapped in the breeze while several guards stood at attention. The double doors stood open and inside the keep they found a narrow hallway that led back to a set of tall doors. Lamps hung along both walls brightened the interior. A throng milled around in the hallway and Pris had to push his way through.

Pris hustled them down the hallway through the wide oak doors into what appeared to have been a large banquet room. The great table in the center of the room was surrounded by people, many of whom Gant knew. Lord Barkmar and Prince Theodore stood near the center of the table, animatedly giving instructions to a continuous line of messengers, both elf and human, who ran the orders outside to the field officers. Zandinar sat at the far end of the table, apparently not taking an active part. Kalmine was there, along with Captain Hesh, huddled near Lord Barkmar. Gant followed Pris, sidestepping a departing messenger.

Lord Barkmar straightened up and caught sight of Gant. "Gant, we need the knights assembled at the rear of the barracks. They will receive their choice of weapons from the main cache."

Gant looked around. Was that it? Had the Elf Lord requested his presence? "Right away," he answered. Gant turned and started back outside where he'd seen the knights waiting.

Pris tugged at his elbow. "Send Zandinar," he whispered in Gant's ear. "The people I brought you to see are in the back, away from all this commotion."

"What?" Gant balked. Pris' knowing wink convinced him. "Okay," he said and waved at Zandinar. "Take the knights to the back of the barracks," he shouted above the din. "I'll join you soon."

Zandinar nodded, and without answering, the blond swordsman stood, rounded the table and headed outside.

Pris guided the group around the crush of people clustered in the middle of the room, slipping behind them near the far wall. At the back of the chamber was a concealed door tucked in behind piles of logistical paraphernalia. Gant followed Pris through the doorway into a cubbyhole furnished with portable cots, stools, and a small table laden with fruit, cheese, meats, and wines.

In this anteroom there were about a half dozen, scraggly, unkempt men and women. Gant's eyes immediately locked on a gray-haired, stoop shouldered man sitting alone at the table nibbling on bits of fruit and meat. The old man savored each bite, chewing slowly, deliberately, only reluctantly swallowing, as if he'd never eaten before. The once muscular frame had thinned, his cheeks hollowed. His face was lined anew from tremendous strain but he was still Gant's father.

His heart pounding in his throat, Gant started toward the smith. His steps faltered, his knees weakened. The frailness, the lack of fire in his father's eyes was disturbing. And where was Gant's mother? Had Barlon killed her?

The old man rose, staggered slightly, and hobbled to Gant, tears streaming down his cheeks. Gant reached him, hugged him. For a long moment neither spoke.

"Father," Gant finally whispered.

"Gant," rasped his father. "I am so happy to see you."

"Not nearly as happy as I am to see you. I was afraid I'd never see you again."

"Son," said his father, retreating heavily to his stool. He motioned for Gant to sit next to him. "All this time, I knew somehow fate would see you cleared. Wendler is a poor excuse for a man and now everyone knows it. I am so proud of you. Gant, I love you more than anything.

"Besides, if your mother had married a nobleman, you would have been a noble, learning swordsmanship as you were born to do. Instead you had to sneak out with your uncle and run rather than stand up to Wendler when the time came. In the end you became a warrior despite me. I tried to be the father you deserved, but after all, I am only a smith."

"Father, your love was all I ever needed. All I ever wanted. Mother loved you. Nobody else would have been good enough for her."

Gant leaned over and wrapped his father in another hug. His father hugged back, the old man's strength fading. Behind them, Pris smiled, caught up in the moment. He hugged Dalphnia who laughed and said, "Aren't you a bit young for me?"

Gant let go of his father and motioned for Dalphnia to come over.

"Father," he said, with one arm around Dalphnia's waist while his other hand rested on his father's back, "this is Dalphnia. She and I are, well, very close."

Gant's father's eyes welled up with new tears. "Pleased to meet you," he choked out. "I'm glad my son has found someone special."

And then, from behind, a new pair of arms enveloped Gant. He turned to find his mother, eyes smiling, and laughter in her voice. "Son, you would have been proud of your father. He never gave in to Barlon's men. Never. No matter what they did."

Gant held his mother. "I have always been proud to be your son, both of you."

Pris pushed his way in. "Don't you think you should take them to your tent?"

"Yes, of course. And oh yes, this is Pris, Emperor of the Eastern Empire."

"The emperor," said Gant's father a touch of awe in his voice.

Pris shook hands with Gant's father, hugged his mother. "Not much of an emperor right now," he mumbled.

"Come on," said Gant, "let's go to my tent where we can talk without the noise. It's much more comfortable."

Gant put one arm under his father's shoulder and helped him hobble out of the anteroom into the main chamber. Dalphnia aided his mother and between them they all managed to work their way out of the keep. Pris led the way, clearing a path for them.

Once outside Gant picked up the shrunken husk that his father had become and carried him out of the castle. Gant thanked Pris when they left him at the castle gates. The boy just smiled and winked.

Gant, his parents and Dalphnia continued on through the maze of activity in the field encampment to his tent.

Once there food was brought in and while they ate, they talked about all that his parents had endured and how they were rescued from Barlon's dungeons. Gant and Dalphnia related briefly how they met, leaving out Egog, and how happy they'd been.

Finally Gant asked, "Do you know what happened to Gwen?"

His parents' smiles faded. "Sorry," they both answered, "we don't know. The day Barlon attacked we were dragged to a prison wagon and carted off before we knew what was happening."

Dalphnia nudged Gant with an elbow. "Who is Gwen?"

Gant subdued a chuckle, surprised at the hint of jealousy. "She's a friend, the reason I ended up an outlaw."

"Only a friend?"

Gant's father broke in. "They were kids playing together."

At that moment, a tumultuous roar rose throughout the camp.

At the same moment, Zandinar stepped into Gant's tent. "Gant," he said, "excuse the intrusion but you are needed at the command center. Uric has returned from Dragon's Home. All the commanders are being called to a meeting."

Gant looked at his parents. Things were moving too fast. There was no time to enjoy each other's company. But, like so many things he had to do, so many choices that had been forced upon him, Gant had to go.

"Mother, Father," he said softly. "I've got to go. Stay here. Rest, eat and regain your strength. I'll be back as soon as I can."

Dalphnia put one arm around Gant. "I'll look after them," she whispered.

"No, someone else can do that. You should be at the meeting."

"Why? I command no army."

Gant grinned. "You command the trees to walk. You ripped the gates from the castle walls. You belong at the meeting."

They said another quick goodbye to his parents and then Gant sent one of his knight's squires to attend them. Gant, Dalphnia and Zandinar wound their way back to the castle banquet hall turned command center.

Instead of messengers, now commanders and high-ranking officers crowded around the central table. Along with Lord Barkmar Gant saw Uric, King Tirmus, King Herzolt, Prince Theodore, Abadis, Amelia, Sarona, and another bewhiskered wizard.

As soon as Gant, Dalphnia and Zandinar entered the chamber, a path opened for them as officers shuffled aside.

"Up here," shouted Lord Barkmar and motioned the threesome to join him.

They crossed quickly to the table amid a ripple of whispers mostly directed at the "lady of the trees."

Gant's heart swelled with pride. She *was* wonderful. More than he deserved. Right now he'd give anything to put an end to this war and go home.

As they reached the table, Gant noticed Sir Jarlz standing next to King Tirmus. He was wearing armor with the Netherdorf crest. Gant angled toward his uncle, bowing to King Tirmus as he approached. The king nodded in return.

Once beside his uncle, Gant asked, "What's going on? Why is everyone here from the Caverns of Darkness?"

"You'll see. There wasn't time to get everyone back there."

Sarona stood at the center of the contingent. She waved her hands for silence.

"Things have taken a turn for the worse," she started. "We must strike now or it will be too late. Each of you must perform the duties that will be assigned to you without question and without regard for risk. Some of us may die this day but we must go willing to make that sacrifice. We hold in our hands not the future of a kingdom or an empire but the fate of all life on this world. We cannot fail."

Sarona paused, scanned the room, making eye contact with each officer in turn, taking the measure of each elf, each man. None wavered.

"Good," said the queen. "The Dragon King will explain our plan."

Sarona stepped back from the table and Uric took her place, a penetrating glint in his reptilian eyes that Gant had never seen before.

"Time draws short," Uric began. "Some of my kin have joined Varg and are now bent on the destruction of all life. Foolishly they believe they will be rewarded."

A moan went through the hushed gathering. Uric continued. "Each minute Varg's army grows. Hordes pour through the portal he created in the tower of Pogor Castle. Soon dragons will guard that gate." Another rustling went through the crowd. "For now the dragons are caught in Homeland. My sons and wife battle them at the crossing but they can't hold them long. We must close the gate before the dragons arrive to protect it."

Uric's voice carried easily through the chamber as stunned silence clamped each throat in a chokehold.

"Gant, Zandinar, Abadis and Valdor," Uric nodded to the robed stranger standing next to Abadis, "will accompany me to the tower in Pogor. We will close the gate if we can. Lord Barkmar and his troops will ride to Chamber Pass to reinforce those already there and ensure that Varg's hordes do not get through the Monolith Mountains. Amelia will go with them as scout.

"King Tirmus and the Knights of Netherdorf will join King Herzolt's army and return to Netherdorf to recapture it, retrieve the weapons stored there, and restore Tirmus' crown. Sarona will journey with an honor guard to the home of the High Elves to cement the peace between their peoples and insure we fight together against this foulness. Any questions?"

The room remained silent. Dalphnia spoke up from behind Uric. "What about me? I'm going with Gant."

"No," said Gant, spinning to face her.

"We had hoped," said Uric turning graciously to the nymph, "that you would take your trees to help block Chamber Pass."

Dalphnia started to protest. Gant's hand closed softly over hers. She hesitated and Gant read her eyes, saw her fear that she would lose him again.

"You cannot help us," said Uric gently, "and your presence would give our enemies a hostage worth taking."

She considered the options and nodded. "If it must be," she said and squeezed Gant's hand.

"I'm going with you," said Pris flatly, pushing his way up to the table.

"No," said Kalmine, reaching for the emperor's elbow.

"Yes," snapped Pris, a bristling determination in his blue eyes. "I am the emperor. I will decide where I go. If this is not successful, my empire falls, too. It is my duty to see that it succeeds."

Kalmine stepped back. A look of surprise widened his eyes, a half grin frozen on his lips.

Pris laid one hand on the old man's shoulder. "You have been as faithful and loyal as any man could ask. Take Captain Hesh and the men and give Lord Barkmar whatever support you can. When I return, we will go to Malathon and set the Empire back to rights."

The old man's wrinkled brown face smiled briefly. "As you wish, Majesty."

Uric turned his attention back to the assemblage. "Then it is set. Go swiftly, and pray for our success. Good luck."

Uric spun from the table and started for the door. He whispered to Gant as he passed, "Make your farewells short. We must go now."

The room emptied quickly as everyone hurried to their assignments. Lord Barkmar and Sarona remained beside the table, carrying on a last minute strategy discussion. Gant hugged Dalphnia. An emptiness filled his heart as he pushed her to arm's length.

"I waited so long to see you again," he said. "I worried that I would never see you again, and now we are already saying goodbye. I'll miss you, even if I'm only gone a few hours. I love you."

"And I love you, Gant." She hugged him.

"Goodbye," he said. "I'll be back. Tell my father and mother I said goodbye." He kissed her once and swept past her out of the room into the hallway and then on into the castle courtyard.

Outside, Gant saw Abadis and Valdor already outside the castle walls, moving steadily down a rocky slope toward the flat shelf where Dalphnia's forest had taken root. There was no sign of Uric, Pris or Zandinar. Gant ran to catch the two wizards.

"Abadis," hailed Gant.

"Ah," said Abadis, turning his head, but not stopping. "I thought you'd be along soon. This is Valdor, High Wizard of Enchantment."

"And you are Ironlimb, the Devonshield Champion," smiled Abadis' companion. "I always admired you swordsmen. Having been a weak child, it seemed so dashing."

Gant nodded, not sure what to say. It seemed like ages since he'd won at Devonshield, hardly worth mentioning now.

"Where are you going?" asked Gant.

"To the trees," said Abadis. "Uric still doesn't like to change form in public if he doesn't have to."

"What about the tower in Pogor? What will we do there?"

"You will kill Varg and we will close the gate," said Valdor.

"How do you know I can kill Varg?"

"Well, if you can't, no one can," answered Abadis, a quiver in his voice. "Just as we don't know if we can close the gate. But, we must try."

"And for that we'll need Uric's help. Spells that powerful are beyond our ability alone," added Valdor. "And if I'm right, Uric will have to assume man form to cast the spells we need."

Abadis' brow wrinkled in thought. "I'm not sure about that. I guess we'll leave that up to Uric."

By now they were nearly to the trees. The trunks were widely spaced and between them Gant saw Uric's massive gold-scaled body squatting in the shade, his wings gently fanning the air.

"I thought you said there were five wizards," said Gant, remembering Abadis' earlier promise. "Where are the others?"

"Couldn't find them. I'm lucky I found Valdor. Without them we will need Uric to aid in the spell casting."

"If we had more time, we might have found them," said Valdor. "I'm glad you found me. In some ways I feel responsible. If I'd been more understanding, Razgoth would still be studying at my keep. Things might not have come to this."

"It would have been someone else," said Abadis, waving off Valdor's self-reproach.

"I hope his soul is at peace," said Valdor.

They went through the trees and found Pris and Zandinar already perched atop Uric's broad back. Zandinar sat stoic, grim faced, silent. Pris, on the other hand, squirmed fitfully, consumed by nervous energy.

"Hurry," boomed Uric. "Time grows short."

Gant helped Abadis and Valdor up onto Uric's back and climbed up himself. He sat straddling a large, raised scale and hung on with both hands. Immediately they were airborne, winging westward toward the blazing sun that sank ever lower near the horizon. They flashed above the rugged, snowcapped Monolith Mountains. The cold air whipped past Gant's eyes, bringing tears and then blowing them away.

Despite the biting cold, Gant looked down at jagged slabs of black rock that shot skyward. It was nature's massive sculpture laid out below him like tiny sand castles on the beach.

Gant glanced at the others. No one else was paying attention to the rugged beauty. They were all intent on preparing for what lay ahead. Clutching a ridged scale, Zandinar sat silent and stiff, almost trance-like, his right hand on his sword, his lips moving imperceptibly. Gant heard the warrior beg for the strength to fulfill his task.

Abadis, Valdor and Uric discussed the gate and how to close it. It was too much magic for Gant. Pris fingered the hilt of his elfin sword and Gant heard soft whisperings from the sword floating in the rushing slipstream while Pris mumbled strange words in the language of magic.

There was something different about Pris, thought Gant. The boyish mischief was gone replaced by cold determination. Something so far beyond his thirteen years that Gant wondered if it were truly Pris. But then Gant couldn't see the hard edge in his own face. His mind replayed so many things. Mostly he thought about the spreading horror. He swore that Dalphnia would never feel that darkness.

They crossed the mountains and Uric descended to a warmer altitude. Abadis chanted arcane words and Gant noticed that they no longer cast a shadow. He turned to the mage, eyebrows raised.

"My new version of invisibility," said Abadis with a hint of pride. "It would be best to surprise them."

Valdor looked down, noticed the missing shadow, and began questioning Abadis about the specifics of the spell. Gant sensed that this was new magic to the older wizard, something worth learning.

Gant turned his attention back to the ground. In the fading light, he saw desolation from horizon to horizon. Huge areas of once rich grasslands were burned black. The stench of sun-baked rotting flesh rose on the night air. It burned his nostrils forcing him to breathe through his mouth. Clusters of dark, hulking shapes roamed the plains. Occasionally hellish shrieks wafted up to his ears. Fires burned out of control and thick columns of black smoke rose skyward, their tops tinted red by the sun's fading rays.

Night swallowed them as they raced unerringly past black shapes that patrolled the skies. Yet no alarm was raised.

Swiftly the ground flashed below and soon they were over the remains of Pogor. Small pockets of dull red embers cast a hellish radiance over the crumbled and broken sandstone that had once been a magnificent city. Strange beasts slithered, crawled, walked and flew around the corpse that was Pogor. Now Uric zigzagged to avoid hurtling black shapes that leapt out of the gloom like caricatures in a fun house. Here and there Gant caught the frozen death smile on a skull as it flashed past.

As frightful as the winged nightmares were, their images were forgotten at the first sight of the main tower of Pogor castle. The top of the tower had taken on a black pulsating aura that even the glow from the city's ashes failed to illuminate. Gone were the glorious reds and yellows of the once beautiful stonework. Now only death and evil radiated from the tower.

As Uric glided toward their target, Gant saw a huge hole blasted through the stone wall on the upper floor. Circling the tower they sailed past the opening. Gant glanced inside. An amorphous cloud of living blackness disgorged a stream of indescribable creatures, each bowing to Varg as they entered this universe, groveling and swearing fidelity as they thanked him for deliverance.

Finally Gant knew his adversary. The demon was huge, tall and broad with four arms and heavily muscled legs. He was black as midnight with flaming red eyes. His ears, much like the Dark Elves, swept up into miniature wings. He was horrifying.

Fear wrenched at Gant's chest as he witnessed the horrors. There were so many, his party so few. How could they stop this? How could they stop Varg? There wasn't time to think. Uric folded his wings and shot straight through the opening in the side of the tower and glided into the chamber. Abadis and Valdor began chanting strange verses. Gant, Pris and Zandinar drew their swords. This was it.

Chapter 46

Inside the tower, Uric landed near the wall opposite the jagged hole. The room was large enough that even as a dragon, Uric wasn't cramped. His riders slid off and Uric regained human shape. Immediately he took up the spell recital that Abadis and Valdor had begun. The wizards retreated with their backs to the wall while the three swordsmen moved out in front as a protective screen. Gant peered around in the inky, unnatural darkness. A faint red glow emanated from the pulsating blackness of the gate between planes. Varg stood on the other side of the portal from Gant, his sweeping black ears turned up like miniature wings, his eyes burning with evil.

At Varg's feet, having just crossed over from the dark realms, a horrible multi-armed, octopus-like monster knelt in homage. On either side of Varg stood massive, man-shaped creatures with four arms that ended in hooked talons. In the portal, lined up as if painted on some mystic canvas, stretching as far as the eye could see, were more apparitions waiting to enter the world of men. There were demonic man-shaped beasts, black flyers, and snake-like monsters with multiple heads.

To Gant's left was a wide stairwell cordoned off by a stout metal railing. Two knights in dark purple armor guarded the entrance to the stairs. The men, if that was what they were, had dark faces and pure white eyes. Gant was surprised to realize that the one on the right was Wendler. There wasn't time to consider how he got there.

For an instant, activity in the tower ceased. Varg turned his head slowly until he glared straight at the intruders. Hatred flared brighter in his red eyes, a sneer spread across his lips.

"You've finally come," he said, his voice a low rumble. "It will do you no good. You will die here, Dragon King, and the world will be mine."

Behind Gant, Uric, Abadis and Valdor chanted in unison. On Gant's left, Pris stood firm, Thantalmos in his hand. The sword's voice growing louder and louder like a rising hurricane wind. On Gant's right, Zandinar kept his eyes glued on Varg and took a half step forward, firm resignation on his face, his sword held before him, its blade glowing with a mysterious white light. Gant held Valorius tightly, the magical blade pulsating with its own light, brighter and brighter until the room blazed with a blinding brilliance that swept away the gloom.

As Gant watched the octopus-thing slithered to the stairwell and started down while yet another creature stepped through the gate and bowed to Varg. An intangible fear wrenched Gant's guts. There was no time to linger in that fear, no time to think. Gant reacted.

"Pris, Zandinar, take the gate. Stop any more of those things from getting through."

At the same time, Gant rushed Varg, intent on driving the demon away from the portal. The Demon-Prince stepped back and waved his two massive guardians to attack. The slayers surged in front of Varg. They leaped at Gant, slashing the air with multiple hooked razors. Gant back peddled drawing them away from the portal while keeping himself between them and the wizards.

From a safe distance, Varg chanted words of magic. The air crackled with the polarized energy from opposite forms of magic. Varg pulled energy from darkness while Abadis, Valdor and Uric called on forces of light.

Pris and Zandinar circled behind the monsters attacking Gant and reached the front of the portal just as two creatures were stepping through. Pris and Zandinar's swords cut them down, slashing in a blur. A hiss of surprise ran through the creatures waiting on the other side of the portal and the line shrank back.

Pris' sword shrieked with an ear-splitting wail. Gant wished he could hold his ears to stop it.

Uric, Abadis and Valdor completed their spell in sync. A glowing, shimmering wall appeared, molding itself into a domed enclosure around Varg. Varg's spell fizzled inside the positive energy sphere. Frustrated, he ripped at the magical barrier with his claws.

Meanwhile, the two four-armed monsters encircled Gant. The first rushed in, slashed and retreated. The second circled to Gant's right. Gant ignored the second slayer and stabbed straight at the one in front of him. It swiped at the sword, trying to knock it aside. Gant twisted Valorius just as Zeigone had done at Devonshield slashing down on the creature's forearm. Valorius bit into the sinewy, black muscle. There was a flash of light and the sword severed the thick limb. Gant watched the quivering claw fall to the floor in a gush of blood.

Just then Varg ripped through the force field. A glittering sprinkle of dust floated down where the sphere had been, disappearing before it reached the floor. Varg roared at his cringing minions still beyond the gate, his guttural voice urging them to attack.

Gant cut through a second arm and then twisted the blade to reverse his stroke. Valorius sliced into the beast's side. Screaming it tottered backward and slumped to the floor. Behind Gant, the two wizards and the dragon unleashed a second force field around Varg.

At the same time, the massed line on the other side of the planal gate rushed forward. Pris and Zandinar set to work, cutting down the creatures streaming through the portal. Pris' sword screamed so loud it didn't seem possible that it could go any higher, yet as the masses pressed against him, the pitch rose another notch. Like waves upon a rocky shore, the charging beasts broke over the two stalwart defenders. Bodies piled up. Pieces of limbs, heads and gore oozed out across the stone floor.

While they plugged the portal, the second slayer leaped at Gant, crashing into him on his exposed right side. The beast raked Gant with inhuman strength. The magic armor held against the vicious claws, but the weight of his attacker bore Gant to the floor. He rolled with the force trying to shed the beast. It didn't work. Its bulk pinned Gant down. Sparks flew as the claws flailed away at the Gant's helm, snapping Gant's head back and forth with each swipe.

Gant lashed out with Valorius. The angle was bad and without leverage but Valorius cut into the leg sinews. The slayer yelped but only lashed out harder.

Behind the beast, Gant heard Pris' screaming sword coming. Thantalmos flashed across the monster's neck and with a sickening splat the monster's head flew past Gant and bounced on the floor. The weight rolled off of him and Gant staggered to his knees.

Across the room, Varg raged inside the new dome, ripping holes in it with his talons. The emperor whirled, a berserk rage in his eyes. He charged Varg just as the Demon-Prince shredded the second barrier. Before the wizards could cage the demon again, Pris was on Varg, a maniacal fire in his eyes.

"No," screamed Uric as Thantalmos came down on the Demon-Lord's left arm.

There was a flash of light and a clap of thunder that shook the stone tower to its foundation. A strange putrescence oozed from the wound. Varg jerked back. Pris staggered as if he'd grabbed a lightning bolt. Biting cold surged through Pris and the fire in his eyes dulled. Thantalmos went silent, the edge dull and nicked.

Now Zandinar stood alone at the gate, holding back the tide. Black flyers gathered at the opening in the outer wall, their screeching and flapping adding to the din. Uric pointed to the black shapes wheeling outside the tower. Abadis nodded.

Uric dashed across the tower and dove out into the black night sky, changing on the way out. Almost before he was through the hole, Uric's body swelled, writhing in its transformation. He hit the flyers as a gigantic dragon, snapping, ripping, and flailing away with his tail. Before one of the airborne killers could land inside the tower, Uric scattered them in a wave of death. Broken and twisted bodies plummeted to the ground.

Meanwhile in the tower, Pris fell against the wall, staggered by the terrible biting cold that hit him when Thantalmos struck Varg.

Gant saw Pris fall and guessed that Varg had the same chilling effect as Egog. He put that thought aside and concentrated on what had to be done. Abadis turned his magic against the creatures pressing to get through the gate while Valdor rushed to the fallen emperor.

Gant righted himself and warily focused on the advancing Demon-Prince whose wounded arm oozed slime. Gant backed across the tower until he came up against the unyielding stone. He gripped Valorius with both hands, glaring up at the towering black fury.

Varg paused a few feet away. His ruby eyes flashed like beacons, the interior of his gaping mouth an intense, radiant orange. There was a pale blue flash from behind Varg as Abadis cast a spell at the tide surging to cross through the portal. Varg glanced at the wizard for only a moment. Not waiting, Gant dodged to the right, trying to gain an advantage. Doubts raced through his mind. How had Pris' sword failed? Thantalmos couldn't be that much weaker than Valorius. And maybe Valorius had lost too much magic.

Resolutely Gant stood firm. Running wasn't going to do any good. He had to stop Varg to spare Dalphnia and everyone else. Valorius had to do it.

Varg charged. With a building fury, Gant met the rush. He slashed at Varg's ribs. Valorius arced toward the target but before it reached the Demon-Prince the sword hit an encapsulating barrier. Valorius' ancient power overcame the protective field in a shower of sparks. The sword's edge bit into Varg's flesh. The demon lurched back, screaming, teeth bared, eyes tight with pain. Varg fought for balance, staggered momentarily, and then righted himself.

As Valorius sliced through the demon's charcoal hide, a numbing sensation flowed like electricity up the blade into Gant's right arm. It was a cold worse than Egog, paralyzing each cell it touched. It was the cold of a demon's heart, cruel and ruthless. In a split second it numbed Gant's right arm almost to the shoulder. By force of will, Gant pulled the sword free from Varg's side only to watch it fall from his frozen fingers. His right hand useless, Gant snatched Valorius out of the air with his left.

Varg snarled, circling warily. Gant turned his left side to the demon, protecting his useless right arm. Fear clouded Gant's mind. To kill Varg he might have to die himself. The cold would be his end. Gant backed up. The demon pursued. Varg slashed at Gant, his claws glancing off Gant's armor in a shower of sparks, like steel on flint.

Varg snatched at Valorius. Gant dodged but Varg caught Valorius under the crosspiece and jerked it from Gant's hand. The sword clattered to the floor. Gant staggered back, crashing into the wall. Varg lurched after him.

Behind Varg, Valdor helped Pris to his feet. The dauntless emperor plucked the dulled Thantalmos from the floor and leaped at the demon. Pris brought the silent blade down on the demon's exposed back. A clang like hammer on anvil rang through the tower. The sword bounced off. Varg whirled and backhanded the emperor as if swatting a fly. Pris flew backward, hit the floor, bounced, and landed like an old rag. Gant ducked under the demon's grasp, leaped to Valorius and snatched it up. Varg turned on Gant.

With Valorius in his left hand, Gant looked for an opening. The freezing sensation in his right arm dulled his will. Sleep, it said, sleep. No, he wouldn't give up. Not now. A flurry of images flashed through his mind, of the life he might have, of Dalphnia, of his parents. He could not fail them.

Blocking out his fear he rushed forward. Valorius whistled through the air. Varg dodged. Gant followed with an overhand slice and then a side slash, the sword a blur of motion. Valorius struck Varg again. The numbing cold swept up the sword, up Gant's left arm. Gant fought against it, willing his limbs to obey, forcing the cold away from his pounding heart.

Varg's eyes dulled, the bright red fading. Gant pressed his attack, mindlessly hacking away, chasing Varg.

The demon retreated faster now, around the room, circling the black portal. Gant pursued, swung and missed. Varg leaped backward toward the gate. Behind the demon, Zandinar turned his attention from the faltering line of creatures at the gate to the demon. He drew back his sword with both hands and plunged it straight through Varg's back.

Varg shuddered, screamed, his arms flailing behind him trying to reach the sword. Freezing cold clutched at Zandinar and he fell to his knees, still holding on to his sword.

Now Gant stabbed Valorius straight into Varg's chest. The demon screamed again. Gant felt the rush of cold, weaker, but still numbing. With his last strength he pulled Valorius free and fell backward with a crash. Valorius' light went out, the sword dulled to a dark gray.

Zandinar released his sword and fell over in a heap. Varg lurched forward, stumbled, and then staggered backward, Zandinar's sword point sticking out of his chest. Dark fluids spilled from gaping wounds.

Gant struggled to his feet. He dropped Valorius, the magic gone. He searched for something to strike Varg with, something magic. There were no weapons left.

Meanwhile, Varg regained his balance. He flailed away with his claws, slashing at Zandinar. Gant dove for the demon, his mailed fists cocked. He hit Varg with his shoulder first, splitting the demon's wounds open. But Gant weighed nothing compared to Varg and his attack barely sent a shiver through the demon. It didn't matter. Gant had gone mad. His fists hammered Varg, raining a staccato of blows on the demon's face and midsection. It seemed impossible but the magic in the armor sent flashes of light with every smashing blow. Numbness trickled up Gant's arms but he was beyond pain. With each blow, the cold grew weaker. Finally it stopped and Varg fell with a thud.

For a long moment the tower was still. Gant stood over Varg's motionless hulk, fists clenched, breathing in convulsive bursts.

Pandemonium broke loose. Every evil creature in and around the tower broke and ran. Those trying to come through the portal retreated into the vast reaches of the dark realms. Those already in Pogor ran or flew for the countryside. Some changed shape to resemble men. The massed flocks of flyers streaked away across the plains.

Gant bent and picked up Valorius. Slowly he turned the sword over and examined the now scarred blade. The magic was gone, his battle madness gone with it. In its place pain and tingling cold washed through his body. Gant sat down, fatigue overcoming him.

He barely noticed the gathering light in the tower. Pinpoints of radiance circled in a swirling pattern that congealed into a glowing sphere of cold, white fire. Inside the globe, a woman appeared dressed in white, so pure, so perfect, so flawless. Gant covered his eyes with the crook of his elbow.

She stepped from the brilliant sphere, tears streaming from eyes so blue that for Gant the blue of the sky would forever remain dull and lifeless. Gant watched in awe. She knelt beside Zandinar. Gently she gathered the fallen warrior in her arms, weeping openly, staring at his face, in death now serene and childlike. Her tears pitter-pattered like silvery, soft rain drops on his chest.

She looked up at Gant. "He died for you," she said, her voice the song of angels, "for all of you that love and kindness might survive. He is my son. He lived for this one purpose. It is done."

A sad smile flickered across her lips, unforgettable and mystic. She stepped back into the sphere of light carrying her burden. Her image faded. The globe broke into sparkling motes of light that dissipated in the night air.

Gant's mind reeled. He looked at Valorius, her edge as keen as ever, the tingling magic running up his fingertips. How? It didn't matter. They had stopped Varg.

Gant fought his way up to his knees, and finally managed to stand. He returned Valorius to her scabbard, swayed and barely managed to keep his balance. Slowly he surveyed the room. Pris stood mouth agape, his back to the now empty portal. Abadis and Valdor gathered beside Pris focused on the black sphere.

Uric swooped in through the opening in the wall, resuming man form as he did so. The sage glanced around, and then approached the mages. "Gant," he said over his shoulder, "guard the stairwell. Pris, take the opening in the wall. Don't let anything past. The spell casting will take some time and we cannot be disturbed."

Without question they went to their posts. There were no intruders. Varg's minions had scattered, disorganized and without leadership, each ran for its own survival.

Gant stepped over to the top of the stairs. Far below he heard the hasty clatter of mailed footsteps receding down the spiral staircase. He peered over the edge and caught a glimpse of a purple shadow moving downward. The figure glanced up once and Gant recognized Wendler but then his magical armor melded with the darkness and he was gone. Gant thought of going after him but his duty was to keep anyone from coming up the stairs and so he held his post.

In the tower, the spell casting proceeded smoothly, though it took a long time. Before they could start Abadis and Valdor rested, meditated and regained strength. Once they had refreshed mentally, they joined Uric and concentrated on the spell that they'd agreed had the best chance of closing the gate. Casting took time but finally the gate was gone, vanished like a bad dream. Uric transformed back into a dragon, lifted the others onto his back and they flew for Chamber Pass as fast as the Dragon King's wings could take them.

Chapter 47

As they flew across the barren landscape, Gant's thoughts turned inward. Death was all around and yet he felt no remorse. Was that bad? Was he so callous that he didn't mind killing? No, he still hated killing. He'd killed to save life. And what about Zandinar and the lady in white? Where had they gone?

"The lady in white, who is she?" he asked Uric.

Uric craned his neck to look back at Gant. "No one is sure. Few ever see her." He paused, licked his lips with his great forked tongue. "I've never seen her before myself so I can only guess. Legends say she appeared at Bartholomew's birth.

"As to what she is, some say she's a goddess. The oldest legends say she is an angel of the Greater God. Other legends say she is one of the five who escaped Tirumfall to the holy realms though there is no proof that any ever escaped that tower. The truth remains a mystery."

"Why did she take Zandinar and what did she mean 'he died for us?'"

"I think now I see," muttered Uric to himself, and then added, "I've heard she can see the future, or maybe she sees possible futures. Probably, like Bartholomew, she saw Varg's return and your rise as a warrior. She knew Bartholomew made your armor and Valorius and that you would use them to kill Varg. But she must have seen what Bartholomew did not, that you alone would not be enough. Maybe she didn't see Pris, or she knew he would not be enough either. Even Thantalmos dulled on Varg's hide.

"She called Zandinar son. How she came by a son, I can only guess. If she returned to this plane from the holy places it was indeed a sacrifice." Uric paused, and then finally added, "That's the best I can offer. The secrets may lie locked in Tirumfall tower. And that is a place better left sealed."

Gant sat in silence. He didn't really understand. He thought of Dalphnia instead. He longed to hold her again. Soon, he told himself.

"What about the swords?" asked Pris. "Varg sucked the magic from them but when she came they were restored."

"That sphere," said Uric and flew on as if that answered the question.

Silently, they passed over the land. Each passenger clung to Uric's broad back, exhausted. The sun was halfway to its zenith when the worn-out band reached Chamber Pass. Towering slabs of rock pushed skyward into broken walls hundreds of feet high.

Uric sailed over the troops clustered near the pass' western entrance and landed far behind the rear guard on a loose gravel path trampled into a roadbed by countless feet, hooves and wheels. On either side of the road only an occasional scrub bush managed to cling to life. Otherwise Chamber Pass was lifeless. The dragon regained man form and the party walked slowly up the winding trail toward the encampment until they were hailed by a brace of guards.

It only took a moment for the group to be recognized and escorted to Lord Barkmar's tent.

"Dragon King," said the Dark Elf Lord as they were ushered into his tent. "You have succeeded?"

"Yes, the gate is closed. Varg is dead."

Lord Barkmar sighed with relief.

"Have any of my family returned?" asked Uric.

"No, we've had no word from the dragons."

Uric's face darkened. Lord Barkmar went on, fighting a tired grin. "Fighting has been light. Jarlz and his knights forayed onto the plain and so far have managed to stem the tide. Because of them, only a half dozen of the black slayers tried to breech the pass and Dalphnia's trees took care of them. Amelia saw some of the flying beasts but none have ventured this far east. She also reports that the destruction of the west seems complete. Everywhere she's gone the villages are burned, the fields ruined, bodies rotting in the open. There's nothing left but evil and death."

"Where is she now?" asked Abadis, his face reflecting his worry.

"Scouting," answered Barkmar. "She said to tell you she'd see you at your house in a few days. She said to watch the mirror. Whatever that means."

Abadis nodded.

Pris cleared his throat. "Can we return to Malathon? I want my throne back."

"Not today," said Abadis. "I'm worn out and casting transport spells in my condition would be a disaster."

Gant noted the wizard, both of them actually, looked thinner, frailer than he'd ever seen them. It was as if they had aged decades in the last few hours.

"You don't look so good," said Dalphnia approaching from behind them. She was flanked by Captain Hesh, Kalmine, Pratt, and Faltern. "Are you all right?"

Abadis sighed. "The strain from our work in the tower has taken its toll. I need to rest and restore myself before anymore spell casting."

"That goes for me too," said Valdor. "But I'd rather do it at home. So if I'm not needed any longer I'll be on my way." Without waiting, he completed a spell and was gone.

"How long will that take?" asked Pris.

"I'll be fine tomorrow," said Abadis. "There are magical spells that can restore vitality. But they take complete quiet."

Shouts from outside halted the discussion.

"Dragons are coming! Dragons are coming!"

Immediately Uric was out of the tent, followed by several others. They spotted three winged shapes rapidly approaching from the north. As they watched, the forms swelled and became Uric's wife Mall, son Pith and his female companion, Valmie. The three of them landed in a clearing behind the main camp. The first thing Gant noticed was the great sadness in Mall's eyes.

"Where's Hamiz?" asked Uric, fighting to control his voice.

"Dead, Father," answered Pith. "Baz killed him." The large silver dragon's head dropped. "We held them as long as we could."

A huge tear slid down Uric's cheek. It fell softly onto the rocky soil. Where the tear ran it turned to pure gold forming a seam that ran deep into the earth.

Finally Uric said, "You held long enough. Varg is dead. Did the others go with Baz?"

"Not all of them," said Mall, "Vee stayed. She talked many of the elders out of this foolishness. Most of the young ones, the brash and reckless, they followed Baz, seeking their own gain."

"We should follow them, wipe them out," snapped Pith, his anger burning fiercely.

Gant fought his own grief. More innocents had died. Rage flamed in him anew. "I'll go with you," snapped Gant, Valorius leaping to his hand. A tear slid down his cheek.

"No," said Mall, even as Uric started to agree. "Vee needs us to back her, especially her king, before any more get ideas of riches easy for the taking."

"Of course you are right," said Uric sadly, "Baz and his band will find the world a cruel place. It'll be a long time before they venture against men of power and it is my duty to see that no others join them. Let us return home, first to secure it and then to bury Hamiz properly."

Uric turned to his son. "Would you and Valmie fly the mountain ridge for a few days? Make sure none of Varg's flyers cross to this side?"

"I'd be honored," said Pith.

"Me too," added Val with a dip of her silver-scaled head.

"Goodbye for now," said Uric. "Perhaps we'll meet again, perhaps not."

"Dragon King," said Lord Barkmar. "We mourn your loss. Your son's life was not wasted. We shall keep the funeral fire lit tonight. Our prayers go with you."

"Thanks," said Uric. He regained his dragon form and the flight of four lifted with a blast of air, stones and sand. In an instant, they were gone over the towering mountain peaks.

Abadis looked at Lord Barkmar. "Is there anything we can do?"

"Yes, get some rest. I'll have an aide take you to tents where you can sleep undisturbed," and the Elf Lord signaled for a guide.

Gant and Dalphnia took one tent, Abadis, Pris and his men another and after a light meal they were all soon fast asleep.

Chapter 48

It was still dark when Gant woke up. Dalphnia stood near the open tent flap looking out. "Did you sleep well?" she asked without turning.

Gant sighed and blinked. "Okay I guess. I was tired. Right now I'm hungry."

"Looks like the meal tent is serving breakfast. Let's go see what they've got."

Gant washed up, put his clothes and armor back on and went hand-in-hand with Dalphnia to the cooks' tent. On the way, she asked, "Do you think things will ever get back to normal?"

"Normal for who? You or the rest of us?"

She elbowed him. "What's that supposed to mean?"

"I don't think things will go back the way they were. Varg's dead and the gate closed but there are uncounted evil creatures loose on the other side of the mountains. Things that are hard to kill. It's unlikely we'll be able to clear them out. Best that I can see is that we have an uneasy peace on this side of the mountains. As for you, well you are stuck with me and I'm not going to be like any other husband you've ever had."

She squeezed his hand. "I'm counting on that."

They entered a large tent and found cooks serving porridge, roast meat, milk, water, and boiled potatoes. They got in the back of the serving line, filled plates, though Dalphnia did not take any meat, and found an empty table. Before they were finished, Abadis, Pris and his men came in, got food and joined them. Gant was glad to see that Abadis looked rested, younger even.

"Are you ready to go to Malathon?" asked Abadis between bites. "I'm ready to get back there myself. I owe Sylvia a visit."

"Not so fast," said Lord Barkmar who now stood at the end of their table. "There are a few things to discuss before you go."

"Like what?" asked Pris. "I want to go home."

"About security at the pass," said Lord Barkmar turning to Dalphnia. "Will the trees stay?"

"Yes, they are quite happy. Their enchantment will last for many months as long as they remain rooted. By then, maybe I'll stop by and wake them up again."

"Thank you, Lady of the Wood," said the Forest Lord, bowing low. "And Gant, your uncle returned while you were asleep and asked to see you before you leave. He's in the Netherdorf bivouac area. I promised him you'd visit."

"I'll go now. It'll only take a few minutes."

"I'll go with you," said Abadis. "Anything else we should know?"

"That's it," said Barkmar and left the tent.

"Let's meet at my tent in half an hour," suggested Gant.

Since there were no objections, Gant and Abadis rose and walked to the area marked by the Knights of Netherdorf's banner. It was a string of small tents clustered around a horse corral. It took only a minute to locate Sir Jarlz who stood near a larger tent where the commander's guidon flapped.

"Uncle Jarlz," yelled Gant, running up to the knight. He threw both arms around his uncle and hugged him. Letting go he stepped back. "We're leaving and I just wanted to say goodbye."

"Me too, old friend," said Abadis only a step behind Gant.

"Well, I won't be here much longer myself," said Jarlz, a broad grin sweeping across his bearded face. "The king will soon regain Netherdorf. Already the people are rising to his banner. We cleared the plain at the mouth of the pass and Lord Barkmar gave us leave to join King Tirmus. We are going to bring a quick end to the fighting. I heard the city council in Blasseldune sent their militia to help."

"Then you'll see Chamz," said Gant. "He's leading them. Tell him I'm all right and I'll see him soon."

"Sure. And when you get to Netherdorf, you better visit Mistress Fallsworth and me. I plan to be seeing her a lot. In fact, plan on attending the feast the king will have to celebrate victory."

"Wonderful," Gant clapped his uncle on the shoulder. "So much has happened since Blasseldune. Do me a favor and check on Gwen when you can?"

"I will. I'm sure she's all right. She has a way of taking care of herself."

"Enough," shot Abadis. "Let's be off."

"See you in Netherdorf," said Jarlz as the two turned to leave.

A few minutes later, at Gant's tent, the pair rejoined the anxious group. They linked hands in a circle and Abadis started his verse. As the last words died away, they flashed through space to appear in the same second floor bedroom at Sylvia's that they'd entered before. A young woman jumped at their appearance, dropping the armload of sheets she carried.

"Sorry to disturb you," said Abadis and led the group down the stairs to the parlor.

Several women lounged on the chairs and couch in the parlor, which was empty of clients.

"Where's Sylvia?" Abadis asked a delectable blond girl at his elbow.

Just then Sylvia burst into the room from the kitchen. "What's all the noise? Oh!" She eyed Abadis suspiciously. Then smiled a sly, knowing smile and winked at the wizard. "Did you come in through our bedroom again?"

"Well, yes," said Abadis sheepishly.

"You old goat." She ran up and threw her arms around him. "Sometimes I wonder if keeping that space open for you to pop in whenever you feel like it is a good idea."

"I can't just appear on the street outside. What would people say?"

Sylvia cocked her head and examined the wizard. "Okay, it's worked fine to this point so we'll leave things just the way they are. So, did you come to stay a while this time?"

"Yes, for a few days. Then I think you should come to my house."

"What?" gasped Sylvia. "Who'll run the house? Er, there's so much to do here, I. . ."

"Don't give me that," smiled Abadis, "you've got lots of good help and a vacation would do you good."

A couple of the girls still in the room chided her for trying to avoid a man.

"Okay, okay. But just you and me."

"My idea exactly. Of course you'll have to meet my granddaughter but she won't be staying long."

"I guess I can manage that," and something in her eyes said she was looking forward to it.

They disentangled and turned to the others.

"I think you remember the emperor and his attendants, and Gant," said Abadis, indicating each as he went, "but I don't think you've met Dalphnia. Dalphnia, this is Sylvia."

Pleasantries were exchanged and then Abadis went on. "Pris, that is His Majesty, has returned to regain control of the throne. *And*, I will be the new Imperial Wizard so I'll be visiting Malathon regularly." He winked at Sylvia.

Sylvia's smile extinguished. "Regaining the throne may be harder than you think. The High Minister has declared you dead and anyone posing as the emperor is to be killed as an imposter."

"Chantel," spat Pris. "Who has he appointed as the new emperor?"

"No one," said Sylvia, "but most believe he'd like to assume the title himself."

"We're going to change that right now. Please accept my apology for refusing your continued hospitality but this has gone on long enough. I shall return when possible to thank you officially for your assistance." Pris turned toward the door.

Before Pris could leave, Abadis asked, "Do you want me to go with you?"

"No," answered Dalphnia before the emperor could respond. "You stay here. Gant and I will go with him. I don't think this will take long."

"Let's go," said Pris, and was out the door.

Gant and Dalphnia bowed to Sylvia and dashed to follow. Kalmine, Captain Hesh, Patt and Faltern were right behind them. Before they'd gone far, Pris motioned Kalmine to take the lead and the emperor fell in behind his advisor.

As they approached the outer palace wall they met two guards, one on each side of a heavy bronze door. Gant noted that they approached the palace from the Royal side, opposite from the entrance he'd used to obtain an audience with Pris. As the group approached, the two guards stiffened and pulled their short swords.

"Oh, put those away," said Pris, advancing to within a few yards of the pair. "You can plainly see I am the emperor. Now stand aside and let me pass."

The two guards wavered, glancing at each other. The one on the right let his sword point dip.

The other said, "We are to kill anyone claiming to be the emperor. On sight! The High Minister has proclaimed the emperor dead."

Both men pointed their swords at Pris but without conviction.

"Did you see the emperor's body? Was there a funeral?" demanded Pris.

"No," said the nearest guard.

"And you must recognize Captain Hesh, and Kalmine, my personal advisor. Or have they been declared dead, too?"

"No, but. . ."

"Then let us pass."

"W-we can't do that," stammered the second guard. "Chantel will have us tortured."

"Then you can die here," snapped the emperor, yanking Thantalmos from her scabbard.

Immediately the sword began to hum. A low wailing echoed off the high walls. Gant thanked the Lady in White that Thantalmos was as sharp as ever.

On sight of the screaming sword, both guards lowered their weapons, their mouths open.

"It is the lost Sword of Emperors," said one.

"He must be the emperor. No one else can hold that sword," said the second. "Forgive us, Majesty." They both knelt. "We were only following orders."

"Orders from a fool," added Kalmine.

Pris sheathed Thantalmos. "You stay here," he said, pointing to the guard on the left. To the other he said, "You escort us to the Council Chambers. I don't want to have to repeat this needless confrontation with every guard I meet."

Both guards bowed low. The one ordered to lead pulled open the bronze door and hurried through. The others followed. The last one closed the door. The group went through a high vaulted tunnel through a thick stone wall and came to a second bronze door. The guard swung it open and held it for Pris who marched through. Two royal guardsmen on the other side casually turned toward the door as it opened. One sat beside a beautiful marble fountain drinking from a half empty wineskin. The other leaned casually against the inner wall, his razor-edged halberd propped beside him.

"Don't move," ordered Pris, glaring at them. "So this is the way you guard my palace. Captain Hesh, take their names. Have them reassigned to a frontier outpost. Someplace where they'll either remain alert or end up dead."

Pris brushed past the two surprised sentries. His quick strides took him swiftly past the fountains that adorned the broad expanse of the Royal Palace Gardens. The rest of the party hustled to keep up. Captain Hesh dropped behind to deal with the two lax soldiers.

On the far side of the gardens, they came to a small door made of expensive, polished wood bound in shiny brass. A lone guard stood in the shadow of the overhang, half dozing in the coolness. Pris was upon him before he could move. The emperor shoved him aside with a sweep of his right arm, catching the startled sentry off balance and sending him sprawling.

"Patt, take his post. No one except Captain Hesh comes through until I personally give you the order."

Patt dropped out of the procession and took up the post at the door, a menacing glare in his eye for the displaced guard.

Now they were inside the palace and Pris was running. The others hastened to keep up. Down one corridor after another, dashing past surprised servants and men carrying out routine duties. They went up a flight of stone steps, around a bend and down a long narrow corridor blocked at the end by a heavy, red velvet tapestry. Pris motioned to Faltern to take up a position in front of the tapestry. "No one comes through," he whispered.

The soldier nodded.

Pris shoved aside the thick cloth and the party entered the vast complex where Gant had first met the emperor. There was a guard inside the tapestry dressed in a strange uniform. He reached for his sword. Gant was quicker. Valorius leaped into his hand, and with a practiced chop using the flat of the blade, he knocked the guard's sword from his hand. It clattered noisily to the floor. The conversation in the room died like a snuffed candle flame.

For a long moment, everything stopped. Those in the chamber turned to see who dared make such a noisy interruption. Gant scanned the room. It was circular, as he remembered it, with numerous entrances, all guarded from the inside by serious-looking armored soldiers, in uniforms that Gant did not recognize.

"Mercenaries," whispered Kalmine through clenched teeth.

An exquisitely dressed merchant had been pleading his case and now turned to stare at the newcomers, his mouth frozen in mid-sentence. On the dais several old men dressed in pompous robes stood around the throne. On it sat an older man dressed in white, a venomous glare aimed at Pris.

"Chantel," shouted Pris, an accusatory tone in his voice. "Get off *my* throne."

For a moment the room remained silent, even the air seemed reluctant to move.

"An imposter," yelled Chantel, leaping from the throne. "Kill him!"

The guards at the doors nearest Pris jerked out their swords and turned to attack. Other guards drew their weapons and surrounded the party. The first mercenary to reach them swung his sword at Pris. Gant stepped between them, Valorius held aside. The two-handed stroke crashed squarely on Gant's breastplate.

Instead of cutting through, the blade shattered off at the hilt, leaving the soldier staring at the pieces as they clattered to the floor.

Two more guards attacked. Gant slammed the flat of Valorius against the wrist of the one to the right. The soldier's sword spun across the room.

Dalphnia brought her hypnotic stare squarely on the second man's eyes. "Stop," she commanded and the man froze in mid-stride.

"Chantel, I am the emperor," shouted Pris. "Return my throne to me."

"The emperor's dead," shot back the High Minister, pointing an accusing finger at the boy. "I am the new emperor."

A gasp escaped from those gathered in the Chamber.

"You reveal your true intentions," said Pris. "Are there others who doubt my identity?"

A murmur of indecision rippled through the crowd.

"Then behold the Sword of Emperors." Pris drew Thantalmos. Its voice rose through the assemblage, piercing. "I bring back Thantalmos to the Empire. Are there any who still doubt?" Pris had to yell to make himself heard above the keening of the sword.

No one moved, spellbound by the glittering weapon. Chantel leaped down the steps, screaming, "It's a trick, an elf trick!" He waved his hands wildly, his eyes glazed over. "Stop the imposter. Stop him."

Chantel grabbed the tall scepter of the royal office from its holder at the base of the dais. He raised the heavy metal-headed staff and ran across the chamber toward Pris.

"I'll stop you. If the others are fooled, I certainly am not."

Gant moved to intercept the minister, but Pris acted first. With a gesture of his free hand and a short string of arcane words, Pris loosed a spell. In midstride, Chantel froze as if turned to rock. A gasp of wonder escaped the onlookers that was audible even above Thantalmos.

Pris returned Thantalmos to her sheath and the room fell silent. The boy emperor walked to the former High Minister. The only sound was Pris' footsteps echoing hollowly through the room.

He removed the royal scepter from Chantel's stiff fist. Holding his reclaimed symbol of power, Pris mounted the steps to the dais, Gant, Dalphnia and Kalmine close at his heels. The other ministers still on the dais scattered. Pris turned at the throne and plopped down with little ceremony.

"Someone take Chantel to a holding cell before the spell wears off," he snapped. "Also, have the High Priest report here at once. I think Chantel may be suffering from some form of insanity. We'll see if the priest can cure him."

Now Pris turned and glared at the huddled ministers. "All of you are relieved of your positions. Tomorrow morning, report to Kalmine, my new High Minister, for assignments more befitting your talents."

Whimpers of fear answered Pris and the deposed ministers bowed low.

"Don't worry, no one will be hurt or imprisoned. But lesser positions suit you, I think." Then Pris waved away the cowered group.

"Well, Gant, what do you think?"

"I'd say you did very well, Your Majesty. And you hardly needed us."

"Not now maybe, but I need to build a core of knights. I'd like you to lead them."

Gant looked at the emperor, a touch of sadness in his eyes. "No, Dalphnia and I are returning to her woods. I've had enough adventure to last a lifetime."

Pris' smile drooped, and then brightened again. "But you'll stay a few days won't you? I must throw a feast in your honor. It's the least I can do. And before you go, I'd like to discuss a few things, like how to change this ridiculous system of gaining an audience with the emperor. Everyone should have equal access to present their problems.

"Then, too, I've got to set up a force to rotate with the elves and knights at Chamber Pass. Everyone has to share in protecting the mountain border."

Gant winked at Dalphnia and said, "I think we can stay a few days. We're going to go back to Netherdorf first anyway so I can visit my father. Did you know he's going to be the Royal Smith with his forge in the castle? And, we want to be there for the victory feast."

"Then it's settled. You'll stay a week, no less, and return often. We'll feast every time you return."

Gant smiled and shook the emperor's offered hand. At least this part of the world remained safe. He hoped he could hang up his armor and Valorius, and someday pass them on to his son. He thought of Zandinar and silently thanked him for his sacrifice. Dalphnia squeezed him tight. It brought Gant back to the present. Things were hardly ideal but at least for now the evil that roamed west of the Monolith Mountains was contained. Gant hoped it would stay that way for a long time. It wouldn't.

If you enjoyed reading **Fall of the Western Kings** you might like to read these other works by J Drew Brumbaugh.

Shepherds

War Party

Foxworth Terminus

Ten More

Girls Gone Great
(A children's book co-authored with Carolyn B. Berg)

Get news, updates, specials, and private notes by subscribing at his website:

www.jdrewbrumbaugh.com

About the Author

J Drew Brumbaugh lives in northeast Ohio where he spends his time writing sci-fi, fantasy and suspense novels, teaching and training at the karate dojo he and his wife founded, building a Japanese garden in his back yard, and taking walks in the Cleveland Metro Parks. He continues to work on his next book and always has several stories in various stages of completion. He can be reached at contact@jdrewbrumbaugh.com.

Made in the USA
Columbia, SC
18 May 2019